AMISH PROMISES

Center Point
Large Print

Also by Leslie Gould and available from Center Point Large Print:

The Courtships of Lancaster County
Adoring Addie
Minding Molly
Becoming Bea

**This Large Print Book carries the
Seal of Approval of N.A.V.H.**

Neighbors of LANCASTER COUNTY
—BOOK ONE—

AMISH PROMISES

LESLIE GOULD

CENTER POINT LARGE PRINT
THORNDIKE, MAINE

This Center Point Large Print edition is published in the year 2015 by arrangement with Bethany House Publishers, a division of Baker Publishing Group.

Scripture quotations are from the King James Version of the Bible.

This is a work of fiction. Names, characters, incidents, and dialogues are products of the author's imagination and are not to be construed as real. Any resemblance to actual events or persons, living or dead, is entirely coincidental.

The text of this Large Print edition is unabridged. In other aspects, this book may vary from the original edition. Printed in the United States of America on permanent paper. Set in 16-point Times New Roman type.

ISBN: 978-1-62899-584-8

Library of Congress Cataloging-in-Publication Data

Gould, Leslie, 1962–
Amish promises / Leslie Gould. — Center Point Large Print edition.
pages cm
Summary: "When an English and an Amish family become neighbors in Lancaster, Pennsylvania, their lives are linked in unexpected ways through conflict, then friendship, and finally, love"—Provided by publisher.
ISBN 978-1-62899-584-8 (library binding : alk. paper)
1. Amish—Fiction. 2. Lancaster County (Pa.)—Fiction.
  3. Large type books. I. Title.
PS3607.O89A8 2015b
813′.6—dc23
                                            2015007336

For my friend Marietta Couch,
and for my friend Marilyn Weisenburg

ಬಬ

And in loving memory of David J. Weisenburg,
May 2, 1978–September 13, 2004

October 2004
Lancaster County, Pennsylvania

"*Aenti*! The baby needs you!" Daniel's high-pitched voice carried to the back bedroom of their neighbor's farmhouse as Eve Lehman tucked the corner of the quilt under the mattress.

"Give her to Lila," Eve called out to her eleven-year-old nephew as she stepped around the side of the bed. "I'll be right there."

Trying to ignore Trudy's cries, she stood back and admired the shadow quilt. Abra had made it years ago and gave it to Eve for her marriage bed someday. That would never happen now. She was the old *Maidel*. The spinster Aenti.

The pine trees out the window cast shadows across the walls of the room as the late afternoon *Licht* waned. She hated to see it go. She stepped to the doorway, pulled the bedroom door shut, and started down the hallway.

The home had been vacant since old Mr. Williams died four months before. Earlier in the week his son had left a message on the phone in the barn, asking if Eve would tidy up the place. He said his daughter and son-in-law, who'd been injured in the war, were moving into the house. They needed a quiet place to "regroup."

As Eve turned the corner into the kitchen, her red-faced niece began to scream even louder. Trudy was fair, like Daniel and Lila. "There, there," Eve said as she reached for the baby. The little one lunged toward her—she could hardly bear to have Eve out of her sight. It was no wonder, considering everything the baby had been through in her short eight months of life.

"It's getting dark." Daniel stepped toward the back door.

"Turn on the light," Eve responded as she cradled Trudy in her arms. The baby gulped for air and let out another cry, but this one was halfhearted.

Lila stepped into the kitchen from the living room, carrying a handful of rags. She'd grown taller than her twin in the last year, much to Daniel's horror. He'd seemed skeptical when Eve assured him he'd soon catch up to and then pass his sister.

"Did you two finish the dusting?" Eve asked.

"Jah." Daniel's face was solemn as he inched toward the back door. "I need to go help *Dat* and Simon with the chores."

"In a minute," she said. "Carry the buckets back to the house first. Go grab the ones in the living room."

Daniel obeyed without hesitating. Lila started rinsing the rags in the sink. Trudy hiccupped and grasped Eve around the neck, her chubby hands holding on for dear life, her soft breath against Eve's skin.

"Does the Englisch family have any kids?" Lila asked.

Eve nodded. "They have a twelve-year-old son." She hadn't told her brother, Tim, that part of the news. He'd be leery of an Englisch boy a year older than the twins, not to mention a military family, living so close to his farm.

Trudy began to fuss again, so Eve turned on the ceiling fan, a trick she'd found effective earlier in the afternoon. The baby put her head back, mesmerized again by the movement of the blades. When Eve had been on her *Rumschpringe*, sure she'd leave the Amish for good, she'd been just as enthralled with the Englisch world as Trudy was now. It was more than just the electricity, cars, and independence for Eve. It was the hope of a marriage different than what her parents had. A good marriage, with her Englisch boyfriend. A home with children—all loved and cherished. And perhaps even a career for herself, in teaching.

But none of that was meant to be. She'd ended up joining the church after all, twelve years ago. And she was still paying for having led Abra astray.

Footsteps fell on the back porch. Eve had planned to be long gone before the new family arrived. But she hadn't heard a car.

"Eve?" It was her brother's voice.

"Jah!" Balancing the weight of the baby on her hip, she hurried toward the door and opened it quickly. He stood with his hat in his hands on the top step.

"You startled me," she said.

"We've finished the plowing," Tim said. "We need Daniel's help with the chores."

Simon waited at the bottom of the steps beside his father, his straw hat in his hand and an impish grin on his face. He was two years younger than the twins and full of mischief.

"We're almost done here." Eve bounced the baby. "Daniel will be back by the time you get the horses unhitched."

Tim preferred to have Simon work with him instead of Daniel. The younger boy put his hat back on his head and then grinned at Eve, his chestnut curls poking out from under the brim. He was the spitting image of his father, but his personality was the exact opposite. Tim was serious, while Simon was full of fun, like his mother had been.

Tim had favored Simon over Daniel since the boy was born, even though Abra had discouraged it. Once she passed away, Tim stopped trying to hide it.

"Where's Rose?" Eve asked as she looked around. Her middle niece had gone out to the field with Simon and Tim.

10

"She was tired," Tim said. "I sent her back to the house." She'd been the baby of the family for six years until Trudy came along—and it showed in the girl's *kintish* ways.

Lila had finished rinsing the rags and joined them at the door, followed by Daniel.

"I'll just go with Dat now," the boy said.

Eve shook her head. "Grab the broom and mops."

Tim ignored Daniel and spoke to Eve. "The rain's coming, and your wash is still on the line." He tugged on his beard. "I trust you've already started our supper."

"Jah," Eve answered. "I fixed a roast." She knew Tim wasn't happy with her housekeeping and cooking, but she did the best she could. "We'll meet you back at the house."

The baby began to cry again. Tim pushed his hat back on his head and then turned and strode down the steps. Simon fell in step behind his father, doing a little jig as they walked away from the house.

Eve wiggled into her cape with Trudy on her hip. Then she took the baby's blanket from the counter and covered her. "We'll go out the front." She pushed the back door tight and locked it. Lila picked up the bucket with the rags, and Daniel carried the other two, along with the broom and mop. The twins followed Eve through the kitchen and across the worn hardwood of the dining room and living room.

Eve ushered the children onto the porch and closed and locked the front door, saying a silent prayer that the new family would find peace and comfort in their new home. Things hadn't always been easy with Old Man Williams, but they'd appreciated him all the same. Hopefully things would go more smoothly with his grand-daughter. Perhaps, if Tim didn't mind, she'd run over a pan of sticky buns sometime tomorrow.

She knew how hard a move could be. It had been nearly a year since she came to her brother's home on Juneberry Lane, right after Abra had been diagnosed with breast cancer. Her sister-in-law had been four months pregnant with Trudy at the time.

It wasn't an easy transition for Eve, but there were more important things to worry about. A sick *Mamm.* A baby on the way. And four terrified children.

Now she had five grieving children to care for, to love the way she'd always longed to love her own.

Daniel bumped the bucket against the railing on the way down the steps, causing the wood to shift. Eve stopped and pushed against the rail. It wasn't secure, but it didn't give way either. She would mention it to the new family the next morning.

They hurried to the lane, crunching through the layers of red and orange maple leaves. A light rain began to fall as they passed the tallest cedar tree. Eve breathed in the spicy scent and pulled the baby closer to her chest.

"Is Simon going to work with Dat tomorrow?" Daniel's voice held a hint of jealousy.

"Probably," Eve answered. In the dark shadows of the lane, it seemed dusk was already falling. They walked in silence until they reached the big oak tree, halfway home.

Lila asked to climb it.

"Ach," Eve said. "You're too old for that sort of thing."

But when Daniel, who'd been in such a hurry, put down his buckets and stared up at the tree, Eve changed her mind. They both deserved some fun.

"Oh, bother," she said. "Be quick." She stepped under the canopy of the remaining leaves, seeking cover from the rain. "And climb like a young lady," she said to Lila, smiling after she said it. As if that were possible.

The baby snuggled against Eve and let out a sigh, her body giving way to sleep. Fearing the little one would be up half the night if she slept now, Eve tickled Trudy under her chin, but the baby didn't stir.

Daniel scampered up the tree, propelled by his bare feet. Lila followed him but settled on the bottom branch, tucking her skirt beneath her.

"Not too far," Eve called out to Daniel, thinking of the twins when they were newborns. So tiny and life changing for their Mamm—and for her too.

In the distance she heard the team of horses making their way toward the barn.

"I can see them from here," Daniel called down. "Simon's laughing. And Dat's smiling."

"Shh," Eve responded. Daniel's jealousy only made it worse. He climbed higher. She called up to him, "We need to get going."

Daniel didn't respond.

"Come on," she called.

In a defiant tone, he responded, "What if I don't?"

Lila gasped.

Eve took a deep breath. It wasn't like Daniel to be disobedient. She hardly ever had to discipline him with more than a scolding. "Come down now," she said.

He shook his head.

She couldn't climb up after Daniel, not even if she put Trudy down. She could have a decade ago, when she was still a teenager, but not now. And even if she could, what would she do once she reached him?

It wouldn't do any good to send Lila up either.

She decided to ignore Daniel, hoping he'd soon be over his obstinacy. She needed to get home before the wash got so wet she had to run it through the wringer again.

Shani Beck peered through the rain-splattered windshield, searching for the road sign. It was an hour until nightfall but the autumn rain had darkened the day.

She slowed and then, seeing the sign, turned sharply onto Juneberry Lane. The narrow road tunneled through a thick grove of trees. Shani swerved to miss a fallen branch.

Her husband, Joel, stirred in the passenger seat. He'd slept since Philadelphia. So had Zane. Their son was twelve—no longer a boy, yet far from being a man. He was definitely starting to act like a teenager, but it was hard to determine if his new moodiness was because of his age or Joel's injuries. Probably a dose of each.

She maneuvered around a pothole. The moving van was a few minutes behind them. Thankfully the movers would unload everything, and then Charlie, Joel's Army buddy, would arrive the next morning to help with arranging the furniture and moving boxes. Zane would help too. She wouldn't be much help, except to unpack boxes and clean, and Joel wouldn't be any help at all.

Then she'd only have two days to get everything and everyone settled before she started her job at Lancaster General.

She'd scanned the listings for weeks for an opening in pediatrics there, and after she found one and they offered her a job after a phone interview, she was convinced they were supposed to move to Lancaster County.

Joel sat up straight, wrinkling his nose as he did. "You didn't tell me there was a dairy nearby." Shani had noticed the stench but hadn't realized it was a dairy. Joel grew up in Wisconsin—he'd know.

"There wasn't one here before." It had been over five years since she and Zane had visited while Joel was on a training exercise. Her grandfather had been much crankier than what she remembered as a child, or perhaps her grandmother had tempered him more than she'd realized. She'd intended to come once she and Zane moved to Philly last spring, but then Joel had been injured in Iraq and she'd gone to Germany instead.

Zane kicked against the back of her seat. "Who are *they?*" he asked.

"What are you talking about?" Shani turned the windshield wipers up higher, her gaze focused on the narrow road.

He tapped on the window. "Those people."

Off to the side stood a woman wearing a bonnet and a cape, with a baby in her arms. A girl with blond hair stood near her. Another child, a boy who was also a towhead, hung upside down from a branch halfway up the tree. The woman and girl's dresses and the boy's shirt were all sky blue, as if they'd all been cut from the same bolt of cloth.

"Why are they dressed that way?" Zane asked.

Joel groaned. "You didn't tell me we have Amish neighbors."

"I don't think we do." Shani realized she'd nearly stopped the van. The woman turned toward her, freed one hand from the baby, and waved. The boy tumbled from the limb and then twisted, making Shani gasp. He landed on his bare feet next to a plastic bucket.

"How come the kid doesn't have shoes?" Zane asked.

"I don't know." It was much too cold for such nonsense. The boy and girl both looked close to Zane's age.

"What's with his hair?" Zane asked.

"It's called a bowl cut," Joel answered. "Want one?"

Shani shot her husband a warning look.

Zane didn't answer his father, but asked, "Can I say hi?" Being an only child seemed to make him extra outgoing—he craved the companionship of other children. The fact that Shani was having a baby—a boy—in less than four months wouldn't change that, though. She was afraid twelve years between Zane and a little brother would make it difficult for them to have much of a relationship.

"No, you can't go introduce yourself." Joel stared at the Amish. "They keep to themselves— at least the ones back home did."

Shani inched the van forward again. The girl turned toward them, a slight smile on her face. Then Shani accelerated around the bend and toward her grandparents' two-century-old house at the end of the lane. The home was made of brick, except for the white clapboard kitchen addition.

"I don't know about this." Joel slumped in his seat. "How can another move be good for us?"

Shani kept her eyes on the lane. "Let's give it a year, like we decided."

"Like you decided."

She didn't respond. They'd been over it a hundred times. After Joel recovered enough to return to the US, they'd gone to Texas for his rehab and then back to the Philadelphia apartment she and Zane had moved into while he was deployed.

He grew more and more on edge with each passing day. At first Shani thought he was simply transitioning, but they lived just off a busy street, and she soon suspected the constant noise of traffic—especially the blare of horns—made him hyper alert. She didn't realize how out of sorts he'd become until she came home one night from work to find him at the window, sitting in his wheelchair with his .45 in his hand.

Joel's left tibia had been shattered in the attack, among other injuries, but the docs said more healing would come with time. He'd stopped taking his sleep aids, making up for it with his pain meds, and any little noise made him jump. Even a car door slamming.

Her grandparents' farm had been a place of healing for Shani the summer she turned ten, after her mother left. As her parents wrangled out the divorce, her father sent her to be cared for by his own parents. Shani found out that the country— her grandparents' farm, in particular—could be a refuge. She returned home ready to face a new life, one without her mother.

She was sure the farm would be a place of healing for Joel too.

Zane kept quiet in the backseat. He'd certainly picked up on the tension between his parents over the last few months, and it seemed he was careful not to set off his father.

Shani pulled the van into the driveway and stopped under the red and orange canopy of another maple tree. The grass was trimmed and tidy. The curtains in the front window were pulled back, as if someone were home.

The land was leased to a local farmer, and after her grandfather passed away her father had intended to rent the house out as well. Thankfully he hadn't gotten around to finding a tenant. Her father said they could stay as long as they needed, at least until Joel was well enough to find a job.

"We're home." Shani turned off the ignition, aware of how false her words sounded.

Zane opened his door.

Shani turned toward her husband. "Shall we take a look?"

He didn't answer but opened his door, swinging his good leg out and then moving his bum leg with his hands. He grabbed his cane.

"Wait," Shani said. "I'll help." She hurried around to the passenger side. Joel was putting his weight on his good leg, pushing down with his cane to stand.

The rain fell harder. "I think I'll look around outside," Zane said.

"Don't you want to see the house first?" Shani asked, taking Joel's free arm.

"I'm just going to check out the field," Zane said. "I want to get my bearings."

She thought that was a funny thing for him to say, but if he explored the field first, he'd miss Joel's complaining about the house. "Come back if it starts to pour."

Zane nodded and then, whistling a tune Shani didn't recognize—probably one he'd learned from Charlie—started toward the field.

Joel faltered on the stone driveway, and she reached for his arm. He shook off her hand and snapped, "I'm not one of your patients."

She held her arm in midair for a moment. He was acting like one.

She eyed the steps, wondering how difficult they would be for him to maneuver, annoyed with herself that she hadn't thought through that detail. There were more than she'd remembered.

Joel's arm stiffened, and Shani patted it. He stopped at the bottom of the steps and scowled, his forehead wrinkling under his short hair, still cropped in an Army cut. As Joel struggled up the steps one at a time, grasping the rickety railing that squeaked with each pull, Shani kept close in case he stumbled.

He took a raggedy breath and snarled, "You know I don't like it when you hover."

She winced at his harsh tone.

"I need to sit and rest a minute." His voice was still raw. "You go ahead."

"But it's raining."

His flipped the hood of his jacket onto his head. "I'll be fine." Her heart constricted, and the baby inside fluttered. Joel wasn't fine—not at all.

As he turned and sat, she steadied him until he leaned against the next step. Another benefit of having Charlie around was that Joel behaved better. He'd never lost his temper with his friend —probably because the man had saved his life when he pulled Joel from the burning Humvee.

She continued on up the steps. She'd need to

hire a carpenter to put in a ramp. Joel had only been out of his wheelchair for a week—he still used it when he was tired. She wished Charlie had followed them, as they'd originally planned. She could have used his help at the moment.

Shani unlocked the door with the key her father had sent and entered the house, surprised by the fresh, lemony scent. In the dim light she found the switch and turned on the overhead bulb. The room was completely bare except for the wood stove. She remembered huddling around it as a child on cold mornings.

She peeked into the kitchen at the familiar worn yellow linoleum and Formica counter tops. Turning down the hallway, she pushed open her grandfather's bedroom door. Once cluttered, the room had been totally transformed. The stacks of books and papers were gone, along with the dark drapes. The last light of the rainy day revealed an Amish quilt covering the bed. The jewel-colored diamond shapes—burgundy, emerald, and sapphire blue—danced against the black background, as if casting a shadow. She stepped forward and rested her hand on the soft cotton.

Where had the quilt come from? Who had cleaned the house?

She felt hopeful, for the first time in months. "Please let us be happy here," she whispered. That was all she wanted—all she'd ever wanted. She'd married Joel when she was nineteen and had Zane a year later. Her father had been horrified by both events, sure she'd thrown her life away. But she'd graduated from nursing school as planned, and for the most part, she and Joel had built a good life together.

Until his injury.

Zane and this new baby needed both parents. She'd seen too many families fall apart in the midst of a crisis. And not just military families. Her mother had left when she could no longer handle the monotony of suburban living, or so she'd said. Shani's dad had coped as best he could—and had been both mother and father to her. But she didn't want a one-parent family for her boys. She'd make things work with Joel, no matter how deep his wounds.

She rubbed her hand over the quilt squares as the hum of a truck vibrated through the room, and then the scrape of a branch against metal. She hurried out of the room, down the hall, and to the porch. Joel stood now and took a step down. Shani rushed to his side, taking his elbow, as the moving truck came to a stop.

Joel jerked his arm away.

"Wait here," she said to him, waving to the mover on the passenger side of the truck. He opened his door and climbed down. "That's quite the narrow lane," he said.

She nodded. It had grown over since she had last visited.

The driver hopped down from the other side, headed toward the back, and pulled down a ramp, dropping it just a few feet from where Shani stood. She hesitated for a moment and then started toward her van. The living room furniture was deep inside the truck, and so was the dining room set. She needed to get Joel's chair so he could sit—and soon, before the movers started up the stairs.

As she pulled the wheelchair from the back, Joel called out, "What are you doing?"

"Helping," she called back. She carried the chair toward the porch, the metal back bumping against her belly.

Joel shook his head as she passed him on the steps. "You're going to hurt the baby."

"Light lifting won't hurt the baby."

"The wheelchair isn't light," he said before she entered the house. He worried constantly about the baby. He worried about everything.

She opened the chair in the middle of the living room and then hurried back to help Joel. He turned to face her as she stepped down from the porch, but he stumbled a little as he turned and grabbed onto the shaky railing. She'd need to get that fixed too. In a moment she was beside him, taking his elbow again.

His face darkened, and the scowl returned, but he allowed her to help. By the time they reached the wheelchair, his breath was labored. He'd always been so strong, so independent. She hated what the war had done to him.

He collapsed into the seat. "I'm going into the bedroom."

"Why?"

"I don't want their pity."

"What are you talking about?"

Joel turned the chair around. "The movers. I've had enough of their pathetic looks." Shani didn't think they'd given him any, not just now or when they loaded the truck, but she wasn't going to argue with him. He began slowly pushing the chair wheels.

"You can rest on the bed." She stepped to the back of the chair and followed. "The room is all made up."

He slept poorly during the night, but she hoped he would be able to rest so he would be alert when Charlie came tomorrow.

"The floors need to be refinished," Joel said as they neared the hall. "And the whole place could use another coat of paint."

He was right. It was a little shabby. Not nearly as well maintained as the last time she'd been in the house. But her grandfather had been eighty-two when he died, and not nearly as mobile as he had once been.

"We'll take care of it," she said. "In time."

Joel grunted. "You'll have to hire someone—and we don't have the money."

The truth was, they did have some money. She had saved as much as she could when Joel was in Iraq, but finances were another of his irrational fears. He was sure they'd go broke before he could heal and find another job.

If the processing of his disability payments kept dragging on, he might end up being right. Unfortunately for him, due to his injuries, he was out of the Army for good. Shani, however, was relieved.

She inched the chair through the doorway, grateful it fit, and then stopped beside the bed.

She pulled back the covers, revealing bleached white sheets, but he didn't move.

"I'll sit in my chair," he said.

"Okay," Shani responded, leaving the bed turned down. "Light on or off?"

"Off."

She inhaled sharply. Here he was, back in a dark room—by himself.

The driver of the moving truck called out, "Mrs. Beck!"

She bent down and kissed Joel's forehead.

He stiffened his back. "Go."

The movers said they'd arrange the furniture for her, but she told them to put it all in the living room. She'd rather have them gone as soon as possible and Joel out of the bedroom. Charlie and Zane could move everything around the next day.

After telling the men where to put things, she

said she'd be right back and hurried toward the field, passing by the barn and chicken coop on her way. It was completely dark now, and the rain had stopped entirely. A few stars poked through the clouds, and a half moon rose over the poplar trees that lined the field.

A figure stood at the end of the field, by the gate. It had to be Zane. She began to walk as quickly as she could, tucking a hand underneath her rounded belly. On the other side of the trees, the creek gurgled. She remembered playing along it as a child.

When she reached the halfway point she yelled Zane's name.

He turned toward her and waved.

"Come on," she called out, gesturing for him.

He glanced over his shoulder and then stepped toward her, walking slowly.

"Hurry," she yelled.

Finally Zane began to jog, but he still glanced over his shoulder a few times. When he reached her, he said, "The Amish family was doing their chores."

She hoped he hadn't offended them by watching.

"There are the two kids we saw, plus the baby, and another brother too, younger, and a little girl."

"Oh," Shani said. "They do have big families."

"The dad is huge. Really tall and strong, like he could lift a house if he had to."

Shani smiled. "Don't exaggerate."

"I'm not," he said. "The kids waved, but I didn't think you'd want me to go over without asking for permission first."

Shani nodded. "Good choice."

"The woman pulled the laundry off the line while she held the baby on her hip and the older girl helped," Zane said. "The dad and boys kept leading cows into the barn and then back out."

"They're doing the milking," Shani said.

As they neared the end of the field he said, "It's cool there are other kids nearby."

Shani didn't think the Amish children would be allowed to play with him, but she didn't want to disappoint him so soon. She reached out and tousled his hair. He'd be taller than her soon, maybe even in a few months. Life had been so crazy lately she hadn't kept up with how much he was changing. Hopefully she would be able to enjoy the year ahead with him. "Can you sit with your dad while I sign some papers for the movers?"

He nodded. "What's for dinner?"

She hadn't thought that far. "I'll find some takeout."

Zane increased his pace as they rounded the corner of the field toward the house. "I'm tired of pizza."

Shani groaned. "Definitely a failure on my part," she joked, although she was partly serious.

They ate takeout way too much. That was one of the things she hoped to improve with their move. "Go check on your dad, okay? He's in the back bedroom."

Zane ran up the steps to the porch, as the two movers came out. "There you are," the driver said, holding out a clipboard. The other mover continued on down to the truck.

After she signed the papers, the driver said he hoped her family would be happy in Lancaster County. As he bounded down the stairs, tears stung Shani's eyes. That was all she wanted.

She swiped at her eyes and turned toward the house. Zane stood in the front doorway. "Dad said he didn't want company. He's sitting in the dark, drumming his fingers on the arm of his chair."

"Okay," Shani said. "I'll go ask him what he wants to eat."

"I'm not staying here while you're gone." Zane zipped his jacket. "I'm going with you."

Shani nodded. It wasn't that Joel couldn't stay by himself. She just didn't like it when he did. But she'd soon be back to work and Zane would be in school.

Joel would be by himself plenty then.

☙ 3

Lila slipped the baby into the high chair while Eve pulled the roast from the oven. Tim and the boys would soon be in for supper.

First the moving truck had come and left and then the neighbors had driven away in their van, probably to get something to eat. She wished she'd made two roasts and left one for them, but it was too late now.

She wondered what the woman thought of the quilt on the bed. She'd mentioned her idea to give it away to Tim but he'd hardly acknowledged what she'd said. Obviously, like with so many things, he didn't care.

"They're coming back," Rose called out from the front room.

"What are you talking about?" Lila stepped to the open archway between the two rooms.

"The new neighbors. In that van."

"Rose," Eve said, "stop spying."

"I'm not," the girl said. "I'm just standing at our window."

It had been a long time since they'd had neighbors to watch. Old Man Williams hadn't done much in the area of coming and going.

"Come finish setting the table," Eve said.

Rose skipped into the living room, her braids

bouncing on her shoulders. She grinned as her eyes met her Aenti's. She wasn't quite as gregarious as Simon, but nearly so. She'd just started her first year of the school the Amish children attended and enjoyed the recess and lunchtime the most, unlike Lila, who soaked up all the learning she could.

Eve turned back toward the stove and pulled the biscuits from the oven. She had been caring for others for the last decade. First for her parents until they both died, then for Abra from the time she was diagnosed with cancer until her death five months ago. Now Tim and the children.

Lila only had two more years as a scholar so, theoretically, she could take over the household then. But in a roundabout way Eve had promised Abra, when she was dying, she wouldn't leave. She'd stick by that promise.

Rose started putting the forks and knives around the table. "Did you see that Englisch kid standing on the other side of the gate and staring at us?" she asked Lila.

Her sister nodded. "We saw him in the van when they came up the lane too, on our way back from the neighbor's house. His Mamm was driving, and his Dat was in the front."

A knife clattered to the table. "The mother was driving? That's weird."

"Hush," Eve said. "The Dat was hurt in the war. Maybe he can't drive anymore."

31

"Oh." Rose scrunched her face as if trying to figure it all out. "Simon's going to want to hear all about the war, for sure."

Eve shook her head. A soldier had spoken to him a year ago in Walmart, and Simon had been obsessed with the military since. No, Tim would not be pleased if Simon asked too many questions. In fact, Tim had lectured all of the children several times since on what it meant to be nonresistant—to turn the other cheek, to not defend oneself, let alone attack—but Eve didn't think Simon had listened.

By the time Eve had the biscuits and roast on the table, Tim and the boys came through the back door onto the mud porch, kicked off their boots, and headed to the bathroom to wash.

"Pour the milk," Eve said to Lila. "And, Rose, put on the napkins." The little girl had drifted to the dining room window. She turned, grinning, and did what she was asked.

The children didn't talk about the Englisch boy in front of Tim, but once he'd finished eating and left to go check on a cow that was in labor, Simon said, "That Englisch boy was staring at me every time I came out of the barn. I thought maybe he'd come over to say hello, but he never did."

"How old do you think he is?" Daniel asked.

Simon shrugged. "I don't know. He's tall." He smirked. "Taller than you."

Daniel frowned, but before he could react, Rose said, "His father was in the Army."

"Are you sure?" Simon sat up straight.

"Jah," Rose said. "That's what Aenti said."

Simon looked at Eve. "I believe it's true," she said. "But that's actually none of our business. Our only concern is to be good neighbors. Jah?" After the conflict Tim had with Mr. Williams, she hoped they'd be given a second chance.

The older children nodded in agreement, Rose wrinkled her nose, and Trudy began to fuss.

"I'm going to put the baby to bed. Lila and Rose, you do the dishes. And boys, go see if your Dat needs any help." She stood and smiled. "Be quick and I'll make popcorn before bedtime." She usually only made it on Friday nights, but this particular Thursday evening seemed as if it needed some cheer.

The children scrambled to their feet as she scooped Trudy out of her chair and headed to the hall. She was sure the children missed their mother most at bedtime, although she knew all of them ached for her all the time.

Abra. Eve's father had ridiculed her friend's name, saying it was too fancy, even though it was the feminine form of Abraham. Tim had ridiculed the name too—until he realized he had a chance to make her his wife. By then he was smitten by Abra. Eve was pretty sure Tim had never expected to marry at all, let alone someone as beautiful and full of life as the woman who became his helpmeet.

Eve had met Abra their first year of school. Her friend had seemed like a fairy with her fine blond hair and bright blue eyes. She was gregarious and fun and expected people to be good and kind.

The first time Eve spent the night at Abra's house it all made sense. Abra was deeply loved. Although she was still Amish at that time, that night Abra's mother prayed with the girls, out loud, asking for both of them to be covered by God's grace. After she'd kissed them good-night, she said that God connected people to each other and to him. "That's what love does," she'd said. Eve had never forgotten that. Years later she realized that sin did the opposite—it tore us apart from God and others.

After Eve diapered and changed the baby and tucked Trudy into her crib, she helped the girls finish the dishes and then sent them into the living room to play a game of Scrabble with the boys, who'd insisted that their Dat didn't want any help.

Eve was sure that was true. Tim grew even moodier in the evenings.

Once the popcorn was done she called the children to the table, but just as they sat down Tim came through the back door.

"How's the cow doing?" Eve asked, dishing the popcorn into individual bowls.

"False alarm," he said. "I think she has a few more days."

He headed into the living room, and the kids ate their popcorn in silence. When Lila had finished hers, she stood and said, "I'm going to go read in bed."

"Me too," Daniel said.

"What about our game?" Simon leaned across the table.

"We'll finish it tomorrow," Lila said, patting her little brother's head as she walked by.

Rose's lower lip jutted out. "I don't want to go to bed yet."

"You don't have to," Lila said.

Rose glanced at Eve, who simply shrugged.

The younger children ended up pulling out a puzzle in the living room. A couple of times Rose asked Tim a question, but he didn't answer. After a short time Simon and Rose went to bed too. After tucking them in, Eve sat down with her knitting.

Finally Tim yawned and stretched, and then he stood. "Did you give away that quilt?"

She stared at the yarn in her lap. "Why?"

He stepped in front of her. "Why would you want to give away something Abra made for you?"

She wrapped the yarn around the needle. "From what you said this morning, I didn't think you minded."

"I do mind." He tugged on his beard. "Did you?"

She raised her head, determined to keep her voice even. "Jah, I did."

He turned toward the hallway. "What a waste."

When Shani woke the next morning it took her a minute to remember they'd moved to the farm. It wasn't until she became aware of the quilt against her chin that she realized where they were. She patted the other side of the bed for Joel and then rose up on one elbow. He was gone.

She grabbed her robe from the end of the bed and hurried down the hall, past the row of boxes. He wasn't in the living room. She registered the smell of coffee.

He stood at the kitchen sink, a cup in one hand and his cane in the other.

"Good morning," she said.

He turned toward her. He hadn't shaved, but he was dressed in sweatpants and a long-sleeved T-shirt. He raised his mug. "Coffee? It's decaf."

She couldn't help but smile. He'd been worried about her caffeine intake even though she'd assured him a cup of regular each day wouldn't hurt the baby. "Thanks," she said, pouring herself a cup. It was the first time he'd made coffee since he was home on furlough last April.

"Sorry about yesterday," he mumbled.

"It's all right," she answered, stepping to his side. She started to put her head on his shoulder but thought that might put him off balance.

Instead she reached up and stroked his scraggly chin. "Is Zane awake?"

"Yes, he's outside."

She stepped to the window. "Already?" She hoped he wasn't spying on the neighbors again.

The day was overcast, but it wasn't raining. At least not at the moment. A ribbon of mist hung over the field though, the part she could see, and a breeze teased the tops of the trees. "I'll get dressed," she said, "and go check on him."

Joel nodded.

"Do you want your chair?" she called over her shoulder.

"No, I'm fine."

She pulled on her maternity jeans and sweatshirt, brushed her teeth, and shook out her hair, scrunching the curls. She'd have to deal with it later. A muffled crash startled her.

"Joel!" she called out. She hurried into the kitchen—his mug was on the counter, but he was gone. She rushed into the living room. He wasn't there either, but the front door was ajar. When she reached the porch it took her a moment to realize what happened. But once she did, she scrambled down the steps.

Joel was at the bottom of the stairs, his injured leg turned under at an angle, his face twisted in pain.

"Call 9-1-1." The words came out in a gasp. "I can't get up."

She knelt down beside him, her heart jolting. As a nurse, she was confident about handling any emergency—unless it was someone she loved. She placed her hands on his shoulders, rolling him onto his back.

"No," he gasped. "Just call!"

What had she done with her cell? She stumbled back up the steps and into the house, grabbing her purse from the floor under the front window. As she dug through it, she rushed back out.

She finally found the phone and flipped it open, hitting the nine and the one before she read the words on the screen. *No service.* Why hadn't she checked the night before?

She'd never guessed she wouldn't be able to get service at her grandfather's house. And the landline hadn't been installed yet.

"I'll call from the neighbors'." She ran back into the house, yanked the quilt from their bed, and rushed back through the front door, pulling it shut behind her. She hurried down the stairs, doubled the quilt, and tucked it around Joel.

"I'll be right back," she said.

"Hurry," he groaned.

Once in the van, she swung it around and started back down the lane, driving too fast over the rutted road. She slowed when the first mailbox came into view and turned sharply. Ahead was a white house and behind it a huge barn, a shed, and a silo. All were well kept, nearly immaculate.

When Shani saw the black pants, white shirts, and baby sleepers on the line she groaned. What was she thinking? It was the Amish place. Which probably meant no phone.

She started to turn around but then she saw the woman and the girl from the evening before climbing the back steps of the house.

Shani opened the van door as a light rain began. "I need to make a phone call. It's an emergency."

"In the barn," the woman responded. A smaller Amish girl, with braids sticking out from under her white bonnet, stood on the bottom step.

Shani turned off the engine and ran toward the barn. A man's voice came from inside, but he was speaking words she couldn't understand, another language—their German dialect, she was sure—then he called out sharply, "Simon!"

There was a sickening thud and then something that sounded like an object hitting a wall. She stopped, but then started up again as a massive man came staggering out of the open doorway, holding a boy in his arms. Behind him was Zane. When he saw Shani, he began to cry.

The man yelled something to the woman. The nurse in Shani took over and she swooped in, motioning the man to put the boy on the ground.

The boy's jaw was split and bleeding. She felt the back of his head. There was no blood there—not on the outside anyway—but already a contusion was forming.

40

"Call 9-1-1," she ordered, as she lowered her face to the boy's. "And ask for two ambulances. One for my husband—he fell and . . ." She didn't finish the sentence. The boy wasn't breathing. She checked his airway, positioned his head, feeling the sweat along his neck where his curls met his skin, and carefully breathed into his mouth, taking in his boy scent mixed with soil and rain. She checked for his pulse. Nothing.

The man stood statue still, but the woman passed the baby to the oldest girl and started running toward the barn.

Shani compressed the boy's chest, her hands covering his suspenders and white shirt. She did it again, keeping her thoughts on the boy.

She counted out loud to thirty. Then gave two breaths, followed by thirty more compressions, following the protocol for children.

Shani noted that the Amish woman had returned. "They're on their way," she said in English. "Two ambulances."

Shani nodded as she breathed out again. As she shifted back to the compressions, her eyes darted toward Zane, who stood a few feet away. "I didn't mean to," he said, his chin trembling.

She couldn't stop to ask him what he was talking about, but her heart raced even faster. Was he responsible for the boy's injury?

Behind Zane, the four other Amish children huddled together, the oldest girl still holding the baby. The woman joined them. All were terror stricken and wide-eyed.

Shani shifted from the compressions to the two breaths again. As she shifted back to the compressions, she could see the father, frozen in place. He hadn't moved an inch—except his mouth, as if he were praying.

Shani felt for the boy's pulse a second time. It was faint. She began the compressions again with even more determination, continuing with her counting, silently chanting, *Live! Please live!* in between the numbers.

As she paused to take a deep breath she heard the wail of sirens.

Eve drew her nieces and nephews close, taking Trudy from Lila, and Rose grabbed Eve's legs through her long skirt as the ambulances screamed down the lane. The rain came down harder now, and she tucked all the children in front of herself, hoping to shield them.

Tim stood frozen in place, his eyes never leaving Simon and the Englisch woman as the ambulances came to a halt. One of the paramedics hopped out.

She pointed to Simon, and called out. "We need help here. And a man is injured at the next farm also. He's by himself. Hurry."

The man nodded, walked back to the second ambulance, and said something to the driver. The ambulance sped away without the siren. He then opened the back of the first vehicle. It seemed as if he moved in slow motion.

The driver stepped out of the cab and around to the back. A moment later both men appeared, carrying a yellow board and a box.

The Englisch woman kept pushing on Simon's chest and then blowing into his mouth, counting out loud as she did. Eve's own chest contracted. *Breathe, Simon. God, make him breathe,* she prayed. Fear tightened her throat, and she swallowed, trying to stay calm for the children.

Life wasn't easy in the Lehman household as it was. How much could one family bear?

The paramedics reached Simon, and the Englisch woman spoke to them as she continued to push on the boy's chest. The first paramedic knelt down on the ground too, his back to Eve, blocking her view.

The Englisch woman stood and stepped away, her long auburn hair curling in the damp morning air. It wasn't until the woman placed one hand on the small of her back that Eve realized she was pregnant.

Lila began to tremble. "Is Simon dead?"

Daniel crossed his arms. "Don't ask that."

Eve tightened her grip on the children. "He's going to be all right," she said. "The woman—your mother," she said to the Englisch boy who stood a few feet away, "she's been doing the right thing. And now those men will help too." She hoped she was right—that Simon would be okay. It didn't look good, honestly. She took a deep breath. "They'll take him to the hospital, where the doctors and nurses will take care of him."

The Englisch boy flicked his honey brown hair away from his eyes. "My mom's a nurse."

"We thank God that she is." Eve pulled her nieces and nephews closer, as if she could hug the boy and his mother too, with her gesture. "God sent her, to help us," Eve added.

The boy turned and looked at Eve, his brown eyes heavy. "We're only here because my dad got his leg blown up in Iraq." He swiped at his eyes. "I'm the one that scared the horse. I'm the reason"—he gestured toward Simon—"he got kicked."

Tears stung Eve's eyes. She wasn't sure how to respond.

The boy crossed his arms and stared straight ahead. He had a strong build, a square chin, and an air of confidence about him even in his grief.

Daniel pulled away from the other children.

Eve exhaled. "Sometimes God allows things . . ." She stopped, thinking about Abra dying and leaving five children behind. She was sure that was what Daniel was thinking about now too. "Things we can't understand."

Daniel darted toward Simon on the grass.

Lila took a step to follow her brother, calling out, "Stop!"

Eve pulled her back, whispering, "Hush."

Daniel stopped when the paramedics lifted Simon onto the board.

Trudy began to fuss. Eve bounced her as best she could, still keeping her arm around the older girls. Lila's trembling had turned into violent shivering. Eve needed to get the children inside.

But then the group started toward the ambulance. The Englisch woman turned toward Tim, who still stood frozen, staring after Simon. "Come on," she said. "You can ride with me."

Tim stood with his hat in his hand, his hair wet from the rain and plastered to his head. Eve couldn't help but feel concern for what the bishop's response would be when he heard about the accident. Just last Sunday, after he'd preached on parenting, he'd warned Tim about not doting on Simon. He'd even said that if Tim continued to spoil the child, God would intervene. She shuddered.

When Tim still didn't budge, the woman grabbed his arm and pulled him along. Daniel stepped forward, but Tim didn't acknowledge him. Daniel started following them toward the ambulance, until the Englisch woman told Daniel to stay. He stopped but kept his eyes on Simon as the paramedics slid the board through the back door.

"Come on, Zane," the Englisch woman said to her son, as she pushed her hair, now soaked, away from her face.

"He can stay here with us," Eve blurted out. "If that would help."

"Thank you," she said, twisting her hair onto her head and securing it with a band that had been on her wrist. "But he needs to come with me."

But the boy said, "I want to stay."

A troubled look passed over the woman's face.

The Englisch woman looked toward the road, then back at the boy. "Are you sure?"

He nodded.

"I don't know when I'll be back."

"We'll be here," Eve said.

"All right . . ." the woman said. She started to walk away but then turned. "Our friend—Charlie—is coming soon to help us. I'll . . . I'll call when I have service and tell him to stop here for Zane."

"All right," Eve said and then nodded toward the van. "Go with the woman," she said to Tim.

He turned toward her, a blank stare on his face.

Eve reached out her hand, touching his shoulder. "Go."

Tim didn't respond but started walking again. She'd never seen him so helpless.

By the time he reached the ambulance, the Englisch woman was at her van.

"It's a code three," the woman said. "They won't let you in the back with Simon. I'll drive you to the hospital, but we need to go now."

The children and Eve watched the ambulance leave, the siren blaring again. The Englisch woman pulled in behind it, with Tim in the passenger seat. The other ambulance waited on the lane, its siren off. The one with Simon in it took the lead.

The baby began to cry as Eve called out to Lila. "Grab the basket for the eggs. Daniel, you help." The best way to stay calm was to focus on their work.

Lila hurried to the back door of the house, returning a moment later with the basket. She and Daniel hurried toward the coop.

"Come on," Eve said to the Englisch boy.

"I'll help them." He walked after the twins.

Eve jiggled the baby on her hip and led Rose to the house. "We're late for school," Rose said.

Opening the door, Eve shook her head. "We'll miss today. Your teacher will understand."

Rose didn't seem happy with that, but didn't say anything. Eve knew she couldn't fully comprehend what had happened.

A half hour later she had the baby in her high chair gnawing on a cracker, a stack of hotcakes ready to go, and slices of ham warming in the frying pan. Zane and Daniel stood in the kitchen while Lila set the table. The Englisch boy had hardly said a word.

"*Fleicht eah is dum,*" Daniel said to Lila.

Obviously the boy wasn't dumb—more likely he was in shock. Perhaps he should have gone with his mother. Eve, alarmed at her nephew's rudeness, said, "*Sil is net shee,*" she responded, commanding Daniel to be nice, and then because he needed to learn not to hide behind their Pennsylvania Dutch, she added, "*Un shwietz Englisch.*"

Zane turned his head toward her at the word *Englisch*.

48

Aiming to change the subject, Eve said, "Let's eat." She called Rose in from the living room as she lifted the ham slices onto a plate with a fork. As everyone sat down, Lila put the hotcakes on the table. The boy reached for one.

"Wait," Daniel said.

The boy froze.

"We say a blessing first," Eve said. "A silent one." She knew not all Englisch understood their tradition.

"Let's thank the Lord for the food and remember Simon and the Englisch man," Daniel said, taking his role as the temporary head of the house seriously. They all bowed their heads. When they lifted them a minute later, the Englisch boy still had his bowed.

"Amen," Eve said.

He looked up, a confused expression on his face. "That was weird."

Daniel frowned and Eve shook her head at him. Still her nephew asked, "Don't you pray at home?"

"Well, yeah. Sometimes. But out loud. Not all quiet like." As he speared a hotcake, the boy turned to Eve and asked, "What happened to my dad?"

"Your mother said he fell on the steps."

The boy winced. "He was in the hospital and then rehab for three months."

"I'm sorry," Eve said.

The boy shrugged. Even sitting down, he was taller than the twins by several inches.

Lila leaned toward him across the table. "I'm sorry too. That had to have been hard on all of you." She was the most sensitive of all the children.

The boy crossed his arms but his face softened some.

"How old are you?" Lila asked.

"Twelve. How about you?"

"Eleven." She gestured toward her brother. "Daniel too."

"Twins?"

Lila nodded.

"Cool." The boy didn't smile but Lila did. Grief washed over Eve again. Lila was so much like her mother. Beautiful. Compassionate. Trusting. *Oh, Abra. If only you were here.*

ᎾᏫ 6

His truck lurched to the right as Charlie McCall drove down the rutted lane. He'd gotten an early start, just after six, but an accident on the turnpike had put him an hour behind. Hopefully Shani wasn't raring to get the house put in order just yet.

Charlie's muscles tightened as he gripped the steering wheel. It would bug Joel that he couldn't help, which would make for a tense day for all of them. Charlie hoped this move to Lancaster County would be good for the Becks, but he wasn't so sure. In fact, he feared the opposite.

But it wasn't his decision or even his business. His duty was to be as supportive as possible.

"I will never leave a fallen comrade," he said out loud into the misty morning. How many times had he recited that during his six years in the Army Reserve? He'd meant it every time.

Charlie was a medic—and Joel was still fallen. He wouldn't leave his friend. Couldn't leave.

Joel had been one of the AGRs—Active Guard Reserve—in their unit. Charlie was a weekend warrior, except during their deployment, but Joel had been full-time. Until he'd nearly had his leg blown off last May. Joel had been one of the best staff sergeants Charlie had ever known. A born leader. He would have done anything for his soldiers.

The radio crackled, and Charlie turned it up a little, hoping for a weather report. Instead it was the news. ". . . one thousand ninety-one US soldiers have been killed in Iraq."

Charlie snapped the radio off, thinking of the civilians who had been killed too, not to mention all the injuries. He didn't want to think about it today. If only he could stop the memories of the soldiers he'd tried to save.

But Joel hadn't died. The man had a wife who loved him and a son who had once idolized his father. Joel mourned being discharged from the service because of his injuries, but if he could just get through these next few months and figure out his life outside of the Army—even if it was as simple as being able to throw a football back and forth with Zane again—he would be all right.

Ahead a two-story house came into view. He exhaled in relief and whistled a few notes until he realized Shani's van wasn't anywhere in sight. Maybe she'd parked around back or in the shed. He stopped his truck, turned the key, and climbed down. He hoped it was the right house.

A folded quilt was on the doormat. He knocked, but when no one came, he stepped to the edge of the porch and peered in the window. The room

52

was dark. He rapped on the window and yelled, "Joel!" Then, "Zane!"

No one answered. He tried the door. It swung open. He paused for a moment, then picked up the quilt and stepped inside, calling out, "Joel!" Again, nothing.

He pulled his phone from his coat pocket, flipped it open, and hit Joel's number on speed dial. When nothing happened, he looked at the screen. *No service.* He put the quilt on the floor under the window, stepped back onto the porch, and pulled the door shut.

Maybe they'd gone out for breakfast. He'd drive back to the main road. Surely he'd be able to get service there.

He jumped back in his truck and headed up the lane, over the potholes, to the main road. He turned to the right and pulled over under a willow tree, opening his phone again. He had a message —from Shani.

Charlie froze as he listened and then groaned. Poor Joel. He stuffed his phone back into his pocket. First things first. He'd get Zane and then drive to the main road and call Shani back. A few minutes later he turned down the driveway to the neighbors and parked his truck. He wiped his palms on his jeans as he hurried up the steps to the front door.

After he knocked, he heard a child's voice call out, "Auntie!" but with some sort of accent.

After a long minute, the front door opened. A boy stood in front of him wearing suspenders, a white shirt, and black pants. *Amish.*

"I'm looking for my friends' son," he said, but then Zane popped up from the floor.

"Charlie!" The boy hurried toward him. "Dad hurt his leg and Simon got kicked—"

"Who's Simon?"

"Daniel and Lila's brother. I scared the horse." Zane's chin began to quiver, and Charlie drew him close, glancing up as he did.

The Amish boy stood beside an Amish girl. In front of them was a younger girl. A woman, wearing an apron over a long dress and a white bonnet—or whatever it was called—stood behind them holding a baby. His grandparents had belonged to the Brethren Church, and his grandmother had worn a prayer veil over her white hair during church—but not anytime else.

This woman's dark eyes were kind and striking under the bit of dark hair he could see. She had an old-fashioned beauty about her, with faint dimples, smooth skin, and a thin face.

"Ma'am," Charlie said, nodding his head.

"*Hallo,*" she answered, stepping forward. "I'm Eve Lehman." She extended her free hand, and he shook it, still holding onto Zane with his other.

"Pleased to meet you," he said. "I'm Charlie McCall."

The baby began to fuss, and the woman stepped

back and started to sway. "I thought maybe you'd come with word about Simon—and Zane's Dat— but it seems you haven't been to the hospital yet."

"That's right," he said. "I had a message. That's why I came here—to get Zane."

The woman nodded.

He glanced down. Clearly Zane felt horrible. Charlie looked back at the woman and said, "What happened?"

"One of the workhorses kicked Simon in the head," she answered.

"I was just trying to be friendly." Zane's voice was muffled. "I didn't see the horse, not at first."

The woman's eyes grew moist, and she stepped forward, putting her hand on Zane's shoulder. He turned his head toward her. "Don't despair," she said. "You have our forgiveness, whatever happened. We all must trust God—that's what is best."

Zane swiped at his eyes but didn't answer.

Charlie squeezed the boy's shoulder, impressed with the woman's words. "So they're all at the hospital?"

She nodded. "The Englisch woman—"

"Shani," he said.

"*Denki.*"

"Pardon?"

"Thank you."

He nodded, realizing she'd spoken in their language.

The woman continued. "Shani drove. Tim rode with her." She spoke above the little one's cry. "Excuse me a minute," she said. "I need to put the baby down for her nap."

Charlie squeezed Zane's shoulder. "Get your coat."

"I don't have one."

"You can wear mine," Charlie said, taking it off. "We'll go straight to the hospital."

Zane shook his head. "I don't want to go."

Charlie wasn't sure how to answer.

"I hate hospitals."

"Ahh," he said. And no wonder. Shani hadn't taken Zane to Germany with her when Joel was at Landstuhl, but he had gone to Texas when Joel had been relocated to Brooke Army Hospital. The three of them had been there for nearly two months. Charlie had gone down as soon as he could, once he was home from Iraq. He took Zane to the Alamo and the San Antonio Zoo to get him out of the hospital. Both Joel and Shani seemed to appreciate that. He was grateful he could be a friend to the whole family.

"Once we have cell service, we'll call your mom and see what she wants us to do," he said.

The woman returned, her arms empty.

"How old is your baby?" Charlie asked.

Her face reddened. "Eight months. But she's not mine. She's my niece. All of the children are my brother's."

"I see," Charlie said, his face growing warm. He'd been so sure the woman was a wife and mother—although she did seem young to have so many children. "Let's go, bud," Charlie said to Zane. "So I can call your mom."

The woman stepped toward them and asked, "Would you like a cup of coffee before you go?"

The Amish boy gave him a suspicious look, and Charlie wondered, for a moment, if it was appropriate for him to be in the house with Eve. He wasn't looking to cause anyone any trouble, especially not a kind Amish woman who, it seemed, was single.

"Denki," he said with a smile. "But we should get going."

They said their good-byes and headed toward the front door. Although he'd grown up on a farm, he'd had a typical American childhood with all the latest gadgets and electronics, which meant Nintendo and Game Boys by the time he graduated high school ten years ago. But being in the Amish house made him think of his grandparents. They had a telephone in their home but no TV or even a radio. He'd often longed for a life like that growing up, but even more so after serving a year in Iraq.

Shani slipped her cell phone back into the pocket of her damp sweatshirt. Charlie and Zane were on their way.

She leaned against the hallway of the emergency department and wrapped her hands around the sides of her belly, stopping the shiver that threatened to run through her. She shouldn't have left Zane at the Amish house. She'd been too focused on Simon and Joel to deny his request. True, he'd only been a little over fifteen minutes away, but it had still made her uneasy.

Charlie would be a distraction for Zane while they were at the hospital, but that too concerned her. Joel didn't seem to notice that Zane and Charlie had been growing closer, while father and son drifted further apart. That was another reason she was sure the move to Lancaster County would be best for all of them. But now she wondered how Joel would handle another setback. He'd been so fragile since the attack. He wasn't the man she'd married, not at all. He'd played football in high school. A year ago he was still running a six-minute mile. He was an expert shooter. Nothing in his previous life had prepared him for sitting in a wheelchair.

She wrapped her arms around her chest, resting

them on her growing bump. She knew its visibility made Joel anxious. She hadn't been careful when he'd been home on his furlough last April. If she'd known Joel was going to be injured she would have taken precautions, but the truth was she hadn't been careful for years.

She shivered again and then stepped around the corner as the aide pushed the gurney through the curtain. "X-rays," Joel said.

"Want me to go along?" She reached for his hand.

He squeezed hers and then let it slip away. "No. Rest until I get back."

She nodded. But she wouldn't rest; she'd get something to eat instead. She turned the opposite way of the gurney and then ducked into the far room of the ER. It took her a moment for her eyes to adjust to the dim light.

Tim sat in the chair, his head in his hands. Simon was flat on his back on the gurney. The split along his jawline had been stitched. Faint purple bruises had begun to spread around it and under his left eye too.

Shani stepped around the side and addressed Tim. "How is he?"

"Sleeping," Tim answered. He was a man of few words. He'd only answered her questions with a *jah* or a *nee* in the car.

At least Simon was breathing. "Do you know what the doctor ordered, as far as tests?" Shani asked.

Tim exhaled. "X-rays and something else."

"An MRI?" Shani asked.

"Jah," the man said. "That's it."

At the least Simon had a concussion. And a broken jaw. Thankfully his neck didn't seem to be broken, but he could have bleeding in his brain. The MRI would determine that. He was lucky the horse had missed his mouth. Otherwise he'd have a bunch of broken teeth to deal with too.

Shani stepped toward the door. "I'll check in a little later. After the MRI."

The man didn't respond.

She spoke to him directly. "I'm going to get a bite to eat. Care to join . . . me?" She regretted asking by the time the last word came out. The man looked downright uncomfortable. "Or I can bring you something."

He stayed silent.

"I'll be in the cafeteria. It's on this floor." Shani didn't anticipate an answer from Tim, so she simply waved and stepped from the room. Her cell phone buzzed as she reached the waiting room, but when she pulled it out of her pocket she saw Charlie, his cell phone to his ear, leading the way through the sliding glass doors. Zane trailed behind, wearing a coat that was much too large.

Sure enough, the call was from Charlie. She hit End, slipped the phone back into her pocket, and waved.

Zane was at that age where his arms and legs

had outgrown his body. Usually his smile was as gangly as his limbs, but not today. A worried expression had replaced it.

Charlie saw her and lowered the phone. When they met in the middle of the waiting room, he asked, "How's Joel?"

"On his way to X-ray."

"What about Simon?" Zane asked.

"He has a broken jaw for sure. He'll get X-rays too and then an MRI."

Zane bit his lip, and Shani pulled him close.

"Charlie let me steer his truck up to the highway," Zane said.

She smiled. It was like him to switch subjects so quickly. He was already trying to get her to let him drive in a teasing way, even though he had over two more years until he could get his permit.

She hugged him tight as footsteps sounded behind her.

Zane's eyes widened. She turned around as Tim stopped a foot away.

"I need to use a phone," he said. "To leave a message for our bishop."

"You can use mine," Shani said, pulling it from her pocket.

He took it. For a moment she wasn't sure if he'd know how to use it, but he flipped it open and stepped away from them. Shani nodded toward a row of chairs, and Charlie led the way. Once they sat, she kept her eye on Tim. He paced back and forth but then stopped as he spoke into the phone. She expected him to be done quickly, but when he paused and then spoke again she realized he hadn't left a message. He was having a conversation.

Tim paced back toward her. "I didn't expect you to be in the shop," he said. "I just wanted you to know what was going on. I'd rather talk about the rest later."

He listened for a moment, pacing back the other way, then back toward Shani. "Jah, I know you warned me." A shadow fell across Tim's face. Was the bishop blaming him for something?

He paced the other way. When he returned, he flipped the phone shut and extended it to Shani.

She took it. "Hungry?" she asked.

He nodded. "They're taking the boy for the MRI. They said I'd have some time."

Shani stood, introducing Charlie to Tim. "You're Eve's brother, right?" Charlie said as he shook the man's hand.

Tim's expression hardened. "How do you know Eve?"

"I don't," Charlie said, his voice as calm as always, his dark eyes kind. "I just met her when I picked up Zane."

"I'm confused," Shani said. "Who is Eve?"

"The woman who called 9-1-1," Zane said. "The one who asked if I wanted to stay with them."

"Oh." Shani had thought the woman was Tim's

wife, the mother of all the children. Where was his wife?

"Let's go eat," Shani said, pointing toward the hall and leading the way.

Once in the cafeteria, Zane stuck by her side while the men went their separate ways. When it came time to pay, Shani kept her eye on Tim, wondering if he had any money with him.

She smiled when he pulled out a card. She couldn't tell if it was debit or credit—either way it surprised her. She wrinkled her nose. It looked like she had a lot to learn about the Amish.

Charlie chose a table by the window, and the rest joined him. The rain had stopped, and rays of sunshine landed on the wet street. Once they'd settled into their chairs, Tim bowed his head. Zane pressed his lips together as Charlie bowed his head too. Then Zane followed the example of the men. Shani stared out the window at the Emergency Department sign, and spoke silently. *You're up to something, aren't you?* She hadn't prayed much lately, just the plea for happiness yesterday, and she doubted this one warranted much of a response either.

Once everyone had raised their heads again, Shani—as she grabbed her fork—asked Tim if he'd been to this hospital before.

He nodded as he buttered his toast. "My wife had our youngest daughter here. And she came here for the cancer treatments too."

Shani almost dropped her fork. "The baby has cancer?"

"No, my wife."

Shani's stomach fell, and she put the fork back down on the table, unable to ask the next question.

Thankfully Tim didn't let it go that long. "She passed away five months ago." He dipped his toast in his eggs and then took a bite.

"I'm so sorry," Shani said, feeling as if her own baby were cutting off her ability to breathe. Five children, motherless. A husband, left alone. She swallowed hard, trying to push down the intense fear she'd had of losing Joel.

This family, their neighbors, had experienced all of that, plus the realization of that fear—around the same time Joel had been injured.

"I'm so sorry," Shani said again.

Tim swallowed his food. "The Lord giveth and the Lord taketh away."

Shani knew the next line—*Blessed be the name of the Lord*—but didn't say it out loud.

A long silence fell on the table as everyone ate. Finally Charlie said to Tim, "That's a nice piece of property you have."

"God uses it to provide for my family," the man responded. "Along with the land I lease."

"Which land is that?" Shani asked.

"Old Man Williams' property."

"My grandfather's?"

Tim nodded. "How long will you be staying in the house?"

"For as long as we need," Shani answered.

"Oh," Tim replied.

"Why?"

"I thought it was just a short time."

Shani's face grew warm. "No. I mean, I'm not sure." If it was up to her, they'd stay indefinitely, but it wasn't her choice alone.

Tim put his toast down, wiped his hands on his napkin, and took a long drink of his coffee. Then he focused on Zane. "You scared the horse, jah?"

"I didn't mean to," Zane answered.

"Jah, I know. But you did. And then the horse backed up and kicked Simon."

Shani's heart beat faster.

He continued. "And now Simon won't be able to do his chores. The doctor said he'll have to rest in a dark room. We'll see what else they say after the test."

Zane exhaled.

"So now you need to take responsibility for your actions."

Zane squared his shoulders and said, "Eve said I've already been forgiven."

"Jah, that's true," Tim answered. "But you still need to make the situation right."

Shani shifted in her chair. "What are you getting at?"

"The boy needs to do Simon's chores. I'm down

a worker. If Daniel and I have to take the time to do Simon's work, we'll get behind."

Shani couldn't help but look at Charlie. He nodded in return and then said, "That sounds fair." Shani wasn't so sure.

Zane leaned back in his chair. "What chores does Simon do?"

"He helps milk the cows twice a day—all forty of them. And feeds the chickens and gathers the eggs. He waters, feeds, and grooms the horses, and cleans out the dairy and all the animal stalls. Plus he helps in the fields and repairs fences some, although I do most of that." Tim took the last bite of his eggs.

Zane appeared bewildered. "That's a lot of chores. What about Daniel?"

"He does the same and helps Eve around the house as well."

Zane tipped back on his chair, but Shani reached over and placed her hand on the edge of the seat, pushing it back to the floor as she asked, "How do they have time to do all that and go to school too?"

Tim reached for another napkin. "They manage."

Shani felt her face grow warm at Tim's abruptess.

But Zane didn't seem upset at all. "What time do you need me?"

"Six a.m. Sharp."

Shani couldn't help but ask, "For how long?"

"An hour or two in the morning," Tim answered. "And then another hour in the afternoon."

"No, I mean how many days?"

He shrugged. "Until Simon can take over again."

Shani couldn't imagine how that would work once she started her orientation and Zane was in school. But she wouldn't say anything now. She'd talk to Tim without Zane around.

She took a bite of her omelet, wondering how Joel would react to Tim's edict. Then she nearly choked as her name came over the PA system. "Shani Beck," the voice said again. "Please report to X-ray."

"Uh-oh," Zane said.

"Want me to come with you?" Charlie asked.

"Please," she answered. "And you too," she said to Zane.

"I can go with him." Zane pointed to Tim. "And see Simon."

"He's not up to visitors," Shani said.

"The boy can wait out in the hall," Tim answered. "Come find him there when you're done. Leave your trays. We'll take care of them."

Shani nodded her thanks and hurried out of the cafeteria. Charlie's footsteps sounded behind her. Every day she struggled to juggle it all—Joel, Zane, the pregnancy, her job, their finances, the mass of Army paperwork. She thought coming to Lancaster would simplify things.

Not make them worse.

ಬಿ 8

That afternoon Eve opened the oven door and grabbed the first pan of sticky buns, lifting it to the stovetop. Then she did the same with the second pan.

"Grab me a towel," she said to Lila. She'd checked the answering machine in the barn for a message from Tim after she put Trudy down for her nap, but there hadn't been one. There had been one from the bishop though, left for Tim, asking what the results of Simon's test had been. Obviously Tim had called him that morning.

She supposed no news was good news as far as Simon was concerned, but she still wondered how he was doing. That's why she'd decided to go over to the new neighbors' with sticky buns to see if they'd returned from the hospital. She should have thought to ask Charlie to give her an update.

Eve would help Daniel with the evening chores after she delivered the rolls. He insisted he could do it all himself, but she knew he'd need help with the milking.

Lila returned with the towel. "Can I come with you?"

"I need you to stay with Rose and Trudy." She could hear the baby fussing in her crib.

"They could come too. The fresh air would do

them good." Lila spoke with confidence. "I'll tell Rose to get her shoes on. And I'll carry Trudy."

"All right," Eve said. It wasn't as if she planned to spend any time visiting with the neighbors. She just wanted to give them the buns, ask about the Englisch woman's husband, and see if they had any news about Simon.

She spread the towel out on the table, put a couple of hot pads down, and then set the pans on top. By the time she had the first pan wrapped for the neighbors, Lila stepped into the kitchen with her cape on and holding the baby.

Rose sat on the floor, pulling her shoes on.

"Hurry," Eve said to her as she headed to the mud porch for their capes. Rose appeared a minute later.

"Will we see the man from this morning?" she asked, taking her cape.

"Maybe," Eve responded, but of course she didn't know if they'd see Charlie.

"He's nice," Rose said.

Eve didn't answer. She knew Tim wouldn't want her encouraging his children to feel fondly toward an Englisch man, but she silently agreed with Rose. He had been kind.

"Ready?" Lila waited at the door, bouncing the baby on her hip.

Eve doubted Lila was looking forward to seeing the man again. More likely, she had her eye on the boy. Tim wouldn't be happy about that either.

Rose led the way out the door and ran down the steps and toward the lane. "Let's go the back way," Eve called out. "And check on Daniel on the way back." He'd be herding the cows toward the barn for milking soon.

For a moment Rose lagged behind, probably a little miffed at not being able to choose their route, but then she ran ahead again toward the gate, her cape flying behind her.

Eve stopped for a moment. If Charlie was at the neighbors and Shani wasn't, would she appear forward? She wrinkled her nose. Probably not, considering she had the three children with her. That thought made her thankful Lila had suggested tagging along.

As Rose reached the gate, Charlie appeared on the other side. He wore a baseball cap, the same coat, and leather gloves.

"Well, hello, little lady," he said, swinging open the gate for Rose. "Where are you off to?"

"Your house."

"My house?"

Rose tilted her head back as she looked up. "With a pan of sticky buns."

Charlie looked past Rose, first at Lila and the baby and then at Eve. "Well," he said. "That's awfully kind of you. But you'd better hurry." He pointed toward the lane. "Shani is getting ready to head back to the hospital." He waved at Eve. "I was headed to your place to tell you how

Simon is doing—but Shani can fill you in."

"Come on, girls," Eve said. Lila ran ahead, making Trudy laugh, but Rose didn't move.

Eve tugged on the girl, pulling her along.

Lila had reached the lane and was waving. As Eve arrived, Shani stopped her van. She lowered the passenger window and leaned toward it. "Did Charlie tell you how Simon's doing?"

Eve shook her head and stepped forward, bracing herself for bad news. That seemed to be all they'd had lately.

"He's awake but has a concussion. And a broken jaw. They wired it shut, so he'll only be able to eat liquids for six weeks, maybe a little longer. There's no bleeding in his brain, so all and all he's doing amazingly well." She smiled. "He should be fine once everything heals up."

Eve's knees felt weak in relief. "And your husband? How is he?"

The woman shook her head. "He broke his tibia again. And on top of that, he's out of sorts. He had . . . an unsympathetic X-ray technician this morning. I snuck home while he's in surgery to get some of his things."

Eve didn't know how to respond. Should she say she was sorry? That hardly seemed appropriate. Instead she said, "How about Tim? Is he coming home tonight?"

Shani shook her head. "He said he'd spend the night at the hospital."

Eve lifted the pan. "I made some sticky buns for your family."

"Oh, thanks," Shani answered. "I don't know what time I'll be back. Could I get them tomorrow? I'll be around then. I need to start on the unpacking."

"Of course," Eve answered as she stepped back from the car.

"Thank you." Shani waved. "I'll see you then."

As they walked back to their farm, Lila said, "We could help her unpack."

"I doubt we'd do much good," Eve answered. Shani seemed awfully self-sufficient. "I'll put the sticky buns back in the house, and then let's go see how the milking is coming along. I'll stay and help Daniel while you watch the little girls."

A few minutes later, as they approached the barn, her nephew barked, "Just one shovelful of grain."

Eve quickened her steps, wondering whom Daniel was talking to. Lila hurried along too, bumping into Eve as they made their way through the barn door. Daniel leaned against a cow, pushing her head into the stall, while Zane stood back a few feet away, a shovel in his hands. Charlie led a cow out of a stall, directed her toward the exit, and then turned around, his eyes connecting with Eve's.

"What are you doing here?" she asked.

He grinned. "Milking."

"You don't need to do that," she said, reaching for the last vinyl apron hanging from the hook on the wall. "I'm going to help Daniel."

Charlie motioned toward Zane. He stepped back to the grain bin and dug the shovel in. As he dumped it into the trough for the next cow, the boy said, "Tim said I needed to do Simon's chores."

Eve's face grew warm. Leave it to her brother to try to control the neighbors' lives too.

"He's going to help out until Simon is well enough to help again." Charlie's voice was extra kind. He must have sensed her discomfort.

"How about you?" she asked. "Surely you have better things to do than our chores."

"No, I enjoy it. I grew up on a farm."

"Really?" She'd taken him for a city boy.

"Not a dairy, mind you. We raised beef, but my grandparents had a milk cow."

Daniel cleared his throat, looking straight at Charlie. "Are you getting the next one or should I?"

"Daniel!" Eve stepped toward her nephew. It wasn't like him to be so bossy.

"I'm just doing my job, Aenti," he said. "Someone needs to be in charge."

Charlie grinned again and then said, over his shoulder as he hurried the opposite way toward the holding pen, "The boy's right."

Trudy began to fuss. "I can stay and help," Lila said. "I'll trade you the baby for the apron."

73

Eve draped the apron over her niece's shoulder and then hoisted the baby from the girl's arms.

"You can show Zane how to do the feed," Daniel told Lila as he checked the tubing and then headed toward the vat in the milk room.

"Bring everyone in for dinner when you're done," Eve said to Lila, shifting Trudy to her hip. It was the least she could do, considering all that Charlie and Zane were doing to help. And it wasn't like Tim would be getting home anytime soon, although Rose would tell him later that she'd invited the Englischers into the house for a meal. She'd just have to deal with him when the time came.

Charlie herded another cow into the barn.

"If you put the grain in now, it'll encourage the cow to come to the right slot." Lila pointed to the trough, and Zane dumped the grain. The cow moved forward and dipped her head down to eat.

"Good work." Lila scratched the cow between her ears while Zane turned back around to the grain bin.

Eve reached for Rose's hand.

"I want to stay," the girl said. "With the Englischers."

Eve spoke softly. "Not today."

As Charlie approached with another cow, Rose put her free hand on her hip and asked, "What did the lady mean when she said her husband was 'out of sorts'?"

Eve shook her head. "Rose," she whispered. "That's none of our business."

Zane stood at the trough, balancing the shovel in his hands. "Did my mom say that?"

"Jah," Rose answered.

Zane turned toward Charlie. "He's always out of sorts these days."

"Your dad had a rough time with the X-ray technician is all." Charlie pointed toward the shovel. "Dump the grain."

Zane did as he was instructed.

"Come on, Rose," Eve said, leading her niece toward the door. To Charlie, she said, "We'll have supper waiting for all of you when you're done." She'd sit Rose down first and give her a talking to though. Eve had been lax in teaching the child her manners.

"Good-bye!" Rose called out to Charlie. As Eve dragged her through the barn, the little girl called out again, this time to Zane, "Don't scare the cows. They kick too!"

"Rose," Eve chided.

"We'll be careful," Charlie replied, the hint of a smile pressing against the serious line of his lips.

An hour later Eve put the noodles into the boiling water when Lila, Daniel, and Zane came in— without Charlie. "He's going to the store outside of Strasburg," Zane said, "to get some groceries. But he said I could eat with all of you."

Eve's face grew warm. She shouldn't have asked Charlie to supper.

"Then I need to head home so we can move boxes and stuff around," Zane said.

"Why don't you help them?" Eve turned to Daniel as she dished up the green beans.

"I can help too," Lila said.

Eve shook her head. "I need your help here." She put the plates on the table and the children gathered around.

Rose climbed onto Tim's chair. "Do you have a TV?" she asked Zane.

He nodded.

"And a computer?"

He nodded again.

"How about a cell phone?"

"Not yet," he answered. "But Mom said she'll get me one by the time I'm in high school." He sat down next to Daniel. "You don't have any modern stuff in your house, right?"

"Jah," Lila answered. "Just the phone in the barn."

"We don't need anything else," Daniel said. "None of our people have electronic stuff."

That wasn't entirely true. Sure, none of the families in their district had TVs, but some had a computer in their shop or barn, to use exclusively for business. And many of the youth had cell phones they charged with batteries out in their barns, but she didn't need to explain that to Zane.

Eve drained the noodles and placed them on the table along with the creamed chicken, green beans, and applesauce. Daniel led them all in a silent prayer again. As the children ate, Eve started on the pots and pans and listened to their chatter. She wasn't hungry.

After a few minutes, Daniel asked, "What did your Dat do in the Army?"

"He was a staff sergeant in a signal unit."

Eve was grateful Simon wasn't hearing the conversation. Daniel leaned forward. "What's that?"

"They figure out the communication stuff— installing networks, connecting with satellites, teleconferencing, fixing cables, that sort of thing."

"So he wasn't really a soldier?" Daniel said, leaning back in his chair.

Zane shook his head. "He was."

"But he didn't shoot anyone?"

Eve turned toward the table. "Daniel," she said. "There are all sorts of different soldiers."

Daniel shrugged.

"He got shot at," Zane said. "Lots of different times. Then an RPG hit his Humvee."

Daniel sat up straight. "A what?"

"A rocket-propelled grenade," Zane explained and then shoved his last bite of noodles into his mouth.

"Oh," Daniel responded and then asked, "Does he have one of those uniforms?"

"Sure," Zane said. "Lots of them."

Daniel frowned. Zane picked up his plate and headed toward the sink.

"Thank you," Zane said.

" *'Wilcom,*" Eve answered.

"Pardon?"

She smiled. "It's Pennsylvania Dutch for 'you're welcome.' "

"So that's what it's called. It's what Daniel and you were speaking this morning." Zane pointed toward Rose. "And what she speaks, right?"

"All of us speak it, but, jah, Rose more than the rest of us. She hasn't had as much experience with English."

"Will you teach me?" Zane asked.

Daniel harrumphed behind her. "That'll be the day." Eve frowned at him again.

"Zane could learn," Lila said.

"Nah," Daniel said. "He doesn't have any reason to learn it."

"I like languages," Zane said. *"Je parle français. Yo hablo español. Ich spreche Deutsch."*

Rose laughed. *"Jah! Wie alt sind?"*

"Zwölf," Zane replied.

Rose laughed again. *"Ich bin sieben."*

Zane high-fived her, which made her laugh even more. "I don't really speak German, although I am twelve," Zane said. "And I'm pleased to know you're seven." He smiled at her. "I don't speak French either. But I do speak a little Spanish, and I'm going to take it in my new school."

"We study German in our school," Lila said.

Rose grinned. "I'm getting pretty good at it."

Eve shook her head at the little girl, warning her not to be prideful.

"And you study Pennsylvania Dutch too?" Zane asked.

Lila answered, "No, we just learn it. When we're little. It's not a written language so we can't study it."

Zane's expression soured. "Oh."

"Jah, that's why you can't learn it." Daniel headed toward the door.

Lila's voice was low, but Eve still heard her clearly—"I'll teach you."

Zane smiled and then followed Daniel out the door.

Eve called after her nephew. "Check on the cow that is due on your way back."

"I know!" Daniel responded. "You don't have to tell me."

"Denki!" Zane yelled as he ran out the door.

9

The next morning Zane and Charlie headed out to the neighbors' as Shani left for the hospital. Charlie appeared rested, especially for having slept in his truck. She trusted him completely, but she also appreciated his sense of propriety.

Before visiting Joel, she checked in with Tim, who looked like he hadn't slept at all. However, Simon seemed to be doing better. She introduced herself, and through the wires he murmured, "Hallo."

Tim followed her out to the hall. "How long are you staying today?"

"A few hours."

"I need a ride back to the farm."

She contemplated his words, wondering why he'd be leaving. "Will Simon be all right without you?"

"His grandparents are coming." Tim's focus shifted down the hall. "My wife's Mamm and Dat."

"Oh," Shani said. He didn't seemed very pleased about their visit. "Of course I'll give you a ride."

Joel dozed most of the morning, and when she got ready to leave, she told him she'd back in the late afternoon or early evening. He squeezed her hand, but that was all.

Tim hardly spoke on the way home. As she drove up the Lehmans' driveway, she passed a wagon heading toward the house.

"Who's that?" Shani asked Tim.

"Our bishop." Tim squinted out the window and shaded his eyes with his hand. "Gideon." The man stopped the wagon by the clothesline.

Shani shifted into Park in front of the house and turned off the ignition.

"You don't need to stop in," Tim said.

"Eve has something for me."

"Oh." Tim kept his head down and opened the door without looking at her.

She climbed out quickly and pushed up her long sleeves as she strode toward the house. The day had grown warm. Unsure of whether to go to the back door or the front, she glanced at Tim, hoping he might instruct her.

He'd walked back to the bishop, his arms crossed and stance wide, oblivious to her.

She decided on the front door and knocked a few rapid beats. Little feet pattered toward her, and then the door swung open. The little girl, braids sticking out from beneath her little bonnet, turned her round face upward and smiled broadly.

"Is your aunt home?" Shani asked.

"Jah."

"May I speak to her?"

The older girl appeared. A strand of her blond hair had managed to work its way out of her bun at the base of her neck. "Rose, invite our neighbor in." The girl was polite and poised.

Rose stepped back, sweeping her arm in a wide arc. "Come in."

Shani smiled as she stepped over the threshold. The little girl had quite a presence.

Eve stepped into the living room. "Hallo," she said. "How is Simon today?"

"He's doing much better."

Eve exhaled and then asked, "How about your husband?"

"Okay," Shani answered.

"*Gut*," the woman said.

Shani guessed that meant *good*. She looked around as her mouth watered from the smell of something baking.

"We're having lunch. Soup and biscuits. Would you like some?" the woman asked.

Shani'd had a protein bar for breakfast. And then another one midmorning. "Sure."

"Zane and Charlie are here," Eve said.

"Are they staying to eat?" Shani followed Eve.

Eve shrugged. "I invited them."

Shani stepped into the kitchen. Charlie stood by the back door, while Zane sat at the table, along with the baby and the older boy. Zane appeared as comfortable as could be.

"Fancy meeting you here," she said, tousling his hair. He ducked away.

Charlie stepped closer. "We're just taking a

break. All the boxes are in the right rooms and mostly unpacked. We left the kitchen and bathroom for you. Of course you'll have to say exactly where you want the furniture." He grinned.

"Sounds good."

Eve motioned for her to sit down and then pulled a plate and bowl from the cupboard. She turned to Charlie. "Would you like some soup?"

He glanced at Shani. She nodded, hoping she communicated he could go back to the farmhouse and make a sandwich or be gracious and eat Eve's soup.

"Sure," Charlie said, heading to the empty seat by the baby. The baby tried to pick up a slice of cooked carrot on her high-chair tray and fussed when she couldn't. After an odd silent prayer, Charlie speared the veggie with his fork and held it to the baby's mouth. She managed to pry it off with her lips.

Shani couldn't help but smile. The man was a natural. Nikki Hall had been a fool to let him go—and a coldhearted one to do it while he'd been deployed. But, selfishly, Shani knew having Charlie unattached meant he was more available to help Joel. He worked three days each week at a fire department on the edge of Philly and had spent much of his time off the past two months trying to encourage Joel to keep doing his exercises and stay positive.

The two hadn't met until Joel was assigned to

Charlie's unit and moved to Philly to get ready to deploy while Shani and Zane stayed behind in California. Charlie had quickly become Joel's closest friend. Shani and Zane had met Charlie at Fort Hood when they'd visited before the soldiers shipped out. Joel, Charlie, and Zane had played football on the lawn in front of the barracks. They'd all gone out to dinner together several times.

Nikki had come down the last few days they were there. It was the first time Shani had met her, and she liked her.

Over and over, when they'd Skyped with Joel once he was in-country, Charlie had been around, kidding with Zane and telling stories about Joel. Charlie had been a good friend to all of them.

Eve dished the soup into bowls and passed them around the table.

"Daniel, pass the biscuits," she said.

The boy complied. Shani breathed in deeply as she sliced the warm biscuit in half and spread butter on each side, remembering her grandmother's cooking.

"Mom," Zane said, "maybe you could take some cooking lessons."

The other children froze.

Shani smiled. "It's no secret that I'm a really bad cook. My idea of lunch—and breakfast and dinner—is a protein bar. Sadly, my husband and son don't agree."

Eve gasped. "But you're growing—" She stopped, her face reddening.

Shani filled in the blank. "A baby."

Eve nodded.

"Yep. And I really am trying to eat better." If only the drama in their life would stop so she could work out a normal schedule.

"Mom?" Zane was staring at her.

"Yes?"

"What's up with Dad?"

"He's back in traction, and then they'll cast the leg again. They adjusted his painkillers too." Upped them. "The doctor said he'll be able to come home by the end of the week." They'd need a ramp by then. There was no way she could help Charlie lift the wheelchair, and Zane wasn't strong enough to do it either.

Besides, Charlie needed to be back for work on Tuesday.

She turned to Eve. "Do you know a carpenter in the area? I need someone to build a ramp." Shani took a bite of the biscuit. It melted in her mouth.

"I can do it," Charlie said.

"We don't have many tools," Shani said. "And I think all of my grandfather's were sold."

"Jah," the oldest boy said. "Our Dat bought them."

"Tim can do it," Eve said.

"No," Shani said. "He has too much going on."

85

Eve shook her head. "He's quick with that sort of work. He'd want to do it."

"Well, that's not what I intended. I thought you could recommend someone. But I can pay Tim— or someone else." Shani took a spoonful of the soup. It was hearty and delicious.

Eve started to say something more but stopped. The older girl and the boy looked at her. "I'll talk to him," she said.

"I think he'll be in soon," Shani said.

"What do you mean?" Eve stood and started toward the window. "He's here?"

Shani nodded toward the driveway. "He's outside, talking to the bishop."

Eve pulled back the curtain, a concerned expression on her face. "Simon's alone at the hospital?"

"His grandparents were coming this afternoon . . ." Shani said, but she stopped when she realized Eve was shaking her head. Shani's voice quieted but she continued. "So Tim came back here."

Daniel crossed his arms over his suspenders. "He didn't need to come back. I'm taking care of everything here. He just didn't want to spend the afternoon with *Dawdi* and *Mammi*—that's all."

Eve stepped back from the glass, shooting Daniel a sympathetic look. Lila said, "It's good he has visitors besides Dat. Has he been lonely?"

"Not too much," Shani answered. "He'll probably be home by tomorrow. He's definitely traumatized, but considering what happened, he's doing well." Shani glanced toward the window and then at Eve. "Tim said he'd go back tonight after the grandparents go home. When I go back to see Joel."

Eve stepped back to the window, wrapping her arms around herself.

"Is everything all right?" Charlie asked.

Eve nodded.

"I want to go see Dawdi and Mammi," Rose said.

"Hush," Lila responded.

A pout settled on the little girl's face. "Then I want to go out and see Dat and the bishop."

"Wait until we're done eating," Eve said, sitting back down at the table.

Rose didn't seem to be afraid of her father, but Shani wasn't so sure about the twins.

The baby began to fuss again, and Charlie fed her another carrot.

"We have cookies for dessert," Lila said. "Snickerdoodles."

"What are snickerdoodles?" Zane asked.

"I've failed you." Shani sighed, thinking about the cookies her grandmother used to make. "You're in for a real treat."

By the time Tim came into the house, Shani and Eve were doing the dishes while Charlie held the baby and the children ate their cookies. Stepping forward, Charlie held out his right hand while balancing the baby with his left.

Tim shook his hand, although without much enthusiasm. He ignored the baby, and she didn't reach for him or acknowledge him in anyway. She seemed content to have Charlie hold her.

The older children scampered away into the living room.

"Shani needs someone to build a ramp," Eve said to Tim. "So Joel can come home. He's going to be in a wheelchair for a while."

"I was hoping I might hire you," Shani said.

"I can help," Charlie added. "As long as we can use your tools."

Tim didn't answer.

"Wash up," Eve said. "You'd better eat before the soup gets cold."

He started to leave the kitchen without answering, but then stopped and said to Eve, "The bishop said to tell you hallo."

Eve didn't respond. Instead, the woman turned toward Charlie and said, "Do you think the wood for the ramp will fit in your truck?"

Charlie nodded.

"There's a lumberyard nearby," she said. "Daniel and Zane can move the furniture around while you're gone." Eve dried her hands and put out her hands for the baby.

Charlie slid the little one into her arms. "I'll go take a look at where the ramp needs to go."

Shani said, "There's a measuring tape in—"

"I have one in the truck," Charlie replied, heading for the back door.

Eve called out to the children, telling them to come into the kitchen. A moment later Daniel and Zane appeared, followed by the oldest girl.

"Lila can go help you finish unpacking," Eve said to Shani. "Or if you'd rather, she can stay here and I can help you."

"Why don't you both come?"

"The baby needs to nap." Eve bounced the little one on her hip.

"We have a portable crib. She can nap at our place."

"Rose would need to come too," Lila said.

"I'll put her to work." Shani dried the last plate.

Tim returned, with Rose at his side. "Where'd Charlie go?"

"He's going to the lumberyard," Eve said.

"Why didn't he wait for me?"

Eve pursed her lips, and then said to Daniel and Zane, "Go tell Charlie that Tim will go to the lumberyard with him after he eats. Then stay at the house so Shani can tell you where to move the furniture."

The boys rushed out the back door and clomped down the steps.

Shani was anxious to get home, but instead she took the baby from Eve and sat down at the end of the table, balancing the little one on the edge so

Eve could fill Tim's bowl and plate. Shani couldn't figure the man out. Had the grief over the loss of his wife changed him? Much like Joel's injury had turned her husband into a man she hardly knew.

The baby smiled, her blue eyes shining. Shani wrinkled her nose, and the baby giggled. She grinned, and the baby laughed out loud. "What beautiful children you have," Shani said to Tim.

He ignored her, shoveling the soup into his mouth. In no time, he stood, carrying his dishes to the sink. Eve took them from him, and off he went, out the back door without saying another word.

Shani couldn't help but feel that Tim was annoyed. "Everything all right?" she asked.

"Jah," Eve said, glancing toward Lila. "Go pack the diaper bag for me, and get Rose ready." Then she turned to Shani. "I'll be done here in a minute. Then we can walk up to your place."

"No need to walk," Shani said. "We can all go in my van. Do you have a car seat for the baby?"

"Jah, I do," Eve answered. "But do we need it for such a short ride?"

Shani nodded. "I've worked emergency and then pediatrics. I've seen way too many injuries."

A few minutes later, as the girls piled into the back of the van, Eve told Shani she'd be just a minute. Lila secured the car seat, while Eve walked toward the chicken coop with the baby. Tim stepped out from the other side.

Eve spoke quietly but Shani could still hear her say, "We could use the money. The lease on the field is due next month. And you keep saying you want to tear down—"

Shani ushered the girls into the van and climbed in herself, not wanting them or herself to hear any more of her neighbors' private business. A couple of minutes later, Tim stepped through the gate to the field.

Eve called out that she'd forgotten a bottle for the baby. When she returned, she fastened the baby into her car seat and climbed into the front passenger seat.

Shani was overcome with a sense of comfort. It'd been so long since she'd spent time with other women. The girls counted too, even the baby. "So why do you have the car seat?" Shani asked as Eve fastened her seat belt, wondering if they used it in their buggy.

"For when we ride with our drivers."

It sounded as if they had chauffeurs. "Drivers?"

"Jah. We hire them to take us places. Doctors' appointments. Stores in Lancaster. Anywhere farther than we can go by buggy." Eve chuckled. "They call it 'hauling Amish.' "

Shani couldn't help but laugh. "So that's what I've been doing, right? Hauling Tim back and forth to the hospital."

Eve nodded, smiling as she did, and then said, "And now hauling us too."

The baby began to fuss as Shani drove, and Lila sang a sweet melody to her. It took Shani a moment to realize she couldn't understand any of the words. Glancing into her rearview mirror, Shani saw Lila leaning forward. The baby grasped her finger and held on.

As they reached the old farmhouse, Tim held one end of the tape measure while Daniel held the other. Charlie wrote in a small notebook, while Zane bent down on the steps, examining where the handrail had come loose.

Shani rolled down her window and called out, "Thank you!"

Charlie gave her a thumbs-up gesture. Tim didn't respond. Maybe he hadn't heard her.

"Is your friend really as nice as he seems?" Eve had her eyes on Charlie as the men headed toward the truck.

"Nice, yes. But it's more than that. It's a long story . . ."

"I'd like to hear it someday," Eve said.

Shani imagined sitting in Eve's kitchen, and over coffee and sticky buns sharing stories. She'd never had that with a friend. Sure, she and co-workers shared their lives between charting and bed checks and shifts. And she'd relied on other Army wives at different bases through the years, but many of them stayed home to care for their children while Shani always had a nursing job.

After getting acquainted at Fort Hood, she and Nikki had started a friendship once Shani and Zane moved to Philly from California. That was before the woman broke up with Charlie by email, on the same day Shani was arranging for her dad to come stay with Zane so she could fly to Germany to be with Joel.

But Shani had never had a neighbor she could pop over to see or share child care. Or recipes. She smiled. It could happen.

Shani opened the side door and told the girls to wait for her at the bottom of the steps. The baby had fallen asleep and stayed that way as her aunt lugged the heavy seat toward the house.

Shani directed the children to ascend the steps on the opposite side of the broken railing and then warned them not to go near it. Zane rolled his eyes at her, which she ignored. "In fact," she added, "after this use the back door until the railing is fixed."

She reached out to help Eve with the car seat, and together they carried it into the house. Then Eve put it down in the corner of the living room, closest to the window.

Charlie and Zane had already arranged the living room furniture. Her and Joel's bedroom set and Zane's bed were pushed up against the far wall. Both would need to go upstairs. She and

Joel would use her grandfather's bed on the main floor for the time being.

She glanced at the boys, sizing them up. "Daniel, have you ever put a bed together?"

"Of course."

Zane had helped Charlie take the beds apart, but he'd never put one together. "You boys take Zane's bed up and put it together," Shani said. "Then put the queen bed together in the guest room."

"I thought that was the baby's room," Zane said.

She hesitated, surprised to hear him mention the baby. Out of all the changes in their lives during the past months, the baby was the one Zane seemed the most unsettled about. Frankly, the most embarrassed by. None of his friends' moms were having babies anymore. "Pardon?" she said.

"The little guy's room. He can't sleep in a big bed."

She smiled at the thought. "His crib will fit up there too."

Zane nodded, grabbed a hammer and his headboard, and led the way to the staircase, with Daniel right behind him, carrying the footboard.

"How about if we unpack the kitchen?" Shani said to Eve. "And you girls can put the towels in the bathroom cupboard." She pointed to a box along the wall. "Move it together."

As soon as the girls started pushing the box, Shani headed into the kitchen. Eve followed.

Shani opened a box on the counter. Glasses. She pointed to the cupboard closest to the sink. "You can put those in there," she said to Eve.

"So you know the baby's a boy?" Eve said as she pulled the wrapping paper from a glass. "Zane called him 'the little guy.'"

"That's what the ultrasound showed." Shani opened a box of plates. "Sometimes they can be wrong, but not often."

"Jah," Eve said. "We thought Simon was going to be a girl. Tim was so happy the test was wrong."

Shani asked, "Do Amish women usually get ultrasounds?"

"Some do. It depends on her doctor. But Abra had some complications with the twins. Tim was worried . . ."

Shani waited a moment, expecting the woman to say more. When she didn't, Shani said, "Tim said Abra died five months ago. From cancer."

Eve inhaled sharply, the glass shaking in her hand.

"I'm sorry," Shani said.

The woman nodded. "Her death broke our hearts. She's the one who held us all together."

"It's good of you to help your brother out—to care for his family like you do."

"Oh," Eve said, "I'm not doing it for him. I'm doing it for Abra. She—"

"Shani." Lila stood in the doorway of the

kitchen, the empty box in her hands. "Oh, sorry to interrupt."

"No problem," Shani answered. "Are you done with the towels?"

Lila shook her head. "We ran out of room in the cupboard."

"Stack them on the counter in the bathroom for now," Shani said. Rose wiggled her way into the kitchen too. If she sent them to put the books on the shelves in the living room next, they might wake the baby. And she didn't want them in the way of the boys. "When you're done you two can help unwrap the dishes," she said. "Then we'll put them in the cupboard."

Shani didn't want to ask any more questions about Abra when the girls would be right back. She opened the cupboard on the other side of the sink. "Wow, someone put down new shelf paper." When Eve blushed, Shani knew it had to have been her. "Did Dad ask you to clean up this place?"

Eve nodded.

"Thank you." She couldn't figure Eve out. She seemed so capable yet reserved. Humble but complex too. "You must have seen the quilt in the downstairs bedroom, then."

Eve nodded.

"I don't remember it from the last time I was here. I'm guessing my grandmother must have bought it before she died. I can't imagine Grandpa buying it."

Eve blushed.

"What?" Shani asked.

"I'll tell you about the quilt later," Eve said, unwrapping another glass and placing it in the cupboard.

Shani raised her eyebrows but decided she'd just have to wait until Eve was ready. Obviously the quilt had come from her.

"So where are you and Joel from, originally?" Eve asked.

"I grew up near Seattle, and Joel's from Wisconsin. We met my first year of college through a mutual friend. Joel was stationed at Fort Lewis." Shani picked up several plates. "We married when I was nineteen and he was twenty-two. My dad about blew a gasket." She smiled at the memory as she put the plates in the cupboard. Joel had been so certain of his love for her from the beginning. Not in a scary sort of way, but in a steady, strong way.

"What did Joel's parents think?"

"They didn't come to the wedding. We don't see them much . . ." It was hard to explain. Joel's little brother, Johnny, had died at the age of twelve, when Joel was seventeen. It seemed his parents blamed him. He'd left home the next year, right after he graduated. Try as she might she couldn't get him to talk about it through the years. And now after he almost died in Iraq, it was the last thing she'd bring up.

Eve stared at her. "Are you okay?"

"Fine." Shani picked up a stack of dessert plates.

"Well," Eve said, "family relationships can be tricky." She glanced toward Rose and Lila coming through the door and lowered her voice. "I think everyone has something difficult they're dealing with."

After a few terse directions from Tim, Charlie turned on the road to the lumberyard. He flipped the truck visor down against the early afternoon sun. Fields of silage gave way to a wooded area. Maple trees, their orange leaves fiery against the cloudless blue sky, stood interspersed with evergreens.

"Turn right," Tim said.

Charlie pressed on both the clutch and the brake, downshifted, and swung the truck wide. He bounced down a driveway.

"What kind of horsepower does this have? Three hundred forty-five?" Tim held onto his hat.

"Yeah, that's right," Charlie answered.

"I usually only have one," Tim said. "Although out in the field, I sometimes have six."

It took Charlie a moment to realize the guy had cracked a joke. Horsepower. Literally. He smiled.

When he was growing up in Ohio, his friends used to call the Amish "Dutchy." He wasn't sure if it was derogatory or not. Though he'd seen them in and around town, he'd never known any Amish back then or since. Hanging out with Tim was a new experience.

They soon rounded the corner into a parking lot. Beyond was a big warehouse-type building with prefabricated sheds, all barn red, lined up on the right. On the other side was a house with a patch of yard around it.

Horses, attached to two buggies and a wagon, had been tied to hitching posts. There were also a couple of pickups and one car, which Charlie parked beside.

As Charlie climbed down from his truck he breathed in the scent of pine and sawdust, and the hint of cows in the field behind the house. He'd been so determined to leave the rural area where he'd grown up, but now he couldn't imagine why.

A tall Amish boy—nearly grown—helped a man dressed in jeans, a Steelers jacket, and a baseball cap carry a sheet of plywood. Just inside the warehouse, in front of a garage-like doorway, an Amish man loaded a cart with cedar planks. Tim took the lead, and Charlie followed, shoving his hands into the pockets of his coat and whistling a few bars of a song that had been stuck in his head.

As he stepped onto the concrete pad, Tim nodded to an Amish man wearing a work apron and speaking with an older gentleman dressed in coveralls. Tim grabbed a cart and began pushing it toward the back of the warehouse.

He stopped at the two-by-fours first, and spent some time examining the boards. Before he began selecting what he wanted, the Amish boy approached. His face was broken out in acne, and when he spoke his voice was soft. "How is Simon doing?"

Tim stopped and slowly turned. "Didn't your Dat tell you? He was just over at our place, asking me a whole bunch of questions."

The boy's face reddened, all the way up to his hat, and he pushed the sleeves of his burgundy shirt up along his forearm. "I haven't had a chance to ask him."

Charlie surmised the man in the apron was the bishop who'd come to visit. Tim had seemed unsettled about his presence then and now too.

"Simon's doing all right." Tim turned his attention back to the lumber.

Charlie stepped forward and stuck out his hand to the young man.

As the boy took it, Charlie introduced himself.

"Reuben Byler," the boy responded.

"Nice place you have here," Charlie said.

The boy blushed again. "It's my Dat's. I just work here." He glanced at Tim. "What are you two aiming to build?"

"A ramp," Charlie answered. "For my buddy. He and his family just moved into the house close to"—he nodded toward Tim—"the Lehman family."

"I know the farm," Reuben said. "Mr. Williams' place, right? Isn't it his granddaughter and her family?"

Charlie nodded. "Yep. Shani Beck. Her husband,

Joel, is going to be in a wheelchair for a while."

Reuben seemed empathetic. "My Dat just helped the Millers design a ramp for their place. One of their kids is in a chair. Dat gave them all sorts of good ideas. I'll go get him."

Tim said, "There's no reas—"

But Reuben was already on his way.

"Seems like a nice kid," Charlie said.

Tim shrugged and began choosing the two-by-fours, passing over anything with a knot or split.

Charlie stepped forward, taking the first two boards Tim approved of and loading them onto the cart. Tim picked up his pace, and as the Amish man wearing the apron approached, they were ready to move on to the slats.

"I'm surprised to see you here," the man said. "I thought you had work to attend to at home."

"Jah, I do," Tim said. "But my neighbors need some help."

The bishop was a half head shorter than Tim but he stood straight, with his arms crossed over his chest and with an air of authority about him. "Reuben says you're building a ramp."

Tim nodded as he tugged on his beard. "This is Charlie. He's a friend of the new people up the lane. The husband's in a wheelchair."

The man took Charlie's hand and said, "I'm Gideon Byler." Then he turned back toward Tim. "Do you need any help with the ramp design?"

Tim shook his head as Charlie nodded. "I was

wondering about the building codes around here," he said. "Do we need a permit?"

"Not necessarily," Gideon said. "Do you expect it to be permanent?"

"No," Charlie replied. At least he hoped not.

Tim turned to Gideon. "We'll need these cut. The two-by-fours too. That'll save me the time of hauling the saw over."

The man took a notepad. "How long?"

"Forty-two inches."

"What's the rise of the ramp going to be?" Gideon asked.

"One to twelve," Tim answered.

"Better make the railing thirty-six inches," he said.

"Jah, I was planning on it," Tim replied.

"U-shaped or L-shaped?"

"L," Tim answered, handing Charlie a stack of planks. "I know what I'm doing, Gideon."

"Reuben," Gideon called out, ignoring Tim, "we need some cutting done." He went on to ask more of the measurements, and Tim spouted off all the information. Charlie dug the piece of paper he'd written everything down on from his pocket, checking the measurements. Tim had remembered them all, exactly.

"I have plenty of nails," Tim told Charlie as Reuben approached. "I'm not sure about the railing. Do you think we need it?"

Charlie nodded. "Too many kids around, and if

Joel uses the ramp by himself, we'll have to have it." Chances were Joel would be using the ramp by himself before he should, and besides, if the ramp needed to meet code it would need a railing.

Reuben took the measurements from his father and then pushed the cart away. Charlie guessed the shop was in the back of the warehouse. The smell of sawdust grew stronger as they headed that way.

Charlie purposefully trailed behind, giving the two Amish men some space. Even so he heard Gideon ask, "What did Eve say when you gave her my apologies for being in too much of a rush to come in and greet her?"

Tim stopped, turned toward the man, and squinted. "I just passed on your greeting. I didn't have a chance to tell her the rest."

Gideon's hands fell to his side. "Well," he said. "I guess I can tell her myself. Tomorrow evening."

"It won't work for you to come by then," Tim said. "Wait a week."

Charlie focused on the trellis again, guessing Gideon was interested in Eve. He had to be in his late forties or so. Charlie guessed she was in her midtwenties. Gideon seemed like an upstanding guy, though. Probably a real catch in the Amish community.

When Reuben finished with the cutting, Tim inspected each piece and had him redo two of them. Charlie would have accepted them but he deferred to Tim's expertise. Obviously the man knew what he was doing.

While Charlie paid, Tim loaded the truck and then went and found Reuben and collected the last two planks.

Charlie thanked Gideon as he took the receipt and then said, "Maybe I'll see you around."

"Oh?" Gideon looped his thumbs in his apron straps again. "I thought you were headed back home soon."

"I'll go back to Philadelphia on Monday, but then I'll be back next Friday."

"What kind of work do you do?" Gideon asked.

"I'm an EMT," he said. "With a fire department on the west side of Philly." He worked twelve-hour shifts, Tuesday, Wednesday, and Thursday.

"I see." Gideon rocked back on his heels. "You must be a good friend to these people—Tim's new neighbors."

"You could say that," Charlie answered. "Thanks again."

His chief had worried about him when he came home from Iraq and quizzed him about PTSD, making sure Charlie was fit to come back on the job. He was fine, but his boss gave him the easiest possible schedule anyway. Charlie figured he'd take advantage of it until Joel was back on his feet—literally.

By the time he got back to the truck, Tim had the back secured and sat in the cab with the passenger window rolled down.

"See you soon," Gideon called out.

Tim waved but didn't answer.

As he left the parking lot, Charlie pulled the truck wide, close to the house. A young woman stood on the porch, washing an outside window. She waved when she saw Tim, and he tipped his hat.

"So Gideon's the bishop," Charlie said as he pulled out onto the highway.

"Jah, that's right." Tim rolled up the window.

"What exactly does a bishop do?"

"Keeps track of things. Preaches. Helps out."

By the way Gideon had said Eve's name, Charlie was sure he was asking a question he already knew the answer to. But he asked it anyway. "Was that Gideon's wife on the porch?"

"Nee. His youngest daughter, Sarah. She and Reuben are the only two left at home."

Charlie waited for a moment, hoping Tim would say more. When he didn't he asked, "Does Gideon have a wife?"

Tim shook his head. "She passed away last winter."

And the guy was already looking for a new wife. That was pretty fast.

Charlie cleared his throat. "Is he interested in Eve?"

Tim stared straight ahead. "That's none of your concern."

"You're right." Charlie tried to swallow but his throat tightened. It wasn't like he cared or anything. Right? Except that he couldn't stop thinking about Eve at the window, spying on the bishop. Or perhaps she was hiding. The expression on her face hadn't been one of happiness. Not even hope.

By suppertime, Charlie and Tim had the holes dug, the posts set, and had just started framing the ramp. Daniel and Zane had gone over to the barn to start on the chores, but Tim said he'd better go check to make sure they were staying on task.

"Daniel can get sidetracked," Tim said, slipping his hammer into his tool belt. "Always has his head in the clouds. Just like his mother."

"He did a good job this morning," Charlie said.

Tim tugged on his beard. "Is that so?"

"As far as I could tell." Charlie ducked his head. What was it about the man that made him feel as if he were eleven too?

"You can use my tools now, but not tomorrow. We honor the Sabbath."

Charlie nodded. He'd expected as much.

Tim looked toward the house. "I don't suppose those womenfolk have thought about dinner."

Charlie was pretty sure Shani hadn't. And he didn't think she had any food in the house besides the cereal and sandwich stuff he'd bought the night before. It certainly wasn't Eve's responsibility to feed them, not when she and Tim were both helping out. Shani had left for a short time but didn't come back with any grocery bags. "I'll go ask," Charlie said, standing up straight and twisting his back.

The older girls played with the baby in the living room, rolling a ball on the floor to her.

"Where's Shani?" Charlie asked.

Lila pointed to the stairs. "Making the beds. They're almost done."

The little girl grinned. "Then we're going to have pizza. The Englisch lady—"

"Shani," the older girl said.

"Jah," Rose said. "Her. She drove to the highway and called in the order. It's going to be delivered." She clapped her hands together, which made the baby giggle.

Charlie smiled. Rose appeared so sweet with her miniature bonnet and apron, but at the same time she was full of spit and vinegar. He liked that.

"But we're going to eat it over at our house," Lila explained. "Aenti thought that would be easier."

A burst of laughter from upstairs stopped the conversation.

A yearning overtook Charlie. He sometimes wondered if Joel knew how blessed he was. Sure, he'd nearly lost his leg. He'd nearly died. But he hadn't.

He had a wife and son and a baby on the way.

Charlie shook his head. Self-pity was a trap. He wasn't going to fall into it now.

He realized the older girl was staring at him, so he smiled and then said, "Tell your Aenti and Shani that Tim's headed over to help the boys with the chores. And I'm going to keep working here until it's time to eat."

He had a feeling Tim might not be thrilled with pizza. He hoped Shani had ordered the meaty kind—sausage and pepperoni, the works. Not one of those pizzas with artichoke hearts and sun-dried tomatoes.

By the time the women were done, Charlie had a section of framing completed. Shani led the way onto the porch, followed by the girls and then Eve, carrying the car seat. All of them were smiling, as if they'd just had a good laugh. Eve, her eyes shining, said something to Shani that Charlie couldn't hear, and then the women chuckled again.

"Want a ride?" Shani asked him. "We can squeeze you in."

"No thanks," Charlie said. "But I'll send Tim's tools back with you."

Eve started down the steps. Charlie put down the hammer and hurried to help her.

"Denki," she said, passing the car seat to him, their fingers brushing for a moment.

Trudy looked up at him with her big blue eyes and gurgled.

Once he had the baby in the van and Tim's tools in the back, he worked for ten more minutes, using Joel's hammer, and then headed down the lane. When he arrived at the Lehmans' driveway, the pizza delivery car was turning toward the highway. By the time he knocked on the back door, Tim and the boys were approaching, on their way from the barn.

"You know better than to tease a cow," Tim said to Daniel.

"I wasn't, not really. Besides Simon does it all the time."

"Simon would never do something like that." Tim's nostrils flared. "Besides, that's no excuse."

Daniel didn't answer his father. Zane fell behind.

"You'll have to do better tomorrow," Tim said. "I'll be spending the night at the hospital again. You'll be in charge in the morning."

Daniel halted and turned toward his father. "So it's safe for you to go back?"

Tim stopped too but didn't turn toward his son.

"Have Dawdi and Mammi gone home?" Daniel asked.

Tim bristled.

Daniel fisted his hands. "How come they went to see Simon but they don't come see us?"

Tim said something in Pennsylvania Dutch as he started marching away from his son and then

110

stomped up the steps, past Charlie, as if he weren't there, and into the house. Daniel put his head in his hands, knocking his hat off his head. Zane bent down and picked it up and then put his arm around the boy. As Charlie waited, the back door opened and Lila stepped out onto the porch, her eyes filled with tears.

"Are you all right?" Charlie asked.

She nodded.

Charlie opened the door, pulling his eyes away from the boys. "Is dinner ready?" he asked as he motioned for Lila to go first.

"Jah," she said, looking over her shoulder. The boys had reached the steps.

Charlie tried to smile. "So what kind of pizza are we having?"

"Shani said to tell you vegetarian." Lila giggled.

"Great," Charlie responded, hoping his sarcasm was evident. He could smell pepperoni. And he was pretty sure sausage too.

As soon as dinner was done, Tim was anxious to get back to the hospital, but Shani said she needed to rest first. "I think I overdid it," she said.

"I'll take Tim and visit Joel," Charlie offered. "I can take you back to the house first."

"Just stay here," Eve said to Shani. "Charlie can pick you up on the way back. That way you can keep me company."

It seemed as if Shani and Eve had been friends for years. Funny how women could do that, but

111

he wouldn't have expected it between Shani and an Amish woman.

Shani grabbed her purse from beside the couch and dug out her keys, handing them to Charlie.

"Put your feet up while I get the baby ready for bed," Eve said to Shani.

She obeyed, lowering herself to the couch a little awkwardly.

"You okay?" Charlie asked.

She nodded. "Go. Tell Joel I'll see him in the morning."

Charlie nodded and then motioned for Tim to follow him out to the van. The Amish man was silent the entire way into town. Finally, Charlie turned the radio on to an oldies station, but then he wondered if it was offensive to Tim. He switched to a news station instead. ". . . a bomb attack injured five US soldiers on the main highway from central Baghdad to the airport . . ."

Charlie's neck tensed. Injured. No one was killed. That was good news.

The reporter continued. ". . . oil pipelines were bombed outside of the city, and three soldiers were killed in a mortar attack in central Baghdad."

Charlie snapped off the radio.

Tim crossed his arms across his wide chest. "People who volunteer for the military are practically asking for it."

Charlie turned toward him, appalled. "Asking for what?"

"The Scriptures say to turn the other cheek."

"But it also says to love our neighbors, and in our country, we do that by protecting them."

Tim shook his head. "The Iraqi people aren't our neighbors."

"They are in the eyes of God."

"How's that? We're thousands of miles away. Their neighbors are on their borders."

"The world's changed in the last century," Charlie said and then turned the radio back on, switching it to the oldies station. He was tempted to add that people who weren't willing to protect their country got a free ride. But he couldn't. Not because of Tim. But because of his pacifist grandparents.

His nation protected all—regardless of their beliefs.

11

Eve sat down in Tim's chair after she'd put all the kids to bed. They didn't know what time Charlie would be back from the hospital, so she and Shani had decided to let Zane sleep in Simon's bed. Eve curled her stockinged feet up beneath her and picked up her knitting.

Shani scooted to a sitting position on the couch, pulling the quilt up around her. "What are you making?" The woman had twisted her long hair on top of her head.

"A scarf for Lila," Eve answered. The yarn was a dull blue, preapproved by Tim.

"Did you make this quilt?" Shani asked, running her finger over a burgundy block.

"No. Abra did."

"It's beautiful. The green and burgundy really make the black and blue pop. It reminds me of the quilt at my place."

"Jah." Eve reached the end of the row. "Abra had a gift when it came to quilting—her Mamm has a quilt shop. Abra made the one at your house too." She felt awkward talking about Abra's quilts.

"Why did you take it over there?"

Eve smiled. "I wanted you to have it."

Shani sat up straighter. "But you didn't even know me then."

114

"I'd prayed for you though, when I heard about you coming." She looked up at Shani. "I felt it was what God wanted."

Shani shook her head, perhaps in disbelief. "Did Abra make the quilt for someone, originally?"

"Me," Eve answered, hooking the yarn. "But, well, I'm not going to be using it."

"Why not?"

"It's too big for my single bed for one thing . . ." She didn't want to tell Shani that she'd never marry, that she'd never have reason to use the quilt. She was glad she'd put it on Shani's bed, especially now that she'd met her.

"Well, I love Abra's quilt. I'm honored to have it," Shani said. "Will you teach me how to make one?"

Eve laughed. "You don't want me to teach you. I've never been good at it."

"We could learn together, then," Shani responded.

A peal of laughter came from down the hall.

"Those boys." Shani stood. "I'll go tell Zane to knock it off."

"They're okay," Eve said. "They have to be exhausted. They'll be asleep in no time."

Eve found ignoring the children worked best. If they weren't asleep within half an hour, it meant they weren't spending enough time outside. That was her philosophy on bedtime.

Shani leaned forward. "I've been overwhelmed by your generosity—Tim's too."

Eve's face warmed. "It's what neighbors do, right? You saved Simon's life." She smiled. "The least we can do is help you."

"Not all neighbors would build a ramp," Shani said.

"Well, you did say you'd pay him," Eve said. She couldn't help but smile. "Besides, Jesus said, 'Love thy neighbor as thyself.' "

Shani nodded. "Right after he said that the greatest commandment is to love the Lord with all your heart, soul, and mind."

Eve nodded. Her neighbor seemed to know about the Lord, more than she'd expected.

The baby began to fuss.

"They woke her up," Shani said.

"No, she's not a good sleeper."

"Will she settle back down?"

Eve shook her head. She'd tried to ignore her. Over and over. But the baby's screaming would upset Tim and then wake Rose. It was easier to give her a late bottle and then hope she'd sleep through the rest of the night. Every once in a while she would. Eve put her knitting down.

"I'll get her." Shani stood.

"She'll need her diaper changed," Eve said.

"I figured." As Shani headed down the hall, Eve walked into the kitchen, pulling her shawl tight against the evening chill. She took a bottle from the rack, scooped the formula, and poured warm water from the kettle on top.

She mourned for all of her nieces and nephews, but her sadness for Trudy was deepest. In the two months after Trudy's birth, Abra hadn't been able to nurse and care for her youngest daughter like she had her other babies. And Trudy would never remember her mother.

When Shani joined her in the kitchen, cradling the baby in her arms, Eve expected the little one to start screaming. She didn't. Instead her blue eyes stayed on Shani's face.

"She likes you." Eve placed her finger over the tip of the bottle and shook it.

"She's awfully sweet." Shani nuzzled Trudy's fine hair with her nose. Eve handed Shani the bottle, and she slipped it into the baby's mouth. As they headed back into the living room, a car door slammed outside.

"Charlie must be back," Shani said.

Eve took the baby from her and settled back in the chair while Shani put on her shoes. Her belly wasn't big enough to have a problem tying them. Eve thought of Abra when she was pregnant with the twins. She'd had no idea a woman could get that big.

She'd been such a slight girl. Seventeen and just over a hundred pounds when she got pregnant. By the time she was six months along, Eve had to put her shoes on for her.

Spending time with Shani made her miss Abra all the more, but her best friend—and sister-in-law—would have been thrilled that Eve met a new friend. She'd be thankful the children had been distracted from their mourning for her and their worry about Simon too. Regardless of the uncertainties, it had been a good day.

"Is it hard—" Shani stopped.

"Go on," Eve said, her attention still on the baby.

Shani shook her head. "I'm tired. I was going to ask something that's not my business."

Eve met Shani's eyes. "Is it hard for me to take care of my nieces and nephews when I don't have a husband or children of my own?"

Shani wrinkled her nose. "Something like that."

"I get asked that some." Eve stared down at her niece for a moment. "The truth is, I do wish I had my own babies, but if I did I'd be taking care of my nieces and nephews too. They've been the greatest blessings of my life."

"Surely you must be seeing someone," Shani teased. "You'll have your own family someday."

Eve shook her head, remembering the bishop's greeting passed on by Tim. Gideon had been friendly lately. She wondered why, when he knew her story as well as anyone. She couldn't imagine he truly thought she was worthy of him. Maybe there was a scarcity of women available for a new widower right now, but in a couple of months, once he came to his senses, he'd move on from being interested in her. At least, she hoped he would.

"I'm content being single," Eve said to Shani. "I've come to accept it."

Before Shani could respond there was a commotion at the back door. Eve was expecting Charlie to knock gently on the front. Why had he gone to the back?

But then Tim called out her name, adding, "Simon's home."

And Zane was in his bed.

"Oh dear." She inched forward and then stood, still holding Trudy's bottle in place.

"I'll get Zane," Shani said.

Shani stepped into the hallway as Tim reached the living room.

"Why is she still here?" he asked.

"She was waiting for Charlie to give her a ride home."

Tim shook his head, and Eve guessed at what. He didn't think it appropriate for Charlie to be staying down at Shani's. "Where's the boy?" Tim asked.

Eve spoke quietly. "In Simon's bed."

Tim threw up his hands.

"Simon was coming home tomorrow. You were spending the night. Remember?" Eve peered down the hall as Charlie and Simon came into the living room.

Zane let Shani lead him, as if he were sleep-walking, past Eve. Shani said hello to Charlie and Simon and then led Zane into the kitchen.

Simon stood watching, and Eve turned toward him. She put her hand on his shoulder and peered into his eyes as the baby giggled and reached for him. He tried to smile, showing a bit of the metal in his mouth, but couldn't. However, his eyes lit up, as bright as ever. Eve gave him a hug, and whispered, "I'm so grateful you're all right." After she released him, she said, "Now go get in bed."

Tim stood with his arms crossed.

"Go tuck him in," Eve said.

Zane sat on a kitchen chair, pulling on his shoes, while Charlie stood by the counter, talking to Shani. "Joel was missing you."

"I should have gone," Shani said. The lamp cast a long shadow, and Eve couldn't see her friend's face.

"No, he's fine," Charlie said. "How are you?"

"Better."

"See—you needed to rest."

Eve turned the lamp up higher.

Shani turned toward her. "Thank you for allowing me to hang out here."

"Zane and I will be over to help with the chores in the morning," Charlie said.

"That's not necessary," Eve said, hoping the tension in her voice wasn't obvious to Charlie and Shani.

Charlie seemed disappointed but didn't say anything. "Zane will come by himself, then."

She nodded. "But after tomorrow he should only help in the afternoon. There's no reason for him to come before school." She would help, if necessary.

"Okay," Charlie said, directing Zane toward the door. "See you tomorrow."

Eve was pretty sure they wouldn't.

Shani waved and then yawned as she followed Charlie toward the door.

Eve headed down the hall to her room, where the crib was. Tim thought she should move the baby out, but the girls would be crowded if she did. There was more space in her room.

Once she had Trudy settled, she stopped at the door to the boys' room with the bottle still in her hand. Tim had left.

"Aenti?"

She stepped inside. "I hoped you were asleep."

"All I did was sleep at the hospital." Simon's words were slurred and slow. "I'm not tired."

She sat down on the edge of his bed. "I'm glad you're home."

"Me too," he said. His mouth didn't move as he spoke.

She started to tousle his curls but then stopped. Maybe it would hurt his head. "Your Dat said you'll need to be in a dark room. And stay quiet."

"Jah."

"And only drink a liquid diet."

"I'm going to starve," he said.

Shani had a blender. Eve had unpacked it. Maybe she could make smoothies over there for Simon. Or maybe that was just an excuse to see the new neighbors. "Right now, let's concentrate on resting. In the morning we'll figure out the food." She stroked his forehead. He was Tim's favorite, which meant Eve concentrated on the other children more. But there was no doubt that Simon was likeable. Easy to get along with. Funny. And he didn't take advantage of being Tim's favorite the way he could have.

She pulled the quilt up to his chin with her free hand. "Come get me during the night if you need to."

He nodded. "I will." All of the children came to her in the night if they had a bad dream or were missing their Mamm. She didn't know of a single time any of them had gone to Tim.

The living room was empty—she hoped Tim had gone to bed—but when she reached the kitchen he sat at the table, his head in his hands.

"Tired?" she asked.

He dropped his hands. "Jah. It's been a long couple of days."

"Go on to bed. Simon seems settled." Eva turned on the water faucet and began rinsing the bottle.

Tim pushed back his chair. "Why were you going to let the Englisch boy stay?"

"I thought it would be easier for him to help with the chores in the morning."

Tim shook his head. "I never should have asked him to help." He yawned. "I'm going to bed."

"Good night," Eve said as she turned her attention to the bottle in the sink. She washed it and dried it and then scooped formula into it for the next feeding.

Just as she reached out to turn off the lamp, she heard a faint knocking on the back door. She hadn't heard a buggy. Or a car.

She hurried toward the door without any expectation of who it was. All she wanted was for Tim not to hear the knock.

She opened the door halfway. There stood Charlie.

"Sorry," he said. "Shani left her purse."

She peered out into the darkness. "Did you walk here?"

He nodded. "She said it's by the couch."

"Come in," Eve said, wrapping her shawl tighter. "But stay here." She hurried into the dark living room, found the purse, and headed back to the kitchen.

"Thank you," Charlie said, as Eve handed him the bag. "Shani's going to the hospital first thing in the morning, but I was wondering about a church. Is there one close by?"

She thought for a moment. "There's a church on Main Street in Strasburg that might work. Or there are a couple of Mennonite churches—one just outside of town and one in the town of Willow Street. I went there for a short time years ago." She'd gone when she was on her Rumschpringe. It wasn't Old Order Mennonite, that was for sure, but a few of the older women still wore *Kapp*s.

"What time do you have church tomorrow?" Charlie asked.

"We don't," Eve answered. "It's our week off."

By the puzzled look on his face, she knew he didn't understand. "We only meet every other week. Some go to another district's meeting or visit friends and family on our off week."

"Oh," he said. "I see." Charlie held up Shani's purse, which made her laugh. He smiled. "What? You don't think it's my style?"

She shook her head. But she did admire him for being willing to come get it. Tim would certainly never do such a thing—at least not for her.

"Have fun visiting tomorrow," he said. She must have given him a puzzled look because he added, "At another meeting. Or with friends and family."

"Oh, that," she said. "We don't do that sort of thing. We'll be here." It had been a long time since they'd gone visiting, since Abra was diagnosed.

"I'll be working on the ramp in the afternoon," Charlie said.

She nodded. "We don't work on Sundays." She didn't want him to think Tim didn't care. "Just the chores."

Charlie nodded. "Tim told me." He opened the door, but then said, "I'll go home on Monday morning. So if I don't see you before then, thank you for everything."

"You're welcome," she answered. Then, instead of saying good-night, as she should have, she asked, her heart racing, "When will you come back?"

"Next Friday," he answered.

"I'll see you then."

She stood in the doorway and watched him go. When he'd disappeared into the darkness she gazed up at the sky.

She'd never pursue a relationship with a man like Charlie McCall. She'd tried the ways of the Englisch once. She wouldn't do it again. But still, she couldn't help . . . She inhaled, sharply.

Her heart never raced around Bishop Byler.

She pulled the door shut, turned off the lamp, and made her way down the dark hall to her bedroom.

⚘ 12

Shani woke to light streaming through the windows. She shifted to her back and waited to feel the baby move. It was the first thing she did every morning. There were still days when she could hardly believe it was true.

He fluttered a little and then shifted. She rubbed her belly. "Wake up, Baby Boy Beck," she whispered.

She and Joel had hardly talked about a name yet. They certainly weren't close enough to a decision for her to call the little one inside anything else.

He moved again, this time more definitely. Relief flooded over her and she reached for her cell phone, knocking it off the bedside table. She rolled over to the side of the bed and sat up, kicking her foot until she felt the phone. Then she retrieved it. All it was good for inside the house was as a clock. Their cell provider said they wouldn't have service until a tower was installed, and that could still be a couple of years. Thankfully the landline would be hooked up by the next day—at least that's what the representative at the phone company said.

7:10. Goodness, she'd overslept. She grabbed her robe from the end of the bed and wrapped it around herself. Charlie had insisted on sleeping in his truck again, but he certainly wouldn't sleep until after seven. She hoped he'd come into the house and made himself some coffee.

She stepped into the kitchen. No coffee. And no Zane or Charlie. She filled a glass at the tap and heard hammering start up outside. She drank the water, put the glass in the sink, and stepped into the living room. Cinching the tie on her robe above her belly, she opened the door. Charlie nailed a plank down on the ramp.

When he stopped, she called out, "Good morning."

He waved.

"Where's Zane?"

"He headed over to the neighbors to do the chores. Want me to go check?"

Though she was concerned about Zane being at the neighbors', she shook her head. It wasn't as if she thought Tim would hurt Zane, not physically anyway. But she wondered what he might say. She wasn't sure if the man had a mean streak or if he was just obtuse. And he definitely played favorites, at least with his own kids.

Eve seemed to walk on eggshells around her brother, but Shani wasn't sure why. Maybe it had to do with Abra's death.

A half hour later, showered, with her hair twisted on top of her head, she left the house for the hospital, telling Charlie she'd stop by the

Lehmans' house and tell Zane to hurry on home to help him.

"Do you mind if I take him to church with me?" Charlie asked.

Shani stopped on the bottom step. "Where are you going?"

Charlie stood. "A Mennonite church. Eve told me about it."

"Is that where they go?"

He smiled as he shook his head. "But it seems Eve went to the church when she was younger."

"Oh." Another mystery when it came to the neighbors. "That would be great for you to take Zane as long as he wants to go." She and Zane had attended a church in Philly last spring—until Joel was injured. Shani climbed into her van, started the engine, waved, and then backed around and headed down the lane.

Before Philly, while Joel was stationed in California, they'd all gone to church together. Looking back, life had been so easy then. The threat that Joel would be deployed had hung over their heads since 9/11, but it hadn't made him anxious. He'd doted on her and Zane all the more, knowing he might be called up anytime.

But after he'd been injured, Joel had been unable to think much about Zane's needs for the first few months. And she knew he trusted her to take care of all of that. But there were some needs only a father could fill. She hoped this reinjury wouldn't set Joel back even more.

When she reached the Lehmans' place, Zane was grinning from ear to ear as he ran down the back steps with Daniel at his side. Shani waved to her son and motioned him toward her.

Eve stood in the doorway but followed the boys when she saw Shani. She called out, "Hallo!"

Shani turned off the ignition and stepped out of the van.

Eve's smile lit up her face. Shani felt a wave of relief sweep over her. She must have imagined the angst from Tim last night. It was probably just the stress of Simon's injuries. How many times had she seen that in a parent?

"Could I come over and use your blender later today?" Eve asked. "I want to make up a pitcher of smoothies for Simon."

"Sure," Shani responded as she wrapped her arm around Zane.

"Denki," Eve replied.

"You can go over now," Shani added. "The house is unlocked. Charlie's there."

"I'll wait until you get back," Eve answered.

Shani smiled. Eve probably didn't want anything to look suspicious. Shani could certainly understand that. She pulled Zane close. "Charlie wants to take you to church."

"Okay." Zane hugged her quickly and then stepped away.

She kept her hand on his shoulder. "Do you want to go?"

"Sure."

"You have a choice?" Daniel planted his hands on his hips.

Zane glanced at Shani, and she nodded.

"That's crazy," Daniel said.

Eve stepped closer. "Walk Zane home. And then come right back."

Daniel faced his aunt. "Can I go with Charlie and Zane? To church?"

"You could ask your Dat," Eve answered.

Daniel exhaled and nudged Zane. "Let's go."

The boys took off, and Shani told Eve she'd stop by on her way back from the hospital, to let her know she was home. "Do you have ingredients for a smoothie?" she asked.

"Jah," Eve answered. "I'll see you when you come back. Tell Joel he's in our prayers."

Shani's eyes teared up. "Denki," she said and then, realizing what she'd said, began to laugh. Eve joined in until Tim strode out of the barn. She clapped her hand over her mouth and waved at Shani with her other hand as she headed back to the steps. But her eyes danced, still full of fun.

By the time Shani reached Joel's room, she realized she was hungry and pulled a protein bar from her bag. She truly intended to start eating better, but she hadn't had time to even stop at the grocery store.

She peeled back the wrapper of the bar and took a bite as she pushed open the door.

"Finally," Joel said.

"Hi," she answered, her mouth full. His breakfast, only half eaten, sat on his bedside table. She swallowed, kissed him on the lips, and then asked, "How was breakfast?"

"Better than Army food," he answered.

She looped the strap of her purse over the back of the chair and slipped out of her jacket. "Mind if I take a few bites?"

"Help yourself."

Shani pulled the chair closer to the table and speared a bite of pancake, dragging it through the syrup.

Joel shifted, as if he wanted to sit up straight, but the position of his leg in traction wouldn't allow it. "What's Zane up to?"

Shani swallowed. "Going to church with Charlie."

Her husband frowned. "Not the Amish church, I hope."

Shani shook her head. "Apparently they meet in homes. Zane and Charlie are going to a Mennonite church."

"Sounds pretty much the same."

Shani shrugged. "It's just one Sunday. When you're better we can look around." The one in Philly had been a community church. Zane had gone to the youth group quite a few times, but she hadn't gotten involved. Working full time meant Shani didn't go to Bible studies or women's gatherings. And she couldn't imagine Joel ever going to a men's Bible study or even a couple's group. He was strictly a Sunday morning churchgoer.

"Zane really likes Charlie, doesn't he." Joel raised the bed. "But who doesn't, right?" Bitterness tinged his voice. Was he growing jealous of his friend, of everything Charlie could do that Joel couldn't? Especially when it came to Zane.

He'd never been inclined toward jealousy before. "It's like Charlie's the uncle Zane never had," Shani said, reaching for Joel with her free hand.

Joel drummed the fingers of his other hand on the railing of the bed. "Or the husband you no longer have."

"Don't be ridiculous," she said.

"Where'd Charlie sleep last night?"

"Don't make me hate you, Joel Beck." She stabbed another bite of pancake and met his eyes. "Your best friend slept in his truck. You can be paranoid about all sorts of things, but don't you dare insult my love for you or the gift of friendship he's given you."

Joel's face fell.

She dropped the fork on the plate and pushed it away, no longer hungry.

"Hey, I'm sorry," Joel said. "I spend all my time thinking."

"Read. Watch TV. Or pray," Shani said.

Joel sighed. "I've tried. It doesn't work. I can't shut my brain off."

She wished he could call her, even if in the middle of the night, but without the landline up yet that was impossible. Hopefully he could soon.

He'd never been suspicious of her before—even during their months of separation. She shook her head. He was impossible.

Joel smiled a little and then chuckled. "He slept in his truck?"

Shani nodded. "He wouldn't even come in this morning to make a pot of coffee before I was up." She changed the subject. "Has the doctor stopped by?"

"Yeah, about an hour ago."

"What did he say?"

"He'll order more rehab, after I'm out of the plaster."

"How long will you be in the cast?"

"Four weeks."

"Where will you do the rehab?"

"Here in Lancaster." Joel shifted again. "But he said I should check in with the VA back in Philly."

She nodded, glad she'd only be working part-time now. She was taking over for a nurse on maternity leave, who would be returning about the time Shani took hers. The truth was, they could have used a full-time salary, but she couldn't keep up with Joel's appointments and everything else and still work that many hours.

"How are you feeling?" Joel asked.

"Fine. I was tired last night, but I got a good rest." The baby kicked. "He's been moving a lot." She stood. "He is right now. Want to feel him?"

For a moment she thought Joel was going to shake his head, but he reached out and placed his hand on her abdomen. She moved it to the right spot, but of course the baby didn't kick again.

"He moves the most in the morning," she said. "When I first wake up. You'll feel him when you're back . . ." Her voice trailed off. *Home.* She knew it didn't feel like home to Joel.

She longed for things to be the way they'd been before. If she'd gotten pregnant before Joel had been deployed, he'd have been ecstatic. But to conceive when he was home on furlough and then for him to find out she was pregnant when he was in the ICU in Germany . . . Well, it had all been a little too much.

"When does Zane start school?" Joel asked.

"Tomorrow. I'll take him and then start my orientation." She wished she didn't have to start so soon, but her quick availability was one of the reasons they'd hired her. "I'll come see you on my break and then before I go home."

Joel shook his head. "You should go straight home. You know how Zane hates to be by himself."

134

"He'll be fine."

Joel shook his head. "Could he go to the neighbors'?"

She pursed her lips but then said, "I can ask." She wasn't worried about Zane's safety—just his sanity. He did hate being alone. He was too social for that. "It will work out," she said in a lighthearted voice. She didn't want Joel to worry, but she didn't feel as confident about all of it as she tried to sound. For things to work out for them, nothing more could go wrong.

She squeezed his hand—three quick squeezes. Their way to communicate quickly and quietly— *I. Love. You.*

He didn't squeeze her hand back.

What if it didn't all work out? The move. Joel's emotional health. She shivered. In some ways it felt as if he hadn't come home from Iraq at all. Not the Joel she knew anyway.

It was late afternoon by the time Shani pulled up alongside the Lehmans' house. She'd stopped by the market for a roasted chicken and a bag of salad, and then drove home on the main road closest to Zane's school. She didn't want any surprises in the morning.

Eve started out the back door with the box of smoothie ingredients in her hands before Shani had turned off the van's motor, so she left it on. By the time Eve climbed into the van, Lila was standing on the top step with the baby on her hip. Eve rolled down the window. "I'll be back soon," she called out to the girl. "Set the table and dish up the applesauce. I'll mash the potatoes when I get back."

Lila nodded and disappeared back into the house.

"How's Joel?" Eve asked.

Shani wanted to answer *"Depressed,"* but instead she said, "About the same. How's Simon?"

"Ornery," Eve replied. "So nearly back to normal." She smiled.

Shani was quiet for a moment and then said, "I have something to ask you."

"Go ahead," Eve answered.

"I was wondering if Zane could come to your house after school this week, you know, before he starts helping with the chores. I have my orientation at the hospital and won't be done until after he gets off the bus."

Eve frowned.

Shani felt awkward for having asked. She rushed on, speaking quickly. "If not, he can stay at the house until it's time to do the chores. He just doesn't like to be by himself."

Eve shook her head. "No, that would be fine. He's welcome at our place."

Shani exhaled and blinked back the tears threatening her eyes. "Thanks."

Eve nodded and then commented on the bright

colors of the leaves. "This is my favorite time of year."

"Mine too," Shani answered as they reached the house.

Zane and Charlie both had work belts on and were pounding away with their hammers. The planks along the ramp were three quarters of the way done.

When Zane saw Eve, he called out, "Did Daniel come with you?"

Eve shook her head. "He's doing the chores."

"Why aren't you helping?" Shani asked her son.

"Tim told me not to this afternoon. Or in the mornings." He seemed disappointed.

Shani turned toward Eve.

"He can still help after school, though," she said. "I'll talk to Tim."

Shani grabbed the bags of groceries from the back and then led the way. Charlie hurried to take the bags from Shani and, as he did, said to Zane, "Grab Eve's box." But the boy had already started to do it.

Charlie had his sleeves pushed up above his elbows. Shani couldn't help but notice Eve staring at the scars on his right forearm for just a moment before he dashed into the house.

After hanging up her coat and purse, Shani followed the rest into the kitchen. Charlie and Eve were chatting but stopped when she entered. She looked from one to the other. Charlie grinned, and Eve smiled back. Shani tilted her head, surprised at the rapport between the two. Eve turned and began pulling items from her box—a large pitcher, juice, greens, two bananas.

"I have protein mix," Shani said, stepping toward the pantry.

"I have some," Eve replied, taking the container from the box. "It's leftover from when Abra was ill."

Shani cocked her head. "You made her smoothies?"

Eve nodded.

"Where?"

Eve smiled. "Here."

"My grandfather had a blender?"

"Jah," Eve answered. "He bought it because of Abra."

Shani couldn't imagine her grandfather being so generous. Or Eve coming over to his house to make smoothies.

"He died the month after Abra did." Eve took a raggedy breath. "He said . . ." Her eyes filled with tears. "He said when he knew he didn't have long left that he'd hug Abra for me when he got to heaven."

"Ahh," Shani said. "He said that?" That was hard for her to imagine too.

Eve nodded.

Shani and Zane had been in Texas with Joel when her grandfather passed away unexpectedly.

There had been a service, but she'd missed it. "Did you go to his service?" she asked Eve.

The woman nodded. "Jah."

Tears stung Shani's eyes. It had been a hard year—for all of them. There was no way she could have made it to her grandfather's funeral. She and Joel had arrived in Texas the week before. Her father had just driven her van—and Zane—down. He had to catch a flight to Philly and then rent a car to get back to Lancaster to make all the arrangements for the service.

"So all of you were friends with Grandpa?"

Eve nodded slightly. "He was the closest to Abra." She lowered her voice, a twinkle in her eye. "He and Tim butted heads."

Shani smiled. "I can imagine." Her grandfather had been an opinionated man. She could see he and Tim wouldn't have always seen eye to eye. "It appears Tim took good care of the field."

"Jah," Eve said. "All organic. That was one of the things that drove your grandfather nuts. He thought it was going to be overtaken with weeds. But the dairy's organic, so the field had to be too. But Tim wasn't very gentle in his explanations."

Shani shook her head. That figured. She turned toward her son and Charlie. "How was church?"

"Good," Charlie answered.

"Some of the women wore bonnets," Zane added, "like Eve and Lila's."

"Kapps," Eve said. "Bonnets are like my black

139

one—that we wear outside with our capes, usually when it's cold."

"Got it," Zane said, as if he were happy for the information. "But a lot of the women were dressed normal."

Eve laughed at that. "Normal," she said, "is relative."

Zane blushed. "Sorry."

"No need to apologize." Eve turned toward Shani. "Could I use some ice?"

Charlie opened the freezer compartment and took out a tray. As he handed it to Eve their hands touched. Neither jerked away.

Then Eve turned to release the ice into the blender.

That was one thing that would never happen. Eve falling for Charlie. She was Amish, after all. And her brother was Tim Lehman. Sure, Charlie was a nice guy, but they existed in two different worlds.

Monday morning Zane was up and sitting at the kitchen table, eating a bowl of cold cereal with Charlie, when Shani shuffled into the kitchen. She poured herself a cup of coffee from the pot Charlie had made. "I can make a hot breakfast," she said, leaning against the counter.

"With the Lucky Charms?" Charlie grinned. "Or the Wheaties?"

She sighed. "I'll make a run to the grocery after work."

Zane glanced up at the clock. "We should get going."

It was seven thirty. Surely the principal and secretary would be in the school office. She'd called last week to let them know Zane would be enrolling.

"I'll work for a couple of hours and then head out too," Charlie said, stepping to the sink with his bowl. "I'll stop by the hospital and see Joel before I head back."

Shani thanked him for all of his help.

"I'll be back Friday morning." He patted Zane's shoulder.

The boy stood and wrapped an arm around Charlie in a quick hug.

Charlie spoke to Shani but looked down at Zane as he said, "Call me sooner if you need anything."

"Denki," Shani said, and then all three of them laughed.

"Yeah, well, run over to the neighbors and then call me, if your landline isn't connected yet." Charlie headed out of the kitchen, already whistling a tune.

Zane had his nose pressed to the window as they drove up to the school. The brick elementary school, middle school, and high school were all on the same property, with the sports fields out front. Manicured lawns and tended flower beds surrounded the compound.

"This is really cool," he said.

Shani agreed. She could imagine Zane going all the way through his senior year at the school. Playing sports. Going to plays. Joining the debate team. Whatever he fancied. She couldn't imagine a better place for him.

Once she parked, he ran ahead of her into the building and was already talking to the secretary by the time she entered the office. It didn't take long to enroll him and for Shani to be on her way to the hospital.

When she arrived, she pulled a protein bar from her bag and headed toward the entrance, hoping they'd have coffee available during the orientation.

When Eve and the children arrived home after school, she sent Daniel to the highway to meet Zane while she unharnessed the horse and Lila held the baby. "May I go with Daniel?" Lila asked. "I'll take Rose and the baby."

Rose frowned. "I want to stay with Aenti." She was usually cranky after school and ready for a snack.

"Go along, Lila," Eve said. "But come right back. No dawdling." Tim had been out dragging the field all afternoon while she'd finished up the wash. She hadn't told him Zane was coming by after school. She hoped Tim would stay out in the field until it was time to do the chores.

After she put the horse in the barn, Eve and Rose headed into the house. Eve checked on Simon, who was still asleep, and then poured Rose a glass of milk and gave her a snickerdoodle. She turned to the counter to cut a couple of apples for more of a snack and then slice some cheese.

Until Abra fell ill, Tim had worked part-time at the lumberyard. After she died, he'd asked Bishop Byler for his job back, but Gideon had told him to wait until the children were settled again. A week or so ago, he had told her he planned to ask Gideon if he could return, but then the horse kicked Simon. She hoped it had been long enough and Tim would go back soon. The family could use the extra income, but more importantly, it would do all of them good to have him gone a few days a week.

Tim and Eve's Dat had worked construction, besides keeping sheep and growing alfalfa. It was always a relief when he was gone to a worksite. Eve knew quite a few gentle Amish men, but her father hadn't been one of them. Neither was her brother.

After the eighth grade, when their schooling ended, Abra had started to work in her Mamm's quilt shop, but it wasn't until Eve was sixteen and had started her Rumschpringe that she found a job in a bakery in town. Having a good reason to leave the house each day brought Eve some relief.

She'd met Patrick that first morning. He lived in an apartment complex nearby, attended the college on the Old Philadelphia Pike, and stopped at the bakery each morning for a cup of coffee.

He was kind and interested in Eve. She'd simply smile, serve him, and tell him to have a good day. Little by little, he lingered more and more. After a while he asked her out. She declined.

But he persisted and finally she agreed. She'd only planned to enjoy Patrick's attention, but his warmth won her over. She soon moved into her own apartment against her parents' wishes, with a Mennonite roommate, and saw Patrick more and more. Once she moved out her parents didn't contact her, but Tim came by the bakery once and confronted her. He told her their parents' health was failing because of her sin, and she'd surely be going to hell.

Eve spun around at the thud of a glass hitting the table. Milk spread across the top, and Rose jumped to her feet. Eve grabbed two dish towels and hurried to the table, handing one to Rose. "It's all right," Eve said as the two soaked up the milk.

How many times had her father yelled at her for a similar accident?

She sighed. She'd been thinking about Charlie on and off throughout the day, which had made her think of Patrick. She swiped at her brow with the back of her hand. She needed to do a better job of controlling her thoughts.

As she wiped the table down, the other children returned—without Zane.

"He wasn't on the bus," Lila said, bouncing the baby on her hip.

A wave of panic swept through Eve. She needed to phone the hospital and have Shani paged. And the school. Maybe Zane had gotten on the wrong bus. Or thought Shani was picking him up.

The baby began to cry. "Fix a bottle," Eve said to Lila. "I'll go make some calls." But as she hurried down the back steps, Tim came through the gate, followed by Zane.

The boy called out, "I got off at the wrong stop and came through the fields."

Relief flooded over Eve, until she registered the expression on her brother's face. He rolled up his sleeves as he marched toward her.

"Go on in and get a snack," Eve said to Zane. "Do you have homework?"

"Not much. I can do it tonight," Zane responded as he hurried toward the house.

Eve spoke up quickly to Tim. "Did you work on their ramp?"

He shook his head. "The cow finally had her calf." Tim pulled off his hat and ran his hand through his hair. "Why is the boy here?"

"Shh," Eve said, glancing at Zane. He'd reached the porch.

Tim yanked his hat back on his head.

The back door opened, and Lila stood with the baby in her arms, smiling.

Once they'd all scampered into the house, Eve said, in a low voice, "I told Shani he could come by after school until it was time to do the chores."

"Where is she?"

"At the hospital."

"She could've come home in time."

Eve shook her head. "She's orienting for her new job."

"What?"

"She works as a nurse, remember? That's how she knew what to do—with Simon."

"She shouldn't be working," Tim said. "She should be taking care of her family." He stepped back toward the gate but then stopped. "No good's going to come from having that boy around."

"You're the one who insisted he help with the chores."

"Jah, I know," Tim said. "I should have thought it through. Tell him I don't need his help anymore."

Eve crossed her arms. "He likes helping with the chores. And it's good for Daniel to work with Zane. It's teaching him to be a leader."

"If the boy keeps coming over, Daniel will soon be learning more than management skills. Lila too."

"You're not going to be able to keep Zane away. Not when we're neighbors."

"Believe me, I'll do my best." Tim tugged on his beard. "Make sure and tell him what I said, about not needing his help anymore."

Eve shook her head. "You tell him," she said, turning toward the house. She'd been gentle with Tim since Abra had died. Before that, she'd been furious with him for his harshness, but the death of his wife had broken him and he'd been numb.

But the numbness seemed to be wearing off— except for the other night when Simon had been injured. Then it was worse than ever.

Eve marched toward the back door, ignoring

Tim as he called her name. She felt like a fifteen-year-old again, tired of being bossed around. Back then she used to beg God to provide a wife for her brother. She never dreamt it would be Abra.

She never would have wished that on her best friend. She sighed as she trudged up the steps. Tim wasn't abusive—not on purpose, anyway. But he was controlling. Lots of Amish kids called their fathers Dad—he insisted on Dat. Other families simply said thank you. He insisted on the old-fashioned denki.

Those were little things he did. Others were harsh and overbearing. He put down Daniel—and favored Simon. He never hugged his children or told them that he loved them. He expected absolute obedience and agreement.

Her mother used to say that was just the way God made Tim and to let him be. But Eve didn't trust her mother's judgment—after all she'd married Eve's Dat. Most likely the six babies their mother had lost between Tim and Eve, her only two children, had something to do with her mother's feeling toward Tim too.

Eve stopped on the mud porch to collect herself before joining the children, chiding herself for thinking ill of the dead. Her father had died from a stroke four years ago, and her mother passed away from congestive heart failure just before Abra had been diagnosed with cancer. Tim and her nieces and nephews were the closest family Eve had left. Turning, she made sure Tim hadn't followed her. He was nowhere in sight.

Her nieces and nephews were the best that life had given her. She'd do anything for them, including giving up her own hopes and dreams.

That was what she liked about Charlie. He was safe. He posed no threat to her commitment to the children.

His presence also reminded her that, years ago, she'd been her own person, willing to marry Patrick and leave her Amish life behind. Now she knew she'd never marry, never have a family of her own. She'd gotten exactly what she deserved.

If there was any chance of maintaining a relationship with the Becks, she needed to ignore their friend—and her feelings for him. The last thing she wanted was for Tim to turn on the new neighbors.

They were good people, just as Shani's grandfather had been. At one time Tim was ready to break his lease, he was so fed up with the old man. Abra had reminded Tim they needed the field to feed the cows, and then she had patched things up with Mr. Williams. That had all happened a year ago, soon after Abra had been diagnosed with cancer. She was sick and pregnant and still cleaning up Tim's mess.

Eve breathed in deeply, opened the door, and stepped into the kitchen. The baby was in her high chair, and the other children sat around the table, eating apples, cheese slices, and snickerdoodles.

Zane sat in Tim's place, at the head of the table, while all the other children were in their usual chairs, except Lila walked around the table, serving the others.

"How do you say apple?" Zane asked.

"*Opple*," Rose replied.

Zane took a bite of the snickerdoodle. "Cookie?"

"*Cookie*," Lila said, handing him another one.

All the children laughed.

"Cheese?" Zane held up a slice.

"*Kais*," Daniel replied. As he did Trudy clapped her hands together, and all the children laughed again.

"Do you say that too, when you take a picture?" Zane asked.

Lila shook her head and said matter-of-factly, "We don't take pictures."

Eve thought about Patrick again. Of the photo he took of her and Abra, of him calling out "Say cheese." They'd both burst out laughing, having no idea what he was talking about.

She couldn't help but wonder where the photo was now. She wished she had it but guessed it had been with Abra's things. Tim had probably burned it by now.

Daniel and Zane headed outside while Lila cleaned up from the snack and Eve took the smoothie pitcher out of the refrigerator and poured a glass for Simon. She grabbed a dose syringe from the drawer and headed down the hall to the boys' room. If he was still asleep, she'd wake him. She didn't want him to be awake all night.

But he sat up in bed when she entered. She placed the glass on the bedside table with the syringe so she could adjust his pillows.

"Aenti." It was unnerving to have him speak without opening his mouth. "Did the boy come over?" Simon asked.

"Zane?"

He nodded.

"Jah. But he and Daniel have gone outside." She doubted Tim was telling Zane not to come around anymore. For all his harshness, her brother avoided conflict when he could.

"I wish they'd come in and play a game with me."

Eve handed him the syringe. "You know the doctor said you have to stay quiet."

"I've been staring at the ceiling all day."

She smiled. "You were sleeping."

His eyes sparkled. "*Mostly* staring at the ceiling." That wasn't entirely true either. She'd read to him while the baby napped, in between the loads of wash. Eve would send Lila in later, to read to him while Eve cooked dinner.

"Dawdi and Mammi played a game with me in the hospital," Simon said.

"They did?"

"Well, not really. They said it wasn't allowed, so instead we talked about games. They told me my Mamm loved to play games."

"She did," Eve said. Abra loved to have fun, whether it was playing a game, pulling a prank, or telling a joke. Her Dat was like that too. A loving, generous man, and her Mamm, although she didn't come by it naturally, was happy to play along.

"Do you want me to feed you?"

He shook his head. "I can do it." He put the syringe into the smoothie, drew the mixture into it, squirted the smoothie into his mouth, swallowed, and then said, "How come Dat doesn't like that Englisch kid?"

"Did he say that?"

"No. But he said he shouldn't have asked him to do my chores. I told him I could do them tomorrow."

Eve shook her head. "The doctor said you have to rest. No bright lights. No sudden movements. No activity."

He groaned. "I'm going to go crazy."

Eve looked her nephew in the eyes. "You could have been killed. I'm so thankful that the worst of all of this is you being bored." Although she guessed his jaw and neck hurt more than he let on. "God wants you to heal. That's your job right now."

"Mammi and Dawdi prayed for me," Simon said. "Out loud."

Eve smiled, remembering how it felt to be prayed over. She tousled Simon's hair again and couldn't help but say, "Bless them."

He squirted the syringe into his mouth and then refilled it as Eve leaned against the headboard. Abra's parents had left the church soon after Simon was born. *"For several reasons,"* they'd said. But Eve was pretty sure they believed the bishop, the one before Gideon, had coerced Abra into marrying Tim.

After Simon was born, suddenly Daniel and Lila, who were only two, couldn't do anything right in Tim's eyes. And Abra's parents, Leona and Eli, were concerned—they talked to the bishop about it, and to Tim too.

Abra told her parents she thought she could handle the situation and make the marriage work, and the bishop chastised them for meddling. Eve knew it was hard for them to leave the church, but they also felt in the long run they'd be more available to rescue Abra and the children from the outside, if needed.

Tim stopped being as obvious about favoring Simon after that, but he'd shunned Leona and Eli worse than anyone in the district, saying he didn't want them influencing his children.

He couldn't stop Abra from seeing them though, and then when she was so sick and in treatment, after Trudy was born, Leona and Eli welcomed all of them—except for Tim—into their home.

Simon plunged the syringe into the glass again and sucked the smoothie into it. He groaned. "I'm going to become an eighty-pound weakling."

Eve nudged him. "Don't you weigh seventy-five?"

He nodded. "But I've never been a weakling. Nobody wants a weak soldier."

Eve nudged him again. "Hush." She knew he was joking, but it still disturbed her. She waited until he finished the smoothie and then took the glass. "Rest for a while, and then Lila will come in and read to you."

Simon rolled his eyes. "I'd rather play a game with Daniel and the boy."

Eve smiled. "Be thankful you have a sister who likes to read out loud. Count your blessings—there's much to be thankful for."

By the time Shani came to pick up Zane, the boys were done with the chores and were visiting with Simon, sitting in the dark on the floor beside his bed. Eve opened the door for Shani, relieved her friend had arrived before Tim came in from the barn.

Lila mashed the potatoes while Rose set the table and Trudy sat in her chair, chewing on a cracker. Eve motioned to her oldest niece to go get Zane, and she obeyed quickly.

"Thank you," Shani said. "This has been a huge help. Is it okay if he comes tomorrow too?"

Eve nodded.

"Are you sure?" Shani asked. Did she suspect all was not well?

"Jah," Eve said. "He's welcome here." At least until Tim said otherwise, directly to the boy.

Daniel came out with Zane, but it was Lila who told him good-bye. "See you tomorrow," she said.

Zane waved to the older children and then patted Trudy's head. She giggled in return. Eve followed her neighbors out the door and said good-bye, wishing she had more time with Shani.

As Shani pulled the van around and back toward the lane, Tim started toward the house from the barn. Eve couldn't figure out her brother. He was downright gentle with his livestock, coddling them along. One of his milk cows had died in the summer, which was a financial loss, but he was more worried about her "best friend," the cow she spent time with the most. True, he worried about losing another cow and milk production and all of that, but his concern for the animal's emotional state seemed genuine. He empathized with her loss. It gave Eve a small measure of hope. Maybe he could learn to be compassionate with humans too. But she certainly wasn't seeing any inkling of that today.

Eve waited for him. When he approached, she

asked, "Have you spoken to Gideon about getting your job back?"

He shook his head. "But I will. Soon."

She nodded. "*Gut*," she answered, turning toward the house.

✁ 14

On Friday, as Charlie drove his pickup truck across the Lancaster County line, his windshield wipers swept away the last of the rain, and a few minutes later the late morning sun began to poke through the clouds. He'd been thinking about Eve again, without even realizing it.

He shook his head, forcing himself to focus on the scenery instead. To the right cornstalks swayed in the breeze. He downshifted the truck as he came to a curve and took it slowly, mindful there could be a buggy around the corner. There wasn't.

It was just over an hour, as long as there was no traffic or accidents, from his house to where the Becks lived. And another twenty minutes on into Lancaster.

He pressed down on the gas pedal for a straight stretch. When he went through his mobilization training, before shipping out to Iraq, one of the financial officers had warned all of the soldiers against buying a truck with their combat pay. Or a Harley. Either could be ordered on base.

Buying such a thing had been the last thing on Charlie's mind—until Nikki broke up with him via email the day after the attack that injured Joel and killed their buddy Samuel.

That afternoon, with his arm bandaged from his wrist to his elbow, he'd gone down to the dealer on the base and ordered his truck. A Chevrolet Silverado with a king cab and canopy. The biggest rig he'd ever owned. Ever would, he was sure. It was waiting for him when he got back home.

Now he regretted getting the truck. He should have gotten something half the size and half the price. It hadn't made him feel any better, not in the long run. He'd always been a modest person—until then.

And every day the pickup reminded him of May eleventh. Not May twelfth, the day Nikki broke up with him. In retrospect that second awful day paled in comparison to the first. There was no way to explain to someone who wasn't a soldier the wrenching pain of losing one brother and not being able to save the second from horrible harm.

That day stayed crystal clear in his mind. It always would.

Charlie had always been an optimistic person, definitely a glass-half-full kind of guy. And he still was, but he'd had to pick the glass up a few times in the last few months to keep it from tipping over.

His co-workers at the station watched him closely, as if looking for him to break. But the truth was, after being in a war zone, he didn't think there was much that could make him panic. It took a lot to get his adrenaline up now.

On his past three days at work, he'd dealt with several traffic accidents, a few heart attacks, a fall from a ladder, a two-year-old who had wedged his leg through the slats of his crib, and an old man who'd died from natural causes at home. All of it was upsetting, some of it downright tragic, but it still felt minor compared to his time in Iraq.

He downshifted again when he reached the edge of town, taking in the brick houses that soon gave way to brownstones. He appreciated the city of Lancaster with its old architecture and history, going back to colonial days. He wondered if Eve came into the city often—and then slapped the heel of hand against his forehead and sighed. He was thinking about her again. Maybe it didn't matter. It wasn't as if he'd ever act on his feelings —or as if she'd reciprocate them.

By the time he reached the parking lot at the hospital the sky had cleared. He found a spot, backed in, and strolled toward the main entrance. He'd talked to Joel the night before and said he'd be at the hospital long before noon. By the time he stepped into his friend's room, Joel was eating his lunch.

"A little early, isn't it?" Charlie asked.

Joel shook his head. "Not around here. We're on a schedule that mimics a preschool."

Charlie turned and looked at the clock above the door. "So that means naptime is in ten minutes?"

"Yeah, you've got the idea," Joel said. "Except I get to skip it today."

"Says who?"

Joel put his fork down on the edge of his plate of macaroni and cheese. He'd only eaten half of it. "The doc. He's releasing me." He knocked on the cast on his leg.

"That's great!" The railing wasn't on the ramp yet, but he'd still be able to get his friend into his house.

Joel sighed. "I can't get ahold of Shani though. She's in orientation again today."

"I can take you," Charlie said, his mind racing through the details. "Where's your chair? Back at the house?"

Joel shook his head. "In the van. I told her to put it in yesterday so it would be there when they finally released me."

"I can track her down and get the key."

"Chances are it isn't locked." Joel shook his head. Charlie knew that was one of his pet peeves with Shani. While they were in Iraq, Joel used to remind her to lock the front door of their apartment. They'd talked regularly over Skype. In fact, Joel was the first person Charlie knew to use the Internet program so he could talk with and see Shani as often as possible. It was one of the benefits of being a communications specialist.

"I'll go see if I can find her van," Charlie said.

He'd seen the sign to employee parking. He'd start there.

It didn't take long, and sure enough the van wasn't locked. He lifted the wheelchair down, opened it, and headed back to Joel's room. When Charlie visited Joel in Texas, Joel had said his relationship with Shani hadn't changed much but everything was different with Zane. Joel said he didn't know if it was because he'd almost died or because he was crippled, but the kid treated him as if he were invisible.

Charlie hadn't known how to answer his friend and had ended up saying, "Give it time."

Time. What did he know about time healing the emotional wounds of a twelve-year-old? And Charlie was pretty sure Joel's relationship with Shani had changed more than his friend realized. Joel was probably in denial. Still, they seemed to be hanging in there.

Joel sat on the edge of his bed, a nurse beside him, when Charlie reentered his room. "Could you send Shani a text?" Joel asked. "Tell her you sprung me out of here. My cell's in her purse."

Charlie did as Joel asked while the nurse went through the discharge protocol with Joel. He found the sound of his friend's voice comforting even though what he and the nurse were discussing was routine. Medication. Pain levels. An order for physical therapy once he was out of the cast. But it was all music to Charlie's ears.

This was a setback for Joel—but it wasn't nearly as bad as it could have been.

Joel signed the last piece of paper and then took the packet of instructions from the nurse, tucking it along the side of the chair. Charlie pushed him from the room and then down the hall, wondering if he'd be able to get Joel into the backseat of his truck. He hadn't thought about that. It was quite the step up. Joel could always stand on Charlie's toolbox—he'd packed it so he wouldn't have to borrow Tim's tools.

As it turned out he did have to use the toolbox. He was afraid Joel would grow frustrated, but he kept his sense of humor, until Charlie asked what was in the pocket of his jacket. He shouldn't have.

"Just my cigs," Joel said.

"I thought you quit."

"I have, mostly. Especially this week—traction makes it a little hard to get outside." Charlie thought of the smoking area outside the hospital.

Joel swung his cast around on the seat, his back toward Charlie. "Shani didn't notice them in the inside pocket of my jacket when she brought it. Or at least she didn't mention them." He shrugged. "On bad days, a smoke helps me get through it." Charlie wondered what exactly Joel considered a bad day.

As Charlie drove out of the parking garage, he glanced at Joel in the rearview mirror. His eyes were closed, but he was sitting straight up and didn't look relaxed at all.

Joel hadn't smoked before Iraq, but lots of soldiers started over there. Not Charlie. But he wasn't going to be judgmental. Joel was a big boy—and one of the best soldiers Charlie knew.

Joel had been assigned to Charlie's Army Reserve unit a couple of months before they'd been deployed. Joel led the advance team and Charlie went with him.

Joel was a good leader and a good soldier. He was excited at first to go, even giddy. He'd trained for it his entire adult life. They all had. But early on the seriousness of the deployment began to weigh on Joel.

Then losing Samuel took a huge toll on him. Much worse, of course, than his own injuries. Charlie was pretty sure that, if Joel had the choice, he'd have traded places with Samuel. That was the kind of leader he was.

Charlie drove in silence. Eventually Joel leaned back and seemed to relax some. Charlie slowed as he turned down the lane and then slowed even more as he passed the turn to the Lehmans' place. He looked down the driveway, hoping to catch a glance of Eve, but no one was in sight.

Joel breathed in deeply. "Smells just like I remember."

Charlie ignored him. It didn't smell that bad, at least not for a dairy.

As he eased around the bend, the ramp came into view. Half the railing was up. A split second later Charlie could see Tim positioning a slat in place.

A buggy with a horse harnessed to it was parked at the end of the ramp. Perhaps Tim had brought over more tools.

Charlie opened the truck door and called out a hello. Tim waved.

"What's he doing here?" Joel asked from the backseat.

"Looks as if he's finishing up the ramp."

"Oh," Joel responded. "I thought it was all done."

"Mostly done," Charlie countered, trying to keep his voice light. He hurried around the back of the truck, opened the tailgate, pulled Joel's chair to the ground, and quickly popped it open. By the time he'd pushed it to the backseat door, Joel had it open.

"I'll get the tool chest," Charlie said.

"I don't need it," Joel answered as he eased himself down to the ground, holding onto the door. Charlie positioned the chair, put the brakes on, and then helped Joel swing around, thankful Tim was on the other side of the truck and couldn't see the maneuver they had to go through. It was kind of like dancing.

He burst out laughing at the thought.

"Stop it," Joel said, but his voice held a lighter tone than usual, more like the old Joel.

Charlie pushed the chair up to the beginning of the ramp. "Ready?" he said to Joel, just as Eve came out the front door, holding the baby in one arm and a box in the other. A strand of her dark hair had escaped her Kapp, and her face was flushed.

"Hold on," Charlie said to Joel, setting the brake on the chair again. He hurried around the ramp to the steps and bounded up them, reaching for the box.

"Denki," she said, sliding the box toward him. "I was making a smoothie for Simon. Shani said it was okay. You can put the box in the front of the buggy."

Charlie's face grew warm as their hands tangled. He pulled away. "How's Simon doing?"

"Tim took him to the doctor yesterday. He said he's doing well."

Charlie headed toward the buggy, leading the way.

"You can put it on the floor, on the passenger side," Eve said, stopping next to Joel's chair and introducing herself.

Joel offered her his hand, and she shook it. The baby gurgled.

"Nice to meet both of you," Joel said. "Shani's told me about . . . all of you. All good things, of course."

Eve smiled at him, warmly. "Ditto," she said, surprising Charlie with the word. It didn't seem like one an Amish woman would use.

She turned toward Tim telling him good-bye, and then climbed into the buggy, still holding the baby. She turned the buggy around. "I'll see you at supper," she called out to Tim.

Charlie couldn't help but wonder if Shani had gotten any food. He should have brought a bag of groceries. It had to have been a hard week for her. He returned to his friend, placing his hands on the back of the chair to push him up the ramp, but Joel said, "It's nice out. I'd like to get some fresh air."

Tim struck a nail with his hammer. "Not much of that in the hospital, is there?"

Joel smiled. "That's for sure."

Tim stepped toward Joel. "I met you, that day at the hospital."

Joel nodded. "I remember." He glanced at the ramp. "Thank you for your help on this."

Tim tipped his hat and then returned to work.

Charlie opened his toolbox, took out his belt, and started working alongside Tim while Joel sat in the sunshine. None of the men spoke, but the sound of the hammers broke the silence, over and over.

Later in the afternoon, after Charlie had pushed Joel up the ramp into the house and turned on the TV, Zane and Daniel popped through the bushes from the field.

"Eve said you were back," Zane called out.

Charlie nodded and then said, "Your dad's in the house. Go tell him hello."

Zane started up the steps with Daniel beside him.

"Stay out here, son," Tim said. Daniel obeyed, sitting down on the top step.

A couple of minutes later Zane appeared with two of Shani's protein bars. He tossed one to Daniel and said, "We should get a head start on the chores." Zane led the way on down the steps. In fact, he seemed to be leading Daniel most of the time, which wasn't surprising. The kid was more like his father than he knew.

Charlie expected Tim to say something to the boys but he didn't. They took off through the bushes and disappeared into the field. About fifteen minutes later Tim packed up his tools and said he'd go help the boys with the milking.

Charlie kept working until Shani arrived. She opened the sliding door and pulled out a pizza box. "I have a salad too," she called out to Charlie and then smiled. "Who says I can't come up with a balanced meal?"

He laughed.

She started toward him. "Where's Zane?"

"Over doing chores."

"Oh, I thought he'd be here by now," she said.

"I'll go get him," Charlie said. "It's getting too dark to keep working." Thanks to Tim, the ramp was nearly completed. Another hour in the morning would finish the construction. Then he'd just need to stain the wood.

Instead of cutting through the field, he took the lane. When he reached the Lehmans' place, Eve was outside taking diapers off the line. She folded one as he approached. He couldn't imagine how often she had to do laundry.

"I came to get Zane," Charlie called out to her.

She didn't turn toward him as she answered, "They're still in the barn."

He must have imagined what he thought was a spark between them last weekend. She was definitely keeping her distance today.

As he neared the barn, Daniel shouted something in Pennsylvania Dutch and then Zane repeated it. "*Misht.* What does that mean?" he asked.

"Manure," Daniel answered.

Someone laughed—but it wasn't Zane.

When he entered the barn, a boy with curly hair leaned against a shovel, still laughing, but with his mouth closed.

"Hello," Charlie said to the boy. "I'm Charlie."

"Simon." He didn't open his mouth as he spoke either, and his words were slightly distorted but understandable.

"Nice to meet you," Charlie said, feeling silly for not guessing who it was. "Glad to see you up and around."

"Me too," Simon said, his eyes sparkling. It looked as if he'd like to break out in a grin but, of course, he couldn't. "I thought I was going to die of boredom."

"Where's your father?" Charlie asked him.

"In the milk room."

Charlie stepped to the doorway. The man stood next to the huge stainless steel vat, his back toward Charlie.

"I'm taking Zane home," Charlie said.

"*Gut.*" Tim waved his hand, as if dismissing them both.

As Charlie turned back toward the boys, Daniel said another word in Pennsylvania Dutch. "*Hinaendt.*"

"What does that mean?" Zane asked.

"You don't want to know," Simon said, slapping his hind end. Both of the Amish boys laughed at that.

Zane stared for a moment but then laughed too.

Charlie found it amusing that it took Zane a minute to catch the meaning but didn't say anything. Instead he told Zane it was time to head on home.

Zane's tone was full of disappointment. "Already?"

"Yep, your mom brought a pizza home."

"A pizza?" Simon shook his head. "We get one of those once a decade, if we're lucky."

"We had pizza last week with them while you were in the hospital," Daniel said.

Simon took a step toward Charlie, still leaning on the shovel. "Then I should get to have some tonight, don't you think?"

Zane's voice brightened. "Can they?" he asked Charlie.

"They'd have to ask their dad." Charlie headed toward the barn door, doubting Tim would allow it. And Simon wouldn't be able to eat it anyway, not unless Shani processed it through a blender.

"He'd say no," Daniel said, his voice glum.

"Next time, then," Zane said. Then he called out, "See you tomorrow!" as he ran out the door only to stop abruptly and head back to the barn. "Speaking of, want to go trick-or-treating together?"

Simon snorted. "Do you think Halloween's a big deal around here?"

"It's not?" Zane had a baffled look on his face.

"Halloween is an Englisch holiday," Daniel explained.

"Do you have a harvest party?" Zane asked. "The youth group I went to in California did."

Simon snorted again, but Daniel just shrugged.

Zane tried again. "But there are pumpkins on your porch."

"Aenti put them there—but they're not carved." He glanced over his shoulder and then whispered, "Dat would have a fit."

There were beautiful purple mums on the porch, no doubt thanks to Eve too. "Come on," Charlie said to Zane. "We can talk about trick-or-treating on the way home."

Zane waved to the boys again, but as they left the barn he said, "I'm too old for it anyway. I thought it would be fun to go with them, but it's not a big deal." He ran toward Eve, who was headed toward the house with her basket of clean diapers. She stopped to speak to Zane, but when Charlie approached she told the boy good-bye.

"Hurry on home," Charlie said to Zane. "I want to talk to Eve for a moment."

She turned toward him, her dark eyes bright and her cheeks rosy from the cold.

"Zane and I enjoyed the Mennonite church last Sunday," he said.

She nodded. "*Gut.*"

"Afterward we were wondering about your church. Are visitors ever allowed?"

Eve pursed her lips and then said, "We don't have any visitors who aren't Amish or didn't grow up Amish."

"My grandparents were Brethren. I'd visit sometimes when they had services at their house. I'm curious how similar their practices are to yours."

She smiled slightly, her profile toward him. "You could ask the bishop about attending." Her

171

brown eyes weren't as warm as they'd been the week before.

"Gideon, right? At the lumberyard?"

"That's correct."

Charlie nodded. That was the right way to handle it anyway. "Do you think he'll be open to the idea?"

"He might." Eve smiled, wryly. "The Scriptures are in High German, though. And the rest is in Pennsylvania Dutch."

"I know some German," Charlie said.

"Really?"

He nodded. "My grandparents spoke German. And I took it in school." He smiled. "Although the only Pennsylvania Dutch I know, I've learned from what Simon and Daniel are teaching Zane."

She laughed. "Jah, he'll be fluent in our language in no time—at least in boy talk."

"I'll go by and ask the bishop tomorrow." He didn't want to leave yet and scrambled for something more to say. "I've appreciated what you've done for Zane and Shani. What Tim has done too, as far as the ramp."

"Shani has been good to us too," she answered.

"It's a relief, really, that you're close by."

She smiled a little at that, adjusted her grip on the basket, and said, "I'll see you later. If not tomorrow, then perhaps at church."

He nodded and waited for a moment as she

strode toward the house, just until he realized he was staring. Then he turned down the driveway toward the lane.

Saturday, Charlie finished the railing on the ramp and then went to the lumberyard to buy stain to finish the project. When he brought up attending church, the bishop seemed flattered. He gave him the address of Deacon King's farm, where the service would be held.

"There are thirty-three families in our district," Gideon said.

That didn't sound too big until Charlie did the math. If most of the families had five children, like Tim did, that would be one hundred sixty-five people. The Kings would have to have a huge house.

Charlie thanked Gideon and left with the wood stain. He'd ask Zane if he wanted to join him.

He wondered how much his grandparents' faith had in common with the Amish. Both were nonresistant—he knew that. He wondered, if they had still been alive, what his grandparents would have thought of him joining the Army Reserve and then going off to war. His mother had been opposed, but not because of her religion—she'd left the Brethren as a teenager. She was against his going simply because he was her son.

He couldn't help but wonder what Eve thought about the war as well.

He quickened his step as the lights of Joel and Shani's house came into view. He wasn't sure why he felt a ray of hope. It had been months since he'd felt anything more than angst. He thought of his grandfather's prayers, back when he was a boy. He whispered one now. "Father, we desire the greatest blessing of all, the blessing of your daily presence."

He felt that around Eve. In her grief and sorrow, she seemed to trust the Lord. Charlie felt a peace when he was with her.

ᔜ 15

Eve stood in the sunshine at the edge of the King family's shed, rocking Trudy in her arms, willing the baby to go to sleep before the service began. Tim and a group of men stood under the oak tree in the middle of the driveway, while Daniel and Simon scuffled nearby.

Eve had told Tim she'd stay home with Simon, but the boy had wanted to come, and Tim allowed it.

The baby snuggled closer, her eyes closed now. Eve pulled the blanket tighter and kept swaying. Tim and the other men, and then the boys, started toward the shed. The bishop followed, but he stopped before entering, turning toward Eve with a smile.

Her face warmed, and she ducked her head down toward the baby. She felt Gideon's eyes on her for a long moment. Whatever his intentions, they wouldn't last. The sooner he moved on to someone else, the better. When she joined the Amish church she'd done it with a personal vow—never to marry an Amish man. That—coupled with the promise she'd made to Abra, that she'd care for her children—meant she'd never marry at all.

When she finally looked up, he was gone.

Instead she saw Charlie and Zane striding down the driveway. She took another backward step to where she could still see them but hopefully Charlie couldn't see her.

He stopped at the entrance to the shed and smiled at Zane, gesturing for the boy to go first. The two disappeared. She hoped they realized the men and women sat on separate sides. Had Gideon explained that? Apparently he'd given Charlie directions to the King place.

She smiled at the thought of all the things that could go wrong for Charlie and Zane. Gender specific sides. The three-hour service—Gideon had probably neglected to mention that. And no matter how much German Charlie knew, he wouldn't keep up with all that went on in a service.

Trudy relaxed against her, but Eve waited another couple of minutes until she was sure the little one had fallen into a deep sleep. Then she entered the shed, stopping at the back. Charlie had figured out the seating arrangements—he and Zane sat three quarters of the way back on the men's side, along the aisle.

The congregation was still singing *Das Loblied*. " 'O Lord Father, we bless thy name, Thy love and thy goodness praise . . .' "

Zane had his head turned. Was he watching Lila, who sat a few rows ahead? Eve started down the aisle with the baby and slipped onto the bench beside her niece. The baby stirred but then settled again. Lila stroked her littlest sister's fine hair. Rose, on the other side of Lila, popped her head forward, grinned at Eve, and then pointed to the men's side, back toward Charlie and Zane.

Eve shook her head at the little girl and then stared straight ahead.

When the song ended, Deacon King stepped to the front and started reading from Scripture. A starling fluttered in the rafters above. Rose fidgeted. Eve suppressed a yawn. She'd been up with the baby twice during the night.

Halfway through the service the baby woke and Eve gave her the bottle she'd prepared that morning. Then Lila and Eve took turns holding Trudy. She seemed content to look over their shoulders at those seated behind them.

At the end of the service, as Eve stood with the baby back in her arms, she couldn't keep herself from glancing at Charlie. Simon stood between him and Zane, obviously thrilled to see them. Tim stood a few feet away, his arms crossed.

"Come on, girls," Eve said to her nieces, pointing to the side aisle. She wanted to avoid Tim—and Charlie. "Let's go help with the meal."

"Will Charlie and Zane eat with us?" Rose asked.

Eve shrugged. She had no idea.

Rose led the way, and Eve followed the girls into the bright sunshine. Deacon King's wife, Monika, reached for Trudy.

The baby didn't protest and settled into the woman's plump arms. Monika cooed to her, "How's our poor motherless babe?"

Rose kicked at the hay that had been spread across the dirt pathway. Lila drifted away.

Monika squeezed the baby and then said to Eve, "How are things going with the bishop?"

Eve's face grew warm. "*Ach*, Monika . . ." She didn't want her nieces to hear. She reached for the baby. "You probably need to get things ready in the kitchen."

Monika grinned and twisted away from Eve. "My girls have it all under control." She had five girls. The oldest was twenty-three and the youngest, Jenny, was in school with Lila. The two oldest were already married, although neither had babies yet, and the next two were mother's helpers in a neighboring district. All the girls were hard workers like their Mamm.

It was Eve's turn to tease. "Are you practicing being a grandmother with Trudy?"

Monika bent down and kissed the baby's forehead. "Jah. That's right."

Rose pointed to the oak tree. Charlie and Zane stood beneath it, looking a little lost. Lila had started toward them, and Rose ran after her.

"Who is that?" Monika asked.

Eve opened her mouth to explain, but before she could, Gideon stepped to her side and said, "That's the Lehmans' new neighbors."

"Actually the new neighbors' son and their friend," Eve added.

"Oh," Monika said, looking at Eve. "Did you invite them?"

She shook her head.

The bishop spoke up. "Charlie stopped by yesterday and asked if they could visit. I gave him permission."

"Oh," Monika said. "How odd . . ." She squeezed the baby again.

"Mamm," Jenny called from the porch. "Where's the blue serving platter?"

Monika frowned. "I thought they had it under control."

Jenny put a hand on her hip and waited. She and Lila were friends, although Eve suspected it was partly because Jenny had a crush on Daniel. Time would tell whether the girls stayed friends or not.

Eve reached for the baby again, but Monika shook her head. "I'm perfectly capable of giving orders while holding a little one." She grinned at Eve and then strode off toward the house.

Gideon stepped closer to Eve, taking his hat off as he did. His sandy hair had begun to gray at his temples. His blue eyes were warm and his smile kind. He cleared his throat. "I was hoping I'd have a chance to speak with you."

Eve's pulse quickened.

"I've been wanting to spend some time

together." He paused and smiled again. "Soon."

"It's been a busy season," she said. "The kids. Now Simon's accident."

"But he's here today. He's recovered, right?"

"Recovering . . ." She'd been trying to keep him quiet and in his room, along with getting as many calories into him as possible. Both were difficult tasks.

"Could I come over this evening?" Gideon asked. His wife had only passed last winter, but it wasn't uncommon for an Amish man to seek another wife soon. Except for Tim. He seemed to not have given it a thought.

Gideon leaned toward her. "I can come over after supper."

"The baby is fussy in the evenings," Eve said.

"Couldn't Tim take care of her?"

Eve didn't answer. Her brother seldom held the baby, let alone took care of her. She doubted he realized it, but she was sure he subconsciously blamed Trudy for Abra's death. She'd refused any sort of treatment while she was pregnant. Finally, she'd agreed to be induced at eight months, so she could start chemo.

Gideon glanced toward the house, where Monika stood on the porch, holding Trudy and talking to a group of women. He chuckled. "Or maybe Monika would keep her for the rest of the day."

"Lila could watch her," Eve said. She didn't want to involve Monika.

"Perfect," Gideon said. "I'll be over after supper. We'll have time for a conversation then. And hopefully a walk."

A commotion over by the tree distracted Eve. Gideon turned, and she stepped to his side to see better. Simon hung from a branch. Charlie spoke to him calmly, saying, "None of that, bud. But, careful, don't drop." He wrapped his arms around the boy's torso and lowered him slowly. "Now go on over and check in with your aunt. Tell her you should go in the house and sit for a while."

Eve started toward the tree, the bishop behind her. "Thank you," she called out to Charlie. "Come on, Simon. Let's go get you a glass of water and find a quiet corner."

"Are they staying for the meal?" Simon pointed to Charlie and Zane. "I want to ask Charlie about the war."

The bishop frowned at Simon but then said, "You're welcome to stay," to Charlie.

Zane looked pleased until Charlie said, "Thank you, but we need to get back."

Eve took Simon's hand and started toward the house.

"I'll see you tonight," Gideon called out to her.

"See you then," she responded, her face growing warm. She'd turned down a few men wanting to court her over the last decade, but she wasn't sure

181

how to turn down the bishop. Tim wouldn't be pleased if she did, not at all. And she didn't want to reveal her vow—it wouldn't make sense to anyone but her.

Gideon would lose interest soon enough. She'd be polite until then, but not encouraging. What else could she do?

When she and Simon reached the porch, Monika and the baby were gone. They must have stepped inside. Eve looked back at the tree. Charlie and Zane were gone too. She turned toward the driveway. They were headed toward Charlie's truck, and Gideon was walking with them.

Charlie would go back to Philadelphia tonight or tomorrow. She imagined, with time, and as Joel healed, Charlie wouldn't make the trip to Lancaster County very often. She sighed. That would be for the best—for her anyway. But not for Shani and her family.

"What's the matter, Aenti?" Simon asked.

"Oh, I'm tired is all," she said, leaning against the porch railing. Simon squeezed her hand. He was the most affectionate of all her nieces and nephews.

"Come on. Let's get you settled, and then I'll see how I can help." She pulled him along into the house. The sooner the meal was over, the sooner they could all go home. Hopefully she could rest before starting supper and bracing herself for the bishop's visit.

Once they were home and Simon was tucked into his bed for a nap and the baby asleep in her crib, Tim motioned for Eve to join him outside. Daniel, Lila, and Rose looked up from the puzzle they were working on at the table.

"What's going on?" Rose asked.

"Shh," Daniel replied, as Eve followed Tim out the door.

Tim kept walking until he reached the gate to the field. Obviously he didn't want the children to hear. "I was *mortified*"—it wasn't a word Eve had ever heard her brother use before—"that you would invite Charlie and Zane to our service."

"I didn't," she answered.

Tim crossed his arms. "They didn't find the King place on their own."

"Charlie asked Gideon about going. Gideon said he could and gave him directions."

Tim pursed his lips and then said, "He wouldn't have asked about going if it wasn't for you."

Her face grew warm, which she hated. It would only add to Tim seeing her as a naughty teenager again. "That's not true," she said.

"It is. You're just like Abra."

"Why don't you ask Charlie," Eve said, pointing past Tim. "Go over there right now and see what he says."

Her brother's eyes narrowed.

Eve put her hands on her hips.

"Maybe I will," Tim said.

"Please do." She turned toward the house. "I'm going to go take a nap." She started marching toward the house, forcing herself to calm down before she reached the kitchen. She didn't want to alarm the children. "I'm going to go rest," she told the children. "I'll be out to fix supper when it's time."

The three looked at her, their eyes big.

"Everything's fine," she said. "But I'll need your help later . . . The bishop's coming by."

Daniel groaned. "Why?"

Lila crossed her arms. "You know why."

"What's going on?" Rose asked, her eyes darting from Lila to Daniel to Eve.

"Nothing," Eve said. "He's coming by after supper, that's all. Just to visit." She'd make an apple crisp while supper heated and serve him that. It wouldn't impress him—and that was fine.

As it turned out, Gideon was impressed with the crisp or at least he pretended to be. "Delicious," he said, pushing his chair back from the table when he'd finished. Eve imagined the children and Tim listening to every word from the living room. As Trudy began to fuss, Gideon said, "How about a walk?"

"Sure." Eve picked up the plates and placed them in the sink, and then headed to the mud porch and pulled her cape off the peg and led the way outside. The warm day had given way to a cold evening. The moon was waning, but the night was cloudless and still bright. The acrid smell of woodsmoke filled her lungs.

Englisch children would be out trick-or-treating. She remembered that from when she was living in the apartment in town. Abra had been over and they'd been surprised when the doorbell rang. Abra realized when she answered it what was going on and had laughed out loud. "So cute," she'd said to a girl dressed like the Little Mermaid and a boy dressed like a ninja. She'd hurried into the kitchen and came up with a nearly empty bag of peanut butter cups and gave one to each of the children.

The boy asked why she'd dressed up like a Dutchy. That made her laugh too. Then the mom had smiled and suggested they turn off the porch light to keep the trick-or-treaters away. Abra had been sad, but it was either that or go buy candy. Eve had teased her friend about her "costume." By then Eve was wearing Englisch clothes all the time.

"You seem lost in thought," Gideon said.

"Ach, perhaps so." Not wanting him to ask what she'd been thinking about, she changed the subject. "The service was good today."

"Jah," Gideon said. "I thought so too." They'd reached the lane, and Gideon motioned toward the left.

An owl hooted, startling Eve.

"You're jumpy." Gideon's hand brushed against her arm. Had it been intentional? She shivered and wrapped her arms over her chest.

"How are the children doing?" he asked. All along he'd been concerned about them. She'd appreciated his attention to her nieces and nephews. She felt the bishop's example was good for Tim.

"They're still having a hard time . . ."

"Is that so." His voice was kind.

"I think Simon getting injured made them worry again," she added.

"Just keep reassuring them. Once Tim finds a new mother for them, they'll settle back in—or maybe sooner. Lila is getting old enough to start taking over the home."

"She's only eleven."

"She seems older," Gideon said.

"She and Daniel are both eleven."

"That's right," Gideon said. Good for him if he'd truly forgotten Abra's shame. And her own. But Eve doubted it.

"Well, Tim's bound to get married sooner or later," he said.

Later was more like it.

They reached the maples along the lane. Dried leaves rustled above their heads. It wouldn't be long until the trees would be completely bare. She shivered again.

"Cold?" Gideon asked.

She shook her head. She didn't want him to feel obligated to give her his coat.

He pointed ahead. "Those lights must be from the neighbor's house."

"That's right," she said.

"Tell me more about Charlie," Gideon instructed.

"I don't have much to tell," Eve said, hoping her voice didn't give away her feelings. "I think you know him as well as I do." The last thing she wanted was for the bishop to become concerned about her and an Englisch man. Perhaps he'd picked up on Tim's apprehension.

"He seems like an earnest fellow. As if he has a good heart."

"He's been a good friend to the Becks."

"The Becks?"

"Old Mr. Williams' granddaughter and her husband. Their son, Zane, was with Charlie today."

"Ach, that's right. I'd forgotten the last name."

Eve stopped walking. They were only fifty feet from Shani's house. Eve didn't want to go any closer. Gideon took her elbow, steering her around toward him just as the front door opened. Some-one stepped out onto the porch.

Gideon let go of her elbow.

It was Charlie coming down the steps. Eve took a deep breath.

"Hallo!" Gideon called out.

Eve couldn't make out Charlie's face, but he

hesitated and then started toward them. "Is that you, Gideon?"

"Jah," he answered. "With Eve. We're out for a walk."

As Charlie kept coming toward them, Eve took a step backward and then another one. Her right foot landed in a rut. She stumbled, rolling her ankle. The pain shot up her leg. She hopped but then touched the ground with the toe of her shoe, not wanting to land in another rut.

Gideon hadn't noticed—he strode toward Charlie.

But Charlie called out, "Are you okay?" He started to jog toward her.

"I'm fine," Eve said. She hobbled a step. At least she thought she was fine.

Gideon turned. "What happened?"

"I twisted my ankle, is all." How could she have been so clumsy? "I'm sure it's fine."

Gideon offered her his arm.

She took it and said, "We should head back." But as she tried to pivot around she gasped.

"I'll go get my buggy," Gideon said.

"I can take you both in my truck," Charlie responded. "I just need to get my key."

Eve started to say there was no need, but Gideon said, "I think that would be best."

"It's unlocked," Charlie said. Gideon helped her to the backseat door and opened it, but as she started to climb up, Shani yelled "Hello" and started toward them.

Then Charlie called out to Gideon, saying, "Come on up and meet Joel." In a quieter voice, but one she could still hear, he said to Shani, "Would you check Eve's ankle?"

Gideon helped her up onto the seat and then started toward the porch, stopping to introduce himself to Shani, and then continuing on.

Shani wore her hair piled on top of her head again and an oversized sweatshirt that nearly hid her pregnancy. "What did you do?" she asked Eve as she approached.

"Tried to pirouette," she answered.

"Now that's an image. But you forgot your tutu." Shani laughed. "Let me take a look."

Eve tucked her skirt under her legs, turned toward Shani, took off her shoe, and pulled her sock down.

"No, really," Shani said, peering down at Eve's ankle by the light of the interior lamp. "What happened?"

"I twisted it. It's not that big of a deal—although the thought of hopping home did seem a little daunting."

Shani put her hands on Eve's ankle and moved them up and then down. "Could you bear weight on it just now?"

"A little."

Shani pressed against a bone. "Is it more painful here?"

Eve shook her head.

She pressed against another one. "How about here?"

Eve shook her head again.

"It's swelling already. It's probably a sprain. I'll go get some ice."

Eve glanced toward the house. Joel was in the doorway in his chair with his cast propped up, and Gideon and Charlie stood on either side of him. Zane squeezed around his dad and bolted halfway down the ramp.

"Are you all right?" he called out to Eve.

"I'm fine," she said. "Just embarrassed."

Shani asked Zane to get the ice.

He took off up the ramp. Shani stepped back to the truck, leaned close, and asked, her eyes sparkling, "So are you and Gideon dating?"

Eve smiled. "You mean courting?"

Shani nodded.

"No," Eve answered.

"Are you sure that's what *he'd* say?" Shani directed her attention back to the men. Gideon walked toward them, Charlie close behind him.

Eve didn't answer.

"Well," Shani said, "maybe you should be courting him. He seems to be *the* man."

Eve knew exactly what she meant. He was a born leader. The lot had chosen well when it picked Gideon to be the bishop. He had a confidence and air of authority about him. He wasn't arrogant—just capable.

As Gideon approached, Shani said, "I don't work tomorrow. I'll come by in the morning to see how you're doing. I can help with the baby." Then she playfully pushed against Eve's shoulder and whispered, "Make room for your beau."

Eve exhaled, hoping Gideon, who was waiting for Shani to move, didn't hear. It wasn't as if he'd sit in the back with her anyway. He'd sit up front with Charlie.

"Nice to meet you," Shani said, turning toward him, as Zane ran back down the ramp. "I'm sure we'll be seeing you around."

Zane handed the ice to Shani, who handed it to Eve. Gideon told Shani a pleasant good-bye and then climbed up front. Eve propped up her foot and placed the ice on her ankle.

There was an awkward moment of silence and then, thankfully, Charlie asked Gideon where he got his lumber, which led to a discussion on different grades of wood. By the time Charlie turned toward the Lehmans' house, the two were talking about levels of grades of wood.

Charlie pulled up the driveway to the back steps and then, turning toward Eve, announced, "Here we are." She couldn't help but smile at his stating the obvious.

But as he put the truck into Park and then jumped down, Eve felt a pang of sadness. Most likely, he'd head back to Philadelphia in the morning.

He opened the door behind his for her, and she scooted over. He helped her down, gently holding on to her arm, while Gideon retrieved her shoe and sock.

"Denki," she said.

"You're welcome," he answered. "Take care." He waited just long enough for Gideon to take her arm, and then Charlie jumped back in his truck and headed back toward the lane. Then he was gone.

Gideon helped her up the steps and into the kitchen. He pulled out a chair for her to sit and then another for her to prop her foot on.

"Do you need more ice before I go?" he asked.

She shook her head.

He nodded, but instead of heading toward the door he said, "The Englisch family seems nice enough. But, Eve . . ."

She braced herself.

"Tread carefully," he said. "You were influenced once before by—"

She interrupted him. "I'm much older now." She couldn't keep herself from bristling. "With much more to lose."

He exhaled.

"But I appreciate your concern," she added.

His eyes were warm, but he didn't smile. "We all make mistakes. I know that. What counts is what we learn."

Eve nodded. She'd learned a lot.

Gideon said good-night and let himself out the back door. He was good and kind, jah. Even meek, in a confident sort of way. He'd seemed genuinely happy to see Charlie, but he must have sensed something to give her the warning, as gentle as it was.

Gideon was nothing like her father. But when she joined the church, her vow not to marry was to protect any future children. She'd decided it was better to not have them at all if she had to raise them Amish. But perhaps she'd been too rash back when she was eighteen. Not all Amish men were like her Dat and brother.

She struggled to her feet and hopped into the living room. Tim relaxed in his chair. Rose sat on the floor, reading a book, while Simon and Daniel put a puzzle together.

Lila held the baby. "Did you have fun?" her eldest niece asked.

"I twisted my ankle," Eve answered. It didn't matter whether she'd had fun or not.

"What's the matter, Aenti?" Lila asked, alarm in her voice.

Eve wiped the hem of her apron under her eyes. "Nothing," she answered. "Just the cold, from being outside."

ᘛ 16

During the night, Joel had thrown his arm over Shani and muttered something. She rolled toward him and tried to wake him, but he turned his head away from her. The pain meds were heavy duty, and she knew they knocked him out. But she couldn't rule out bad dreams either. Maybe from the meds. Maybe from Iraq.

After he threw his arm over her a second time and yelled, she scooted to the edge of the bed and slept on her side with her back to her husband, cradling her belly with her hands. But then he'd kicked her in the foot, hard, obviously with his good leg, the one closest to her.

She fumbled for her cell: *5:47.*

At 6:30 she finally crawled out of bed and woke Zane. An hour later she yelled, "Time to go!" up the stairs.

"I can take him." Charlie stood in the kitchen doorway, a cup of coffee in his hand.

"Thanks," Shani answered. "But I told Eve I'd check in on her." She also had an envelope with cash to pay Tim for helping with the ramp.

She glanced down the hall. "Joel will sleep another hour or so."

"Take your time," Charlie said. "I can help him. I don't need to leave until afternoon."

"Okay. Thanks."

Zane came thundering down the stairs and lunged toward Charlie, who raised his cup in the air. "Easy, bud," Charlie said, wrapping one arm around Zane in a hug. The boy called out good-bye as he rushed out the door.

"See you soon," Shani said to Charlie, heading out after her son into the misty morning. She was thankful for Zane's friendship with Charlie. It was a good thing, and in a few more years he wouldn't be as enthusiastic about another adult in his life as he was now. But it still made her ache for Joel.

Zane was fastening his seat belt by the time she reached the van. She must have forgotten to lock it again. At least she hadn't left the key in the ignition. She'd been known to do that before too. "Just over two years until I can get my permit," Zane teased.

Shani smiled. It would be here in no time.

When they passed the driveway to the Lehman farm, Zane craned his neck.

"Do you see anyone?" she asked.

He shook his head. "They don't leave for school until eight thirty. Eve takes them in the buggy."

"Oh." Shani had imagined Eve at the house by herself, with just the baby. With Lila there, she wouldn't need Shani's help.

She turned onto the highway and then pulled over to wait for the bus. A few other kids had already gathered.

"You don't have to stay," Zane said.

"But I want to," she answered.

"Mom." He opened the door. One of the girls waved at him. She didn't look like a seventh grader, not even an eighth grader. Her skirt was short and her jacket unzipped, revealing a tight T-shirt. Shani thought of Lila and her cape dress and cap, and the contrast between Zane's two worlds.

Zane climbed down from the van and stepped into the middle of the group. He'd always had an easy time making friends. It looked like this new school was no exception.

She drove to the next lane and turned around to go to the Lehmans' place. She pulled the van down the driveway, squinting against the morning sun. Dew sparkled in the field and on the lawn too. A cat ran toward the barn. Surely milking was long done. Thankfully Zane was still allowed to do the chores in the afternoon. She knew it was the highlight of his day.

Once she'd parked the car and turned off the ignition, she gripped the steering wheel, aware of her baby's kick. A movement caught her eye. Lila hurried toward the house, carrying a basket. She wore a cape and a black bonnet over her cap. The girl waved.

Shani climbed from the car and called out a hello. "How's Eve's ankle?"

"It's swollen," Lila answered as she reached the

steps. "She won't admit it, but I think it really hurts."

A sprain could be more painful than a break. "Does she need anything? I'm going to the store later."

Lila motioned toward the back door. "Come on in and ask her."

Shani followed the girl. By the time she reached the kitchen, Lila had the basket full of eggs on the counter. Eve sat at the table and fed the baby, who sat in her high chair. Rose brushed her own hair.

"Hi, Shani." An expression of relief spread over Eve's face.

"Lila said your ankle hurts." Shani stepped into the room, closing the door behind her.

Eve bit her lip and then said, "Jah." She nodded toward Rose. "Could you help her?"

Shani put her purse down on the end of the table as Rose extended the hairbrush to her, a smile on her face.

"How do you want it?" Shani asked, sitting down in the chair across from Eve and positioning Rose in front of her.

"In a bun, like Lila's."

"Or braids would be fine," Eve said.

"I can do a bun," Shani said. "Do you have bobby pins?"

Rose opened her hand to reveal them.

Shani brushed out the girl's hair, twisted it into

197

a bun, and then pinned it. Rose felt the bun and then smiled in approval.

"Is Daniel getting the buggy?" Eve asked Lila as she gave the baby the last bite of food.

"Jah. Simon's helping him. They should be coming around with it any minute."

Shani was surprised Simon was going to school but didn't say anything.

"Go tell your father it's time to leave," Eve said. "He's working on the fence. Take the lunchbox along with you."

Lila grabbed a small cooler from the counter, motioned to Rose, and headed out the door. The little girl frowned. "Why aren't you taking us?" Rose had put her Kapp on her head and was pinning it in place.

"It's hard for me to get in and out of the buggy." Eve put the cereal bowl on the table. "Give me a hug," she said to Rose.

The little girl obeyed.

"Now grab your cape and go on out with Lila. If your Dat asks why Shani's here, tell him she's just checking on my ankle."

Rose shuffled toward the back door.

"Hurry along," Eve said. "It wouldn't be right to make the others wait for you."

The little girl grabbed her cape and a book bag and closed the door behind her.

Eve let out a sigh, pushed herself up, and reached for the baby.

"I'll get her." Shani stood. "Sit back down and elevate your ankle."

She obeyed.

"Have you wrapped it?" Shani asked, wiping the baby's mouth with her bib and then lifting her from the high chair.

Eve shook her head.

Shani smiled at the baby. "Do you have an Ace bandage around?" she asked Eve.

"I don't think so."

Outside, Tim yelled something. The baby began to fuss. Eve wrinkled her nose. "I just hope none of them comes back inside."

"Rough morning?" Shani patted the baby's back.

"Jah," Eve said. "They're a challenge without a sprained ankle. Nearly impossible with."

"I can help for a little while."

"I don't want to impose," Eve said. "It's easier now that it's just Trudy and me."

Footsteps fell on the back porch and the door swung open. Tim filled the doorway. "I'm going by Gideon's on the way home and then to the feed store. I'll be gone most of the morning."

"All right," Eve said.

The man frowned at Shani but then gave her a nod.

She responded with a cheery "Good morning." She took the envelope out of her purse and extended it to him. "Thank you for your help on the ramp."

He grunted something—probably "Denki"—and took the money. Then he turned and left.

"I hope he asks Gideon about his old job," Eve said.

Shani raised her eyebrows, surprised Tim had worked anywhere besides the farm.

"He used to work part time at the lumber-yard. Gideon wouldn't let him continue after Abra was diagnosed. He said he was needed here."

"Oh," Shani said, wanting to ask Eve if Tim could take the baby with him so she could rest, but she thought she knew the answer. However, she could take the baby home with her.

"You go in the living room and prop your ankle up on the couch. I can take Trudy home with me for a couple of hours."

"But you have Joel to care for."

"Charlie's still at the house. He'll help." It was a good thing he hadn't left yet.

Eve chuckled. "With the baby?"

"Charlie is a man of many talents." Shani meant it as a joke but when Eve nodded, she smiled. Charlie could probably calm a baby just as he seemed to manage to calm everyone else.

"Take some ibuprofen," Shani said to Eve.

"I just did. And in the middle of the night too." Eve stood and began to hobble into the living room as Shani scanned the kitchen, thinking she'd do up the dishes before she left, but Lila must have done them earlier. Except for the eggs, the counters were bare.

Shani called out, "Should I put the eggs in the fridge?"

"Don't bother," Eve responded, already in the living room. "Lila will take care of them."

"Won't they go bad?"

Eve laughed. "You really are a city girl, aren't you? If you don't wash them they'll stay fresh for weeks. They have a protective coating."

"Oh." Shani only bought grocery store eggs—washed ones, it seemed. She glanced at the baby, who contently mashed the toast against her face.

Shani followed Eve. Her friend sat on the edge of the couch, reaching for her knitting bag.

"You could just rest," Shani said.

"Knitting *is* resting." She nodded toward the hall. "Trudy's diaper bag is in my room. Her car seat is in there too. And grab a bottle out of the fridge on your way out. Lila mixed them up this morning."

The other time Shani had been in the baby's room, it had been dark with only a little light from the lamp in the hall. Now the curtain on the window was pulled back and light flooded the room. A twin bed with a smaller version of the quilt Eve had given to Shani was against one wall and the crib against the other. On the bureau sat a Bible, a hairbrush, and a bottle of lotion. Several dresses hung in a small closet with no door. Two pairs of shoes, running shoes and dress boots, were lined up on the floor of the closet.

Next to the crib was the car seat with the diaper bag in it. Underneath it was a baby blanket and a little jacket.

As Shani picked up the car seat and headed down the hall, a wave of empathy rolled through her. Eve had given up everything for her brother, nephews, and nieces. She was a woman, in the prime of her life, with nothing of her own.

Marrying Gideon Byler was a grand idea. Eve deserved some happiness, and the man was both handsome and kind. And well respected. Charlie had said so. Gideon was older, but probably only in his mid, maybe late, forties. He could easily have a second family with Eve.

Eve had her foot propped up on the couch cushions and was knitting when Shani stepped into the living room. "I'll bring Trudy back after I go to the store, before noon," she said.

Trudy fussed as Shani pulled her arm through the sleeve of her little jacket. "I should have thought to bring an Ace bandage over to wrap your ankle," she said to Eve.

"Just bring it when you come back."

"Rest, ice, compress, and elevate," Shani said, getting the baby's arm through the second sleeve. "RICE. Icing it more will help the pain but not the swelling. However, wrapping it will still help." She put Trudy into the car seat and strapped her in. "I'll send Charlie back with the bandage."

Eve shifted on the couch, looking uncomfortable.

"You okay?" Shani asked.

The woman blushed. "I'm fine. Thank you for your help."

Shani grabbed a bottle from the fridge, put it in the side pocket of the diaper bag, told Eve good-bye, and lugged the car seat and baby out the door. After she buckled Trudy into the van, she tickled her under her chin.

Trudy smiled and then laughed, her blue eyes sparkling. Shani looked forward to spending the morning with the little one—she hoped Joel would feel the same.

He was up, dressed, and sitting in his chair at the kitchen table when Shani came through the door with the baby in her arms.

"What do you have there?" he called out, stretching to see her through the doorway into the kitchen.

"Trudy," she said, sliding the diaper bag to the floor in the living room and then walking into the kitchen. "Eve's elevating her ankle. I told her we'd watch the baby."

Joel hesitated and then said, "She's a cutie."

"But?" Shani balanced the baby on her hip and turned to pour herself a cup of coffee, guessing this second pot was decaf.

"Don't you think we have enough going on?" Joel asked.

"It's just for a couple of hours. I need to run to the store later this morning. I'll take her back then." She turned toward him. "Where's Charlie?"

"Putting up grab bars in the bathroom."

"Ahh," Shani said. "Bless him." The guy really was a saint. "Want to hold the baby?"

"Not really," Joel said.

"Just so I can drink my coffee?"

"All right," he said, extending his arms.

Shani slid the baby into them, hoping Trudy wouldn't fuss. She didn't. She craned her head to look up into Joel's eyes.

"Hi, baby," he said.

Trudy didn't smile but she didn't cry either.

"I'm Joel."

The baby reached up and touched his chin.

He smiled. "Maybe she likes my scraggly look," Joel said.

"Yeah well, not if you give her a whisker burn." Shani took a sip of coffee. The baby patted Joel's chin. "Maybe she wonders why you don't have a beard like her Dat."

"Like her what?"

"Dat. Father."

"Are we talking Amish now?"

Shani smiled and took another sip of coffee. The baby inside her rippled, ever so gently, then kicked hard. She massaged her side.

"Maybe he's jealous," Joel said.

"Maybe they'll be friends," Shani responded.

Joel shook his head. "None of us are going to be friends," he said.

"Are you talking about me?" Charlie stood in the doorway.

"Yeah, well, sorry you had to overhear that," Joel joked. "But I guess it was bound to come out sometime."

"Joel doesn't think Amish and Englisch"—she *was* talking like them—"people can be friends."

"Why? Has something happened?"

Joel shook his head. "But it will. Just wait and see. Tim will think of something. There's no doubt about it that we don't meet his standards."

"Hush," Shani said, thinking of the legalistic church Joel grew up in. "Don't talk that way in front of the baby."

"Yeah," Charlie said. "I'd say she's your friend —at least today."

Joel laughed. Trudy smiled.

"Look," Joel said. "She has teeth."

Charlie hurried behind the chair. Shani grabbed her purse from the counter and pulled out her camera. "Hold that pose," she said, snapping the photo of the men and the baby's back. Then she said, "Turn Trudy around." Joel did and she snapped another photo.

"Better not show those to anyone," Joel said.

"Why?"

"Well, not to anyone Amish."

Shani shook her head. "Why not?"

"They don't like photos—something about graven images. You know, one of the Ten Commandments. I remember that from back home."

"There are Amish in Wisconsin?"

"Yeah." Joel nodded. "They're everywhere, except the West Coast." He turned to Charlie. "Right?"

"Pretty much," he said.

"Oh," Shani said, slipping her camera back into her purse and going back to her coffee. "I didn't know." Her face warmed. Joel was probably right. Even though her grandparents had lived in Lancaster County, Shani hardly knew anything about the Amish. She needed to do some research.

When she'd finished her coffee she found an Ace bandage in the bathroom drawer and returned to the kitchen. Charlie sat next to Joel, trying to teach Trudy patty-cake. The baby girl flung her hands around, giggling as she did.

"Sorry to interrupt the fun," Shani said to Charlie, "but would you take this over to Eve and wrap her ankle?"

He put his hands up as if protesting his innocence. "Are you trying to get me tarred and feathered?"

Shani laughed. "You're a professional. You can wrap a woman's ankle."

"Not that woman's. Tim would kill me." His face reddened.

Shani put her hand on her hip. "Charlie McCall, are you blushing?"

"Not on purpose."

Joel hooted.

Shani smiled. "Tim's out running errands."

"In the buggy?" Joel laughed.

"What's so funny?"

"I don't know. Just seems like it would take all day."

"Isn't that what they do in Wisconsin?"

Joel shrugged. "We didn't live *that* close to a settlement."

"They've been making it work for a few centuries now," Shani said. "I think they have it figured out." She tossed the bandage at Charlie. He fumbled it but caught it before it hit the floor.

"You do it," he said.

"I don't want to haul the baby over there and back."

"Leave her here. She's doing fine," Charlie replied. As if on cue, the baby began to fuss.

"I told Eve I'd watch her." Shani scooped up Trudy. "Besides, Eve's courting the bishop." Shani winked. "It's not like she's going to think you're interested in her . . . unless you are."

Charlie held up the bandage as if he was going to toss it back at her, but he was smiling. "Believe me, if she wasn't Amish, I would be." He patted the baby's back. "No offense, Trudy. You'll understand someday."

↬ 17

The morning mist had stopped but the clouds still hung low as Charlie tossed the Ace bandage in the air and turned down the Lehmans' driveway, half expecting to see Tim. But no one was in sight. Once he neared the house and could confirm the buggy really was gone, he sighed and relaxed—just a little.

He'd wrap Eve's ankle and leave. That was it. He wouldn't instigate a conversation with her. Or look into her deep brown eyes. Or think about how long her dark hair was, all tucked under her cap-like thing. He jogged the rest of the way and then ran up the steps, knocking quickly.

Then he waited. Finally he tried the door. Of course it was unlocked. "Eve?" he called out.

"Coming," she said.

He groaned. He was making her hobble to the door, but it couldn't be helped. He wasn't going to wander into the house.

"Come on in," she finally said, her voice closer.

He opened the door to find her leaning against the kitchen table. He held up the bandage. "Shani sent me."

"Denki," she said. "I can wrap it myself."

"Do you know how?"

Eve pursed her lips. "Not really."

"It will just take a minute," Charlie said.

"All right," she said, sitting down on a chair.

He pulled a chair across from hers, sat down, and patted the edge of the seat. "Put your foot here," he said.

She did, tucking her skirt around her leg as she positioned her heel.

Charlie's face warmed, but as he started winding the bandage around her ankle he relaxed. Shani was right. He was a professional. He wouldn't think about the smoothness of Eve's skin. The way she held her skirt modestly around her leg. Her dark eyes watching him.

He worked quickly, pinned the bandage in place, and then gently patted her ankle. Finally he looked up into her eyes.

The expression on her face startled him. It wasn't the demure look he'd seen before. He leaned back, fearing if he stood he'd knock over his chair. But then a rush of cold air swept into the room. It took him a moment to realize the back door was opened.

Eve's eyes stayed on Charlie's as Tim boomed, "What's going on here?"

Eve seemed as calm as could be, although her face pinked up some. "Charlie's a medic. He wrapped my ankle." She put her foot to the floor.

Charlie stood, his heart racing. Perhaps he'd imagined the look on her face—fantasized it even. "I was just leaving." He turned toward Tim and grimaced. It was a stupid thing to say. He sounded guilty as sin. He'd done nothing wrong.

Tim crossed his arms, filling the doorway. If he was trying to intimidate Charlie, it was working.

"Close the door," Eve said to her brother.

He didn't budge.

Charlie headed toward Tim. The man didn't move. Finally he said, "Don't come here again if I'm not home."

"He did no harm," Eve said.

Charlie turned to Eve and said, "Good-bye."

"Thank you again," she said, her eyes still warm.

Charlie faced Tim, his heart pounding against his chest as he nodded toward the door behind the man. "Excuse me."

After a long moment of silence, Eve said something in Pennsylvania Dutch. Tim replied harshly. Charlie couldn't even guess at the words.

"Good grief," Eve said. And then, "*Stoppen.*"

That Charlie understood. Tim stepped aside, and Charlie strode onto the mud porch with as much confidence as he could muster and then down the stairs. He walked slowly, not wanting Tim to think he was scared.

Joel was right about something setting Tim off. Charlie expected Tim to follow him, but when he hadn't heard any footsteps by the time he reached the lane, he turned around.

Tim stood in the middle of his driveway, his

210

arms still crossed, his feet spread wide, and his hat tipped back.

Charlie waved to Tim, but the man didn't respond. Instead he rolled back on his heels and glared.

Joel sat in the living room with the baby on his lap again, giving her a bottle, when Charlie returned. "How'd it go?" Joel asked.

"Fine," Charlie answered.

Shani stepped out from the kitchen. "Looks like you survived."

"Barely," Charlie said.

"What happened?"

Charlie's face warmed again. "Tim came home."

"Uh-oh." Shani peered out the kitchen window. "Oops. Looks like he followed you here."

Footsteps fell on the porch followed by a rapid knocking.

It'd been months since Charlie had felt any kind of fear. Until now.

"I'll get it," Shani called to Joel. Charlie followed her.

Shani opened the door, the dish towel still in her hand. "Hi," she said.

Tim took off his hat. No matter how upset he was, he seemed to be minding his manners. That was a good sign. "I came to get my daughter," he said, scanning the room.

"I was going to bring her back in a little bit," Shani said.

"I'll take her now." Tim's eyes landed on Joel and the baby.

Shani stood with her hand on the door. Charlie had never, in all the time he'd known her, seen her at a loss for words or action. But she seemed to be now.

"Excuse me," Tim said stepping around her toward Joel.

Joel stared him down. "Shani, get the baby's things while she finishes her bottle." He motioned to the chair a foot away. "Have a seat, Tim."

Incredibly, Tim followed Joel's instructions.

Charlie stood against the wall. The men all watched the baby while Shani gathered up the diaper bag. "I'll drive you home," she said. "This is a lot to carry."

"I can manage," Tim said.

"The car seat is in the van. I can drop it off later."

Tim shook his head. "I'll take it now." Once the baby drained the last of her bottle, Tim reached for her. Joel let her go, handing the bottle to Tim at the same time. Trudy looked even smaller in her father's big burly arms. He took the diaper bag from Shani and slung it over his shoulder.

"I'll get the car seat," Shani said, heading toward the door, giving Charlie a pleading look. He shrugged. Tim nodded a good-bye to Joel and then followed Shani out the door.

Charlie followed. He stood at the bottom of the stairs while Shani retrieved the car seat and headed back with it. Tim slipped the baby into it, but then struggled with the straps. Shani did it for him. He scooped the seat up with one arm and slung the diaper bag over his shoulder.

"We won't be needing the boy any longer in the afternoons," Tim said.

"Oh." Shani stepped backward. "But he enjoys it so much. Couldn't he keep helping?"

Tim shook his head.

"It's good for him," Shani said. "And your sons enjoy having him."

Tim shook his head again.

Charlie cleared his throat. "If this has anything to do with me, please don't take it out on Zane."

Tim ignored Charlie. "The boy's made amends," he said. "We're grateful for his help, but Simon is doing fine now." He started to walk away.

Shani hurried to his side. "How is Eve going to manage, with her ankle sprained?"

"I'll go get Lila at school if I need to," Tim said. "We can manage."

"Why won't you accept our help?" The sound of his own voice surprised Charlie. He hadn't intended to say a word.

"Your *help?*" Tim spat the words. "I saw your *help* on my sister's face. I lost her once—I won't lose her again."

"You have nothing to be afraid of," Charlie said. "I wouldn't harm Eve. Not for anything."

Tim shook his head. "It's her harming herself that I'm worried about." He turned to Shani. "Tell the boy I'm sorry. I've appreciated his help. But it's for the best. For him too—you'll see." Then Tim marched away, covering the distance like a giant lumbering down the lane.

Charlie stood completely still. A breeze teased through the leaves above their heads. Shani put her hands on top of her bun, squishing it down. "What happened with Eve?" she asked, her voice too loud.

"Shh," he said.

Her voice dropped to a whisper. "I don't want Zane to lose those boys. I don't want to lose Eve's friendship."

"I don't want that either," Charlie said.

"Why would he turn us away when we can help? There are three of us adults . . ."

Well, two, Charlie thought. He needed to return to Philadelphia—and the sooner the better.

Tim had reached the cedar tree. "He can't hear us now," Shani said. "Tell me what happened."

"I don't know," Charlie said. "I was wrapping Eve's ankle—being professional, I promise."

"I believe you," Shani said.

"And when I was done, I looked up and she was staring at me, and then Tim walked in."

"Staring at you? How?"

214

Charlie swallowed hard. "I-I don't know, Shani. She was just staring at me."

"How?"

He shook his head. "I don't know." But he did. *Desire.* That's what it looked like. Tim had seen it too.

Charlie hadn't imagined it.

He couldn't tell Shani though. He wouldn't betray Eve. Charlie started back toward the house.

Shani grabbed his hand. "We have too much to lose."

Charlie shook his head. "I didn't do anything." At least he didn't think he did.

"She's courting that bishop. Tim must have misinterpreted how she looked at you. . . ." She hesitated. "Whatever it was he thought."

Charlie headed for the house again, and this time Shani followed.

"What was that all about?" Joel asked as they trudged back into the house.

Shani glanced at Charlie and then back at her husband. Her tone changed, probably because she didn't want to upset Joel. "I guess you were right about Tim," she said. "It just happened sooner than we thought."

"That's a shame," Joel said.

"You fell for the baby, huh?" Shani sat on the arm of his chair.

Joel turned toward her. Charlie stepped into the kitchen, his heart hurting. He wiped down the counters as Shani entered. "You make such a good maid," she said.

"Yeah, well, I like to earn my keep."

"When are you leaving?"

"Soon," he said.

"I'm going to run to the store. Can you stay for an hour?"

"Sure," he answered.

He needed to do some grocery shopping when he got home and throw in a load of laundry, but that wouldn't take long. Mostly he needed some time to think.

After Shani left, Charlie wheeled Joel down the ramp and out into the sunshine.

"Wheel me up the lane," Joel said.

Charlie shook his head. "There are too many ruts." He pushed Joel to the edge of the driveway, where he was still in the sun. Charlie sat down on a nearby stump.

"The road's not as bad as the ones in Iraq."

Charlie nodded. "You're right about that."

After a long silence Joel muttered, "Did we do the right thing?"

"We did what we were asked to do—for each other if nothing else."

"Do you think that's how Samuel's wife feels? And his parents?"

Charlie stared off into the trees, not knowing what to say. Joel had always been more philosophical than he was. "Did we do the right thing in joining up? Going to Iraq? Sending the gunner with the other Humvee instead of keeping him with us?" He'd helped Joel make that decision.

"Yeah, all of those things."

"What does it matter?" Charlie asked. "We can't change anything."

"Except how I feel about myself." Joel shaded his eyes.

Charlie certainly couldn't change that.

Joel cleared his throat and then asked, "Have you heard from any of the guys lately?"

"Yeah. Rogers sent me a text last week." Charlie hesitated, not sure whether to keep going or not.

"What did he say?"

"Samuel's baby was in the hospital with pneumonia."

Joel cursed.

"No, she pulled through. She's gonna be okay."

Joel exhaled. "How old is she now?"

"Five months." Charlie rubbed his hands together. He was pretty sure Joel knew—he just didn't want to do the math. She'd been born the day before they were hit. Samuel had been so green—so naïve about everything, but in a funny way. He'd come from a conservative background. Went to some church that Charlie never got the whole story on. Married young. He should have had his whole life in front of him.

Joel shifted his gaze toward a flock of starlings swooping toward the field.

Charlie wasn't sure whether he should say more or not, but he guessed it would come better from him than someone else. "Samuel's parents moved to Lancaster not too long ago."

"You're kidding?" Joel tightened his grip on the arms of his chair.

"Nope. Seems they wanted to be closer to their grandchild, without moving to Philly."

Joel shook his head.

"You looked good holding Trudy today," Charlie said, hoping to lighten the mood.

Joel shook his head again.

"You're a natural."

"That's what Shani said." Joel kept his eyes on the distance.

"Yours will be here before you know it."

Joel's eyes clouded over. Charlie looked away.

"I don't deserve it," Joel said. "God knows I don't. Samuel should be with his baby. I shouldn't. . . ." He didn't have to say it. Charlie knew what he was thinking.

Joel thought it should have been him instead of Samuel.

Charlie hit traffic just before the exit to Valley Forge. He kept thinking about the Lehmans. About Tim lumbering down the lane with the baby and car seat in one arm and the diaper bag over the other. About Joel giving Trudy the bottle. Of Zane joking around with Simon and Daniel, learning all the wrong words in Pennsylvania Dutch. About Shani lamenting that she didn't want to lose Eve's friendship.

And most of all, about that unexpected look on Eve's face.

"But she shouldn't have sent me over there," he said out loud and then sighed. "No, I shouldn't have agreed to go." Shani didn't have any reason not to send him over, regardless of their joking.

Joel was right. It was inevitable that Tim would find some reason to stop the friendships between the two families. Maybe Tim overreacted or maybe he was looking for a reason to disengage from the Becks.

He couldn't help but wonder what the man meant when he had said, *"It's her harming herself that I'm worried about."* What had happened in the past to make Tim so suspicious?

His heart constricted again. What was the matter with him? He should have asked Joel to knock some sense into him before he left.

That made him smile. Joel could probably still take him down. He'd done it to Samuel just outside of Tikrit. They were on a mission to set up a communications antenna when word came that Samuel's wife, who was seven and a half months pregnant, had gone into early labor. Samuel freaked out. Joel told him to stop, but Samuel started yelling and kept it up until Joel tackled him and held him down, calmly saying, "Get a grip or you won't be any good to your wife and kid. They need you."

Joel kept him pinned until Samuel finally stopped fighting. Back at base that night, after the baby had been born, Joel called the hospital, got through to the maternity ward, and managed to talk someone into helping Samuel's wife get on Skype.

The baby was in the NICU, but her chances looked good. She just needed some extra care. The last thing his wife said to him was, "You'll see her soon. I promise." Samuel was scheduled for a furlough in six weeks, during the time the baby was originally due.

He couldn't sleep that night after talking with his wife and was bouncing all over the place. Joel threatened to take Samuel down again if he didn't stop it.

The next day the rocket-propelled grenade hit the Humvee. Samuel never saw it coming. And he never saw his baby girl either. He had a photo waiting in his inbox that arrived while they were out. When Charlie found it later, he couldn't bear to open the attachment.

All Charlie could think of were Joel's words. *"Get a grip or you won't be any good to your wife and kid. They need you."* He was pretty sure that was what haunted Joel too.

As the traffic crawled along, dark clouds rolled in. A big raindrop splattered against the windshield and then another. Soon the black sky opened up, and the deluge brought traffic to a standstill. There were bound to be accidents.

His chest constricted again, but this time in anticipation of danger. Of things gone wrong. That was the tragedy of what had happened with the Lehmans. The friendship had the promise of something good. Now that had all changed.

It was seven thirty by the time he reached his little brick house on the west side of Philly. It wasn't exactly a great neighborhood—but it wasn't horrible either. It was eight by the time he'd unpacked and started a load of laundry. *Forget the store.* He had enough lunch meat to make a sandwich. He'd grocery shop after work the next day.

As he scrounged the cupboards for dinner—a can of tuna, a jar of peaches—his landline rang. Maybe Eve was calling from the barn phone.

He answered it quickly.

"Hi." It wasn't Eve.

"Who is this?" he asked.

"Guess."

His stomach sank. He didn't reply.

"I can't stop thinking about you." Nikki paused. "How are you? I heard about the bad stuff that happened. I feel horrible. It sounds like it all came down right after . . . you know."

"Uh-huh," he said.

"So, are you doing all right?"

"I'm fine," he said, tucking the phone under his chin. "How are you?"

"Good. Listen, I'm thinking about going back to the church group. Are you still going?"

"I haven't yet, but I plan to."

"Do you mind if I go? This week?"

He wanted to say it was a free country, but the cliché made him cringe now.

"Charlie?" Her voice sounded the same.

"Go if you want," he said. "I may make it, depending on what time I get off work."

"I hope I'll see you," she said.

"Maybe," he said. *Or maybe not.* His chest constricted again. Not in pain. And certainly not in desire—at least not for Nikki.

He fell asleep that night thinking about Eve but woke up in the middle of a dream about Nikki. At least he thought it was about her. He couldn't remember it for sure. Just her long blond hair.

He punched his pillow and then rolled over to his back, staring at the ceiling. He didn't have much to complain about. He was alive. He didn't have a messed-up leg. He wasn't disabled with a family to support and a new baby on the way.

But nothing felt right. Helping Joel and Shani and Zane had felt good until the stuff with Tim blew up. He knew he shouldn't have gone to help Eve. Why hadn't he just told Shani it was a bad idea?

Because he'd wanted to go down—that was why. He wanted to see Eve. He glanced at the clock: *1:45.* He definitely needed more sleep.

He must have drifted off, because sand blew around him. A blown-out car blocked the road. He could almost smell the diesel. Dusk fell. A scream pierced through him as he jumped out of the Humvee.

His heart thumped as his eyes flew open. Sweat dripped down the side of his face. He turned toward the clock: *4:03.* He took several deep breaths and blew them out slowly, like the emergency training video had shown. Still his heart raced.

After a minute of more deep breaths, he got up. He'd shower. Fix some eggs for breakfast. Make his lunch.

As he stumbled into the hall, he groaned. He'd done a fine job helping the Becks. He'd only made things worse—not better. And for himself too. He'd forget about Eve. He'd try his best to go to the church group and see Nikki. He needed to get on with his life.

He needed to move forward. *Now.*

ಯ 18

Early Tuesday morning Eve woke before Trudy and listened to the rain drum against the window and a branch scrape against the side of the house.

Once the baby stirred, Eve slid her legs over the side of the bed and sat up, putting a little weight on her ankle. The bandage had come loose. She bent over and tried to rewrap it, but it was too dark to see what she was doing.

Trudy started to cry.

"I'm right here," Eve said. "Hold on." She stood, putting more weight on her ankle. It didn't feel any worse than the day before. She slipped her robe on and then, putting her weight on her good foot, pulled the baby from the crib. Hobbling into the hall, she made it to the bathroom, changed Trudy's soaked diaper, and headed to the kitchen to light the lamp and heat up a bottle.

She started the kettle for coffee while the bottle heated. She considered putting Trudy down and letting her cry, but that might wake up the other children, when they could sleep another half hour.

She put the filter and then the coffee in the French press. "You get your bottle," Eve whispered to the baby. "And I get my coffee."

Trudy reached toward the stove, opening and closing her fist.

"Patience, little one," Eve said. "All in good time." The thought depressed her. All in good time for everyone but her, it seemed. She'd ruined everything by feeling what she did for Charlie. And not just for herself, for the children too. It would have done them good to have Englisch friends. She understood Tim's concerns, but there was no stopping life. His children would come to know Englischers sooner or later, unless he locked them in the house.

Trudy must have sensed her unhappiness, because she patted Eve's cheek and then smiled, showing her bottom teeth.

Eve pulled the baby close, causing Trudy to squirm and then laugh.

Once the bottle had heated, Eve retrieved it, turned off the burner, and turned the kettle down to a simmer. She wouldn't risk pouring the boiling water with the baby in her arms, not when she was so unstable.

She settled into the chair in the living room, the weight of the baby's body against her own comforting Eve. Once the baby was fed, Eve put her on the floor with her toys, made the coffee, dressed, rewrapped her ankle, and started breakfast. By then Tim and the boys had gone out to the milking, and Lila was getting ready.

Eve woke Rose. Trudy, still in her sleeper, began to fuss. A minute later Lila came into the kitchen with her.

"Put her in the high chair," Eve instructed as she mixed eggs and milk together. "And give her a cracker. I'll make her cereal in a minute."

Lila obeyed and then began setting the table. "Why didn't Zane come over yesterday?"

"Your Dat doesn't need the help anymore." Eve didn't dare look at Lila. The girl had a way of knowing when something more than what was being said was going on.

"Daniel was cranky all evening." Lila reached for the plates.

Eve nodded. They were all cranky.

"I think it was because he misses Zane."

Eve didn't bother to nod this time. They all missed Zane. He'd lightened their afternoons with his constant chatter and questions. She regretted that Tim had come home when he did yesterday. But on the other hand, she was thankful he had. What had come over her?

Poor Charlie. He was such a nice man. She'd known she was attracted to him, but the longing she'd felt for him surprised her. Shocked her, really. It was having him so close. It was his tenderness. His care. She hadn't intended to feel so strongly for him.

But she wasn't surprised an Englisch man would make her feel that way. Apparently, neither was Tim.

Rose shuffled into the kitchen, dressed but sleepy-eyed. Eve greeted her, but then the sound of a wagon rolling over the gravel distracted all of them. Rose hurried to the window. Tim had gone to the lumberyard the day before after he came home with Trudy. She'd thought it was just to talk with Gideon, but maybe he'd ordered wood for a new chicken coop. He'd been wanting to rebuild it.

She hoped it was Reuben making the delivery.

She realized in all that had gone on yesterday, she'd forgotten to ask Tim if he'd gotten his job back.

"It's the bishop," Rose singsonged. "He's getting down." She turned toward Eve, patting her heart as she grinned.

"Stop it." Lila glared at her little sister as she spread slices of bread on a cookie sheet to toast. "We don't want Aenti to get married and move away." It was quite the outburst for Lila. Her face grew red as she turned toward Eve and then whispered, "I'm sorry."

"No, don't be." Eve reached out her arms for the girl, giving her a hug. Eve's parents weren't affectionate with Tim or her. She'd learned to be loving with the children from Abra, who'd learned it from her parents.

Eve kissed the top of Lila's head. Her oldest niece had far more insight, of course, than Rose. "Go tell your dad the lumber's here." Hopefully they were almost done with the milking.

As Lila hurried out the back door, Gideon came

227

in wearing a rain slicker. "*Guder Mariye,*" he said, taking it off and hanging it on an empty peg on the mud porch.

"Morning," Eve answered.

Rose hurried to his side and took his hand, pulling him to the table. The child had always been outgoing, but since Abra's illness and death she seemed downright needy. "Want some breakfast?"

"No," he said. "I already ate. But I'd love a cup of coffee."

"I was just going to make another pot," Eve said, hopping over to the stove.

"How's your ankle?" Gideon asked.

"Getting better," she answered, although she wasn't sure it was. She did know it would though, in time.

As the water boiled for the coffee, she scrambled the eggs, stealing glances at Gideon. He *was* kind. And spiritually grounded. Far more than she.

She hoped Tim wouldn't tell Gideon about her behavior the day before. That's all she needed— for the bishop to get involved. She finished the eggs and set them on the back of the stove.

Tim wouldn't say anything. He cared far too much about what others thought to divulge such information. They'd all been under the magnifying glass since Abra fell ill. Tim wouldn't want to bring any more attention to their troubles.

"How is Simon?" Gideon asked.

"Good," Eve answered, pouring the hot water to make the coffee. "He's going to school. And helping with the chores more. He seems to be doing fine."

"And how is Tim—" Gideon hesitated— "doing?"

Eve guessed he wondered if Tim had learned his lesson in regard to favoring Simon more than the other children. She doubted he had or ever would, but it wasn't her place to judge her brother. "Jah, better," she said as Tim came through the back door, taking his hat off and then slipping out of his coat. Thankfully she hadn't elaborated on her answer, not that she would anyway, and especially not in front of Rose.

After telling Gideon hello, Tim thanked him for bringing the lumber.

Gideon simply smiled.

"Have you decided about my job?" Tim asked.

Gideon leaned against the back of the chair. "I've been thinking about it. Why don't we start with two days a week and see how that goes?"

Tim nodded and then retreated to the bathroom to wash up. Eve imagined her brother was pleased. She certainly was.

A few minutes later Simon, Daniel, and Lila came in. The boys shed their wet coats and hats and headed to the bathroom to wash up too.

Tim returned and asked, "Are we ready to eat?"

"Jah," Eve said, pouring two cups of coffee.

Gideon stepped to the counter and retrieved the cups while Eve dished up the eggs.

"Can you drive the children this morning?" Tim asked. "So I can help Gideon unload the lumber."

"I'm not in a hurry," Gideon said. He turned to Eve. "No need to do it if you're not up to it."

"I can manage," Eve responded as Simon and Daniel returned to the kitchen. "As long as the boys hitch the horse—and help me into the buggy."

Simon groaned, but his eyes lit up. She missed his smile.

Lila put the eggs and toast on the table as the boys sat down. After the prayer, Eve told them all to hurry. "We need to leave in fifteen minutes," she said as she sat down to feed the baby.

When they reached the school, Monika King stood at the bottom of the steps, her umbrella over her head. Jenny stood with her, but when she saw the Lehman children, she waved and hurried up the steps of the school, stopping by the front door. She let the other children go ahead of her and then walked in with Daniel.

Eve expected Monika to head toward her own buggy, but instead she walked toward Eve and then stepped up into the buggy. "Ach," she said, taking Trudy, "she's so sweet in her sleeper."

"Jah," Eve responded, "it's been one of those mornings." Just like every morning, it seemed.

"I heard you twisted your ankle."

Eve nodded.

Monika's eyes sparkled. "While you were with the bishop. What in the world was going on?"

Eve laughed. "Is there a rumor spreading already?"

"Already? It happened two days ago."

"Jah, but I haven't said anything to anyone."

"Tim did. When he dropped the children off yesterday." As Monika spoke, Trudy reached for the woman's mouth. Monika laughed and then continued. "We all wondered why you were being lazy." She kept moving her lips once she'd stopped talking, smiling at the baby as she did.

Eve knew Monika was joking. Kind of. She also thought a lot of women found a perverse satisfaction in seeing her struggle with taking care of Tim and his family. Some of them, surely, felt it was her comeuppance to be responsible for a family without the comfort of having a husband.

"He said you were out for a walk with Gideon when it happened." Monika nudged Eve with her elbow.

Monika was different than some of the others in their community though. She'd forgiven Eve for her sins of more than a decade ago.

"Jah, we were on a walk."

"I'm so relieved," Monika said as she shifted on the buggy seat. "When I saw that Englisch man at our place on Sunday, I was sure, by the way he looked at you, that he was wanting to court you."

Eve's face warmed even in the cold.

"I know Gideon's a bit older than you, but he's a fine man." Monika smiled. "I can't think of anyone, besides the Deacon, who would make a better husband." She had a quirky habit of referring to her husband as *the Deacon*—as if he were the only one. The thing was, in Monika's eyes, he was. She adored him.

Monika continued. "And Gideon's taken with you. I can tell." Monika paused a moment to smile at the baby again. "I shouldn't say this, but he spoke about you with the Deacon, asking his advice. He wanted to know if he thought there were any red flags."

Eve's face grew hot.

"Of course there aren't. You've been in good standing. You've proven yourself over the years. Look what you did for Abra and what you're doing for these kids."

Tears stung Eve's eyes.

"Ach, I'm sorry," Monika said, patting Eve's shoulder.

"It's fine . . ."

"Tim will find a new wife," Monika said. "He might not be ready yet." She chuckled. "Look at how long it took him to marry the first time. I know he's not like Gideon. He can't—" she struggled for the right word—"*adjust* that quickly."

Eve nodded. That was true.

"But he will. In the meantime, you need to

move ahead with your life. That will force Tim to find another wife."

Eve pursed her lips.

"God will work it out," Monika said, her eyes kind.

Eve appreciated the woman's optimism—even if she didn't share it. There were lots of things that God never worked out. Oh, she certainly believed he could—he just seemed to choose not to when it came to her.

"Let me take Trudy home for the day," Monika said. "I'll bring her back when we pick up the kids."

"I don't have a change of clothes for her. And probably only one diaper." She did have the baby's bag with a bottle in it and the emergency can of formula.

"I saved some of the girls' old clothes. And diapers. For those grandbabies I'll soon have." She grinned. "You need to rest your ankle. You can't do that packing a baby around."

Tears threatened again. She never would have guessed a decade ago that Monika King would become so important to her. "Denki," was all she managed to say. For a moment she was tempted to speak honestly about the vow she'd made never to marry an Amish man—even how she felt about Charlie—but she knew that would change how Monika felt about her.

After Monika had climbed out of the buggy with the baby and the diaper bag, the tears started to

233

roll down Eve's face. As she pulled onto the road, she cried for the children. For herself. Even for Tim. Then she cried for Charlie. And for the Becks.

She hadn't intended to go to Shani's, but when she looked down the driveway and saw that Gideon's wagon was gone, she guessed that Tim would be consumed with his new project and wouldn't miss her until the noon meal. She'd be home long before then.

So she kept on going.

Shani's van was parked in its usual place. As Eve parked the buggy on the other side of it, Zane came out of the house. He should have been at school. He waved when he saw her.

A wave of awkwardness overcame Eve. What was she thinking, just showing up at their house?

Shani came out of the house next, wearing a raincoat with the hood on her head. She waved too. "Is everything okay?" she called out as she hurried down the steps.

Eve nodded as tears welled up in her eyes again. Shani was just a few steps away now. "Zane," she said. "Go ahead and get in the van." Then she turned toward the buggy. "You've been crying."

Eve ran her fingers under her eyes. "It's that obvious?"

Shani nodded.

"I'm fine," Eve said. "Is Zane all right?"

"Stomachache," Shani whispered. "Psycho-somatic."

234

It took Eve a moment to remember the meaning of the word, but when she did she whispered back, "We call that *faking it*."

Shani smiled. "So do we. He's just been so . . ."

Eve waited for her to continue.

"Upset."

Eve's own stomach began to ache, guessing Zane's pain was over Tim not wanting him to help with the chores.

"Why did you stop by?" Shani asked.

"Oh . . ." Eve paused. "I was hoping you'd have time for a cup of coffee."

Shani's face brightened. "Come with me. We'll drop Zane off first and then go out."

Eve nodded toward the horse. "I can't leave him here."

"Zane and I'll take care of him," Shani said. "We'll put him in a stall."

As Eve hobbled to and waited in the van, she couldn't help but be impressed with how quickly they unhitched the horse and led him into the barn.

When they climbed into the van, Zane said, "I gave the horse some fresh water and hay."

Eve thanked him. Shani's grandfather had kept goats the last few years of his life, saying he needed some sort of livestock around. The hay was most likely left over from them.

Zane was extra quiet, much as he had been the evening when Eve and the children first met him.

"See you after school," Shani said when she pulled up by the school.

"I'll take the bus home," Zane said.

Shani shook her head. "No, I'll pick you up, like I said. I want to touch base with your teachers."

Eve thought about the one-room school her nieces and nephews went to. There was one teacher and a helper for thirty-three students. It was much less complicated than the massive buildings in front of her.

Zane politely told Eve good-bye and then grunted at his mother. He wasn't downright rude—but he certainly wasn't respectful.

Eve anticipated a harsh response from Shani, but she simply said, "I love you."

Zane closed the door harder than necessary and headed toward the front door of the school. Shani sighed as she accelerated the van. "The Lehman kids probably never act like that, do they?"

"Oh, they have their moments," she answered. They had sometimes acted that way for Abra, and every once in a while for her. But never for Tim.

"What time do you need to be back?" Shani asked.

"Around ten thirty, I suppose," Eve replied.

"So Tim's watching the baby?" Shani pulled back onto the highway, heading toward Strasburg.

Eve shook her head and explained about Monika. "She hopes to be a grandmother soon and likes to practice on Trudy."

Eve didn't get into Strasburg often, but she liked the little town with its brick buildings, restaurants, and shops. It was often filled with tourists who had no qualms about staring, but she did her best to ignore them.

Shani found a parking place across the street from the coffee shop and deftly backed her van into it without any effort. Eve limped along beside her as they crossed the street at the light. They entered the shop, ordered their drinks, and then Shani chose a table by the window. Eve almost suggested a table farther in the back, but didn't speak up. If she was going to have an Englisch friend, she wasn't going to try to hide her. Not that it would be possible anyway. Anyone could have seen them walking across the street together.

When the coffees were ready, Shani told Eve to sit tight while she got them. She returned with the coffee first, darted back to the counter, and then arrived with a cinnamon roll. "I couldn't pass it up," she said, cutting it in half with one of the two forks she'd picked up.

"Thank you," Eve said, thinking of all the goodies she and Abra had shared through the years.

"So what happened with Charlie yesterday?"

Eve grimaced. She'd known some Englisch who beat around the bush. It didn't seem Shani was one of them.

"Tim overreacted, is all."

Shani cocked her head, and Eve nodded. She wasn't going to tell Shani what had really happened. The last thing she wanted was for Shani to tell Charlie anything about how she felt, not when Eve was doing her best to turn her thoughts away from him.

"Is that what's going on with Tim? Just an overreaction?" Shani asked. "Or does he really not want Zane to come over at all?"

Eve took a bite of the roll and tried to figure out her answer. She decided honesty was best. "Most likely he is most concerned about Charlie, but I doubt he'll come out and say that. Send Zane over to play after school. I'll work things out with Tim."

Shani exhaled. "That's exactly what Joel doesn't think we should do. He's afraid Zane's going to get hurt—worse than he is right now." She wrapped her hands around her mug. "What's Tim afraid of?"

Eve met Shani's eyes. "The past."

"Anything specific?"

Eve held onto her coffee cup. She'd guarded herself for so many years against talking about the running around she and Abra had done. There was enough talk about them without her contributing to it. "Have you heard of our Rumschpringe?"

"Someone mentioned it during my training. It's when Amish kids go wild, right?" There was a sparkle in Shani's eyes.

Eve smiled. "Some do. Some don't. Let's just say Tim didn't . . . but Abra and I did. Me more than she. He's afraid of that for his own kids."

Shani shook her head. "I don't understand."

"I had an Englisch boyfriend. He and his buddies had a pretty big influence on Abra and me." That was how it started, anyway. How it ended was Eve's fault. She'd set a horrible example for Abra.

"Oh." Shani leaned forward. "And Tim's afraid Zane will be a bad influence on Daniel?"

Eve's face warmed.

Shani smiled. "He's afraid Charlie's going to be a bad influence on you too. Right?"

Eve shrugged and tried her best to sound nonchalant. "Who knows exactly what Tim thinks."

"But why would you . . . What do you call it?"

Eve shrugged, unsure what Shani was talking about.

"When you date someone," Shani said.

"Court?"

"That's right. I mean, there's no way you'd court Charlie or even be interested in him." Shani held her mug with both hands. "You're courting Gideon, right?" Shani smiled. "Even though you denied it the other night."

Eve's face grew even warmer.

Shani sighed. "I have to say Charlie's the nicest guy I know. I've never even heard him cuss, which is saying a lot for a soldier. But selfishly, I wouldn't even want you to court him—if you fell for him you'd end up leaving." She smiled and then took a sip of coffee. "Although I wouldn't mind if he found an Englisch woman just like you. His ex—girlfriend, not wife . . ." She grimaced. "Anyway, she dumped him while he was in Iraq. Can you imagine?"

Eve shook her head. She really couldn't.

"Really, I'd give anything for him to find someone like you—but Englisch."

Eve didn't respond.

Shani put down her mug, picked up her fork, and speared a piece of cinnamon roll. "Gideon seems like a great guy from what I saw the other night. Attentive. Thrilled to be with you. All of that." Shani put the bite in her mouth.

Eve tried to think of what to say, but before she did, Shani swallowed and started up again, "I guess I'm just saying that it seems Gideon really cares for you."

Maybe Eve did need to reevaluate her vow never to marry an Amish man. Maybe her confusing feelings for Charlie didn't really have anything to do with him—maybe they were to show her it was time to rethink her life.

Shani wrinkled her nose. "I wouldn't be surprised if Nikki tries to get Charlie back. Some women can't handle war, and I guess I should admire her for not pretending she could. It's weird, some feed off the drama of having their man gone and then break up with him when he

240

gets back. Others break up while they're gone. You'd be surprised how many relationships don't survive a deployment." She cut off another bite of cinnamon roll. "It takes work."

Eve nodded. She imagined it did.

"Anyway, I've obviously had too much caffeine today, since I can't seem to stop talking."

Eve smiled.

"But," Shani said, "as far as Charlie and Nikki, they were a good fit in some ways. I just wonder if he can trust her now. What if they get back together and then something bad happens again? She would probably bail."

"People change," Eve said. She certainly had. "Maybe she was just really afraid. I think we all know what that's like."

Shani pushed the plate toward Eve as she said, "Didn't Jesus say not to be afraid?"

Eve smiled and cocked her head. He had. Why was it so difficult for her to obey that command? She'd give anything to stop living in fear—fear of Tim, fear of the church, fear of messing up again. It seemed she'd been living in fear for a long time.

"I know a little about the Bible." Shani smiled. "I went to a Christian group in high school. Joel grew up going to church, and once we married, we went together. The chapel on base. Places like that." She shrugged. "We'll find a church here, once things settle down."

Eve nodded. "That's *gut*. There are lots of choices around here."

"That's what Charlie said."

They talked more about churches, and then Shani took a sip of coffee and changed the topic to Zane's school. "He missed the fall dance, but apparently there will be a winter one before Christmas break. I told him he's not going unless I'm a chaperone. You should have seen his face. . . ."

Relieved for a change of topic, Eve leaned back in her chair and listened, but not with her full attention. Her thoughts went back to Charlie's girlfriend dumping him. Poor guy. She knew what it felt like to be rejected.

She hadn't been serious about anyone since Patrick left her over ten years ago. Her thoughts went back to Charlie. Maybe he and Nikki would get back together. That would definitely help Eve manage her feelings.

She smiled at Shani, to encourage her to keep talking. It was good to be with her new friend. A blessing from God. She was glad the woman was so talkative. The more she said, the less likely Eve was to say something she'd later regret.

Her thoughts kept bouncing from Charlie to Gideon. If she was going to stay a part of her nieces' and nephews' lives, she couldn't leave the church. The most logical answer was to accept Gideon's interest, and perhaps, some day, his love.

∾ 19

Shani slowed at the Lehmans' driveway. She didn't want to turn down it and risk an encounter with Tim. "You're certain you want to do this?"

Zane nodded.

"Go to the house first, even if the boys are outside. Let Eve know you've arrived." Eve had sounded so positive during their coffee date that Zane should stop by that Shani had been won over. But now she wasn't so sure.

Zane opened the door and jumped down.

"I want you to head home before it's time for chores. So only stay an hour."

He nodded and then slammed the door shut.

Shani accelerated and continued on down the lane. She would have liked to have stopped by the Lehmans' herself. She enjoyed the time she spent with Eve and hoped all of their friendships could continue, although she'd felt downright silly when she'd brought up Charlie to Eve. Even though neither of them would talk about it, something *had* happened when he went over to wrap her ankle.

But then when she'd brought up Gideon, Eve wouldn't talk about him either. She'd seemed respectful enough toward him the other night, but she certainly didn't seem starry-eyed. And not today either. Maybe that was the way it was with the Amish.

Joel would tell her it wasn't any of her business—and he'd be right. It wasn't. Still, she couldn't help but wonder.

She parked the van in their driveway and headed up to the house. She could hear the TV before she opened the door and guessed Joel had been watching sports all day.

Joel turned the volume down when she entered and asked, "Where's Zane?"

"At the neighbors'."

"Shani, you've got to learn to say no to him."

"It was Eve's idea."

"Did you think about asking me?"

Actually she hadn't. "I'm sorry." After getting used to not asking his opinion about daily life, she'd simply forget to. "He won't be there long," Shani said. "He's coming home in an hour."

Joel frowned. "What did Zane's teachers say?"

Shani was surprised that Joel remembered. "I only spoke to one. The others were in a meeting. She said he's doing fine—he just needs some time to adjust."

She paused for a moment and then said, "I'll try to do better—"

His eyes drifted back to the TV.

"—at asking your opinion." Clearly he didn't want to talk anymore.

Shani hung up her purse and then her coat. Part

of her problem was she wasn't sure what to bother him with and what to handle on her own. She didn't want to burden him when he was dealing with so much already, especially when he'd seemed so distant. Most of the time he didn't seem very interested—and certainly not engaged —in the daily life around him.

Joel wheeled a little closer to the TV as the announcer started talking about the Milwaukee Bucks. It was his favorite boyhood team.

Shani yawned. "I'm going to take a nap." She was scheduled to work the day shift in the morning, as part of her orientation. She figured a little extra rest would help.

She awoke from a deep sleep to Joel saying her name from their bedroom doorway. The room was nearly dark. It took Shani a moment to realize where she was. Her grandfather's house. Lancaster County. Zane was at the neighbors'.

Joel wheeled a little closer. "Zane's not home. You should go check on him."

The baby kicked. Maybe he was annoyed at being awoken. Or maybe he was trying to get her out of bed. She swung her feet to the floor.

"Take the flashlight with you." He already had it in his lap. "And the umbrella. It's raining again."

She yawned, stood, and followed Joel as he wheeled his chair to the front door, where she slipped into her boots, wrestled her coat on, grabbed the umbrella, and took the flashlight from Joel.

"Did you have any dinner ideas?" he asked.

She shook her head. "I'll order pizza."

"I'll do it," he said. The landline had finally been installed.

"Denki." It had become her joke—one Joel didn't share. She started out the door and then stopped. "Think like Zane. Do you think he's still at the Lehmans' place? Or do you think he's in the pasture or along the creek?"

"Are you trying to decide to take the van or not?"

"Yes," she answered, holding the flashlight and umbrella tightly.

"Wouldn't Eve have sent him home by now?"

She nodded.

"Go through the field." Joel rolled back a little in his chair, expecting her to close the door.

She patted his shoulder. "He's fine," she said. "Don't worry." Then she hurried on down the ramp. Losing Samuel had changed her husband.

Shani shone the flashlight along the field and the line of poplar trees between her and the creek. An animal, probably a raccoon, darted away, but besides that she didn't see anything else. Once she reached the neighbors' she decided to go to the house first. She knocked several times on the back door before Rose finally answered it.

"Is Zane here?" Shani asked.

"He went home." Rose motioned for her to come in.

Eve sat at the table, peeling potatoes. "He left about a half hour ago."

Shani pressed her lips together. "Where are Daniel and Simon?"

"Doing the chores," Eve answered as Lila stepped into the kitchen, Trudy in her arms.

"How about Tim?" Shani asked.

"He's working on the new chicken coop."

"In the dark?"

"He has a lantern."

"Oh," Shani said. "I'll go ask the boys if they've seen Zane."

"You go too," Eve said to Lila. "Put Trudy in the high chair."

A minute later Lila and Shani headed toward the barn. Shani could see the lantern casting a soft glow behind the old chicken coop, and the sound of hammering rang out in the night.

"How was school today?" Shani asked Lila, even though her thoughts were on Zane. Surely he couldn't have gone too far.

"*Gut.* We had a kickball tournament during recess."

"What do you like best about school?"

"Art," Lila said. "Our teacher does a lot of it."

"What kind?" Shani asked.

"Drawing. Watercolor. Sculpture."

The information surprised Shani. It seemed too impractical for the Amish. "Do you sew and quilt?" she asked the girl.

"Some. My Mamm taught me."

Shani suspected the girl was being modest. "My grandmother tried to teach me when I was close to your age."

"The one who lived here?"

Shani nodded.

"I remember your grandfather, but I don't remember your grandmother at all," Lila said.

"She died a long time ago. When I was a few years older than you are now." Shani stopped talking when she heard laughter in the barn.

"Wait here," Lila said. Shani stopped a few feet from the barn while the girl continued, but then the rain started again and even though Shani had the umbrella she stepped under the eaves of the barn, to the side of the door.

"Hurry home," Lila was saying, her voice low. "Your Mamm's outside."

One of the other boys giggled.

Shani felt both relieved and annoyed.

"Stop it," Lila said. "Do you want to get caught? Then Zane won't be able to come over at all." Her voice grew harsher. "You should have gone home when Aenti told you to."

"Ach, don't be *bays*," Zane said.

Shani stepped closer to the door. *Bays*? What in the world was he talking about?

"I'm not angry," Lila hissed. "Just annoyed. Now go out the back."

There was more giggling.

"Stop it, Simon. You two hurry up. Dat's bound to come check in a minute."

There was a rustling, the sound of feet running, and then Lila's steps over the concrete threshold. "Daniel and Simon said they built a fort down by the creek today. Zane grabbed a couple of boards to add to it on his way home. He's probably there now."

Shani's mouth dropped open. She'd never expected Lila to lie to her. "Sweetie . . ." she said.

Lila inhaled.

"Zane was in there. I heard."

Lila's expression faded into a blank look.

"I'd never want you to lie for him."

Lila didn't respond, but by the light coming through the barn door Shani could see tears pooling in Lila's eyes. "I'm sorry," the girl said. "I wanted you to let him come back."

"Lila!"

Shani turned toward the voice, realizing the hammering had stopped. Tim strode toward them. "Who are you talking to?"

"It's me. Shani." She stepped forward, in front of the girl. "I was just looking for Zane. He hadn't come home."

"He's not here," Tim said.

"I know," Shani answered. "It sounds as if he's down by the creek."

Tim nodded and marched into the barn, calling over his shoulder. "Get back to the house and help your Aenti."

Lila, without saying anything, stepped away from Shani.

"Wait," Shani said, reaching for the girl.

Lila turned toward her and Shani whispered, "No more lying, okay?" Shani let go of the girl. "We all need to be honest."

Lila nodded and took off for the house.

Shani started toward the field. She hadn't exactly been honest with Tim. She sighed and headed back toward the barn. When she entered, Simon shoveled grain into a trough, Daniel led a cow out the other side of the barn, and Tim knelt down beside another cow. No one was talking or giggling or laughing.

"May I speak with you?" Shani asked Tim.

Startled, he bumped his head against the cow.

"It'll only take a minute," Shani said.

"I thought you went home."

"I will," she said. "After we talk."

"Go ahead."

She nodded toward the barn door. "Outside." She didn't want Simon and Daniel to hear.

Tim stood and followed her out. The rain was coming down harder. She opened her umbrella

250

and raised it high so Tim could join her underneath it. He didn't.

"Zane *was* helping with the chores earlier," she said. "I didn't intend for him to, just to play with your boys in the field after school."

He didn't respond.

"But he was in the barn when I got here. I think he's on his way home now."

Tim still didn't respond.

"I just wanted to clarify that," Shani said, growing more uncomfortable with each second. "I implied he'd been down at the creek for a while. I shouldn't have. I want to be honest—and have you be honest with us too."

Tim crossed his arms.

Shani rubbed her free hand on the thigh of her maternity jeans. "Can he and your boys play down by the creek together after school? I understand that you don't want him helping with chores . . ." Shani's voice trailed off. She couldn't bear the thought of Zane being ostracized, not when the Lehman children were such a good influence on him.

Tim stared straight ahead, without making eye contact.

"I work tomorrow and the day after. Two days a week, mostly. Zane will check in with Joel after school, but if it's nice out, he's not going to want to stay at the house." Did she have to spell it out to Tim? She couldn't control exactly where Zane

251

went after school, and it wasn't as if Joel could track him down and force him to stay home. They could discipline him, sure, but it would be after the fact.

Perhaps Tim was starting to understand because he said, "Jah, I don't want him helping with chores. Simon is well enough to do them. And I don't want your boy distracting mine . . . from their work."

Her pulse quickened, but she nodded.

"If they bump into each other down by the creek . . . then I suppose that's all right." He uncrossed his arms. "Now, I need to get back to my own chores."

"Of course," Shani said. "Thank you."

Instead of going through the field, she headed toward the lane, stopping by the house first. When Lila answered the door, she looked up at Shani, a sheepish expression on her face.

"I clarified things with your father," Shani said.

Lila nodded solemnly.

"That Zane was in the barn."

Lila's expression didn't change.

"I'd like to come in and talk with Eve a minute."

Lila nodded and stepped aside.

Eve stood at the counter slicing bread, while Rose fed the baby. "Shani," she said, "is everything all right?"

"I think so. Zane's probably home by now. I talked with Tim—he doesn't mind if the boys meet down by the creek to play, after school. I'll tell Zane. I work tomorrow," Shani said. "Day shift." She'd move to swing shift soon. "So I won't be around. But Joel will be home. Call our landline if you need anything."

Shani put the flashlight on the table. Rose grinned at her. Trudy sputtered food, sweet potatoes, maybe, from her mouth. Shani turned toward Lila. "Do you have a piece of paper and a pen?"

The girl nodded and darted into the living room.

"Can I leave you my work number?" she asked Eve. "And Charlie's number in case you can't get ahold of me? If there's an emergency."

Eve nodded as Lila returned with the paper and pen.

Shani wrote down the numbers quickly and handed the paper to Eve, who slipped it into her apron pocket. "Of course, if anything happens"— she meant to Joel—"Zane should call 9-1-1 first."

Eve nodded. "If Joel needs help with anything, tell him to call our number. Someone might be in the barn and hear it."

Sincerely, Shani said, "We appreciate that." Then she told Eve and the girls good-bye and hurried out the door.

By the time she reached home, the pizza delivery person was leaving. By the time she reached the kitchen, Zane had the paper plates and napkins on the table and the root beer opened.

"Let's say grace," he said.

"Let's talk about what just happened first," Shani responded.

Joel backed up his chair so he was close to the table. "He lost track of time."

"No. Eve sent him home. But instead of obeying her, he went to the barn with Simon and Daniel. Poor Lila lied to me to cover for Zane." She glared at her son. "What's that all about?"

He hung his head.

"Son." Joel's voice was harsh.

"It was Simon's idea," Zane said.

"It doesn't matter whose idea it was," Joel replied. "You didn't obey Eve. Tomorrow come straight home after school. Then we'll talk about you hanging out with the neighbors—or not."

It was the first time since he'd been home that Joel had taken the lead in disciplining Zane, and she wasn't about to question his decision.

"Let's pray," Shani said.

"I'd rather not," Zane replied.

"Tough." Shani bowed her head, giving Joel a chance to say grace. When he didn't she took a deep breath and recited the prayer from her childhood, "Come, Lord Jesus, be our guest. Let this food by thee be blessed." It was one her father had said when she was a child.

After she ended with "Amen," Zane said, "I like the silent prayers better."

"Tough," Joel responded.

Zane reached for a piece of pizza.

"Serve your mother first." Joel glared at Zane until he complied.

Shani took the plate from her son. Life was never easy. She sincerely believed that Zane's friendship with the Lehman children was a good thing, but it was almost unbearably complicated. She didn't like tiptoeing around because of Tim. And she couldn't help but share Joel's fear that it would all blow up in Zane's face.

Later, as Shani made lunches for the next day, the telephone rang. Zane, who sat at the kitchen table doing homework, popped up. "I'll get it."

"I've got it," Shani said, wiping her hands on a towel as she walked toward the phone on the far wall of the kitchen.

It was Charlie, just calling to check in.

"How are you?" Shani asked.

"Good," he answered. "I went back to that group at church I used to go to. For the first time since getting back."

"How was it?"

"Fine." He sounded a little out of breath. "Is Joel around?"

Shani headed into the living room, where Joel was watching a basketball game.

"It's Charlie," she said, handing him the phone.

She couldn't hear the conversation while she finished the lunches, but it lasted for a while.

She heard Joel say good-bye as Zane closed his

social studies book. "Go on to bed," Shani said to him. "I'll come up and wake you before I leave in the morning."

He stood and gave her a hug. She kissed the top of his head. In a few months he'd be too tall for her to do that. "Go tell your dad good-night."

She watched from the kitchen doorway as Zane, his expression blank, bent down and hugged Joel. Then he slipped on up the stairs.

Shani turned off the light to the kitchen. "Come on." She put her hand on Joel's shoulder. "Let's get to bed."

"Give me a minute," he said, pulling a pack of cigarettes out of his pocket.

She groaned. "I thought you'd stopped."

"Mostly."

"But you've been smoking again, when I'm at work?"

He shrugged. "Not much—it's not like I can drive down to the closest convenience store and buy more. All I have is what's left." He dropped the pack in his lap and headed toward the back door. She guessed he had a stash in his footlocker. She tossed the dish towel on the counter.

He'd started smoking in Iraq. He'd been honest with her about it right away, over Skype, when Zane wasn't in the room. Said it calmed his nerves. He'd laughed and said it was the safest thing he did all day. She didn't think that was funny.

She went on into the bedroom and changed into her nightgown.

He must have only smoked half a cigarette, because he came in right away and put the pack in his drawer. "I'll stop," he said. "I hardly ever do it anyway. Just on especially bad days."

She didn't reply as she helped him get ready for bed. It had to be his decision. Time would tell— but it irked her.

Once they were in bed, the baby began to swirl around. She took Joel's hand and placed it on her abdomen. He patted her and then pulled away.

She rolled toward him and brushed his hair from his forehead. It was longer than usual. He'd be asking for a haircut in a day or two.

He inched away from her. She tried not to take it personally. They didn't have the same relationship they'd had before. He was distant. Tired. And with good reason—he was still recovering. He wasn't the same Joel. Not at all.

Since his return, he'd not once placed his hand on her belly—or anywhere else on her—without her initiating it, and then he'd put off her advances since he reinjured his leg. But there were ways. If he wanted.

She'd been so faithful in praying while he was in Iraq. In fact, that was what had kept her sane. Right after she'd found out about the attack and during the first few days in Germany, she'd been so grateful that he'd survived, so full of praise. But the ongoing impact of the death of Samuel and Joel's injuries—mainly the emotional ones—made her, over time, afraid to pray.

She was pretty sure her prayers didn't have any sway with God. She inhaled sharply. Was that the kind of woman she'd become? One that didn't pray? One that didn't trust? One that would, in the end, give up?

She swallowed hard, weary of thinking about what was—and wasn't—going on around her.

"What's Charlie been up to?" she asked.

"He saw Nikki tonight."

Shani propped her head up on her hand. "You're kidding?" It was so much easier to talk about other people's lives than their own.

"Nope."

Her prediction to Eve about Charlie and Nikki nagged at her. "Did he see her at church?"

"Yep."

Shani rolled to her back. "How'd it go?"

"He said it was fine. She's apologetic for how she handled everything."

"And he probably forgave her. Right? Just like that."

She could tell Joel was shaking his head. "I don't know, Shani. I didn't ask him."

"Do you think they'll get back together?"

"I hope not," Joel responded.

Shani stared at the ceiling. She'd liked Nikki,

but she thought she'd been a fool—a mean fool—to dump Charlie the way she had.

Shani started to ask Joel if Charlie sounded happy that he'd seen Nikki, but his breathing had already changed. He'd probably taken a pain pill after he'd had his smoke.

She checked the alarm, making sure it was set, and then pulled the quilt up to her chin. She really did wish Charlie would find an Englisch girl like Eve.

Charlie glanced at the clock on the dashboard of his pickup: *3:42*. Zane would be home by the time he got there.

He'd done his laundry, grocery shopped, and cleaned in the morning, telling himself he couldn't leave Philly until it was done. Being gone two weekends in a row had taken its toll on his domestic well-being, and he'd determined to set it straight before a third weekend wreaked complete havoc.

Last night, Charlie had considered not going back to Lancaster for the weekend at all. Nikki had invited him to dinner at her house on Saturday with a few friends from their group, but he'd already told Joel he'd visit and chop enough wood to last the family for a few weeks. He couldn't back out now. But he wouldn't return to Lancaster for a while after this trip.

Before he'd left for Iraq, he and Nikki had talked about getting engaged when he returned. That seemed so long ago now. He couldn't fathom why she'd stepped back into his life. Perhaps it was pity. Or maybe she felt she needed to make up for dumping him the way she had.

He turned off the highway onto Juneberry Lane. The day was clear and bright but cold. The maple trees were nearly bare, while their leaves covered the lane in a collage of yellow, orange, and red. Winter wasn't far away.

He slowed, glancing down the Lehmans' driveway, but didn't see anyone. A minute later, as he neared the cedar tree, a branch came sailing across the hood of his pickup. He slammed on the brakes.

Simon appeared.

Charlie rolled down his window. "Did you throw that?"

"It got away from me," Simon slurred, his jaw still wired shut. "We're playing Romans. It's my javelin."

"Who's *we?*" Charlie asked, opening the door and climbing down from the truck.

"All of us," Simon said as Rose came running out of the bushes. Daniel followed, greeting Charlie with a wave.

"Zane too?" Charlie asked.

"Jah, he's across the field," Simon said.

"Zane!" Rose yelled, her voice much louder than Charlie would have predicted.

A moment later, Zane appeared, followed by a bright-faced Lila.

"Does your dad know you're playing Roman soldiers?" Charlie asked, looking directly at Lila.

"We have permission to play after school," the girl replied.

"But probably not a game with soldiers, right?"

261

Charlie glanced around the circle of Amish kids. Simon and Rose both met his gaze with grins but Lila and Daniel hung their heads.

"Ach," Zane replied. "Don't spoil our *Shposs*."

"Pardon?"

Zane sighed at his ignorance. "Our fun. We're not hurting anyone."

Charlie grimaced. "Except my truck." He patted Simon's shoulder. "Will you be home soon?" he asked Zane.

"Around four. That's how long we're allowed to play."

"See you then."

The children scurried away toward the creek on the other side of the field. Lila and Zane ran ahead, leading the way. The girl could really run, considering she wore a dress. She pulled ahead of Zane.

Then again, maybe he let her.

Charlie climbed back in his truck and drove the rest of the way, slowly, his thoughts falling on Eve. How many times over the week had he told himself he wouldn't think about her anymore— only to find his mind wandering her way again? That was another reason to stop coming down to Lancaster.

The smoke coming out of the chimney greeted him as Charlie parked his truck. He jumped down and breathed in the acrid smell, thinking of fall days with his grandparents. He'd raked leaves with his grandfather and then helped him burn the piles. After they'd finished, his grandmother served hot cider and they all played Chinese checkers.

He knocked on the door and immediately heard Joel call out, "Come in."

He did. His friend sat in his chair in front of the TV, but he turned it off and wheeled toward Charlie. "How was your trip?"

"Good." Laughter from the kitchen distracted Charlie. "Who's here?"

"The Amish chick." Joel grinned.

"And the baby?"

Joel nodded. "Yeah. She wasn't as keen on me as last time."

"Oh, you didn't give her a chance," Shani said, sweeping into the living room with the baby perched on her belly. "She just had some apple-sauce. She'll be fine now." She plopped the baby down in Joel's lap and grinned at Charlie.

"Oh, hey," she said.

"Hey, to you too," he responded. "Looks like you have visitors."

She nodded. "Come on in and say hello."

Feeling awkward, he followed her into the kitchen, glancing back at Joel. What had changed? Everyone was acting as if the encounter with Tim last Monday hadn't happened.

Joel didn't seem to notice his questioning look. The baby was lunging at the armrest, her mouth open, and Joel was trying to wrestle her away.

"Look what the cat dragged in," Shani said.

Eve stood, turning an apple peeler that was attached to the tabletop. She looked up as he entered. "Hallo there," she said.

Charlie stopped in the doorway.

"The kids picked the apples off those trees out back," Shani said.

"Isn't it late for apples?" he asked.

Eve licked her finger and headed toward the sink. "These are the last to ripen."

"*Ripe* is the important word here," Shani said. "That's why we'll be making applesauce out of all of them."

"Well, I'll leave you ladies to your work," Charlie said, turning away.

"Eve's a good influence on me," Shani called out. "I'll actually be cooking meals soon."

Charlie chuckled as he headed back to the living room. The baby had settled down in Joel's lap and was staring at the TV.

"Is that all right?" Charlie asked.

"What?"

"For Trudy to watch TV."

"It's just basketball. It's not like it's *The Simpsons* or *King of the Hill* or anything like that."

Charlie shook his head. "That's not the point. She's probably never seen TV before."

"Actually, she has." Eve had stepped to the doorway of the kitchen.

"Where?" Charlie couldn't hide the surprise in his voice, but he hoped he'd disguised his hurt at Eve's snippiness.

"At Abra's parents'. They're Mennonite. Right after Trudy was born, Abra and I went there with all the children."

Charlie tilted his head, trying to understand.

Eve nodded. "Jah, the kids didn't watch any of those shows Joel mentioned, but they watched *Sesame Street* and things like that. And sports." Eve stepped forward and reached for the baby. "It's chore time. We need to head home. I'll tell Zane to hurry this way," she said to Joel.

"Thanks," he answered, giving up the little one.

Eve grabbed the diaper bag and headed into the kitchen with the baby. It was one thing, back in Philly, to resolve not to be interested in her but quite another to control his feelings when she was so close. He took a deep breath, fearing she was mad at him. Probably about Monday. Tim had probably been worse toward her than anyone. Still, Charlie couldn't get the expression on her face out of his head.

He exhaled. Joel smirked.

"Don't," Charlie said.

"I wouldn't think of it," Joel chuckled. "So how's Nikki? Are you giving her a second chance?"

Charlie shrugged. She was the last thing he wanted to talk about, especially with Eve so close.

There was more laughter from Eve and then Shani. Then a round of good-byes and the sound of the back door closing.

"Well, things seemed to have relaxed around here," Charlie said to Joel, except for Eve. She seemed uptight, with Charlie at least. But he wasn't going to mention that. "What happened since Monday?"

"Tim's got a job at the lumberyard. He's working a couple days a week. Seems the bishop's trying to win his favor."

"Oh," Charlie said.

Joel grinned. "Jealous?"

Without responding Charlie stepped toward the door. "I bet you need more wood chopped, right? Is the axe outside?"

"Where else would it be?" Joel teased.

Charlie headed to the front door. "I'll be back."

"Don't forget the wood," Joel called out as Charlie closed the door behind him.

He'd resolved to let go of his feelings for Eve after what happened on Monday, but now—after seeing her—he had to know. She was limping toward the Lehmans' home, so she hadn't gotten far. Charlie jogged toward her, calling out, "Let me help with the baby."

She turned around. "Thank you, but I'm fine."

Trudy waved at him and smiled. Charlie slowed as he reached the two. "The extra weight can't be good for your ankle."

The baby lunged toward him, drool cascading over her lower lip. Charlie grabbed for her, and Eve let go.

Charlie matched Eve's pace, which wasn't very fast. "May I ask you something?"

Without looking at him she said, "No."

He persevered. "About what happened last Monday."

She stopped and turned toward him. "I said no."

He stopped too. The baby wiggled in his arms as if she wanted him to keep going. When he didn't move, she leaned toward Eve, who took the little one back.

Charlie hung his hands at his sides. "You seemed annoyed with me just now."

"I'm sorry."

"I only intended to help you with your ankle on Monday."

"I know."

His eyes burned.

"You didn't do anything wrong," she said. "It was me." She kissed the top of the baby's head and turned away.

Charlie caught her elbow. "I understand the differences between us."

"Jah," she said. "That's why it's no use."

He inhaled sharply. "Can we be—" his breath caught—"friends?" Saying the word pained him. But he'd rather have her as a friend than nothing at all.

She hesitated. Their eyes met. Her gaze was resigned. Nothing like it had been on Monday. "It's no use," she said.

"Eve . . ." He swallowed. He couldn't say more than her name.

She shook her head. "Years ago, before I joined the church, I became friends with an Englisch man. We ended up dating, for quite a while. We became—too serious. No good came from it." She shook her head. "The consequences would be even greater now."

"I don't intend—" Charlie stopped. That wasn't entirely true. He wasn't sure what he intended. When Nikki broke up with him, he'd responded in an email, telling her that was it. He wouldn't give her a second chance. It had been a stupid thing to write, but he'd meant it.

He felt different with Eve. He'd give her as many chances as she needed. Even if it was just to be friends.

"I heard you saw your old girlfriend this week," Eve said.

Charlie looked past Eve, out into the field. Shani must have told her.

"Are you getting back together with her?"

He shrugged but then answered, "No."

Eve nodded. He got the feeling she saw right through him.

"I'd really like to be your friend." He couldn't hope for anything more than that.

Eve looked down at the top of the baby's head. "We really can't," she said. "Friendly, jah, but not friends."

He'd wanted more than that but he'd have to take what he could for now. He stuck out his hand to her. "Friendly, then?"

She smiled, balanced the baby with one arm, and took his hand. Hers wasn't soft—how could it be after all the hard work she did? But it was warm and strong. And tender.

"Do you mind holding the baby again?" she asked, her voice softer. "Then I think I can make it home. Shani carried her over."

As she slid Trudy into his arms, Charlie's heart contracted at the loss of what might have been. He swallowed hard. He'd still try to be Eve's friend, but respect her boundaries.

As they started to walk up the lane again, the voices of the children grew loud. Rose squealed, and Zane yelled, "To the creek!"

Eve called out to her nieces and nephews, telling them it was time to get home and do the chores. They came running.

"We'll walk them home," Charlie said to Zane, "and then go back and chop wood."

Rose skipped along and took Charlie's free hand. Ahead Zane walked between Simon and Daniel, while Lila fell into step beside Eve, but after a minute Zane slowed until Lila caught up with him.

"You run along, Rose," Eve said to her niece. "See if you can catch up with Lila."

As soon as the girl skipped ahead a few paces, Eve sighed. "Life is much calmer with Tim working away from home some days." He expected her to say more, but she didn't.

The baby snuggled against him. "So does Tim work tomorrow?" Charlie asked.

"Jah," Eve said.

"Will you be around?"

"I'm going on an outing."

"With the bishop?"

Rose stopped and spun around as Eve nodded. "Is the bishop coming to take you away?" the little girl asked.

Eve shook her head. "No."

"I don't like the bishop." Rose's lips curled into a pout.

"You liked him earlier this week, when he brought the lumber," Eve said.

Rose shook her head. "I like Charlie."

Charlie grimaced.

Rose, the pout still on her face, spun around and started jogging. "Lila, wait," she wailed. The older girl and Zane both slowed down until Rose caught up with them.

"The children are going with us," Eve said. Again, Charlie waited for Eve to say more, but she didn't.

Gideon Byler seemed like a man who knew

what he wanted—most likely he wouldn't want to court for long. No wonder Eve had said it was no use for the two of them to become friends. Charlie didn't realize he'd stopped walking until the baby started to fuss. He started again, catching up with Eve in just a few steps.

They shuffled the rest of the way in silence. He should have stayed in Philly and taken Nikki up on her offer of dinner.

"Sunday's a no-church day, right?" He wouldn't have wanted to attend their service again, even it wasn't.

"Jah," Eve said. "I'm going to take the children to see their grandparents."

"Your parents?" Charlie asked. No one had mentioned them before.

"No, they've both passed. Abra's parents. Simon saw them in the hospital, but the other children haven't seen them in months."

"Oh." After a long pause Charlie managed to ask, "How come?"

"Tim—he's been against it. But Gideon convinced him it's important." Each time she repeated Gideon's name, it seemed she said it with more respect. Charlie doubted if he'd be able to even be friendly with Eve for much longer. No doubt she'd be married soon.

The next morning, as Charlie flipped the last of the pancakes, Shani said, "There's a farm auction this morning, out on the highway."

"That's nice." Joel stuffed a sticky forkful into his mouth.

"We already have a farm," Zane said.

"They auction off what it takes to run a farm," Shani replied. "Equipment. Supplies. Livestock."

"Cool." Zane pushed back his chair and headed to the fridge with his cup.

Joel swallowed and groaned. "What are you thinking?"

She pushed up the sleeves of the oversized shirt —most likely Joel's—she wore. "Not anything big. Chickens. Rabbits. Maybe a couple of goats that Zane can milk. We have the small pasture we can use."

Joel shook his head. "You have no idea . . ."

"Of course I don't, but you do." Shani nodded toward Zane as he poured more milk. "It would be good for him."

"Goats are a pain in the—"

"Hinaendt?" Charlie asked.

"Jah," Joel said. "What he said." Everyone laughed.

Shani ignored him. "Then we can go into Strasburg for ice cream."

"It's too cold for that." Joel cut into the last half of his stack of pancakes.

"It's never too cold for ice cream," Shani said. Joel used to love the stuff. "We can drive by Zane's school too."

It was Zane's turn to groan. "Ach, are you trying to ruin my weekend?" Charlie couldn't help but marvel at the way Shani coordinated everything. And she was right, even if Joel thought it would be too much, having a few chores closer to home would be good for Zane.

A half hour later, as Charlie wheeled Joel down the ramp, Shani tossed her keys at him as she said, "How about if you drive?"

Charlie caught the keys with a backhanded grab, unsure of what she was up to. But he figured it out once she and Joel were in the back and Zane was up front with him. Joel had been the kind of guy who always drove his family around—until he got injured. He hadn't driven since. Having Charlie drive didn't make it all so obvious.

And that way Shani could ride in the back with Joel.

As they passed the Lehmans' driveway, Zane peered down it.

"Do you see anyone?" Charlie asked.

Zane shook his head. "I bet the boys will be down by the creek later . . ."

Charlie nodded. It was a beautiful early November day. A perfect day to play down by the creek. It made him wish he were twelve again. Shani told him to turn left on the highway and then to turn right after the willow tree.

"Take another right at the stop sign," Shani instructed a few minutes later.

Next she said, "Now a left."

Ahead was a field full of cars, pickups, and buggies. Off to one side was a canopy with tables underneath. One row seemed to be food booths, and behind it were tables and chairs.

A banner hanging from the canopy read: School Auction.

"I thought you said this was a farm auction." Joel's voice fell flat.

"I thought it was," Shani responded.

"Looks like it's for an Amish school," Zane said, and then, his voice rose, "I wonder if the kids are here."

It was pretty obvious whom he meant by *the kids*.

"Probably not," Charlie said. "Eve"—he couldn't seem to manage to say *and the bishop*—"was taking them somewhere today." He frowned. Maybe she was taking them to the auction, with the bishop.

He looked in the rearview mirror at Shani. Had Eve told her they'd be here? Was that why Shani suggested it?

Charlie wanted to groan, but he stifled it. Better to go along as if he hadn't put any of it together.

"I'll pull up by the sidewalk over there," Charlie said. Concrete ran in front of the food tent and along a graveled area where more booths were. Beyond that, in the next field, were buggies and farm equipment. In the opposite direction was the barn with a homemade banner hanging over the doorway that read: Livestock.

The ground was dry and solid, thanks to the cold nights. It wouldn't be a problem to push Joel's chair all the way to the barn. Charlie wasn't sure if he wanted to be along if Joel and Shani got into a dispute about what constituted "livestock" though.

Charlie put the van in Park and jumped out to retrieve the wheelchair. By the time he had it opened and in position, Shani was trying to help Joel but he was brushing her away. Charlie stepped forward and took his friend's elbow to help him pivot to the chair and sit. By the time he pushed him onto the sidewalk a group of kids was staring. One of them, an Englisch girl, waved at Zane, who still sat in the front seat, but he didn't seem to see her. His eyes were on a group of Amish people standing a few yards behind the Englisch girl. Lila waved at Zane, and he waved back. Then he opened the door and jumped down.

Next to Lila was Eve. She wasn't waving. In fact, the look on her face didn't appear to be welcoming at all. Gideon stood beside her. The expression on his face was pure confusion, but then he started toward Joel and Shani, his hand extended.

Charlie continued on toward the driver's side. If it were up to him, he'd walk back to the farm, but Zane was urging Charlie to hurry and park the van and join them.

❧ 21

Alarm filled Eve as Charlie parked Shani's van and then started toward their group. Gideon was shaking Joel's hand, though Shani's husband looked as if he'd rather be just about anyplace except the auction.

Lila pulled on her arm. "Come on."

Eve, holding Trudy, allowed herself to be dragged along, limping as she walked. She was happy to see Shani and Joel. They weren't the problem. Neither was Zane.

"Hi, Eve." Shani gave her a hug, pulling her and the baby close. "I thought this was a farm auction —I didn't realize it was for a school until we pulled up. Is it for your school?"

Eve nodded.

Shani placed her hand on Joel's shoulder. "That's all the more reason to buy something, right?"

Joel shook his head but then smiled, just a little. Trudy finally noticed her friend and let out a squeal, reaching for Joel. He put up his arms, and Eve eased the little girl into them. Joel settled her on his lap.

"How's the leg?" Gideon asked.

"Better, I hope." Joel held on to the baby with both hands.

"I'll keep praying," Gideon said.

"Thank you," Joel responded.

Eve was touched that Gideon would pray for Joel.

Eve turned toward Shani. "What are you wanting to bid on? Quilts? Furniture? Plants?"

"Livestock," Shani said as Charlie approached.

Eve stepped back, bumping into Gideon. "Cows? Horses?"

Joel shook his head. "We're thinking smaller."

"Goats," Zane said. "And chickens. Maybe some rabbits."

"Do you plan on eating rabbit?" Gideon asked.

Charlie, without glancing at Eve, tousled Zane's head. "Maybe not rabbits."

"But chickens for sure," Zane said.

Joel exhaled.

"We'll walk over to the barn with you," Gideon said.

"Here," Eve said to Joel, "I'll take Trudy back."

"She's fine," he said. "I'll hold on to her."

Gideon led the way. Zane caught up with Lila. The boy hadn't asked about Daniel or Simon—who were off mucking out stalls. Charlie put his hands on the back of the wheelchair and began to push, glancing at Eve as he did.

"You shouldn't have come," Eve whispered.

"I didn't know you'd be here," he said softly.

"I told you yesterday."

He shook his head. "You just said 'an outing.' I didn't ask where, and you didn't say."

Joel looked over his shoulder. "Could you two speak a little louder? I'm having a hard time eavesdropping."

Shani gave him one of her looks. Eve hoped Gideon hadn't heard. Without replying to Charlie, Eve increased her stride as best she could and walked with Shani for a moment and then continued on to catch up with Gideon. Charlie was probably right—chances were she hadn't said where they were going. She shouldn't have thought the worst of him.

"Come on," Eve looked over her shoulder and said to Shani. "I want to introduce you to the wife of one of our deacons." The two women branched off while the others continued toward the barn. After Eve introduced Monika, she added, "She's known me since I was Trudy's age."

"Jah," Monika said, "and I couldn't help but think how happy your Mamm would be today to see you and Gideon and the children together. God works in amazing ways." Monika's eyes teared as she spoke.

Eve stepped to the side of the table and put her arm around the woman.

"What went on before . . ." Monika swatted away the past with her hand. "That was too much for your sweet mother."

Eve's face began to grow warm.

"But this . . ." The woman paused for a moment and then rushed on. "It's God's redemption. You've proven yourself these last years."

Eve let go of Monika as the old shame returned. She knew Monika meant to be positive—but bringing up the past always hurt.

"To see you with Gideon and the children—I haven't seen anything so reassuring in . . . I don't know how long. He is a good man, Eve Lehman. Don't you forget it."

Shani stirred, and when Eve glanced at her she smiled.

Monika dabbed at her eyes. "It won't be long until you're married."

Eve shook her head, wanting her friend to stop. It felt especially awkward in front of Shani.

Monika seemed to get the hint, because she said, "Well, we'll just take it a step at a time."

A baby's crying made all of them turn. Gideon traipsed toward them with Trudy.

"Ach," Monika said. "She can't stand to be away from you." The baby had tears rolling down her face. Eve stepped forward and took Trudy in her arms.

"She was fine," Gideon said, "until she realized you weren't with us." He smiled.

"You've lost the touch," Monika said, her hands on her hips.

"I'm not sure I ever had the touch." Gideon grinned. He and his wife had had six children, two still at home. He stepped backward and turned to rejoin the others.

Trudy hiccupped. Monika reached for the baby as her husband approached, but Trudy clung to Eve. Deacon King nodded at Eve and smiled at Trudy. Eve introduced Shani and then said they needed to catch up with the rest of their group. Eve glanced over her shoulder as the deacon wrapped his arm around Monika and pulled her close. Most Amish weren't very affectionate, but the Kings were. Monika patted his cheek. Both were short and a little plump. And they had to be the cutest couple Eve had ever seen.

She sighed, pulling Trudy close. Monika didn't mean any harm in what she'd said. As they turned back toward the barn, Shani said, "Monika really likes Gideon, doesn't she?"

Eve nodded. "Everyone likes Gideon." She did too and had for years. When he was on the school board and she applied for the teaching job after she joined the church, he was the only who wanted to give it to her. He'd been willing to give her a second chance long before anyone else was. Of course, back then he was a married older man—not anyone she'd ever consider as a husband.

Shani slowed, and Eve matched her pace. "Are you two as serious as Monika makes it sound?"

"No," Eve said. "We haven't talked about anything, not seriously. But . . ." Eve stopped.

Shani did too. "But what?"

Eve pulled Trudy even closer. "Some things aren't talked about much. They're just expected."

The others had all stopped at the door to the barn. As Shani and Eve approached, Gideon and Charlie each took a side of the wheelchair and lifted Joel over the lip of the doorway.

By the time Eve and Shani reached the others, Zane hung over the railing of a pen with three ewes. "Can we get them?" Zane asked.

"No," Joel replied.

Eve chimed in, "They'd be easier than goats."

"But what purpose would they serve?" Joel asked.

"Responsibility," Shani answered.

"They've most likely been bred," Eve chimed in. "You'd have lambs in late winter."

"Ahh," Shani said. "Not too long after I have the baby."

Joel didn't respond and instead turned his head toward Gideon. "What do people do with sheep around here?"

"Sell the wool. Sell the meat. But if you want to make any money, you need a flock."

Joel crossed his arms.

"We could bid and see what happens," Shani said. She patted Joel's shoulder. "Let's go look at the chickens."

As the group moved on, Charlie bumped Eve's shoulder with his arm. "Sorry," he mumbled.

A tingly sensation crept up her spine. She

stopped. Why did the briefest touch from Charlie send her reeling? Shani glanced over her shoulder and gave Eve a puzzled look.

Eve followed the others.

"These are Rhode Island Reds," Gideon said, pointing to a small coop. "They're young and will make good laying hens."

"Where would we keep them?" Joel asked.

Shani stepped forward to get a closer look as she answered, "The coop."

"One push would knock it over."

Joel was exaggerating. Eve didn't think it was that bad.

"How about if we bid on these too?" Shani asked, ignoring him.

"As long as we don't get a rooster," Joel replied.

"But then you'll never have chicks," Eve said.

"Exactly."

Zane didn't seem to hear his father, saying, "I can't wait to take care of all of them."

"Let's get whoopie pies here while we wait to see if we win the bid," Shani said. "Instead of going into town for ice cream."

Lila turned toward Eve with a questioning look on her face, but Eve shook her head. She didn't have the money to buy treats for everyone.

"I'm buying," Shani said, taking Rose's hand. "Whoopie pies for all."

The thought that Shani may have seen her exchange with Lila mortified Eve, but there was nothing to do about it. "Denki," she said. "That's very kind."

Shani did win the bid on both the chickens and the sheep, but she hadn't thought about how she'd get them home. "Oh," she said with a laugh. "I thought maybe someone would deliver them. But they can ride in the van with us."

Joel groaned.

"We get the crate with the chickens, right?"

Gideon assured her that she did and transporting the chickens wouldn't be too hard but hauling the sheep in the van could be a problem. Then he came to the rescue. He'd brought his wagon— Eve and the children had all ridden with him. "Charlie and Zane can ride with us," he said. "And hold onto the sheep." He grinned.

Eve's mouth grew dry. The last thing she wanted was to spend more time with both Gideon and Charlie.

"Great," Shani said, pulling out her checkbook. "But can you take the chickens too? That way Joel and I can go on home."

Gideon assured her that would work fine. She wrote a check for the amount of their bids, folded it, and handed it to Eve. "Thank you," she said.

"You're welcome," Eve answered.

Joel told everyone good-bye as Charlie continued to push him toward the parking area. Gideon hurried alongside the two, talking away, probably about caring for the sheep and chickens. Would Charlie tell him that he grew up on a farm?

Shani gave Eve a quick hug and then followed the men. Zane and Lila spotted Daniel and Simon at the back of the barn and took off after them, with Rose lagging behind. Monika's daughter Jenny saw Lila—or maybe Daniel—and followed the group. Eve lost sight of them as Monika approached. This time Trudy was willing to go to her. Eve covered her up with her blanket, tucking it between Monika and the baby. "She'll probably fall asleep," Eve said.

"I need a rocking chair," Monika answered.

"How about a lawn chair?" Eve pointed to several that were available for the elderly on the other side of the food booths.

"Oh, goodness, I'm too young." Monika laughed but then made her way toward the chairs. Eve followed her and then stood, as if waiting for something, but she wasn't sure what.

She'd almost decided to go check on the children, when Charlie started toward her, without Gideon.

"There's that Englisch man," Monica said. "It looks like he's headed this way."

Eve didn't reply.

"What's he doing?" Monika's eyes crinkled in a squint.

"Gideon's giving him a ride home," Eve explained.

Monika clucked her tongue. "That Gideon has such a good heart—don't you think?"

Eve nodded.

Charlie must have seen the children because he veered off toward the barn. Eve exhaled, relieved that Monika wouldn't have the chance to see the two of them together.

A few minutes later, Gideon pulled up with the wagon. "I guess we're leaving," Eve said. "I'd better go turn in Shani's check. I'll be right back."

As she headed to pay, Charlie led the children toward the barn as if he were the Pied Piper. Rose held his hand. Lila skipped alongside. Simon poked at Daniel with a stick. Zane increased his stride, most likely to catch up with Lila. The outing with Gideon certainly hadn't gone as planned.

"Meet you at the wagon," she called out to Charlie, pointing back at Gideon.

He nodded, called out to the boys to head to the barn with him to get the sheep and chickens, and then started toward it himself.

Fifteen minutes later they were all situated, mostly. Eve held Trudy and rode up front with Gideon, with Rose and Lila between them. Charlie held on to one of the sheep, while Zane and Daniel held on to the other two. Simon sat with his arms wrapped around the chicken crate.

Lila spent most of her time looking at the crew behind them and laughing.

The sheep made a racket with their bleating and the chickens sounded as if a fox had slipped into their crate.

"Thank you," Eve said to Gideon.

He nodded and then turned his head toward her. "I look forward to us seeing more of each other." He smiled. "With or without the interruptions." His expression spread into a wide grin.

Lila squirmed, bumping against Rose, who elbowed her sister. Eve put her hand on the younger girl's leg and pressed down as she tried to smile back at Gideon, but she was afraid her expression appeared more as a grimace. They rode on in silence.

After supper, as Tim dozed in his chair and Eve and Lila finished up the dishes, a knock sounded at the back door. As Eve hurried to answer it, she expected it to be Gideon. It wasn't.

It was Charlie.

"One of the ewes is sick," he said.

Eve clenched the dish towel in her hand. "I thought you grew up on a farm."

"I did, but we only had cattle." He held a flashlight in his hands. "Does Tim know anything about sheep?"

"I'll go see if he'll help." Eve headed into the living room.

She said his name, but he didn't budge.

Lila said, "Dat, Aenti's talking to you."

He still didn't respond.

"Tim," Eve said again, putting her hand on his shoulder. He brushed it away. "The neighbors have a sick ewe. Would you go take a look?"

He shook his head, his eyes still closed. "The neighbors don't have sheep."

"They do now."

He groaned. "You know as much as I do about them," Tim said, turning his head away. "You go."

Their Dat had raised sheep. Tim swore he never would, but Eve liked the animals. "All right," she said.

Eve stepped back into the kitchen and told Charlie she'd go with him.

He gave her a puzzled look.

She shrugged. "I grew up helping my Dat care for our ewes."

"How's your ankle?" Charlie asked. "I could go get my truck."

She shook her head. "I'm fine." She'd already put the baby to bed. Hopefully she'd stay settled. If not, Lila could take care of her.

She grabbed her cape and then followed Charlie out the door into another clear, crisp night. A crescent moon hung in the sky like a cradle, and the stars shimmered around it. She pulled her cape tight.

"I know this doesn't look good," Charlie said. "I promise I'm not stalking you. I thought Tim would be the one to come help."

She didn't answer.

"It's just that Zane's beside himself and Shani doesn't want to call a vet unless she has to," Charlie said. "Because Joel's worried about money . . ."

"I'm happy to help," Eve said. "If she needs a vet, I'll give Shani the number of ours. He's reasonable."

They walked in silence until Charlie led the way into the barn, which was well lit with overhead lights. "They're in the back."

She followed him to the last pen. Zane sat with the ewe's head in his lap and Shani knelt on the floor next to both of them. "She seems depressed," Shani said.

Eve knelt too and patted the sheep's belly. It was hard. The ewe stirred, lifting her head to look at Eve, but then she dropped it again in Zane's lap.

"Did you give her grain?" Eve asked.

Zane nodded. "I found it in the barn."

"A lot?"

"Not too much . . ." Zane glanced down at the ewe.

"I'm guessing she has acidosis," Eve said. "She's probably only been grazing to this point. The grain has to be introduced gradually."

Zane hung his head.

"You couldn't know. She'll be all right." At least Eve hoped she would be. "Get a pop bottle, fill it with water, and add two tablespoons of baking soda. Then feed it to her. She'll take it straight from the bottle."

"Denki," Zane said, standing.

She patted his shoulder. "This can be serious, but I expect she'll be okay. After you give her the soda water, check on her before bed and first thing in the morning."

Zane nodded and hurried out of the barn.

Shani reached for Eve's hand, took it, and squeezed. "What would we do without you?"

Eve smiled. "You'd get by."

"I'll walk you home," Charlie said.

As they headed back up the lane, Eve asked Charlie if he was planning to go back to the Mennonite church the next day.

He shook his head. "I'm going back to Philly, to my church, in the morning."

Eve wasn't sure what to say.

They shuffled along. Eve pulled her cape tighter. She stopped herself from asking when Charlie would come down to Lancaster County next. He'd helped the Becks with moving, the ramp, chopping wood. He probably needed to start focusing on his own life again.

Eve's heart contracted at the thought of not seeing him again.

"I'll be thinking about you and the kids visiting Abra's parents tomorrow," Charlie said.

"Thank you," Eve said.

They continued on in silence. When they

reached the driveway, Eve said she could go the rest of the way by herself. "I have every pothole memorized. I promise."

Charlie smiled. "I'll pray that the visit with the grandparents will be a good one," he added. "Some day I hope you'll tell me how it goes."

Eve's eyes began to burn. "I'd like that."

Charlie extended his hand and she took it. They shook. She didn't want to let go but quickly did.

"Take care," Charlie said.

Eve managed to whisper, "You too."

He took a step away and then turned back. "Shani gave you my number, right?"

She swallowed hard.

"You could call," he said. "Sometime. And tell me how things go tomorrow. I promise not to be anything more than friendly if you do." He smiled, a little wryly.

She nodded, knowing she wouldn't call. He turned and strolled back down the lane. She waited until he disappeared in the dark and then, finally, continued up the drive. "So this is how it ends," she whispered. "Before it ever started."

It was for the best. Monika was right. Eve's behavior had brought her mother great pain. It probably had contributed to her illness. Eve could never make up for what she'd done, but she'd do the right thing now. Her mother had adored Gideon Byler. And Eve did too. In time, she was sure she'd come to love him.

Vowing to never marry an Amish man had been a foolish promise.

The next afternoon, Eve poured herself and Abra's mother cups of hot tea as she listened to Rose chatting away with her grandmother. Leona, who held Trudy on her lap, didn't wear a Kapp anymore, but her salt-and-pepper hair was still pulled back in bun. She wore a print dress and a white apron.

The older children had gone outside to do the chores with their grandfather. When they returned it would be nearly time to head for home.

"I like school, most of the time," Rose said. "Aenti helps me with my letters and numbers. She said I'm getting really good."

The visit had gone well, and Eve knew it would be hard for the children to leave. She guessed they felt the safest at Leona and Eli's house. It was the last place they'd been with their mother when she'd been strong enough to help care for them.

When Abra was eight months along with Trudy, she'd had a C-section and surgery to remove the tumor at the same time. Afterward she insisted on staying with her parents to recover, with all the children. A month later she started chemotherapy. Every morning Eli would drive the children to school and then come back and take Abra, along with the baby, to her treatments. Eve would go along too, to care for Trudy.

Tim stayed away during that time. He'd been angry with Abra for delaying the treatments until after Trudy was born. Then he'd been angry with her for going to her parents' home. And he'd been angry with Eve for going with her.

Looking back, they all should have stayed at Leona and Eli's longer, but after it was evident the treatments weren't working, Abra felt her place was with Tim. Abra hadn't loved Tim when she first married him—but she said she grew to love him. Eve still couldn't fathom how or why. Abra could stand up to him like no one else, but she honored him and respected him.

He was ill equipped to handle her quick decline though, and he wouldn't let Leona stay with them. Abra's parents had left the church—he wasn't going to allow them in his home.

Instead Eve struggled to care for Abra, newborn Trudy, the other children, and Tim.

Her hand shook as she put Leona's cup down, just thinking about how trying that time had been.

"Aenti's going to be leaving us soon," Rose said to her Mammi.

"Oh?" Leona asked.

"But we don't know who she'll decide to marry —Gideon or Charlie," the little girl said. "I'm hoping for Charlie."

Eve shook her head at the child, and Rose averted her eyes, a smile spreading across her face.

"Who's Charlie?" Leona asked as she shifted Trudy away from the table and her hot cup of tea.

Eve shook her head. "No one."

"He's Englisch," Rose said.

"Eve." Leona's eyes were filled with kindness instead of disdain. "What's going on?"

"Nothing. He's a friend of our neighbors—that's all." The children had told their grandparents all about Zane and Shani and Joel and his wheelchair.

"And Gideon is Bishop Byler, right?"

Eve nodded.

"Lila said the bishop would take Aenti away from us," Rose said.

"Oh?" Leona leaned toward Eve, her eyes bright. "Unless Charlie takes you first?"

Eve shook her head, her face growing warm. "It isn't like that—really."

"But the bishop is serious?" Leona asked.

Eve inhaled. Leona would be a safe person to talk with, safer than Monika or Shani.

"Rose," Leona said, "would you go out and check on the others? Tell them to come into the house so we can have a snack together before it's time for all of you to leave."

Rose frowned.

Leona spoke softly, saying, "I made peanut butter and chocolate bars."

Rose clapped her hands together and scooted off her chair, heading to the back door for her cape.

"Be quick," Leona called out.

"I will!" Rose waved as she hurried out the door.

Leona turned back to Eve. "I ran into Monika at the store the other day." Leona wasn't a gossip by any means, but she did seem to be accomplished at gathering information. "She said things were pretty serious between you and the bishop."

"You know how it is," Eve said. "We've hardly talked but already there seems to be the expectation . . ."

"Tim must be happy about it."

Eve nodded. It was the first time Tim had been mentioned all afternoon. "He's working for Gideon again."

"Good," Leona said. "Tell me, though, how do you feel about the bishop?"

Eve sat up straight. "He's very kind. And gentle." Her face grew warm. "Very different from my Dat."

Leona nodded.

"I respect him." Eve paused and then blinked. She tried to swallow back the tears, but they flooded her eyes.

Leona spoke softly. "Do you love him?"

Eve shrugged but then shook her head.

"Oh, sweetie," Leona said, tilting her head, saying the words in the exact same tone she'd used with Abra over the years. "How about this Charlie? Do you love him?" She scooted her chair closer, still holding Trudy, and wrapped her arm around Eve.

Eve dabbed at her eyes and whispered, "I don't know."

"Is he a believer?"

Believer wasn't a term most Plain people used, but it was one Leona did. "Jah," Eve said. "And he's a *gut* person. Much better than I am."

"That isn't true," Leona said. "We're all in need of salvation, every one of us."

Eve nodded. She knew that.

Leona continued, "Remember what Paul wrote in Romans: 'There is therefore now no condemnation to them which are in Christ Jesus.' And in Ephesians, he wrote, 'For by grace are ye saved through faith; and that not of yourselves: it is the gift of God.' "

Eve knew that Leona could quote Scripture all day long, all out of love, never out of judgment.

The older woman leaned closer. "You have cared for others for so long, Eve. God has good things for you too."

"Jah, caring for the children is very *gut*. I'm blessed."

Leona sighed. "You are, but this should be temporary. Not for the rest of your life. Tim is more capable than you think."

Eve wasn't sure why Leona would think that but she stayed quiet.

"I need to say this to you, even if it's unsettling,"

Leona said, her voice a little ragged. "And it's nothing against Tim. Although as you know, we did have our concerns."

"I know," Eve said. "I did too." She'd begged Abra not to marry her brother.

"It's more against the bishop at the time. He put so much pressure on her to marry—anyone, really. We didn't think it was right, not at all. And it was one of the reasons we ended up leaving the church."

Eve nodded.

"Don't give in to manipulations," Leona said. "You are a grown woman. No one else should make a life-changing decision for you." She met Eve's gaze. "You must make your own choices—out of love, not fear."

Eve inhaled sharply. If only it were that easy.

"May I pray for you?" Leona finally asked.

With all of her heart, Eve wanted to decline. She didn't deserve Leona's prayers.

But she couldn't tell the sweetest woman she knew that she felt so unworthy. "Okay" was all she could manage.

"Dear Lord," Leona prayed, "please guide Eve. Please show her your will. . . ."

A sob welled up inside of Eve. The children's needs had to come first. She couldn't risk being shunned and having Tim treat her the way he did Leona and Eli. She'd never see the children. She had to honor her promise to Abra.

"We ask these things in Jesus' name," Leona prayed. "Amen."

The woman reached over and squeezed Eve's arm. "Abra would want you to marry the man you love—whether he's Englisch or Amish."

Eve shook her head. She was pretty sure Abra would want her to marry Gideon.

Leona stood and, with Trudy still in her arms, hugged Eve just as the children crashed through the kitchen door.

At bedtime, as Eve took off her apron, she felt for the slip of paper in the pocket. She'd been transferring it from her dirty apron to her clean apron each day since Shani gave it to her.

She read Charlie's number again, but the truth was she had it memorized. It was nine fifteen. He'd be awake. Maybe out with his old girlfriend. Or perhaps at his house, alone.

He'd said he would pray that the visit would go well. He'd asked her to phone him. She'd been clear about their relationship. Could it hurt to call?

Phoning Charlie just to tell him the afternoon had gone well wouldn't hurt anything. He probably wouldn't be coming back to Lancaster anytime soon. She might not ever see him again. A last conversation would give her the closure she needed to turn her thoughts toward Gideon.

She wouldn't tell Charlie she'd broken down in tears in front of Leona—or about Leona's advice to marry for love. That wasn't anything he needed to know. She'd simply give him an update and then tell him good-bye, for good.

She slipped the piece of paper back into the pocket and retied her apron. She glanced at Trudy again. She slept on her back, her arms over her head, settled into a deep sleep.

Eve put her nightgown on her bed and turned off the lamp. Then she stepped into the hall and listened. A rattle came from down the hall—Tim was snoring. She listened a little longer. The older children must have all been asleep too.

She tiptoed down the hall, through the living room, and into the kitchen, slipping her feet into her boots and then grabbing her cape and the flashlight. She carefully opened the door and just as carefully shut it behind her, slinging her cape over her shoulders.

A light drizzle fell, and the dark cloudy sky hid the stars and moon. Eve hurried along, not turning the flashlight on until she reached the barn. One of the horses snickered as she entered, and a starling fluttered above her head. She flicked on the flashlight and headed toward the room where Tim kept his files for the dairy business. On his desk was the phone.

Picking up the receiver, she took a raggedy breath, trying to calm herself. Her fingers fell to the numbers but didn't move. Finally she dialed, slowly.

After the first ring, her heart began to race. After the third, she contemplated hanging up. After the fifth she was relieved. God was protecting her against her own foolish decision. But as she moved the phone away from her ear, someone came on the line.

"Hello?"

It was Charlie.

"Hallo," she said.

"Eve?"

"Jah, it's me."

"Is everything all right?"

She stepped to the side of the desk and leaned against the wall, calmed by the sound of his voice. "Jah, everything's fine. I just called to say thank you for praying for our visit with Abra's parents. It went well."

"I'm so glad." The relief in Charlie's voice was noticeable. "Let me call you back," he said. "So the call isn't on your dime." She knew he meant Tim's. She hadn't thought about him seeing the call on his bill. At least that would be a month away.

She hung up and Charlie called back. She briefly described the visit—Rose talking about school, the older children helping their grandfather, Leona holding Trudy. Then she said, "I wanted to tell you about the children because you said you'd pray, but I also called to tell you good-bye."

"Good-bye?"

"Jah, you won't be coming down as much anymore, right?"

He didn't answer.

"And even if you did, it's not a good idea for us to even be friendly with each other." Her heart began to race. "This is the last time we should talk." She pressed the heel of her hand against her forehead.

"In that case," he said, "couldn't we talk a little longer?"

She exhaled. Charlie kept on talking. About the sheep. He said the ewe was fine—Zane had called that afternoon. He talked about his job as an EMT and how much he enjoyed caring for people. He asked what jobs she'd had in the past.

She gave in and told him at one time she'd wanted to be a teacher. Then she found herself telling him about Abra and how they'd met their first day of school and had been friends since they were younger than Rose.

Her voice choked up a little, and Charlie said, "I'm sorry."

Eve swallowed hard. "I should let you go."

"I should let *you* go," he said. There was an awkward moment of silence when she wondered if she should simply say good-bye and hang up, but then Charlie cleared his throat. "Could we talk tomorrow?" he asked. "You can call when it's convenient for you and then hang up. I'll call back."

She didn't answer.

"I understand if it won't work," he said quickly. "Or if you change your mind."

"What more would we talk about?"

He was silent for a moment. "Our work. The children. Even about Gideon, if you'd like."

She didn't want to talk about Gideon.

"I can give it a try," she finally said, her heart racing again.

"Tomorrow, then," he said.

"Jah," she answered.

On the way back to the house, the clouds parted, showing the quarter moon above the bare maple trees on the other side of the field. Eve hummed as she hurried along, her step quick. She wouldn't think of what the ramifications of the call might be. Not now. Charlie was her friend. Like her friendships with Monika and Shani and Leona. That was all.

‌ၷ‌ 22

Wednesday after work, as Shani drove her van down the lane, she peered into the field. Tim's getting a job at the lumberyard was the best thing to happen to her son. It seemed Tim wasn't home most afternoons. Pretty much every day after school Zane played with the Lehman children for an hour, and when it was time for them to go do their chores, he went home to take care of the sheep and the chickens.

It was Shani's last day shift. She'd asked for the next day, Veterans Day, off and then she'd start working swing shift on Friday. She'd be able to take three months off when the baby came. Hopefully, after that, Joel's leg would be healed and he'd be able to—with Zane's help—care for the baby.

She reached the house without seeing any of the children, but as she climbed out of the van, Rose stepped out onto the porch. The little girl ran down the stairs and gave her a hug. "We were just using the bathroom," she said, her face red and cheeks chapped.

The older kids followed her, all except Simon with an apple in their hands. Zane tossed one to Rose. No wonder Shani couldn't keep any food in the house. Simon stopped in the middle of the porch, turned back to the house, and said in his stilted way, "You can tell me more about the war tomorrow."

Joel sat in the open doorway. "See you then."

Shani cringed. Joel hardly spoke about the war at all. Why in the world would he talk with Simon about it?

"It's time for chores," Shani said to Zane.

He hurried down the steps. "Can't we head back to the creek for a while?"

She shook her head, pulling her jacket over her bulging belly. The late afternoon had grown chilly. "Walk the kids home—then come right back and put the sheep in."

Simon bolted toward the field. Daniel shouted, "Last one home is a rotten *oy*." Lila took after her brothers. Rose started running but dropped her apple. Zane scooped it up for her as Shani headed up the steps into the house.

The lights in the living room and the TV were off, but the kitchen light was on. "In here," Joel called out. He was moving faster and faster in his chair.

Shani found him with the dishwasher open and one hand clasping knives, forks, and spoons. "You're home early," he said.

"A little bit. We got through report faster than usual."

With his free hand, he turned the wheel of his chair around to the drawer.

"Zane should've unloaded the dishwasher," Shani said. "Before he went to school."

"He was running a little late." Joel sorted the silverware. "One of the chickens got out. He had to sprint all the way to the bus stop as it was."

"Sorry the kids all traipsed through here." Shani put her purse on the table and then started stacking the clean plates.

He shrugged. "It breaks up the monotony."

"Do they come in often?" Shani asked.

"A couple of times an afternoon."

That was pretty often, considering they only played together for an hour.

"Do we have a supper plan?" Joel asked.

"Oh, it's *supper* now?" she teased. They'd always called it *dinner* before.

"Jah," he answered, "the neighbors are rubbing off on me."

"How about grilled cheese sandwiches and tomato soup?" She put the plates in the cupboard.

"Too bad Eve's cooking isn't rubbing off on you," Joel teased.

She ran her hand through his hair. "What do you mean? That's practically a gourmet meal for me."

He reached for her hand and squeezed it.

"So what were you telling Simon about the war?"

Joel let go of her hand. "Not much. Just answering his questions."

"Like?"

"How old I was when I joined the Army. Have I ever shot anyone." He shook his head. "Just the basics."

Shani groaned.

"Don't worry. He won't say anything to Tim."

Shani wasn't so sure. "Maybe you could change the subject next time."

Joel shrugged. "I'm just trying to be honest. It's not like anything I say would encourage him."

She wasn't so sure about that either.

After Joel finished putting away the silverware and the plastic bowls in the bottom cupboard, he drifted back to the living room and the TV, turning the volume up too high.

As darkness began to fall, she looked out the window for Zane. She headed out the back door to check if he was in the barn. The sheep were still grazing in the side field.

"Zane?" she called out.

The ewes lifted their heads and then startled as Tim shouted, "Daniel!" He sounded furious.

"Jah, Dat!"

"Hurry!" It was Lila's voice.

Simon hooted. The sheep ran toward the fence.

Shani hurried to the edge of the field. In the dim light, she could make out Tim's shape marching down the field. He looked like Goliath.

Daniel and Simon walked ahead, followed by Lila, who held Rose's hand. Zane waited in the trees along the creek.

"Daniel, you're neglecting your responsibilities," Tim shouted.

Daniel didn't reply but started to run. Simon kept moving at a slower pace.

Shani watched as Daniel headed straight toward the direction of the barn, followed by Simon, and the girls veered off toward the house, all of them bypassing their Dat without saying anything more. He caught up with Simon, said something, and then put his arm around the boy's shoulder as they continued on toward the barn.

"Come on," Shani called out to Zane.

"He got home early," Zane said.

"It's nightfall." Shani put her arm around him, brushing her hand against his cold face as she did. "You need to keep better track of time."

He nodded. "We were finishing up our fort."

"Do your chores. Hurry."

He grinned. "I will."

He'd always been a content child, but she didn't think he'd ever been this happy. He adored the Lehman children, all of them. And caring for the animals had brought out a tenderness she didn't know he had. With all of their moving, they'd never even had a cat or dog before.

When she stepped back into the kitchen, Joel called for her.

"I'm here," she said, hurrying into the living room.

He sat in the dark, the TV off. "Where'd you go?"

"Just out to check on Zane. He's doing his chores." She headed for the floor lamp and turned it on.

Joel was pale.

"Are you feeling all right?"

He nodded. He didn't like dusk. And he often grew anxious if she was late or he didn't know exactly where she was.

"Do you want to go to one of the American Legions tomorrow?" She'd done a search at work, because the Internet at the house still wasn't working, and she'd found one close by.

Joel shook his head.

"How about breakfast out tomorrow? Zane doesn't have school."

He shook his head again. "I don't like you swinging my chair in and out of the van."

"Zane can do it."

Joel shook his head again, his eyes heavy. She put her arms around him. "Come in the kitchen with me while I fix our gourmet dinner."

He shook his head a third time but didn't say anything. Shani let go of him and walked away, thinking of Joel with his gun in his lap back in Philly.

She hoped she wouldn't be finding him sitting in the living room with a gun in his hand again. She wasn't sure she could bear it.

Veterans Day morning got off to a lazy start with a late breakfast of waffles. Zane couldn't believe

307

the Amish children had school. "Why don't they get it off?" he asked.

Joel sighed.

"It's a private school," Shani said, prying another waffle from the iron. The first one wasn't done enough but this one was nice and crispy— probably too crispy. "They don't have the same holidays."

"And they don't honor veterans," Joel added. "They're pacifists. They don't believe in war."

"Actually," Shani said, "they're nonresistant. It's not just that they won't fight, they refuse to retaliate or even defend themselves." She'd researched it on her break at work.

"Simon's not nonresistant when we're playing Roman soldiers." Zane grinned.

"You play Roman soldiers?" Shani almost dropped the fork in her hand.

"In the field. After school."

"Zane . . ." Shani glanced at Joel and then back at her son. "You need to play something else. Like the Oregon Trail—"

Joel laughed.

"Or . . ."

"How about Manifest Destiny? Or American Colonialism?" Joel asked. "Or, I know, the Reformation!"

"Stop it," Shani said. "Because, in fact, lots of Anabaptists were murdered during the Reformation because they wouldn't fight back." She'd found some horrendous stories during her Internet search. "That's how they ended up here."

"Yeah, because there are those of us who have— through the centuries—fought for the religious freedom of our neighbors." Joel wheeled away from the table. "I'm glad the Amish can be so idealistic, while the rest of us are forced to live in reality."

Shani didn't reply.

"Keep playing Roman soldiers," Joel called over his shoulder to Zane as he wheeled away from them. "Or choose something else. Just know, no matter what, it will involve conflict. And no matter how hard you try, you'll never really win." He rolled through the door. "That's the way life is and has always been."

Zane gave Shani a confused look.

She didn't address it, but instead said, "Tim would be really upset if he knew his children were pretending to be soldiers."

"But we chose the Romans because there weren't any guns back then. Just spears and bows and arrows. Well . . . and daggers. And catapults."

Shani shivered. "Can't you play farmer?"

Zane shook his head. "They are farmers. What fun would that be?"

"How about explorers?"

Joel called out from the living room, "Explorers without conflict? Didn't happen. Life without conflict? Impossible. Speaking of—don't you

309

think the neighbors' dairy smells worse than usual?"

Shani ignored him, and then was grateful when the phone rang. Zane popped up to answer it. Clearly it was for him. After a few seconds he said, "I'll ask and call you back. But I'd have to be home by three." He grabbed a pen and scribbled something on the pad of paper on the counter and then hung up.

Turning toward Shani, Zane said, "Anthony wants me to come over and hang out."

Hang out. Funny that he used the word *play* when he was talking about the Lehman children.

"Who's Anthony?"

"One of the bus-stop kids."

"When?"

"Anytime. I just told him I had to be home by three."

"Is his mother home?"

"I think so . . ."

"What would you be doing?"

"Basketball. Football. Video games."

"What kind of video games?"

"Not bad ones—I promise."

"Let him go," Joel called out from the living room. "The kid needs to have some normal friends."

Shani lowered her voice. "Do you want to go?"

He shrugged. "It's not like I'm doing anything around here today."

●●●

Shani drove Zane to Anthony's house and walked with him to the front door. Anthony's mother was home. So were his three younger brothers and his older sister—who turned out to be the eighth-grade girl at the bus stop who was friendly to Zane.

The mom seemed a little overwhelmed but nice. "As long as it's not raining, they'll be playing outside," she said with a sigh. "Why they have a day off in the middle of the week is beyond me."

Shani almost launched into an explanation about the importance of remembering veterans and their sacrifices but bit her tongue. She wished she'd gotten one of those red poppies to wear on her jacket.

Having a family day turned into a nap on the couch and then leftover tomato soup and another grilled cheese sandwich with Joel. She thanked Joel for his service, but he just shook his head.

When it was time to go get Zane, she asked Joel if he wanted to ride along.

He gave her a wilting look.

"Your chair isn't that heavy."

"That's all we need—for you to hurt your back or make the baby come early."

When she arrived to pick up Zane none of the kids were outside. And it wasn't raining. She knocked on the door several times before Anthony's sister finally answered. "They're back in the den," she said. "I'll go get them."

Shani followed her. "Where's your mom?" she asked the girl.

"Probably in the laundry room."

When they reached the den, Zane glanced up from where he sat on the couch next to Anthony, who was playing a game. The girl plopped down in an easy chair. Shani's eyes fell to the TV. "What are you playing?"

Zane stood. "Let's go."

"Zane . . ."

"Thanks for having me," he said to Anthony, who grunted.

"Anytime," the girl answered.

"Tell your mom thanks," Zane added, heading toward the doorway.

Anthony waved and said, "See you tomorrow."

Neither of the kids walked them down the hall to the door. As they let themselves out, Shani heard a child cry from upstairs.

"Did you have fun?" Shani asked as they climbed into the van.

"Not really," Zane answered.

"What game was Anthony playing?"

"One you wouldn't like."

"Zane . . ."

"I didn't play it, okay?" He was silent the rest of the way but brightened up when he peered down the Lehmans' driveway. "Stop!"

Shani did.

"They're home," Zane said, opening the door.

As he jumped out, he said, "We'll be down for a snack in a few minutes."

By the time she'd parked the van and started toward the house, Simon and Daniel came running through the hedge of the field. After a quick hello they scampered up the steps to the porch, where they stopped.

But then Joel yelled, "Come on in."

The boys glanced at her for permission. "Go ahead," she answered.

She started toward the field. Zane and the girls couldn't be far behind. They weren't. "How's Eve doing?" Shani asked Lila as they approached.

"She's fine."

"What's she up to?"

"She said she had some phone calls to make—she took Trudy to the barn."

"Oh." Shani had thought a cup of coffee with Eve sounded good, but she didn't want to interrupt her calls. She followed the children to the house but stayed out of the kitchen. They didn't need her.

Joel had the TV off and wheeled his chair toward her when she entered. "Charlie called."

"Oh?"

"You know, happy Veterans Day and all that . . . Misht."

Shani shook her head. "I see Zane's been giving you language lessons."

Joel smirked. "I'm a good student."

313

She hung up her purse. "Did Charlie say anything besides that?"

"He asked if he could come down on Friday."

"Really?" Shani thought he'd planned to spend the weekend back home.

"I told him yes. He wants to chop more wood."

Maybe Charlie would lift Joel's spirits. "Did he say anything else?"

"Nope. He said he'd phone back later. He had a call coming in."

Shani hung up her coat. It was probably a call from Nikki, but if he was coming back this weekend that meant he wasn't pining after her. Otherwise Shani was sure he'd stay in Philly.

Friday on her way to work, Shani stopped by the Lehmans' place. The buggy was gone. She hoped Tim was off somewhere and not Eve. As she hurried up the back steps, the door swung open and there stood Eve with Trudy on her hip. Both were smiling. The baby reached for Shani.

"You two look so happy," she said as Trudy fell into her arms. She should have offered to watch the baby the day before, to cheer up Joel.

"Want a cup of coffee?" Eve asked.

"I'd love one," Shani answered. "But I'm on my way into work." She made a face at Trudy, and the baby giggled as she followed Eve into the kitchen. "It seems like the kids have a system worked out as far as getting a snack at our house and then getting home on time."

"They get a snack at your house?"

Shani nodded. "It's fine. I stocked up on fruit and crackers and cheese sticks. Joel seems to like having them come in." Not that he would admit it.

Eve crossed her arms.

"He turns the TV off," Shani added. "But I wanted to let you know that the kids have been playing Romans."

"Romans?"

Shani nodded. "As in soldiers."

"Oh." Her eyebrows shot up. "I see."

"I told Zane to choose something else, but I wanted you to know. In case you wanted to . . ." Shani stopped.

Eve was smiling. Her friend chuckled and then said, "I remember playing World War II when I was little, with Tim. He was usually a fighter pilot, and I'd pretend to jump out of his plane and storm the creek bed."

"You're kidding."

"No. Of course he'd never fess up to it now. And he wouldn't be happy about the Roman soldier thing—he'd let it go with Simon but not with Daniel."

Shani cocked her head. "Why's that?"

Eve blushed. "It's a fault of his. Gideon has talked with him about it. In fact, Gideon warned him not to favor Simon." She sighed. "I wish he'd change. I know other Dats who don't show any favoritism to their biological kids and—"

"What?" Shani asked.

"Favoritism?"

"No. The biological stuff. Tim's not Daniel's biological father?"

Eve shook her head. "Nor Lila's, of course."

Shani placed her hand on the side of her belly. The twins had blond hair, but so did Trudy. "When did Tim marry Abra?"

"When Daniel and Lila were fourteen months old."

"Wow."

Eve wrinkled her nose. "It's not a secret. The kids know—although no one really talks about it."

"Who's their biological father?"

Eve's eyebrows shot up. "Well, we don't talk about that at all. He left the area before Abra knew she was pregnant." Eve seemed a little uncomfortable. "And then she didn't want him to know. She was afraid he or his family might try to get custody, or something like that." Eve blushed even more. "She didn't have much of a relationship with him . . ."

"So I take it the father was Englisch."

"Jah," Eve said.

"Wow." Shani's hand went to her throat. "No wonder Tim doesn't want Englischers influencing his kids."

Eve nodded. "I've probably said too much."

"Don't worry," Shani said. "I won't say anything to Zane or anything like that. It's not our business." She didn't want to offend Tim—not for any reason, but especially not when he'd been more tolerant of Zane in the last couple of weeks.

"Denki." Eve raised her eyebrows again. "And I'll talk with the kids about playing Roman soldiers."

"Thanks," Shani said. She was grateful for the information about the twins. It made her want to be a friend to the children all the more.

Eve nodded.

Shani smiled. "How's the bishop?"

Eve shrugged. "I haven't seen him all week."

"Oh." She searched Eve's face, but she wasn't giving anything away. "But you'll see him this weekend?"

"Maybe," Eve said.

"How's Tim's job going?"

"Good. One of Gideon's staff quit, so Tim's working five days a week now. Tuesday through Saturday."

Shani suppressed a smile. That was why Eve seemed so much more relaxed.

Traffic going into Lancaster was slower than usual, putting Shani a little behind. And finding a parking place during the middle of the day was harder than she expected. By the time she rushed onto the pediatric ward she was nearly late for the shift change. The day-shift charge nurse took it

317

easy on her, waiting to give Shani her assignments until last.

The first was a thirteen-year-old boy who'd had an appendectomy that morning. That would be pretty straightforward. The second was an eight-year-old girl with brain cancer. That would be heartbreaking. The third was a baby girl, just six months old, with pneumonia.

"She and her mom were visiting the grandparents—and the little girl fell ill. This is the second time she's had pneumonia this fall, so they're running tests. She won't be back in the room for a couple of hours."

Shani's name was already on the whiteboard, with the patients listed below it. All the other nurses had four or five patients. The charge nurse was being nice to let her ease into it. Not that she couldn't handle the work—she'd been working in pediatrics for four years—but it always took a while to get used to where everything was on a new ward and how things were done.

After she'd checked in with the older children, she poked her head into the baby's room, just in case they'd made it back from the tests. It was empty.

Fifteen minutes later, as she filled in the chart for the boy, a transportation specialist pushed a crib down the hall. Behind it walked a young woman with short strawberry blond hair, wearing jeans and a sweatshirt, and a middle-aged couple.

The older woman wore a dress and a cap much like the Amish did, except the material was a print, not solid. And the cap was rounded, not heart shaped.

Shani finished her notes and started down to the room. When she rounded the corner, she almost bumped into the young woman. She stood facing the couple, saying, "You should go home and get some rest. I'll call you if anything changes."

"Do you want us to come up this evening?" the man asked.

The young woman shook her head. "Come back in the morning. I promise I'll call if I need you sooner."

Shani slipped by as the three hugged. "Thank you for everything," the young woman said. "I don't know what I'd do without you."

Shani stole a last look. The older woman was dabbing at her eyes. The younger woman hugged her again. "She'll be all right. She's a strong little girl."

"You've been through so much," the older woman said. "Too much."

"I'm okay," the younger woman said. "As long as she's going to be all right, I will be too."

Shani had forgotten the baby's name, so she checked the chart. *Samantha Johnson.* The little one was asleep.

Shani pulled her stethoscope from her shoulders, but a sound at the door distracted her. The young woman leaned against the doorframe, her hands to her face.

"Are you all right?" Shani asked.

The woman nodded, but it was clear she was crying.

Shani stepped to her and put her arm around her. "I'm Shani. Samantha's nurse for the evening."

"I'm Karina," the woman said through her hands. "Samantha's mama."

Shani wondered why the young woman had her parents leave, but she didn't ask. If there was one thing she'd learned in her years of nursing it was, if there were problems in a family, they were bound to come out under the stress of a hospitalization.

Shani stepped toward the baby, who was under an oxygen tent in the crib. The woman followed. "You're visiting in Lancaster, right?"

"Yes." Karina dropped her hands away, revealing a tear-streaked face, and stepped to the end of the crib. "We're from Philly. Visiting my in-laws."

"Oh," Shani said. They weren't her parents.

Karina continued. "Samantha's grandparents moved here from Illinois, to be closer to us. They didn't want to live in a big city, though. So they chose Lancaster."

Shani nodded, wondering where Samantha's father was. "So Samantha's had pneumonia before?"

Karina nodded. "She's been sickly since she was

320

born—seven weeks early, but the pneumonia was a new thing. She recovered, and her pediatrician said it was fine for us to come down for a visit. He thought it would do both of us good."

Shani stood with the earpieces of her stethoscope in her hands. "What about Samantha's father? Where is he?"

Karina's eyes filled with tears again.

"I'm sorry," Shani said.

"No. It's okay. He was killed, last May. In Iraq."

Shani whispered, "Samuel Johnson?" Her knees grew weak and her mouth dry. "The eleventh of May?"

Karina's face contorted with what looked like pain. "How do you know that?"

Shani put her hand her chest. "My husband is Joel Beck. He was injured that day too."

"Samuel's sergeant?"

Shani nodded.

Karina swiped at her eyes. "How is he?"

Shani hesitated and then said, "He's recovering."

"I hear from Charlie McCall every once in a while," Karina said. "He calls to check up on us."

Shani's heart contracted. If only Joel had called her as well. "Charlie's coming down tonight. Could I tell him you're here?"

Karina nodded. "I'd like that."

Shani reached for her hand. She hadn't gone to Samuel's funeral, and of course Joel hadn't either. They'd both been in Germany. When they got back from Texas, she'd asked Joel a couple of times if he wanted to visit Samuel's wife and see the baby, but he'd said no, without any more of an explanation.

"I'm so sorry," Shani said. For so many things.

"I know," Karina said. "I got the card Joel sent. That meant a lot. And Charlie's told me about Joel. . . . I know it hasn't been easy." She brushed a strand of hair behind her ear. Shani wondered if she was as young as she seemed.

Shani checked on Samantha, along with Karina, as much as she could through the evening, and insisted Karina take a break and go down to the cafeteria to eat a proper meal. "You're nursing," Shani said. "You have to take care of yourself."

When she came in at the end of the shift, Karina was in the recliner with a blanket covering her. "Tell Joel hello," Karina said. "We never met, but Samuel spoke highly of him. I'd like to meet him someday."

"I'll tell him," Shani said. "He's back in his wheelchair—and not getting out much."

"I'm sorry," Karina said.

Shani shook her head and tried to say it was nothing compared to what Karina had been through but choked on the words.

Karina's eyes were full of kindness. "When is your baby due?"

"The end of January," Shani answered. "He's a furlough baby." As soon as she said it, she wished she hadn't. Karina probably could have done the math on her own.

"I'd like to keep in touch," Shani said, "to see you and Samantha again sometime."

"She'll be okay, right?"

Shani nodded. "Depending on the test results, you should be headed home tomorrow or Sunday. You'll want to stay with your in-laws for a few days. Do you have a good relationship with them?"

Karina nodded. "They weren't happy when Samuel and I married. They're . . . pretty conservative. Religious, you know?"

Shani nodded.

"I didn't grow up that way. And Samuel is— was." Karina took a deep breath.

"You don't need to go on," Shani said.

Karina shook her head. "I'm okay," she said. "He was their only child. We met our first year of college and got married young—at twenty. When he joined the Army, it was too much for them. And they didn't see him . . . us much."

She made eye contact with Shani. "But they've been good to me since . . . They'd do anything to help. Samantha is all they have left."

Shani gave the young woman a hug, thankful for the support she had. "I'll stay in touch."

"Thank you," Karina said. "I'd like that."

As Shani drove home, she contemplated telling Joel that little Samantha was on her ward. If she did tell him, he would worry Samuel's daughter might die as well. But how could she not? She'd ask Charlie what she should do. Hopefully he'd still be awake.

The night had turned clear and cold. She parked on the other side of Charlie's truck and hurried through the front door. The TV was on but no other light. She squinted to see if anyone was up. Zane was sprawled out on the couch, and Joel dozed in his chair. She hung up her coat and purse, covered Zane with a blanket, and then touched Joel's shoulder.

He turned his head toward her. "You're home."

She placed both hands on the handles of his chair. "Is Charlie already in bed?"

Joel yawned as he shook his head. "He's out for a walk."

"This late?"

Joel nodded. "He said he needed some fresh air."

She pushed the chair toward the hallway. "What did you guys do today?"

His voice had an edge to it. "Charlie and Zane tossed a football around for a couple of hours."

"Seriously?"

"Yep. I watched them until it got too dark to see."

Shani hurt at the thought of Joel sitting in his chair at the window as he watched them play.

The next morning when Charlie came down the stairs, the blanket Zane had been under last night was on the floor, and there was no sign of the boy. He was probably out doing his chores.

Charlie yawned and started the coffee. He'd stayed up too late. The night had been so bright and clear he'd walked longer than he'd meant to, trying to clear his head. Talking with Eve on the phone was one thing but being so close to her, just down the lane, was another. He wanted nothing more than to see her in person. A part of him had hoped she'd sneak out last night and try to find him. He didn't feel good about the wish—but it was there.

He wasn't sure what had happened in the last week, but something had. They'd talked about everything over the phone. Their childhoods. Her Rumschpringe. Her Englisch boyfriend, Patrick. Abra.

"She wasn't wild, not like I was. I'm the one who should have been punished."

But then she'd said, *"Not that I see the twins as a punishment now. God's the one who chose to bless the world with Lila and Daniel. There'd be no giving them back."*

Charlie agreed. That was the way God worked.

He'd told her a little about what had happened

in Iraq—that Samuel had been killed and that Joel nearly had been.

He poured himself a cup of coffee and headed out the back door with it. The sheep were already turned out into the field, but the chickens were squawking as if they hadn't been fed. Charlie stepped to the edge and peered down the field. The grass glistened from the frost. In the morning light it appeared as if diamonds had fallen during the night.

Zane, Daniel, and Simon huddled at the end of the field. Then Eve appeared. The boys gathered around her. Tim must have left for the lumberyard already. Charlie started up the field.

Eve had on a faded blue dress, her cape, and a bandana instead of her white Kapp. Simon saw Charlie first and broke into a big smile followed by an enthusiastic wave. The rest turned toward him too. Eve smiled. Even at a distance he could make out her dimples.

Charlie's heart began to race. The boys started running toward him. Eve followed at a respectable pace.

"Are you done with your chores?" Charlie called out.

Daniel yelled that they were, but Zane said he still needed to feed the chickens and gather the eggs.

"We're going to help him," Simon said. It would take all of three minutes.

They passed Charlie and kept on running.

When Eve neared, Charlie feared for a moment that there would be an awkwardness between them. But once they met, she smiled, her dimples deep.

He longed to reach for her hand. "How are you?" he asked.

"*Gut.*" She stepped closer.

His heart raced. "What do you have planned for today?"

"Housework. Lila's going to help me scrub the floors. And wash the windows. We have church at our house in two weeks, the Sunday after Thanksgiving."

"Where will you have the service?"

"In the shed, but we won't start cleaning that out until next weekend."

"How about the meal?" He hadn't actually seen how it worked the day he went to Deacon King's house, but he could imagine how hard it was to feed that many people.

"In the house. We don't really have enough room—everyone will have to walk sideways." She smiled again. "I wish Gi—" She paused. "That we'd been given a time in the summer."

Was the pause to avoid saying Gideon's name?

Shani's voice interrupted them. "There you are!" she called out.

Charlie turned. Shani wore sweats and Joel's jacket. Eve and Charlie started toward her.

"Good morning!" Shani beamed, obviously delighted to see Eve. "I see your boys are helping Zane with his chores, as if he needs it."

Charlie trailed behind Eve, sorry to see their brief time alone come to an end.

"You'll never guess who I met last night," Shani said.

It took Charlie a moment to realize she was talking to him. "Who?"

"Karina Johnson. And Samantha."

Charlie couldn't comprehend what she was saying. They lived outside of Philly. "Where?"

"At the hospital. Samantha has pneumonia again. They'd been visiting Samuel's parents."

"Wow," was all Charlie could manage to say.

"She'd like to see you."

Eve gave Charlie a concerned look. Without thinking, he said, "Samuel's wife and baby."

"Oh." Eve's eyes filled with compassion.

If Shani thought their exchange odd, she didn't say anything. "They'll be at the hospital another day at least. The baby's oxygen is pretty low. I haven't told Joel yet." She turned toward Charlie. "Do you think I should?"

"It would be natural to tell him."

Shani shrugged. "Then why do I feel so unsettled? Why do I feel as if it's just going to make him worse?"

"It might make him feel bad," Charlie said. "But telling him later would make him angry."

"Not if he doesn't find out at all." Shani took a long drink of coffee.

It wasn't like her to be secretive. That was one of the things that Charlie had always admired about her—her honesty.

"Don't treat him like one of your patients," Charlie said. "He's a lot stronger than he seems."

She shook her head. "Sure, he's strong in some ways. But he's really fragile in others." She held her chin high.

Charlie softened. "We could tell him together."

"Thank you," Shani said. "That's what we'll do." Then she turned toward Eve. "Karina's in-laws are Mennonite . . . maybe. . . . Something like that. And they just moved to this area."

Charlie tilted his head.

"Karina seems so young," Shani said. "She could use a friend like you, Eve."

Charlie couldn't disagree with that, but Eve didn't have time to take care of anyone else.

"Maybe we could go up to see her," Shani said.

Charlie thought of all the housework Eve needed to do, but she surprised him by saying, "I'd like to meet Karina and her in-laws—I'll call Monika and see if we could drop the kids off at her house."

"Why don't I just stay with the kids," Charlie said. "Lila will help with Trudy."

"We can go while she's napping." Eve pushed up the sleeves of her dress. "The kids could all be over here." She nodded toward the Becks' house.

Charlie thought that was a good idea. Trudy could nap upstairs in the room Shani had set up for her baby.

"Should we go around eleven, then?" Shani asked.

"Jah, that will give me time to do my chores," Eve said, turning around and heading back up the field.

A few minutes later, while Joel drank his coffee, Shani told him about Samuel's baby.

He put his head in his hands.

"She's going to be okay," Charlie said. "Right, Shani?"

"Yes. She's getting good care. Karina's a great mom. She has a lot of support from Samuel's parents." She hesitated for a moment and then said, "They were at the hospital last night too."

Joel looked up. "What did they say?"

"I didn't realize who they were until after they left."

"Oh," he said.

He seemed surprised by the information but not overly upset.

"Do you want to go up to the hospital with Eve and Shani?" Charlie asked. "To see them?"

He shook his head. "You should go though."

"I'm going to watch the kids," Charlie said. "Trudy's going to nap over here."

"Go," Joel said. "I can be in charge. I'll keep the landline in my hands at all times."

Shani shook her head.

"We know how quick the paramedics can get here," Joel said. "Trudy will sleep the whole time, right? And Lila will be here. The kids can play board games inside. I promise I won't watch TV."

Shani shot a look at Charlie. He shrugged. It was the most responsibility Joel had been willing to take since the attack. They might as well let him step up and be in charge.

Shani insisted on driving her van. "That way Eve can sit up front with me," she said. Charlie would have liked to sit next to Eve, but he knew it was a foolish wish.

By the time they reached the hospital, the gray clouds had grown dark. "Looks like a storm is on the way," Eve said.

They found Karina in the baby's room, her in-laws with them. Shani introduced Eve as a friend and then Charlie as Samuel's Army buddy. Shani had been right—the in-laws were Mennonite. Not Old Order but fairly conservative.

Charlie listened in as Eve figured out that they went to the same church as Abra's parents.

"You know Leona and Eli?" the mother-in-law asked.

"Jah," Eve said. "I'm their grandchildren's Aenti. I was Abra's best friend."

The woman bit her lip and then said, "Leona mentioned their daughter. I know they understand our pain over Samuel."

Charlie tried to remember what Samuel had said about his parents. Not much. Just that they didn't want him to join the Army. Now it was clear why.

Samantha was under the oxygen tent—an IV hooked up to her hand and a finger probe to measure her oxygen and monitor her pulse. She'd grown some since the last time he'd seen her, but she was still really small.

"The doctor said she'll probably be able to go home tomorrow or at least by Monday, but we'll stay in Lancaster for a while," Karina said. "At least past Thanksgiving."

"Where are your folks?" Charlie asked her.

"Colorado," she answered. "We'll go out for Christmas, if Samantha is doing all right."

He remembered now that Samuel had met Karina when he was in college in Indiana.

Eve, Karina, and Shani talked softly while Charlie visited with the in-laws for a while. They'd sold their farm in Illinois and the father-in-law was now working at a nursery. "It's worth it," he said, looking at Samantha. "We already had quite a few friends here." They seemed like good people and Charlie was relieved Karina and Samantha had them in their lives.

He knew Karina had been a dental hygienist before she had the baby. He couldn't imagine her returning to work now and putting Samantha in daycare, not when she was so ill.

"Does Karina plan to stay in the Philly area?" Charlie asked her in-laws.

The mother-in-law gave her husband a furtive glance. "We're not sure," the man answered.

Charlie quickly said, "I didn't mean to pry."

"Oh, it's fine," the woman responded. "It's been hard for her to decide."

Charlie guessed Karina didn't plan to go back to Colorado—otherwise the Johnsons wouldn't have relocated.

After a half hour, Shani said they should go. After telling everyone good-bye, as they walked out into the hall, Charlie thanked Eve for accompanying them.

"I'm so glad I did," Eve answered. "I'll call Leona tonight so she knows to check in on the Johnsons."

"Do we have time to get some lunch?" Charlie asked.

Shani glanced at her watch. "I told Zane to make sandwiches—and a smoothie for Simon." She turned toward Eve. "How long will Trudy nap?"

"For another hour or so."

"A quick lunch in the cafeteria and . . . Uh-oh." Shani stopped. "I forgot to check my schedule. You guys go on ahead. I'll catch up with you."

There was a bench in the hallway ahead, before the entrance to the cafeteria. "We'll wait for you here," Charlie called out as Shani headed back toward the elevator. He turned to Eve. "If that's all right."

She smiled. "It's fine."

His hand brushed Eve's arm as they sat. "Sorry," he said, inching away. He longed to convey how much he'd enjoyed their phone calls, but he couldn't come up with the right words. Instead he kept quiet.

After an awkward silence, Eve asked, "What happened the night Samuel was killed?"

Her question caught him off guard.

She must have sensed his discomfort. "I'm sorry. I shouldn't have asked."

"No," he said. "Are you sure you want to hear it?"

"Positive," she answered, folding her hands in her lap.

"It was the eleventh of May," he said. "The day after Samuel's baby was born. We were headed back to base at dusk after checking on a faulty antenna. Joel had sent the first Humvee, and the gunner, from our unit on ahead because they were done with their work.

"Samuel should have been driving our Humvee, but Joel was at the wheel because Samuel was exhausted and fidgety and wired all at the same time. They both sat up front, and I sat in the back. As sunset fell, it cast a pale pink hue across the horizon, and Joel told Samuel it was in honor of his baby girl. Samuel and his wife were going to decide on a name, via Skype, the next morning.

"Then, just as dusk fell, a rocket-propelled grenade hit the engine, stopping the Humvee and hurling shrapnel through the windshield. I bailed out of the vehicle."

Charlie paused for a moment, and Eve leaned closer, as if to encourage him.

He continued. "I yanked open Samuel's door and checked his neck for a pulse. There was none." Charlie inhaled sharply. "It was obvious by—" He paused again. "There wasn't anything I could have done to save him."

He told her how he ran around to Joel's door, managed to get it open, and put his fingers to Joel's neck. Relief flooded through him. He had to get Joel out of the Humvee.

He wrapped his arms around Joel's chest and yanked him out as bullets zoomed by, most hitting the Humvee. Darkness was falling quickly. It was his only hope to get Joel to safety.

He dragged him across the road and behind the closest palm tree. Joel was unconscious, and the shrapnel had torn up his leg. It was bleeding badly. Charlie ripped open Joel's medical kit and yanked out the tourniquet, putting it on as fast as he could. Then he threw Joel over his shoulder and ran up the bank, taking cover behind another tree, hoping there were no snipers behind them.

A big boom shook the ground. Charlie threw

himself on top of Joel and raised his head, holding onto his helmet. A second rocket-propelled grenade hit the Humvee, blowing it apart. Then a third. That's when the shrapnel hit Charlie's arm.

He radioed for help and then tried to rouse his friend. Joel slipped in and out of consciousness. Charlie prayed over him, in a whisper. He recited the Lord's Prayer in German, the way his grandfather had taught him. He tried not to think of Samuel, his wife, or new baby. Or Shani and Zane.

It seemed to take forever until a helicopter landed.

"God bless the medivacs who risk their lives over and over," Charlie said to Eve. "Because of them, Joel got out in time."

"I'm so sorry," she said.

"Thanks," Charlie said, "but I was the lucky one."

She touched his arm as she asked, "How bad was your injury?"

"Not bad. I was only in the hospital a few hours. Got it cleaned out and stitched up. I was back in the field in a few days." Charlie had been looking straight ahead as he told his tale, but he turned toward her now. "You're the only civilian I've told this to," he said.

"Why?"

His eyes grew moist. "It's not easy to talk about. I'm not sure most people would understand—I came through it fine. But it's still the hardest thing I've ever gone through."

"Of course," Eve said, tightening her grip.

His heart lurched. Sitting next to Eve on the bench felt too close, too intimate. "Let's wait for Shani in the cafeteria," he said, standing. They could sit across the table from each other instead of side by side.

Although she had a confused expression on her face, she followed.

Charlie saw Gideon first, coming around the corner. He grabbed Eve's arm to keep her from crashing into the man, pulling her closer to him, sending a shiver down his spine. She looked back up at him with her beautiful doe eyes for a split second before she realized Gideon was beside them.

"Oh." She pulled away from Charlie. "Hallo."

Gideon's eyes filled with worry.

"Why are you here?" she asked.

"Deacon King was admitted in the middle of the night with chest pains," Gideon answered.

Eve's hand went to the top of her cap. "Is Monika here?"

Gideon shook his head. "She went home to try to get some rest." Gideon glanced from Eve to Charlie and back to Eve. "What are you doing here?"

"Visiting a young widow and her baby. Her in-laws go to Leona and Eli's church." Eve blushed as she spoke.

"And what is your relationship to the young woman?" he asked Charlie, though he was looking at Eve.

Charlie stepped forward. "Her husband was in my unit, in Iraq. Joel was our staff sergeant."

"Oh." Gideon's eyes were still on Eve. "I'm going to put some prayer and thought into this. In the meantime think about your nieces and nephews. About your obligations. Your responsibilities. I've given you the benefit of the doubt because—" He shook his head. He didn't seem angry. Just befuddled.

She took a step backward. Charlie wanted to reach for her hand but stopped himself.

"I'll see you tomorrow," Gideon said to her. "At church." He stepped around Eve without saying anything more to Charlie.

Eve leaned against the wall, her head down. Charlie stepped to her side.

They stood silently outside of the cafeteria, Charlie wanting to reach out to her, to talk to her, but he feared Gideon coming back down the hall. Charlie was tempted to remind Eve they weren't doing anything wrong—that they were just being friendly. But that was a lie. They'd moved on to being friends, close friends. And if it was up to Charlie, they'd be more than that soon.

Instead he whispered, "Eve, is being with Gideon what you really want?"

She met his eyes.

"You left the Amish once." He spoke as softly as he could. "Are you sure you're meant to stay?"

"I've been a fool," she said, her voice louder than his.

"What about?" Shani had snuck up on them.

Charlie grimaced. How much had she overheard?

"What's going on?" she asked. Maybe she'd only heard what Eve had said.

"Gideon saw us—together." Charlie stepped away from Eve. "A few minutes ago."

"Oh," Shani said and then shook her head. "Why does that matter? It's not like . . ." She glanced from Charlie to Eve. "It's not like anything's . . ." Her voice trailed off.

Eve stepped away from the wall. "We should get back. I don't want Joel to be overwhelmed by the kids. Or for Tim to come home unexpectedly."

Shani stepped to her friend's side. "Do you think Gideon would call Tim at the lumberyard? Just because you and Charlie were alone for a few minutes?"

"Maybe," Eve answered.

"I'm so confused," Shani said.

"So are we." Charlie shoved his hands into his pockets. He led the way, hoping Gideon wouldn't call Tim.

But it wouldn't surprise him if he did.

ॐ 24

"Do you want me to drop you off at your house?" Shani asked Eve as she turned her van onto Juneberry Lane. "Trudy's probably not up from her nap. I can bring all the children when she wakes up."

"Denki," Eve said. Charlie stirred behind her in the middle seat. After Eve told Shani about Deacon King, the three had stayed quiet. Shani had tried to make small talk a few times, but mostly they'd all been silent during the ride from the hospital.

Shani turned down the Lehman driveway. "I'll get out too," Charlie said.

Eve didn't protest. She at least owed him an explanation.

Shani stopped the van and put the vehicle into Park. "One of you needs to tell me what's going on," she said.

Eve looked down as Charlie opened the side door.

"Give us a few minutes," he said.

Shani gripped the steering wheel.

Eve opened her door, but then said to Shani, "Sorry. We haven't meant to be secretive."

Shani raised her eyebrows. "Is something going on between you and Charlie?"

Eve shook her head. "We were just talking. Thank you for taking care of Trudy."

"I'll see you in a little bit . . ." Shani said.

Charlie held the door for Eve and she climbed down. After he'd shut it, she said, "We shouldn't go inside."

He nodded.

"Let's go sit on the front porch." She led the way. Charlie stole a look at her, but she didn't meet his eyes. They walked side by side up the steps and then sat down on the top one.

She tucked her dress under her legs. "I never should have called you that night."

Charlie leaned toward her. "I asked you to call, and I'll always be thankful that you did."

She shook her head. He wouldn't be. In another month or so he'd think of her as that crazy Amish girl that had put him through the wringer in an awkward one-week friendship.

"I'm sorry," she said.

He inhaled deeply. "Don't keep apologizing. It's not your fault."

But it was.

"I don't think we are meant to be just friends, Eve," he said. "I think we are meant to be much more."

His words stabbed at her heart.

When she didn't respond, he asked, "Do you love Gideon?"

She didn't answer. He didn't understand what he was up against.

Gently, he said, "Eve."

She tried to inhale, but her breath caught.

"Do you love Gideon?" he asked again.

She struggled for air.

"Eve?"

Finally she managed to sputter, "I need to try to explain something to you." Staring down at her hands, she said, "I can't leave the Amish."

"Because of what happened before?"

She shook her head. "Well, that's how it all started. That's when I made a commitment to the church because Abra was determined to join, and I was determined to stand by her and be a good friend. To help her and her babies."

Charlie nodded.

"But this is more. When Abra was dying she asked me to promise that I'd care for her children, which means I can't leave."

"Wow," Charlie said.

Eve bowed her head and stared at her hands. "The children need me." Charlie didn't need her, not compared to the kids.

"Why would you promise her that?"

How could she explain to Charlie that it was part of her penance? She loved the children—that was true—but she owed Abra.

Back when Eve was with Patrick, Abra came over to his apartment one night, hanging out with a friend of his visiting from Virginia. Abra'd had too much to drink, and the young man offered to take her home. Eve had said no, Abra needed to spend the night, at Eve's place. But Abra said she worked the next day and needed to go. Eve insisted she and Patrick take her home, but Abra said that wasn't necessary.

The boy from Virginia went back home a few days later. When Abra figured out she was pregnant, Eve had been afraid the young man had raped her. She said no, she'd been stupid but willing.

Eve was sure if she hadn't been willing with Patrick, Abra never would have gone that far. Eve, it turned out, had been a horrible friend—and Abra had paid the price.

"Eve?" Charlie touched her arm.

"Sorry," she said. "I owe Abra that. I let her down in a way that altered her entire life. What else could I do but promise to care for her children?"

"Did you promise her you'd never marry?"

She shook her head again. "No."

"Why didn't you marry years ago, then, after you came back to the Amish?"

She hesitated, not sure if she wanted to answer him.

"Eve," he prodded.

Finally she said, "My parents had an awful marriage. And I'd seen others where the husband was domineering and harsh. I knew the damage it did to a child—I experienced it. When I finally joined the church, I vowed never to marry an Amish man."

"So, basically never to marry at all?" Charlie asked.

She nodded, although back then she hadn't been absolutely sure she'd never leave the Amish again. That was why Abra had made Eve promise.

"And now you feel you're stuck," he said. "You can't leave the church and you can't marry in it. Except that doesn't explain Gideon."

Her face grew warm. "Jah, I know."

Charlie's voice was still even. "He's a kind man though, right? Not like your father? Or . . . others."

She nodded and raised her head.

He met her eyes. "Do you love Gideon?" he asked for a third time.

She whispered, "No."

"Then why would you marry someone you don't love?"

"To be close to the children." Her eyes swam with tears. "And, for a short time, I hoped I'd come to love him."

He leaned closer. "Abra might have been too ill to even realize what she was asking. Or it could have been the medication she was on. From everything you've said about her, it doesn't seem like the kind of request she would have made in her right mind." Charlie paused and then asked, "Would you consider rethinking your promise to Abra?"

"I can't," she answered. "There's too much at stake."

She could feel his breath as he said, "I wouldn't come between you and the kids."

"I know that," she said. "But Tim would make it impossible. I wouldn't be allowed to see them. He'd turn them against me, and Gideon wouldn't intervene, not like he has for Abra's parents." The sound of a vehicle stopped her. She headed down the steps, alarmed that Tim would arrive so soon.

But it wasn't Tim. It was Shani, with the children. The kids piled out into the rain as soon as Shani stopped. Lila was last, holding a screaming Trudy.

"There, there," Eve said as she took the baby, pulling the blanket over her head to protect her. She turned toward the children. "Everyone go inside." They all obeyed.

"I'll head back," Charlie said. Eve could tell he was hurting.

"No, stay," Shani said, pulling her hood onto her head. "I want to know what's going on."

Charlie shook his head slightly. Before Eve could say anything, the sound of another vehicle stopped her. It was the driver Gideon used, with Tim in the front seat.

Eve's shoulders tightened. Neither Charlie nor Shani said anything. They all stood still as the driver parked the car and Tim climbed out.

Finally he broke the silence, "I was a fool the first time. Not the second." Tim glared at Charlie. "Leave my property."

Charlie glanced at Eve. She nodded. The baby fussed and then quieted again.

"Good grief," Shani said. "Can't we talk this out? We're all adults. Not junior highers."

Tim crossed his arms.

"Thank you for coming over," Eve said, turning toward Shani. "Please go," she whispered, not daring to look at Charlie.

Charlie stepped toward Tim, as if he might extend his hand, but Tim stuffed both of his under his arms. Eve felt as if she might be sick.

"Don't come back," Tim said to Charlie. "Eve is my responsibility. She's none of your concern."

"No, she is," Charlie answered. "I care about Eve—more than I've ever cared about anyone."

Eve's heart raced. No one else had ever stood up for her like that.

"You have no idea of our ways," Tim said. "She's under my authority."

"She's a grown woman. She can make her own decisions. I want what she wants."

"She wants to marry the bishop."

"Maybe that's what you want," Charlie said. "Have you asked her what she wants?"

346

Tim's eyes narrowed. "You're no longer welcome here," he said.

Shani wrinkled her nose. "Tim Lehman, you may think you can control everyone and everything around you, but you can't. Someday, sometime, this will all backfire on you."

"Don't . . ." Eve didn't know what else to say. No matter what her friend said, it wouldn't do any good.

Shani turned toward Eve. "Should I call for help?"

Eve shook her head, wondering who Shani would call.

"Will you come with us?" Charlie asked as he stepped toward her.

Eve shook her head. "Go," she said again. The baby grew heavier in her arms by the minute.

"We'll wait in the van," he said loudly. "As long as you need us to."

Tim wouldn't do anything to physically hurt her, but he would berate her with his words. "Please go," she said again.

Charlie walked toward the van, his shoulders square and his head high.

Shani stared Tim down as she followed Charlie. Once she'd slammed the van door, Tim started toward the house. Eve followed him up the steps to the mud porch.

Trudy sighed, relaxing against Eve. The baby helped her stay calm as Tim began to rant.

"Gideon wanted to know how long you and Charlie have been courting."

"We're—"

"Don't lie to me. Gideon said it was obvious, clear as day on both your faces. That day Charlie was in the kitchen, I thought it was just you who had feelings for him, but it sounds as if I was wrong."

"I never meant to hurt Gideon," Eve said.

"He'll forgive you."

Eve shook her head. "I don't want his forgiveness. I want—"

Tim bristled and banged his fist against the wall of the mud room. Trudy began to cry.

"To leave this family? These children?" His eyes were furious. "To deny Trudy the only mother she's ever known?"

"If I married Gideon, I'd—"

"*If* you married Gideon?" he snarled. "*When* you marry Gideon."

"I'll leave the children then, anyway." Although she wouldn't go nearly as far as if she left the Amish. Eve bounced Trudy as she began to scream.

Tim shook his head. "Gideon said you can care for them . . . until I . . ." He stopped. *Find another wife.* He couldn't say it. She knew he couldn't fathom replacing Abra.

She shook her head. "How will that work? I'll come over here every day? What about the evenings? And the nights?"

"You've spoiled Trudy—she'll sleep through the night with you gone. And Lila can take care of the mornings and the evenings."

Eve didn't respond.

Tim's eyes narrowed. "I'm going back to work. We'll go to church tomorrow. You'll do your part. Gideon will do his. None of us will speak of this again."

Tim threw open the back door and stomped out. After he slammed it shut, Trudy stopped crying. Eve stepped into the kitchen and then over to the window. Tim climbed into the driver's car without glancing at Charlie and Shani, who both stared straight ahead.

Once the driver had backed up and headed down the driveway, Charlie opened the van door. For a moment, Eve was tempted to gather up all the children and go with him to Philly. But then she imagined the headlines the next day. *Amish Aenti kidnaps nieces and nephews.* No matter Tim's faults, she couldn't take his children away from him. And she couldn't bear it if he took them away from her. Tim hadn't let her finish, but if he had, she would have said she wanted to be allowed to make her own decisions *and* have a relationship with her nieces and nephews.

Charlie stepped down and started toward the house. Eve rapped on the window and shook her head. He threw up his hands. She shook her head again. Charlie turned toward Shani, who jumped out of the van and hurried to the door.

Eve opened it, tears spilling down her face. "I can't see him," she said. "Tell him I'm sorry."

Shani pulled Eve and the baby into an embrace. "I didn't realize . . ." she said, "that you two felt this way about each other."

"I never meant to hurt him."

"Shh," Shani said. "None of us can help who we fall in love with."

Eve swiped at her eyes. "But we can help how we act on that love." She'd feared, at first, that her attraction to Charlie was simply that he was Englisch. First because he was safe. Then because he reminded her of her past. She knew that wasn't true now. He was attractive because he was kind and confident and good with the kids. Because he listened. Because he cared. For her.

Shani hugged her harder. "Something will work out. Charlie wants you to call—tonight."

"I can't." Tears flowed from her eyes. "Ask him to forgive me," she said, letting Shani go as the baby began to fuss in her arms again.

The next day after the church service in Gideon's shed, Eve turned Trudy over to Lila and walked toward the bishop's house. Monika was at the hospital, but her girls had come to church. She gave Jenny a hug, and they headed toward the kitchen to help. "How's your Dat doing?" Eve asked.

"Better. They're doing a procedure today—with a stent."

"Sounds like he has blockage," Eve said.

"Jah, that's what Mamm said."

Gideon's daughter, Sarah, had everything under control in the kitchen. She was a quiet girl but capable and efficient. She had Reuben in charge of moving the benches into the house, and he'd recruited Simon and Daniel to help. As Eve put the bread in baskets, she noticed Lila standing in the doorway to the living room, holding the baby. Trudy's blanket fell to the floor, and Reuben quickly picked it up, handing it to Lila.

Eve watched the two. Reuben was four years older than Lila—a significant gap at their current ages, but it wouldn't seem so wide in a few years. He was a nice boy. Kind and considerate. Not as outgoing as Gideon, but he had some time before he was a man. He'd probably be a lot like his father when he was full grown.

Lila smiled at the boy as she tucked the blanket around her sister.

Eve didn't see Tim or Gideon until toward the end of the first sitting for the meal. Tim came in first and sat down beside Simon, rumpling his hair as he did. Eve couldn't see Simon's face, but Daniel sat across from his brother, and she could clearly see his frown. Gideon came in a few minutes later, and Eve dished up a bowl of bean soup for him.

"Denki," Gideon said, looking her in the eye.

Her face warmed.

"I appreciate you taking charge of the kitchen," he added.

"Sarah's in charge," Eve replied. "I'm just helping."

Her awkwardness grew as he continued to stare.

"How about a piece of bread?" She took a step toward the baskets. "And some apple butter. Monika made it."

He stepped around to the other side of the counter. "Speaking of, I was wondering if you'd like to go the hospital with me. This evening."

Eve swallowed.

"I know Monika would like to see you."

Eve exhaled, wondering if he was testing her. "Let me check with Tim," she managed to say.

A pained expression passed over Gideon's face. Thankfully Lila approached with Trudy, who had begun to fuss. "Have you eaten?" Gideon asked Lila.

She shook her head.

"Take my soup," he said. "I'll take the baby."

A couple of minutes later, with Trudy asleep in his arms, Gideon sat down next to Tim. The boys left the table, leaving the men to talk. As the second group entered to eat, Eve caught Tim looking at her a couple of times. Once the rest of the members were served, Eve went to take the baby from Gideon.

"Denki," she said as he scooted Trudy into her arms.

Tim leaned back on the bench. "He has a way with the little ones, jah?"

Eve nodded.

Tim sat up straight. "I didn't help Abra enough when Simon and Rose were babies. It's time I learned now. Starting tonight." He fixed his eyes on Eve. "Go with the bishop to the hospital. Nothing would make Monika happier, I know."

Eve nodded. It was true Monika would be pleased to see her. But she grew anxious at the idea of going with Gideon.

"I'll be by around four," Gideon said.

"Better get the kitchen cleaned up so we can go home," Tim said. "I'll take the baby."

Eve slid Trudy into his arms. She expected the baby to protest, but she didn't. She settled against her Dat, turning her face against his chest. When Tim smiled down at the little one, Eve realized she couldn't remember the last time she'd seen a positive expression on his face. She wasn't sure if it was the comfort Trudy brought or the fact he'd manipulated her into going with Gideon.

Monika was delighted to see Eve, especially with the bishop. She said their arrival took her mind

353

off Deacon King. "How's the baby?" Monika asked. "Did she miss me today?" Before Eve could answer, Monika cooed, "Who's watching her now?"

"Tim," Gideon replied.

"Oh, good for him," Monika said. "Now we just need to find that man a wife. Then everything will be as it should."

Deacon King was a little groggy but was happy to see Gideon. He nodded toward Eve, but that was all.

The nurse came in and said he needed a break. "Let him rest," she said.

"Let's go out to the waiting room," Monika said. "The bigger one, where I can get a cup of coffee."

Gideon paid for Monika's coffee after she ordered it from the little stand, and then the three stepped into the waiting room. In the back, Eve saw Karina and her in-laws sitting with Shani. Gideon saw her too and took Eve's elbow to direct her the other way, but she waved, and once Shani saw her she stood and hurried toward her.

Eve gave her a quick hug and then asked, "You remember Monika? From the auction?"

"Of course," Shani said turning toward the woman. "Eve told me about your husband's heart attack. I'm so sorry."

Monika gave Shani a one-armed hug.

Karina stood across the room and asked, "Would you join us?"

Eve glanced at Gideon. He nodded, although it seemed with some reluctance.

After all the introductions had been made and everyone crowded onto the two couches facing each other, and the side chairs, Gideon and Monika fell into a conversation with Karina's in-laws, while Shani explained that she'd just finished a half shift.

"Where's Charlie?" Karina asked.

"He went back to Philly today," Shani said.

Eve hoped her face remained expressionless.

"Are you and Charlie dating?" Karina asked Eve.

Eve shook her head at Karina, and Shani mouthed, "I'll explain later."

Gideon glanced over at the three women. Karina was rightly confused and said, "Sorry."

"No worries," Shani said. Eve's face grew warm.

Karina scooted to the edge of the couch, and said she was going to head back up to Samantha's room. Her in-laws stood too, just as a nurse hurried into the waiting room, her eyes falling on Monika.

"Mrs. King," she said, motioning for Monika.

"Oh dear." Monika stood.

"We'll go with you," Gideon said.

Eve stood and put her arm around Monika, walking alongside her. Gideon led the way, passing Karina and her in-laws, who all had concerned expressions on their faces.

Gideon, Monika, and Eve didn't speak as they hurried down the corridor to his room. When they reached the nurse's desk a woman Eve hadn't seen before stepped toward them. "He's coding."

Monika fell into Eve's arms.

"How bad is it?" Gideon asked.

"They're working on him now." She motioned toward the grouping of chairs. "Please wait."

Eve held onto her friend, and Shani joined them. None of them said a word as Gideon stood watch. They sat like that for twenty minutes. Then another woman approached, and introduced herself as one of Deacon King's doctors. Her face was red, and she clutched a stethoscope with both hands. "I'm sorry," she said.

He was gone. Monika turned white and gasped. Eve tightened her grip on her friend.

The doctor used some medical terms Eve didn't understand and then said she'd be back in a few minutes.

After the woman left, Monika shuddered. "How am I going to tell my girls? Jenny's so young to lose her Dat."

Gideon stood, following the doctor.

"It's okay to cry," Eve whispered to Monika.

Monika shook her head.

Eve pulled her close. "Don't feel as if you have to be strong," she said. Shani leaned forward and put her hand on Monika's arm.

The tears began to flow. "Will I get to see him?" she asked.

Shani pulled a small packet of tissues from her purse. "Yes, in a few minutes."

Monika dabbed at her eyes. "I didn't think it was that serious."

"Something more must have happened," Shani said.

Monika shuddered. "He was the one person I could trust completely. The only person I truly felt I belonged to. I should have been with him—"

Eve pulled her friend tight. Monika had been surrounded by family and friends her entire life, yet Deacon King had been the one who made her feel as if she belonged.

"You have so many people who love you, who care," Eve said as Gideon approached.

"The doctor said you can go into the room," he said.

Shani walked with them down the hall. When they reached the room, Monika took Eve's hand and started inside.

"You come too," she said to Shani.

The three women stood at the end of the bed for a moment, and then Monika stepped forward and took her husband's hand. "Denki," she said. "For loving me."

Shani put her arm around Eve, and both women cried.

Finally, Monika moved away from the bed,

and Eve and Shani stepped to her side, embracing her. Gideon cleared his throat from the doorway. "Eve and I could go tell your girls," he said.

Monika nodded in agreement. "The older ones are all at the house with Jenny."

"I'll stay here with you," Shani said. "In fact, I'll stay until you're ready to go, and then I'll take you home."

Eve was overcome with love for her new Englisch friend. "Denki," she said, as she hugged Shani good-bye.

As Eve and Gideon rode with the hired driver to the King residence in silence, Monika's words kept replaying in Eve's mind. *"He was the one person I could trust, completely. The only person I truly felt I belonged to."* That was it. She would never belong with Gideon. He *was* a good man, but she felt no connection to him.

After she and Gideon had told the girls, the driver dropped Eve off at home. Trudy had been cranky all evening and Tim was out of sorts, even more so after she told him Deacon King had passed. Finally, after Eve got the baby settled down and Tim had gone into his room, she put her cape back on. She had to talk to Charlie.

As she opened the back door, Tim's footsteps fell across the kitchen floor. "I thought you'd been sneaking out," he said.

"I'm just going to get some fresh air."

Tim continued forward, stopping a foot from her. "You'll stay in this house."

"So I'm a prisoner now?"

"You will not call the Englischman."

Eve crossed her arms, defiance surging through her.

"If you go out that door, you won't come back inside." Tim's face reddened with each word. "And you'll never see the children again." As he spoke the rain started again, coming down all at once in torrents.

Tim reached around her and slammed the door shut.

Eve didn't move. Finally, Tim returned to his room.

She stood for a long time, staring at the closed door, her cape still on. She wanted nothing more than to call Charlie and ask him to come get her. She wanted nothing more than to escape with him to a place where she was valued for who she was—not for who she was supposed to be. As unhealthy as the situation had been, she'd felt that during her time in the Englisch world—valued.

As hard as she'd tried all these years, she'd never fit in, let alone belonged. The morning she was baptized she was doing it for Abra, not for God. By that time, she'd come back to him. Felt his grace, as much as was possible. She knew joining the church wouldn't make her relationship with him any better. But she owed it to Abra—

after everything that had happened—to remain by her side.

And she wasn't sorry she'd done it.

But she knew no matter how hard she tried, she'd never feel as if she belonged in the Amish world. Not even with Gideon by her side. Especially when she didn't love him.

But she couldn't abandon the children. She wouldn't go back on her word to Abra.

She took off her cape and hung it on the peg.

❦ 25

When Shani stopped by Monika's the day before the service, the oldest daughter advised her to come to the burial not the actual service. "It will all be in Pennsylvania Dutch," she said. "And long. Come to the cemetery instead." She gave Shani directions.

On her way home she stopped by Eve's. She wanted to double-check with her to make sure it was okay if she went to the burial. But Tim was home and came out of the house into the rain without even his hat as she stepped down from the van.

"I don't want you coming around," he said.

"I have a question for Eve."

Tim crossed his arms. "She's busy."

Shani replied. "Then I'll ask you."

"I won't answer."

Shani shook her head. The man was a brute. "I'll see you tomorrow," she said, yanking her door shut. Her stomach lurched as she backed her van around and headed to the lane. The baby must not have liked her rising anxiety, because he hauled off and kicked her, hard.

She turned right at the lane instead of left, figuring she had enough time to get to the grocery store before Zane got home, but as always, it took longer than expected. When she reached the farmhouse she anticipated he'd be down at the creek with the kids, but he wasn't. He was watching *SportsCenter* with Joel.

"How come you're not out with the kids?" Shani asked as she carried in the bags of groceries.

Zane shrugged.

Joel spoke up. "Because Tim met him in the field and told him his kids wouldn't be playing anymore."

Zane's eyes didn't waver from the TV screen.

"How come Tim's not at work?" Joel asked.

"I don't know," Shani replied, stepping into the kitchen, her blood pressure rising again.

The next day, at the cemetery, she saw Eve across the gravesite but didn't wave, feeling as if it wouldn't be proper. But she smiled at her friend, and Eve smiled back—until Gideon stepped to her side.

Shani exhaled. It wasn't just Tim who had grown hypercontrolling.

Charlie had called last night, asking if Shani had spoken to Eve. He sounded heartbroken, saying she hadn't called.

After the burial, Monika sought Shani out and gave her a hug. "I don't know what I would have done without you that night—" Jenny, the youngest daughter, joined them, clasping her

362

mother's arm. Shani knew what it was like to have only one parent to cling to.

"You have my number," Shani said. "Call me. If you need a ride. Or someone to talk to. I'm happy to help."

After she gave Monika a hug, Shani searched for Eve but she'd disappeared. She'd probably gone back to Monika's house to set up the meal. She didn't see Gideon or Tim either. The children, it seemed, hadn't attended at all.

On her way home, Shani slowed down by the Lehmans' driveway but didn't see anyone. When she arrived home, she found Zane watching an old rerun of *Bonanza* with Joel.

Between work and caring for Joel, Zane, and their home, the days zipped by for her—but Shani couldn't seem to pull all of them out of the funk they were in. Zane was lonely without the children, Shani felt lost without Eve, and Joel's nightmares and generally negative disposition grew worse. The last time Shani had asked him to see the therapist, he'd cursed. When he calmed down, he'd said, "Don't bring it up again. I'm fine."

Shani felt as if she were holding her breath. She wished she could talk to Eve. Or at least ask her to pray.

Charlie didn't come to visit, not even for Thanksgiving. He called and talked to Joel, saying he'd had dinner at Nikki's that day. Shani got on the phone and told him to get his butt down to Lancaster to see Eve, but Charlie said he still hadn't heard from her. He wasn't going to be one more man in her life trying to control her.

"You're right, but she does need one man in her life who truly loves her."

He didn't answer for a long awkward moment. Finally he said, "She doesn't want me."

"So you're going to go back to Nikki?" Shani said. Joel frowned at her.

"No," Charlie answered. "I told her that we couldn't see each other any longer."

Shani handed the phone back to Joel without saying good-bye.

The next morning, on the way to the grocery store, she stopped by the Lehmans', but they were all gone. She imagined they were off visiting— probably at Gideon's. Her heart sank as she drove away.

When she returned, Joel said Charlie had called and planned to come down for the afternoon. "Why?" Shani asked.

Joel shrugged. "He misses us, I guess."

Charlie arrived midafternoon. He sat with Joel and watched college football on TV for over an hour but then asked Zane if he wanted to go outside and toss a ball around. Zane jumped at the chance.

Shani headed into the kitchen to heat up the

turkey breast from the day before. She'd thought Joel was going to the bathroom when he headed down the hall, but when she came back out to the living room, Joel sat at the window, the TV off and his .45 in his hand.

"Hey," she said, walking toward him. "What's going on?"

"I hate this time of day," he said. Dusk wasn't far away.

"Give me the gun," she said. "I'll put it away." She knelt beside his chair. "We're safe here."

"There's always a threat," Joel said.

"Joel . . ."

"Leave me alone."

If they'd had cell service in their hollow of a farm, Shani would have texted Charlie to come in through the back door. But then what? She needed to stay calm.

She followed Joel's gaze outside. Zane caught the ball and then ran with it, back toward Charlie, zigzagging this way and that. Charlie reached over and slapped Zane's shoulders with both hands. Next Zane threw the ball to Charlie.

"I'm no use to any of you," Joel said. "Not as a husband. Not as a dad. I won't even be able to carry the baby when he's born. You'd be better off without me."

"Stop," she said, reaching for his free hand. He jerked it away. Back when he was in the hospital, she'd succeeded at quieting his suspicions about her and Charlie. But there was no proving him wrong in his recognition that Zane and Charlie had become close. It was totally appropriate—but it was still hurtful. Maybe she should have intervened—asked Charlie to be careful not to make it so obvious.

"We love you." She pulled herself up from the floor, using the arm of his chair. "And you are getting better. You'll be out of the cast soon and back in rehab. This is just a setback." Somehow she had to get him to agree to mental health help too.

She started to wheel the chair away from the window.

"I want to stay," he said.

"But why sit here and watch if it makes you feel worse?" She kept her eyes on the gun as she spoke.

"Leave me alone," he snapped.

"I'm going to go get Charlie," she said, starting toward the door.

"Don't." The gun was still in his lap. He sighed. "We need to figure out how to get through life without Charlie."

Her eyebrows, involuntarily, shot up. "Then give me the gun."

He shook his head. "Just let me hold it. I'm not hurting anyone."

"I'm going to go check on the turkey," Shani

said, walking slowly into the kitchen. She passed the oven and opened the back door as quietly as she could, hurrying down the steps and motioning to Charlie. She was confident Joel wouldn't use the gun on any of them—but she wasn't positive he wouldn't use it on himself.

She put her finger to her lips, hoping it wouldn't be obvious to Joel that she'd called them in, but both Charlie and Zane looked straight at her.

"Shani!" Joel yelled. He must have caught on to what she was doing.

She hurried back up the steps. "I'll be right there," she called back to him.

Zane came up behind her first. "Wait a minute," she whispered to him, catching his arm. She whispered to Charlie what was going on.

He nodded and said, "I'll go talk to him."

"Stay in the kitchen with me," Shani said to Zane. "Wash up and set the table."

At first the voices coming from the living room were soft murmurs, but then Joel's voice grew louder. "We don't need you to keep coming here anymore."

Zane's eyes grew wide.

Shani put her hand on his shoulder. "It'll be all right." She hoped she wasn't lying.

Charlie's voice stayed calm. "I'll be on my way after dinner. How's that?"

"But you'll be back. You and Shani treat me as if I can't do a thing by myself. And the thing is—

you're right. I can't do anything without one of you."

"Your leg is healing, Joel. You'll be walking soon and out playing football in no time."

"Who are you kidding? I'll never play football like I used to."

"No, but you should be able to play. With Zane. And your new son."

Joel grunted. Shani stepped to the doorway of the kitchen. Joel stayed at the window, but Charlie sat down on the couch.

She shot him a questioning look. He shrugged.

When it was time to eat, Joel said he wasn't hungry. Shani asked Charlie to fill his plate and eat in the living room while she and Zane ate in the kitchen. The reheated turkey was dry, and the stuffing was still mushy. No wonder Joel didn't want to eat.

When Charlie came in with his empty plate, Shani sent Zane upstairs and then asked what they should do. "Call the police?" she asked.

He shook his head. "That will only make things worse. Let's wait until he gives it up or falls asleep. I'll take it home with me." Charlie ran his hand through his hair. "He obviously needs some help."

Shani nodded.

Charlie headed back to the living room, and Shani went as far as the doorway again. Joel had his head turned toward them, a pained expression on his face. Charlie settled back on the couch and Shani headed up the stairs to Zane. Maybe he was faking it, but he appeared to be asleep.

Shani returned to the kitchen, cleaned up, and then sat at the table, waiting. For once she wished she knitted or crocheted.

An hour later, Joel wheeled into the bathroom. Shani hoped he took his pain meds—that would mean he'd be asleep soon. Sure enough, fifteen minutes later he started to doze in his chair. Once he was sound asleep, Charlie slipped the .45 from his grasp.

Charlie's eyes glistened as he looked up at Shani.

She swallowed hard.

Joel stirred but didn't wake. Charlie grabbed his coat and started out the door. Shani followed.

"He's going to be furious," Charlie said.

"I know." Shani wrapped her arms around herself.

"If he gets volatile, call for help."

"I will," she answered. And she'd make an appointment with a therapist first thing Monday morning.

"I'll call him tomorrow," Charlie said. "Hopefully we can talk things through."

"Thank you," Shani said, fighting back her tears. "For everything."

She told him good-bye and headed back in the house, fearing they would soon be losing his friendship too. She'd been so sure her grandfather's farm would be the answer to their problems. Instead they were becoming more isolated than ever.

She checked on Zane again. He'd crawled under the covers and seemed genuinely asleep now. She sat on the edge of his bed and ran her fingers through his bangs, sweeping them from his forehead. He turned away from her, toward the wall.

Joel didn't wake as she rolled him down the hallway to their bedroom. But when she started to transfer him to the bed, he asked, "Did you put the gun away?"

"It's safe," she answered.

The next morning, while Zane was doing the chores, she asked Joel if he remembered what had happened. He nodded.

"Charlie took the gun," she said.

He cursed. "Why'd you let him?"

"Because we need help," she said. "I was scared last night. I'm going to find a therapist on Monday."

Joel shook his head and wheeled into the living room. That afternoon Charlie called, but Joel refused to talk with him.

On Sunday the Lehmans had church at their house. Shani couldn't imagine what a big job it was for Eve—all the cleaning and setup and food preparation. The thought overwhelmed her. A constant parade of buggies came down the lane in the morning and then left in the early afternoon. Shani stood on her porch and watched them go, feeling lonelier than she ever had in her entire life.

On Monday she made several phone calls. By Wednesday, she had a therapist in Lancaster lined up through the VA and made an appointment for Friday. But Joel refused to go. She went alone. She left with a list of mental health emergency numbers to call and pamphlets about PTSD. The therapist suggested getting his platoon sergeant involved, but Shani wasn't sure that was a good idea. Joel would be absolutely humiliated.

During the next couple of weeks, probably because he didn't want to talk with a therapist, Joel stabilized again. His cast came off, and though he still relied on the wheelchair, he sometimes walked with a cane when he felt strong enough. He started physical therapy, which meant Shani helped him with his exercises and took him to more appointments, trying to coordinate them with her own prenatal appointments. She didn't have the energy to keep nagging him about seeing a counselor.

The second week of December Shani stopped by to see Eve again, this time with a plate of brownies, made from a mix, of course. Even at that they were dry.

Lila came to the door. The girl brightened up when she saw it was Shani but still had a forlorn look about her. "How's Zane?" she asked.

Shani said he was lonely.

Lila teared up. "Us too."

Just as Shani reached to give Lila a hug, Tim's booming voice stopped her. "Who's there?"

"Go," Lila said.

Shani shook her head. "I want to say hello to your dad."

Lila stepped back. "Please go."

Shani hesitated but gave the girl the brownies and then walked slowly back to her van. She wasn't going to make things worse for Lila. She climbed into the van and sat back a moment. The curtains fluttered. The baby shifted inside of her, kicking toward the steering wheel. Her own eyes filled with tears.

Zane had refused to go to the school dance, even though Shani had actually encouraged him to attend. He needed some friends. He needed to spend time with people his own age. "The kids at school are all lame," he'd said. "I'd rather hang out with Daniel and Simon. And Lila and Rose. Even Trudy."

Shani hadn't responded. She preferred he hang out with the Lehman kids too.

Three days before Christmas, Shani's father came out from Seattle. The early afternoon of his first full day with them, he said he was going to walk up the lane to talk with Mr. Lehman about whether he wanted to lease the land again the next year.

Joel leaned against his cane. "Good luck with that."

"Want to come along?" he asked.

Joel shook his head.

"I do," Zane replied.

Shani looked at Joel to get his opinion. "It's fine," he said. "Tim's not going to say anything in front of your dad."

Shani had an extra tin of butter cookies for Zane and her dad to take with them. She was tempted to go herself, but Joel seemed anxious, and she needed to leave for work in an hour.

Joel settled into the recliner they'd bought the week before and turned on the TV while Shani finished up the dishes. After that she made a lunch for herself and stared into the fridge trying to think what the rest of them could have for dinner. She decided her dad could make eggs, bacon, and hash browns. That was his specialty.

Shani had been drinking a lot of smoothies lately, following Eve's recipe. At least she was doing better as far as nutrition for the baby. If only she could get Joel and Zane to drink them too. Coming up with meals was the task she hated the most.

She closed the fridge, thinking through Christmas dinner. She'd need to go to the store the next day. She'd get a ham—that was easy. A bag of potatoes, a couple of jars of gravy, rolls, frozen beans, and a ready-made salad. Oh, and a pie.

The phone rang. It was Charlie, asking for Joel. Shani took the phone into the living room and handed it to her husband without saying anything. He said hello, but as soon as he heard Charlie's voice he handed it back to her.

Shani held it like a hot potato. "Come on, Joel. It's Christmas."

Joel's eyes narrowed, and he shook his head.

Shani waited until she was back in the kitchen before she said she was sorry.

"It's all right," Charlie said. "I just thought I'd try."

"How have you been?" she asked.

"All right."

"Have you heard from Eve?"

"Nope," he answered. "Have you talked with her?"

"No," Shani said, the word catching in her throat. She changed the subject. "How about Karina and Samantha?"

"Good. Karina's looking at going back to work part-time. She has a lead at a good day-care center."

"Tell her hello," Shani said.

"How's Zane?" Charlie asked.

"My dad's here, so that helps."

Charlie asked about her and the baby, and Shani answered everything was fine. Then she said, "Joel's better than he was that night. We haven't had anything like that again."

"Good," Charlie answered. "I should let you go."

Shani wanted to say how much they missed him, but that wouldn't go over well with Joel. Instead she said, "Merry Christmas," and then told him good-bye.

A few minutes later, as Shani put on her coat, her father and Zane came up the front steps. She opened the door. "How did it go?"

"It was weird." Zane stepped around her and kicked off his boots.

"It was fine," her father said, taking off his hat. "Tim's going to lease the land for another year."

"Did you see Eve?" Shani asked.

Zane shook his head. "Lila told us Tim was in the barn. We went out there to talk."

"How's Lila?" Shani wound her scarf around her neck.

Zane shrugged. "She said Simon got his jaw unwired a couple weeks ago. That's a good thing."

She agreed.

Her father pressed his hands together. Weeks ago she'd told him about the troubles with Tim. He'd told her it was the man's duty to protect his family, and they shouldn't take it personally.

"I didn't grow up with Amish neighbors," her father had said over the phone. "But I did grow up in Lancaster County. Some Plain people are okay with the influence of outsiders. Others aren't. Let it be."

That was easy for him to say. He hadn't grown

close to Eve and fond of the children. He hadn't seen Zane make the best friendships of his life. And he hadn't witnessed the attraction between Eve and Charlie. Shani had pondered that one a lot. She, selfishly, hadn't wanted them to have a relationship. She didn't want Eve to leave Juneberry Lane. Instead her family had lost both of them.

Now her father looked at her with a serious expression as he stood with his coat still on and his stocking cap pulled over his gray hair. "Tim Lehman is a good man. He has his own struggles. You'll just have to see how this all works out. There's not anything you can do to make it better."

Her dad walked her out to the van, and when she stopped at the driver's side, he cleared his throat.

"What is it?" she asked. "More about the Lehmans?"

He shook his head. "I'm worried about you and Joel."

"We're fine," Shani said, opening the door. She hadn't told him about the gun incident.

Her dad narrowed his eyes at her, the way he had when she was a teenager, lowering his bushy eyebrows as he did. "Tell me the truth."

Shani shrugged. "He's stressed. No doubt he has PTSD." Her eyes filled with tears, and her father wrapped his arms around her. "Yeah," she admitted, "things aren't so great. I tried to get him to see a counselor, but he refused."

"What are you going to do?"

She shook her head. "Wait it out, I guess."

Her dad shook his head. "Zane told me about the gun."

"I wondered," Shani said. "I'm sorry. I should have . . . I didn't want you to worry."

"I just want to make sure you and Zane and the baby are safe."

"We are," she said, climbing into the van. At least she thought they were. As long as Joel wasn't driving, he couldn't get another gun. She slammed the door but then rolled down the window. "There's breakfast stuff in the fridge. Do you mind making dinner?"

Her dad smiled. "Drive carefully."

It started to snow as Shani drove down the lane. She slowed and glanced up the Lehmans' driveway, just as she did every time she drove by. Eve was grabbing sheets off the line. Shani stopped. Eve waved and smiled. Shani rolled down the passenger-side window and waved back, shouting, "Merry Christmas!"

"Merry Christmas to all of you too," Eve yelled back, her black cape open. Snow swirled around her, and a white sheet flapped in the wind.

Shani drove on, her stomach sinking. Nothing felt right. She'd felt so hopeful when they'd moved to Lancaster, but with each passing day that hope diminished more and more.

• • •

The Beck family managed to get through Christmas and the days after. Shani's father chopped wood every day, helped Zane with the chores, shoveled the ramp, and made sure the pipes were all well insulated.

Shani was sure Joel could have helped with some of it—or at least thanked her father—but he didn't. He watched TV, mostly *SportsCenter*, while the rest of them worked.

On New Year's Eve, after they all went to bed, a few fireworks went off. Shani felt Joel stiffen. "You okay?" she asked.

"Yeah, I'm fine," he answered, rolling away from her. "I just wish tonight that all of our neighbors were Amish."

Shani dozed, but at midnight more fireworks exploded, waking her. A dog howled in the distance. Another barked. Joel swung his feet over the side of the bed.

"Where are you going?" Shani asked.

"Out to the living room."

"Want me to come?"

"No," he answered, shuffling toward the door, his cane thumping against the floor. "You should sleep."

Shani's dad left the Saturday after New Year's, and on Monday, Shani and Joel drove to Philly. Joel worried it was too close to Shani's due date for them to travel that far, even though it wasn't much over an hour. He worried the roads might get bad and they wouldn't make it back before Zane got home from school. He worried the doctor would have bad news.

Shani found Joel's despondency harder and harder to take. "Let's make an appointment with a mental health provider while we're at the VA," she said as she maneuvered through traffic.

"I told you I don't need to see a shrink."

"It's no different than seeing a doctor for your leg."

"My brain isn't broken, Shani." He slumped against the seat and closed his eyes.

After the medical exam, the doctor said that the leg was healing. "There'll be more healing as far as the nerves and muscles. It's never going to be perfect though. You'll always walk with a cane, but you can start driving when you feel up to it."

Shani asked Joel if he wanted to drive home. He said he didn't feel ready.

They reached home a half hour before Zane did. Joel collapsed in his recliner and fell asleep and didn't do anything the rest of the day.

The next morning he didn't do much either, besides watch TV. When Shani left for work, she told him there was soup in the cupboard and sandwich meat in the fridge. He grunted and said they'd be fine.

The next day she asked him to drive himself to physical therapy, but he said he'd rather not go if she wasn't going to take him. She ended up going, but her resentment grew.

That evening Zane was grumpy too. She couldn't get him to talk, but finally at bedtime he said he'd ventured into the Lehmans' yard on the way home from school, and Tim had told him to go on home. "Daniel and Lila were at the new chicken coop, and they both stared at me."

Shani gave him a hug.

"They looked so sad," he said.

"We're all sad," Shani answered.

"Except for Tim. And, well, Dad. I mean, he's sad but not because he misses the Lehmans— except maybe Trudy."

Shani sighed. The only time Joel had seemed positive about their baby was when Trudy had been around. Now he fretted about their little one more than ever.

The next morning she asked Joel if he'd help around the house. "Like empty out the wood stove," she said. "The ash has really built up." She didn't think lifting the bucket would be any harder for him than it was for her.

"I'll get to it," he said.

By afternoon Shani felt tired and took a nap. When she woke, she could hear voices. Zane was home.

It seemed extra dark. She glanced at the clock, *4:10*. She decided a storm was blowing in. Thankfully she didn't have to work the next day.

The baby shifted, and she put her hand on her belly, trying to feel a foot or elbow. Tears filled her eyes. Another couple of weeks and Baby Boy Beck would arrive. What would Joel do then?

She shuffled out to the living room. All the lights were off except for the TV. She turned on the lamp.

Zane still had his coat on.

"How was school?" she asked.

"Fine." He was becoming as uncommunicative as his dad.

But then he perked up a little. "Anthony said we might get an ice storm," Zane said.

Joel stared at the TV. "That's what they're saying on the news too. By this evening."

Every few years, when she was growing up, Seattle was hit by ice storms. It shut down the entire city. She wondered if the same thing happened in Lancaster County. It didn't matter. They'd hunker down. None of them needed to go anywhere.

She called in a pizza order, doubling it. If there was going to be a storm, they'd need leftovers. They were watching the local news when the ice started to fall. First it pinged against the windows and then the roof.

Shani gathered candles, matches, and flashlights and put them all on the coffee table. "Zane, go get more wood for the stove," she said.

"I let the fire die down," Joel said. "So I could clean out the ashes."

It wasn't as if they used the wood stove to completely heat the house. Her grandparents had installed electric heaters way back when, but Shani preferred the wood stove. And they'd need it if they lost power.

"This would be a good time to do it," Shani said, heading to the bathroom. She'd get a shower now, in case the lights went out. She didn't want to do that by candlelight.

As she turned off the water, the lights flickered but didn't go out. But a cracking noise from outside startled her. Probably a tree branch. She hoped they wouldn't have too much clean up to do after the storm. She dressed in a hurry.

When she came out of the bathroom, Zane sat on the couch with a slice of pizza in his hands.

"Where's Dad?" she asked.

"Taking out the ashes."

"Put the pizza back. We'll all eat together." She started down the hall to the bathroom to dry her hair. She didn't want to catch a chill. "Tell Dad to get a fire started. In case the electricity goes out," she called out over her shoulder.

When she came out again, Joel and Zane were working on building a fire. She moved the pizza from the kitchen to the coffee table, along with plates and napkins. Before they were ready to eat, Zane asked if he could say the prayer.

"Sure," Joel said.

Shani expected him to recite the prayer they usually said but instead he said, "Dear Lord, thank you for this food and how you take care of us. Please keep us safe. And please make things right with our neighbors." He paused, as if there was something else he wanted to add, but simply said, "Amen."

Zane took his half-eaten piece of pizza from the box and then said, "He works things for good, right? That's what Eve says."

"Oh, I don't know," Joel said, patting his bad leg. "I'm still waiting to see what good he works from this. And I can't fathom how he'd work good from Samuel . . ." His voice trailed off and he turned toward the stove.

Zane wrinkled his nose, started to say something, but then kept quiet.

Joel held a piece of pizza in midair. "Son, it's good to trust God. I have nothing against that. But God wants us to take action too—he doesn't want us sitting around doing nothing."

Shani cringed. That's all Joel had been doing—sitting around.

Zane sat up straight. "What should we do to make things right with the Lehmans?"

Joel shook his head. "That's just it—you have to figure out what you have control over and what you don't. We don't have any control over Tim Lehman."

Shani quickly added, "So we have to leave it up to God."

Zane frowned.

"Thanks for making the fire," Shani finally said to her husband and son. Neither responded.

After dinner Shani felt crampy but chalked it up to the pizza. She didn't have problems with indigestion, but there was always a first time. She decided to go to bed early. Zane went out to check on the ice and said everything was coated with it. "There's no way there will be school tomorrow."

"You might have a late start," Shani said. "It could melt in the morning."

"Not according to the news," Joel said. "They're predicting more—a lot more."

"Go to bed on time anyway," she said to Zane, grabbing one of the flashlights to take with her, just in case.

When she woke it was pitch-black. No lights from the alarm clock. No crack of light under the door.

Her heart raced. Something was wrong. She was wet. And in pain.

"Joel," she said, patting the bed beside her. He wasn't there. "Joel," she called out. Still nothing.

It was dark but not quiet. The ice still fell, pinging the windows and side of the house.

She swung her legs out of bed, pulling the quilt around her. A contraction tore through her. She grasped her belly, in pain. They'd have to call

9-1-1. She couldn't drive, not in the ice, not while having contractions. And Joel shouldn't attempt it either.

The last thing she wanted was for the baby to be born in the van on a freezing cold night.

Fumbling for the flashlight, she turned it on and then made her way out of the room and down the hall. When she reached the living room she swung the beam of the flashlight to the couch. Zane was sprawled out on it. She moved the light to the recliner. Joel stirred.

"The baby's coming, Joel."

He bolted upright. "What?"

"My water broke. I'm having contractions—close together." She held her belly. Another one tore through her. "And they're strong."

"I'll go scrape the van."

"No, call for an ambulance. I'll get changed."

A minute later, Joel came down the hall. "The landline's down," he said. "I went out on the porch and tried to get service, just in case, but of course couldn't."

"Send Zane to the Lehmans', to call from their phone." As she spoke, Zane appeared in the doorway of the bedroom, another flashlight in his hand. "Sweetie," she said to him, "if their phone doesn't work, ask Eve to come help me."

Joel shook his head. "Do you think Tim will let her help?"

Tears filled Shani's eyes. "He has to."

ᖇᖇ 26

Eve stood at the crib, patting Trudy's back, singing "Jesus Loves Me" in German. *"Jesus liebt mich, dies weib ich."* She sang just loud enough for the baby to hear her. *"Denn die Bibel sagt es mir."*

The ice hit the window as she sang. It had been a few years since they'd had a bad ice storm. She'd been dreaming about Charlie when Trudy's cries woke her. The storm had most likely woken the baby.

She still thought about Charlie all the time. She kept hoping she'd stop. Eventually she'd stopped thinking about Patrick. He'd given her the ultimatum to leave Lancaster County with him or be done with their relationship for good, but Abra had just found out she was pregnant and was still in shock. Eve had chosen to support her friend.

It had been difficult for Eve to tell Patrick good-bye. She mourned not hearing from him after he left Lancaster County without her, but she never regretted her decision. At least not any longer than a day or two. Still it had hurt.

It wasn't as if Charlie had given her an ultimatum. She'd given it to herself. She thought of that night in the hospital, two days before Abra had passed, when she'd gripped Eve's hand

and over the beeps of the medical equipment whispered, "Promise me you'll take care of my children."

"Of course," Eve had said.

Abra squeezed her hand harder, searching Eve's eyes.

"I promise," Eve added. "You have my word."

She'd honored her promise, but she couldn't seem to make herself stop obsessing about Charlie, no matter how hard she tried.

Trudy sighed and wiggled a little. Eve kept patting her back. She wondered if the storm was hitting Philly too and hoped Charlie was safe at home. She'd seen his truck go by the day after Thanksgiving, down the lane to the Becks', and had hoped beyond hope that he'd stop to see her. He hadn't. And what would she have done if he had? Begged him to take her with him?

No.

A pounding startled her. Was it a branch against the house? No, it sounded like a knock. Surely no one was out in the storm. She lifted her hand from Trudy's back. The baby stayed still.

Eve grabbed her robe, slipped it on, and hurried down the hall. The pounding grew louder. By the time she reached the kitchen the back door was open and the beam of a flashlight blinded her.

"I can't see," she said, covering her eyes.

"Sorry." The beam fell to the floor.

"Zane?"

He closed the door. Ice hung from his hood and eyebrows.

"What's wrong?"

He was breathless. "Mom's in labor and our phone won't work. I need to use yours."

"To call for help?"

He nodded. "Mom doesn't want to drive in this."

"Of course not. No one should." Except an ambulance driver. "I'll go out with you." Eve said a prayer as she pulled on her boots and slipped her cape over her robe. "Come on," she said to Zane.

He led the way down the steps, waving the flashlight back and forth. Eve moved slowly and carefully. The world had turned into a sheet of slippery glass, although it didn't seem to slow Zane down.

"Wait," she called after him. Her ankle had healed, but she feared spraining something else on the ice.

He stopped and turned toward her, putting out his arm for her. He'd grown taller and broader since she last saw him. With his help, she made it to the barn as the ice pelted them and the wind howled through the trees. Zane pushed the door open and shone the light on the stoop. Eve stepped over it. One of the horses nickered and a cow mooed. Tim had put all of them in the barn when the ice began to fall.

Zane led the way to the office, and then Eve took the phone off the receiver and lifted it to her ear. There was no dial tone. She pressed down the receiver and let it back up. Nothing.

"I should have brought Mom's cell phone and gone to the highway," Zane said.

Eve shook her head. "It's too dangerous," she said. "I'll go back with you. We'll figure it out." She'd been with Abra for the delivery of all of her babies, and as a nurse Shani would know what to do.

"Help me back to the house," she said to Zane.

Zane took her arm as they reached the barn door. Tim wasn't going to be happy with her. She'd take the baby with her and Lila too, just in case it took all night.

When they reached the house, she woke up Lila first and told her to dress. "And pack a couple of bottles for Trudy."

Eve dressed herself and then lifted the baby from the crib and wrapped her tight in two blankets. When she reached the back door, Lila had the diaper bag ready and already had her boots, cape, hat, and mittens on. Eve handed her the baby.

She decided to leave Tim a note. There was no way she'd wake him up to tell him where she was going. As she grabbed a notebook and pen from the drawer, she didn't hear his footsteps. Just his words. "What's going on?" He stood in the middle of the kitchen in his long underwear.

"Shani's in labor. Neither of our phones are working—I'm going to help."

Tim's eyes narrowed, and he started to speak, but Eve stopped him. "She needs an ambulance."

He crossed his arms.

"Take the sleigh to the gas station. Maybe the pay phone is working."

He shook his head. "I don't have a quarter."

"There are some quarters in the box of Abra's things we brought home from the hospital."

He tugged on his beard.

"You'd want someone to help Abra, wouldn't you? If she was in labor on a night like this."

Tim said nothing, just crossed his arms again.

Exasperated, Eve said, "Could you at least try to help?" She blew her breath out slowly and then added, "Remember, the Lord told us to love thy neighbor as thyself. What better way to love the Becks than to help Shani and her baby right now."

Tim tugged on his beard but then headed back to the hall. He reappeared a few minutes later with a flashlight as Eve fastened her cape. He had a couple of quarters in one hand and a piece of paper in the other. "I'll go call," Tim said, holding up the coins.

"Denki," Eve said, wondering what else he'd found. It didn't matter. She was just relieved he was willing to help. She slung the diaper bag over her shoulder and reached for the baby. Lila took the flashlight, while Zane carried the garbage bag of blankets and sleepers and offered his arm to Eve. She took it.

It was slow going down the steps and then along the driveway. Lila slipped and almost fell.

"Hang on to me," Zane said, offering his other arm. He nodded toward the field. "It's less slippery that way."

Ice clung to every blade of grass. The uneven surface meant it wasn't as slippery, but it also made for a rough walk. Eve's ankle turned, but Zane caught her before she fell.

Lila gasped.

"I'm okay," Eve said.

Trudy stirred but didn't cry.

They continued on in silence, concentrating on each step. Finally they reached the Becks' house.

"Let's take the ramp," Eve said. "We can hold on to the rails."

Once she grabbed hold, Zane ran ahead, racing up the sheet of ice to the door. Lila followed him, although not as quickly. Eve took it slowly, a step at a time, gripping the baby tightly.

As Zane threw open the door and rushed inside, he yelled, "Their phone is down too! But Eve is here. And Lila and Trudy."

A moment later he returned and headed back down the ramp, grabbing Lila's arm and helping her all the way up. Then he returned to Eve, taking the baby and her arm. "Mom's in her room," he said. "Dad's with her."

When Eve and Zane stepped into the house, Lila took Trudy from Zane and headed to the wood stove, bouncing her little sister. A single candle burned on the coffee table, casting shadows around the room.

"I'm here," Eve said as she hurried down the hall. A dim light shone through the bedroom door, which was wide open. Joel stood at the end of the bed, leaning against his cane.

A flashlight sat on a low table. Shani knelt against the side of the bed. She wore a nightgown and her hair was caught atop her head in a loop. Eve knelt down beside her. "How far apart are the contractions?"

"Three minutes."

"Okay."

"Zane said Tim was going to go call for an ambulance."

"Jah . . ."

"It's what we get for moving to the middle of nowhere," Joel said, stepping to the window.

"He's not helping," Shani whispered. "He used to be so good in a crisis."

Eve stood. "Joel, go tell Zane to put some water on the stove."

"The pump isn't working."

Eve inhaled sharply. "You didn't fill pitchers or the tub when the storm started?"

"We didn't realize . . ." Shani said.

Eve shook her head. "It's not a problem. Zane can go get ice from outside and melt that. Joel—I need your help. Go give Zane the instructions."

Maybe her tone got his attention. He stood up a little straighter and stepped into the hall.

"As soon as Zane left he got all worked up," Shani explained.

"Hush." Eve swept a strand of hair away from Shani's forehead. "Concentrate on the baby."

"I can't believe this." Her face contorted as she spoke, and then she took a deep breath.

"Did another one start?"

Shani nodded.

Eve picked up the watch on the bed in front of Shani. By the time Shani relaxed eighty seconds had gone by. That was pretty long.

Sweat beaded on her friend's forehead even though the room was freezing. Eve shuddered at the thought of trying to keep the baby warm.

"At least you know how all of this works. I know some of what to do, but make sure and give me suggestions," Eve said.

"Oh, no. I'm great when it comes to taking care of other people—or even myself. But when it comes to my family, I'm a mess." She took a sharp breath. "And apparently, this isn't about me. It's about this little guy . . ." She gasped. "Because I'm not coping very well." By the expression on Shani's face another contraction had started.

Eve extended her free hand, and Shani grabbed it, squeezing tight.

When the contraction ended, Eve said, "I'll be right back." She hurried into the bathroom and grabbed towels and washcloths from the shelf. When she returned, Shani still leaned against the side of the bed and had tensed up again.

"Another one?" Eve grabbed the watch.

Shani nodded, breathing heavily.

They were two minutes apart now. Eve watched the second hand in the dim light.

After ninety seconds, Shani said, "Done."

"They're closer together and stronger," Eve said.

Shani nodded. "I'm feeling a lot of pressure."

"To push?"

Shani nodded.

Eve's stomach fell. Even if Tim had reached the phone booth and the line was still up, the ambulance wouldn't make it in time.

Another contraction hit before Shani could say anything more, and this time she yelled. "Sorry," Shani panted. "It caught me off guard."

"No reason to apologize." When the contraction ended, Eve said, "I'll be right back."

Joel, balancing himself with his cane, held the lid of the pot high, checking the water. Zane and Lila, holding Trudy, stood on the other side of the wood stove.

"I need a pair of sharp scissors," Eve said. "And string."

"Get it from Mom's sewing basket," Joel said to Zane.

The boy pulled the flashlight out of his pocket and ran up the stairs.

"How's it going in there?" Joel asked, replacing the lid.

"Fast," Eve answered.

Joel nodded. "I'll stoke the fire and be right in." When Eve returned to the bedroom, Shani was in the middle of another contraction.

When it ended, Eve asked, "Do you want to get back on the bed?"

Shani shook her head. "This feels better."

When she heard Zane thundering down the stairs, Eve stepped into the hall. He handed her the scissors and embroidery thread. That would have to work.

"Take the scissors to your dad and tell him to hold them over the candle flame."

His eyes grew wide.

"To sterilize them. Then wipe them off." She handed him one of the washcloths.

Shani let out another yell, Zane's eyes grew even wider, and Eve hurried back into the room.

"It's really hurting," Shani said.

"Worse than with Zane?"

"I had an epidural with him." She managed to smile.

Eve smiled back. "It's supposed to hurt," she said. Not that she'd ever know.

Shani grimaced again and put her arms on the bed, leaning against it. "Oh no."

"What?"

"I need to push." She gasped and then let out another yell, pushing her forehead down against the mattress.

A knock came from the hallway. "Here are the scissors," Zane called out.

Eve hurried to the doorway.

"Is Mom all right?" Zane asked.

"Jah." Eve took the scissors from him.

Zane's voice was low. "Is the baby going to be okay?"

Eve nodded. God willing.

"We need the ambulance, right?"

"Yes, but if they don't come, God will provide."

Zane nodded. "But he wants us to take action, right? Not just sit by."

Before Eve could respond, the boy was gone, hurrying back down the hall.

Eve rushed back to Shani's side.

"Get Joel," Shani said. "And then help me onto the bed. I don't think it's going to be long."

Eve hurried out into the living room. "Come on," she said to Joel, who was putting another piece of wood in the stove. A look of panic passed over Zane's face, and he shoved his hands deep into the pockets of his jacket.

"You two, rest," Eve said to the children. "We'll come get you when the baby's here."

Lila nodded, and then patted Trudy's back as she moved toward the couch.

"Do you need more ice?" Zane asked.

Eve shook her head. What was on the stove was probably enough. "But thank you."

She followed Joel down the hall, but then waited as he shuffled into the room. She gave them a minute alone and then stepped on through the doorway. Shani gasped as another contraction seized her. Joel was at Shani's side, leaning against the bed with one hand, massaging her left shoulder with the other. Shani put her hands on the bed and pushed. Eve hoped the baby would at least wait until they could get her on the bed. It did.

When the contraction stopped, Shani sputtered, "Help me." Joel stepped back and took one of her arms while Eve took the other, and together they slid her onto the bed.

"You go around and support her other leg," Joel said. Pleased that he was taking charge, Eve hurried around the bed.

Shani positioned herself against the headboard and Eve and Joel both grabbed her legs. Joel leaned against the bed for support.

Another contraction hit her, and she pushed hard.

"I can see the head," Eve said. "You're doing great."

The contraction stopped, and Shani leaned back

against the headboard and closed her eyes. Both of her legs began to shake. Eve tightened her grip. Joel repositioned himself and then took Shani's leg again.

Another push. Shani grabbed her knees and pulled forward.

She pushed harder. Eve thought for a moment that Joel might catch the baby, but then she realized, because of his leg, he couldn't get in the right position. She slipped onto the bed as the head delivered and slipped her hands under the baby's body.

"It's your boy," Eve said, looking up into Shani's face.

"How is he?"

"Pink." Eve rubbed his chest. The baby opened his eyes and began to fuss. "Lean back," she said to Shani and then placed the baby on her chest just as she remembered the nurses doing for Abra. Thankfully the cord was long enough.

"He's so small," Joel said, as he pulled the quilt up over his wife and baby.

The baby wasn't that small. He was much bigger than the twins had been. Eve scooted off the bed and grabbed an extra blanket off the bureau. She slipped it around the little boy, under the quilt. Then she tied and cut the cord. "Where are more blankets?" she asked Joel.

He stepped toward the door.

"I'll get them," she said.

"In the hall closet."

Eve hurried from the room, going on to the living room first. The candle sputtered and was nearly out. "It's a little boy, and he looks healthy," she said, squinting toward the couch.

Lila stirred. "Oh, good." She was propped against a pillow, Trudy in her arms, an afghan wrapped around both of them. The other side of the couch was empty. So was the recliner. Zane wasn't by the stove either.

"Where did he go?"

"Outside." Lila yawned.

"Why?"

Lila shrugged.

Eve checked the water. It was still cool. She'd wait. But she needed a bowl for the afterbirth. She made her way into the kitchen, in the dark, and opened the bottom cupboard, managing to find a mixing bowl.

She caught a whiff of smoke. The wind must have pulled the chimney smoke to that side of the house. On the way back down the hall, she grabbed two blankets from the closet and returned to the bedroom. She spread them out on top of Shani and the baby. "How's he doing?" she asked.

"Okay, as far as I can tell." Shani pulled the blanket back a little. "He's alert, and he's breathing okay."

"I don't think I should clean the two of you up yet," Eve said. "It's too cold."

Shani nodded. "I'll see if he'll start nursing. And let's get the placenta out." She patted the bed next to her and then looked at Joel. "Get up here and get a closer look at our son. And keep us warm."

Joel struggled up onto the bed as Eve folded the blankets up from the bottom. Both parents peered down at the baby. Joel stroked the side of the little one's round face. Tears filled Eve's eyes as she took a moment to gaze at the tender moment.

As soon as the placenta was out, Eve threw another blanket over the mother and baby. She caught another whiff of smoke. "Do you smell that?"

"What?" Shani asked.

"Smoke."

Shani shook her head, but Joel scooted off the bed and stepped toward the window, pulling back the curtain.

Eve caught a glimpse of the orange flames as Joel cursed. He started toward the door, his cane thumping against the floor. "Zane!" he yelled. He stopped in the doorway though, looking back at Shani.

"Go!" She tried to sit up in bed.

Eve was torn between getting Shani and the baby out of the house and helping Joel. "I'll be right back," she said as she ran out of the room and down the hall.

Joel yelled again, "Zane!"

"He's outside," Lila said.

"Still?" Eve asked.

Lila nodded.

"Out back?"

Lila shook her head. "He went out the front."

Eve started toward the back door, toward the flames.

"Stop," he called out. "We need to go around from the front. Opening the back door will pull the flames in. And there's not any water anyway, since the pump's not working."

Eve turned and followed him to the front door.

"We need to get everyone out of the house," he said. "Into the van. We can back it away from the house. The heater will keep Shani and the baby warm."

Eve would grab Abra's quilt to wrap them in.

Joel froze for a moment. "The fire—it's my fault." He gestured back toward the kitchen.

"It doesn't matter," Eve said. She couldn't imagine how it could be. "Don't think about it now."

He nodded and seemed to refocus. "We have to get everyone out."

Eve grabbed Shani's purse. "I'll get the key."

Joel looked back down the hall and then put his hand out for the purse. "I'll look. You go get Shani and the baby. Lila, take Trudy to the van."

"Take the afghan with you," Eve said.

Joel started digging through Shani's purse. Lila

hurried to the front door and swung it open. She peered out for a moment and then stepped forward, still holding onto the door.

Joel dumped the purse on the floor. "There's no key."

"Go," Eve said to Lila, squatting down beside the contents in the dim light, panic rising in her throat.

"The van's gone," Lila said.

Eve looked up at her niece. "What?"

"It's gone."

Joel moaned, "Who would have taken it?"

"Zane." Lila's voice was so soft that Eve could hardly hear her. "He said he was going for help, but I didn't think that meant he was going to drive."

◈ 27

There was a fine layer of snow on the highway, but that was all until just past Gap. That was when Charlie hit the ice.

Tim's phone call had come through as Charlie was getting ready to leave the station, just over an hour ago. The weather had been fine in Philly—overcast but no precipitation. He'd stayed most of the night shift, covering for a buddy.

The phone number that popped up on his cell wasn't one he recognized. It had the same prefix as Shani and Eve's—but it wasn't either of their numbers. It turned out Tim was calling from a pay phone out on the highway.

"Come quickly," he said, without even saying who he was. "Shani is having the baby, but we have a terrible ice storm going on. I've called for the ambulance, but they're not sure if they can make it."

"Tim? Is that you?"

"Jah," he answered. "Eve went over to help. I'm out in my sleigh—but it's rough going in the ice. It's the worst I've seen."

"Why are you calling me?" Charlie stuttered.

"Love your neighbor, remember?"

Charlie recalled their discussion on the way to the hospital. It seemed like ages ago. Tim added,

"Eve told me the same thing tonight. The Becks are right next door—not thousands of miles away. It's my duty to help them."

"Thank you," Charlie said. "For calling. I'm on my way."

Tim had hung up without saying good-bye, and Charlie had made good time until now. His headlights revealed a world—trees, fences, roads—covered in ice. It was a miracle Tim had been able to get a call through. Ahead, along the side of the road in the range of his head-lights, a tree limb cracked. Charlie flinched but kept his grip on the steering wheel. It fell to the ground, bouncing to the edge of the pavement. He slowed even more, gripping the steering wheel harder.

Joel had to be beside himself. He felt helpless all the time, but in an ice storm with his wife in labor . . . Charlie feared what his reaction might be.

About a mile from the turnoff, the truck slid, and Charlie slowed even more. He hoped no one came up fast behind him. When he reached Juneberry Lane he slowed to a crawl and took the turn as carefully as he could. Still he slid toward the ditch. He pumped on the brakes, but it didn't do any good. In slow motion, he kept on going.

The truck came to a stop once it dipped down in the ditch. Charlie turned off the engine, grabbed his hat from the passenger seat, and jumped down. Before he knew it, he was on his Hinaendt, flat on the ground.

He stood, slid, and then grabbed hold of his truck until he felt steady enough to walk. He made it over to the other side of the lane and walked in the grass.

As he passed the Lehmans' driveway, he looked down it, as always, but didn't see anyone. He started jogging, crunching the grass with each step. As he rounded the first curve his stomach lurched. There was Shani's van—in the ditch.

He bolted toward it. The key was still in the ignition but no one was inside. Hopefully whoever was driving had been going slow enough to avoid injury.

As he ran, the first light of dawn crept over the trees—along with a large column of smoke. It was more than that of the wood stove. Charlie's heart raced as he breathed in the acrid scent.

The scene unfolded in front of him as the road curved. A sleigh and two workhorses. A fire truck with a tank. And the old farmhouse, charred and burned on the wooden kitchen side. The adjacent bricks were blackened. One firefighter held a hose and sprayed water, while two others chopped the charred remains of the back porch.

"Where's the family?" Charlie called out as he approached the fireman with the hose. And where was Eve?

The fireman looked around. "The women went in the ambulance."

Shani had gotten help. Charlie felt some relief. "There were some Amish folks here too . . ."

The second fireman nodded toward the fire truck. "There's an Amish man over there."

Charlie jogged toward it. The door swung open, and Tim leaned his head out and said, "You made it."

"Is everyone okay?"

"Jah," Tim said. "Shani's probably at the hospital by now. Eve's with her."

Genuine relief flooded through Charlie. "How about the baby?"

"He seems to be fine," Tim answered.

Charlie exhaled in relief. "Where's Zane?"

"I took him and Lila and Trudy back to my place. I found him in the van—in the ditch."

Charlie groaned.

"He's fine," Tim said. "I'm sorry about the house."

"The important thing is that everyone is okay." Thank goodness most of it was made out of brick.

"Jah. I'll pull the van out on the way back to the house."

Charlie tilted his head. "Can you pull my truck out too?"

"Sure," Tim said, glancing to his side. That was when Charlie saw Joel, standing at the back of the truck, leaning on his cane. He'd assumed he'd gone to the hospital too.

Charlie stepped around the truck to Joel's side. He wore his heavy coat but no gloves or hat. A blanket lay in a heap at his feet.

"Let's get you in the sleigh," Charlie said, putting his hand on Joel's shoulder.

Joel stepped away. "I want to talk to the firemen first."

Charlie followed Joel over to the captain, while Tim headed toward the sleigh.

"We'll have to investigate," the fireman was saying.

Joel leaned against his cane more.

"Besides the damage to the porch and kitchen, there's a lot of smoke inside the rest of the house. Call your insurance and go from there."

"Thanks," Joel said.

"Sure thing," the man answered. "Sorry for the fire, but it sounds like things could have been a lot worse. Count your blessings."

Joel frowned and shook his head.

A few minutes later, Charlie helped Tim hitch the horses to the van while Joel waited in the sleigh. The horses were strong, and the van was out with seemingly little effort. Once it was back on the lane, Joel said he'd drive it. "Zane left the key in the ignition, right?"

"Yep," Charlie said and then went to help his

friend. If Joel put it back in the ditch, they'd just pull it back out again. Tim waited for Joel to go first. He didn't put it back in the ditch, but when he reached the turn to the Lehmans' he kept going.

"Did he say anything about going to the hospital?" Charlie asked.

Tim shook his head.

Because if that was Joel's plan, Charlie would have liked to go with him. He dug in his pocket for his phone and hit speed dial for Joel. He didn't pick up.

By the time they reached Charlie's pickup truck, Joel was out of sight. He'd already turned onto the highway.

After Tim pulled his truck out of the ditch, Charlie called Joel again, this time leaving a message. "Call me," he said. "As soon as you get this. Once you get to the hospital." If he reached the hospital. The storm had stopped, but it was still a treacherous drive.

After he ended the call, he turned toward Tim. "So are you okay if I come in?"

The man shrugged. "As long as Eve isn't around."

Charlie found Zane sleeping on the couch. He tried to rouse him, but the kid wouldn't budge.

"He's fine here," Tim said.

"Thank you," Charlie answered. "I'll be back for him as soon as possible."

The closer Charlie got to town the better the roads were, and by the time he reached Lancaster they were fine. He didn't see Shani's van in the parking lot and tried to call Joel again. Still no answer.

He found the maternity ward and checked in at the desk. They called down to Shani and, with her okay, sent him down the hall.

He knocked on the door. It swung open. Eve stood before him.

She whispered, "You're here."

"Are you all right?" Charlie leaned against the doorframe.

She reached for his arm. "I'm fine."

Charlie wrapped his arm around her, pulling her close. "Tim called me, after he called the ambulance."

"How did he know your number?"

"Probably from his phone bill, back in November."

Eve blushed. "Jah. I knew he'd see that call sooner or later, but he never said anything."

Shani cleared her throat. "I thought you came to see the baby."

As Eve pulled away, Charlie grabbed her hand. He didn't want to let her go. She led him to Shani's side.

In her arms was a tiny bundle.

"Is he really okay?"

"He's perfect," Shani said. "But he certainly

picked the worst night of the year to make his appearance."

Charlie pulled Eve close. "So you delivered him?"

She smiled. "Shani delivered him. I caught him, is all."

"And cut the cord. And wrapped us in the quilt. And got us out of the house and kept us warm until the ambulance arrived."

Eve frowned. "If I'd been on my toes, I would have realized there was a fire sooner. I smelled smoke right after Shani delivered, but I thought it was from the stove."

Shani shook her head. "It was Joel's fault."

"The fireman said it will take a while to know what happened."

Shani grimaced. "Joel's been smoking, out on the back porch."

"Let's wait and see what the investigation turns up," Charlie said, his heart sinking.

"Zane took our van—put it in the ditch." Shani shifted the baby in her arms.

Charlie nodded.

"Tim took him to their home," Shani added.

Charlie nodded again. "I checked on him before I drove here."

"Thank you," she said. "He was so desperate to do something." Shani sighed.

Charlie reached down and touched the baby's face. The little one's nearly translucent eyelids fluttered but didn't open. "Have you decided on a name?"

Shani shook her head. "I'm waiting for Joel to make up his mind." Shani's eyes fell back on the baby.

"Where is he?" Charlie asked, looking around.

Shani's head shot up. "What do you mean?"

Charlie shook his head. "He left in the van. I assumed to come—"

"He hasn't been here." Shani groaned.

Charlie exhaled, trying to think. The roads were better toward the hospital. He hadn't seen any accidents on the way. "I'll go look for him," Charlie said.

Shani squeezed her eyes shut and then said, "He's still a mess, even worse."

Charlie took a step forward. "Shani . . ."

Her eyes opened slowly. "It's true. And he won't get help." Her face grew pale as she spoke. "Go find him."

"I'm sorry," Charlie said. "This is awful timing for you."

"I'm fine." Clearly she wasn't. She turned toward Eve. "Charlie can take you home."

"I don't think that's a good idea," Charlie said. "Tim was accommodating this morning—but if I show up with Eve, I think that could change." He turned toward her. "I'll get you a taxi."

"I can call for a driver."

Charlie shook his head. "A taxi will be faster.

You have to be exhausted." He suppressed a yawn.

Eve picked up her cape from the back of a chair.

"Take the quilt," Shani said.

Eve grabbed the one she'd given Shani off the window seat. "It's the one I used to keep Shani and the baby warm," she said. "While we waited for the ambulance."

Charlie grimaced. He didn't even want to imagine that scenario. He exhaled and turned toward Shani. "Where would he go?"

Shani shook her head, her eyes hard. "I don't know. He's been just as bad as he was that night, just without the gun. Depressed. Despondent. Last night he started out negative, but during the birth he was nearly back to his old self, helping me, doing what he could. But then the fire . . ."

"I will never leave a fallen comrade." But Charlie had. He'd left Joel because the guy was mad at him, instead of coming back down and working it out. *No, God,* he prayed. *Please.* What would Joel do?

"I begged him to come with us in the ambulance—the driver said it would be okay, under the circumstances—but . . ." Shani inhaled sharply. "Charlie, he's said several times we'd be better off without him."

Charlie took his phone out of his pocket and dialed Joel's number again. When it went into voicemail, he said, "Hey, buddy, me again. Give me a call as soon as you get this."

"I doubt if he has his phone. We didn't grab anything on the way out." Shani's eyes glistened. "Please call me when you find him."

Charlie and Eve headed straight to the emergency department. He knew the woman at the desk couldn't give him any direct information, but he spelled out his concerns and told her Shani was up on the maternity ward. He made sure she got the last name and Shani's room number, just in case Joel ended up in the ED.

Then he called the Lancaster County sheriff. After the dispatcher picked up the line, Charlie said, "I know it's too early to file a missing person report, but I need to alert you anyway." He recited all of the pertinent information and then said, "He's an Iraq vet. Injured. Recovering. Just went through a traumatic event—a house fire that he blames himself for after his baby was born—early this morning."

"I understand," the man said.

Charlie left Shani's hospital phone number and his cell number, even though he didn't expect they would call him.

Then he walked Eve to the entrance to the hospital, put her in a taxi, and paid the driver. He wanted more than anything to hug her good-bye, but of course he didn't.

He drove as slowly as he could once he reached the ice storm area, peering across the other lane of traffic into the ditch. The ice was melting, dripping off the telephone wires and the trees and turning into slush on the pavement. There was no blue van anywhere that he could see.

Once he neared the farm, he turned around and took another possible route into Lancaster, but there was no blue van that way either.

Finally he decided to go back to the Lehmans' to see if perhaps Joel had returned there, but first he pulled over and called Shani's room.

"Would he go back to Philly?" he asked her.

"I don't know where to . . ."

"Would he go to his parents'?"

"Wisconsin's a really long way. I don't think he could drive that far with his bum leg."

Charlie agreed. Besides, he didn't seem very close to his folks. They wrote to him a few times when he was in Iraq, but neither Joel nor Shani had talked about taking a trip out there, and as far as he knew his parents hadn't come to see him since he'd been home.

"I'm going back to the Lehmans'—and then I'll check the house," Charlie said. "Maybe he just went to the pay phone to call the insurance company." He hoped to God that was the case.

"I was mad at him about the fire," Shani said. "I yelled. I'd asked him to stop smoking."

Shani had a lot to be stressed about. Giving

birth in an ice storm, having to evacuate her house right afterward because of a fire, and then finding out that Zane had put the van in the ditch. Not to mention all the physiological stuff going on. She'd probably felt like a mama bear, ready to tear someone apart.

"Why didn't he go to the hospital with you?" Charlie asked.

"He said it was his responsibility to stay until the fire was out. He asked Eve to go." Shani took a ragged breath. "What if he buys another gun? Or what if he's headed to your house to get his?"

Charlie's stomach sank. "I don't think he'd do that." He reached for the gearshift. "After I check the Lehmans' and your house, I'll go back to Philly—just in case he headed there. I'll call as soon as I find anything out."

༄ 28

Eve thanked the taxi driver and climbed out of the back of the cab, the quilt in her arms. She'd need to wash it to get the smoke out.

There was no sign of Shani's van.

Ice dropped from the trees on the south side of the house. The day was finally warming. Still, she carefully climbed the steps, not wanting to fall. She yawned as she opened the back door and stepped onto the mud porch, placing the quilt on the top shelf of the cupboard, kicking off her boots, and then taking off her cape. The house was cozy warm, and something smelled good. Really good.

Apple strudel.

She shuffled into the kitchen, yawning again, as Monika hurried into the room with Trudy. "You're back," she said to Eve.

"Jah, what are you doing here?"

"Helping." She grinned. "Tim called Gideon . . ."

Which meant the bishop knew she'd been at the hospital with Shani. "Thank you," Eve said to her friend.

Trudy gurgled at Eve but seemed content with Monika. After Eve updated her on Shani and the baby, she asked, "How is everyone here?"

"*Gut.* Tim's resting, and Zane's still asleep on the couch," Monika said.

"How about Lila?"

"She and Jenny helped me with the strudel, but now they're playing a game in Lila's room. She'll probably be asleep soon." The woman smiled. "She certainly is capable."

Eve nodded. She was—but she was also still a girl.

"You should go sleep," Monika said. "While you can."

Eve nodded. "I'll get something to eat first."

Monika's eyes lit up. "I was just going to take the strudel out." She stepped closer. "Take the baby."

Eve reached for her, but Trudy ducked, making them laugh.

"You know how to make a woman feel needed, don't you," Monika said, kissing the top of the baby's head and then scooting her into Eve's arms.

As Monika grabbed the potholders and opened the oven, she said, "I was tidying up and saw the note to you from Abra."

Eve's heart stopped for a moment. "What note?"

"It was between the refrigerator and the counter. It looked like it had fallen there."

Eve shook her head. "I don't know what you're talking about."

Monika took the pan of strudel out of the

oven, placed it on top of the stove, and then took a piece of paper out of her apron pocket. "Here," she said.

It looked like the piece of paper Tim had in his hand when he left to call the ambulance. Eve took it, holding it away from Trudy. Monika put her hands out to the baby, who fell back into her arms, and Eve unfolded the piece of paper. It was dated May 1, 2004. The night before Abra passed. She was in the hospital, and Eve had been home with the children.

Dear Eve . . . It was written in Abra's schoolgirl hand, but shaky, like an old person's. Eve was amazed her friend could write at all at that point.

> *Please forgive me. I shouldn't have asked you to promise to care for my children.*
> *I have to trust God for that. And trust him with you too.*
> *My prayer is that God will bring you a husband who follows Christ and loves you. And a houseful of your own babies. I know you will always love mine—that's all I can ask.*

Tears filled Eve's eyes, but she continued.

> *Another thing I regret is not talking about my love for Tim with you. At first I struggled,*

as you know. And then later, when we found our way, it seemed too private to talk about. Rough at times, true, clear to the end. But he's been good to me, as much as he was able. And I love him. God has assured me that he'll find his way in caring for our children—God will provide.

You have been more than a sister to me. I'm sad to leave all of you but ready for heaven. Please assure my children of my love for them.

My greatest privilege was being their mother, Tim's wife, and your friend.

Love,
Abra

Eve swiped at her eyes as she raised her head.

"Did you read it?" she asked Monika.

The woman blushed. "Yah. I didn't . . ."

"No, it's fine." It wouldn't have been if it was anyone but Monika, but Eve trusted the woman. She folded the paper. No wonder Tim had been inspired to call for the ambulance and then call Charlie in the middle of the night. He'd just read about Abra's love for him. Perhaps it had helped him love his neighbors.

Eve swiped at her eyes. Abra had released her from her promise.

How had she missed the note all these months? The nurses had probably packed it in with Abra's things, and it had simply been overlooked.

"Are you all right?" Monika put her arm around Eve.

She nodded.

Monika squeezed Eve's shoulder. "You're free to marry Gideon now."

Eve nearly laughed. That wasn't what she'd been thinking at all.

Monika added, "I'm sure Abra would agree that Gideon is a fine man."

She held the note up. "Denki," she said and slipped it into the pocket of her apron. "I think I'll take a shower and then get something to eat."

She'd towel dried her hair as best she could, twisted it into a bun, put on a fresh Kapp, and then returned to the kitchen just as a knock fell on the back door. She hurried to it, swinging the door open to Charlie—all alone.

"You haven't found him?"

Charlie shook his head. "I'm going to head to my place in case he's there."

"Come in and get something to eat first," Eve said.

He shook his head.

"At least a cup of coffee."

He shook his head again.

She smiled. "Tim's asleep, but Monika is here."

"In that case," he said. "I really could use a cup of coffee."

Monika, with Trudy still on her hip, gave him a hug as he stepped into the kitchen, and then directed him to the table. She served him coffee and strudel. "You sit too," she said to Eve.

"Tim said he'd get a crew—an Amish crew—to fix the house," Monika said to Charlie as she put a piece of strudel down in front of Eve.

"You're kidding," Charlie said, glancing at Eve as he took a bite of the strudel.

Eve smiled. "They'll get it done in no time. Probably next weekend." It didn't surprise her that Tim planned to do that.

"So has he had a change of heart?" Charlie asked.

Eve shrugged. "He's good in a crisis, and we grow up being taught to help when things get bad." She didn't want to tell Charlie about the note from Abra in front of Monika. She'd give too much away.

But then the baby began to fuss and Monika headed down the hall with her.

Charlie took the last bite of his strudel and asked quietly, "Where are things at with you and Gideon?" There was a hint of bitterness in his voice. The last two months had worn on him too.

"I told Gideon I can't court him." She hesitated. "I don't love him."

Relief filled his eyes but then he asked, "And he believed you?"

She shrugged. "He said he'd give me more time." She took the note from her pocket then but didn't risk handing it to him in case Tim or Monika came into the room. "Tim found this last night. It's from Abra to me, before she died, releasing me from my promise to care for the children. He didn't tell me about it, but Monika found it and gave it to me. Tim must have left it on the counter."

Charlie leaned toward her. "What are you going to do?"

"For now?"

He nodded.

"Care for the children. And pray." She swallowed hard and slipped the note back into her pocket.

"I'll pray too," he said.

"Denki," she answered.

He met her gaze. "When I saw the smoke and then the house, I . . . Well, I was terrified for everyone, really, but . . ." He placed his hand, palm down, on the table. "If anything had happened to you."

"None of us were in danger," she said, although she felt shaky thinking about it.

"You could have been," he said, leaning

forward. "I want you to know that I'll wait for you, for as long as it takes. For as long as you need. I know you only wanted for us to be friendly with each other—but we became friends anyway." His eyes glistened. "And I want to be your friend, but more than that too, if you'll have me."

"Denki," she whispered.

"I've fallen in love with you," he said.

Her heart constricted. "Shhh," she said as Monika bustled back into the kitchen with Trudy. The woman didn't say anything, but she stood for a moment and then grabbed the coffeepot and said, "How about some more?"

Charlie exhaled sharply. "I need to get going. I'm headed to Philly to try to find Joel."

"Does he have a key to your place?" Eve asked.

Charlie shook his head. "But he knows where I keep the spare." He took a last drink of the coffee and then said, "Is it okay if Zane stays here?"

"Of course," Eve said.

"When I come back—when *we* come back—I'll get a hotel room. Zane can stay with us."

Monika shook her head. "You can all stay at my house," she said.

"Wouldn't that be frowned on?" Charlie asked.

Monika smiled, slightly. "I'm on the other side of middle-aged. No one's going to make a fuss about it. Shani and the baby can stay too once they're out, until you and the other men can get that house fixed."

"Thank you," Charlie said to Monika.

Eve stood and walked him to the door, trying her hardest to treat him as she would anyone else as she said good-bye. She must have failed though because as she turned back toward the kitchen, a concerned look passed over Monika's face.

Patting her pocket, Eve said, "I'm going to go try to get some sleep. Thank you again for everything."

She wouldn't talk with Tim about the note from Abra. Not yet. Not when he was doing his best to help the neighbors.

ನಲ್ 29

Before leaving, Charlie called his buddy Ron, who'd served with them in Iraq as a chaplain. He asked him to go over and check out his house for a blue van. Fifteen minutes later, Ron called back and said he didn't see one. "Let me know when you find him," he added. "I can help."

Charlie decided to head out anyway. He'd get a shower and pack a bag. And maybe Joel would still show up. If not, he'd make more phone calls, starting with the state police.

He hadn't expected the van to be at his house, but it was. First relief flooded through him. Then fear. He'd locked Joel's gun in his safe—but that didn't mean Joel hadn't figured a way to break the lock.

He bolted from his truck around to the back of the house, but he slowed as he came through the door, saying, "Hey, Joel."

No one answered. Charlie hurried through the kitchen.

Joel sat on the couch, slumped to the side, his eyes closed. Fear surged through Charlie. What if he'd grabbed his meds on the way out of the house and had overdosed?

Joel opened one eye.

Relief flooded through Charlie. "You okay?"

425

Joel yawned. "Tired."

"Why didn't you answer your phone?"

Joel held up both hands. "I don't have it."

Charlie downplayed his concern, choosing his words carefully. "We've been a little worried."

Joel shook his head. "I didn't know what else to do." His eyes were red and watery. "I burned the house down. I almost killed my family. After everything Shani's done for me, I couldn't even help her get out the door. And I can't help her"— he shuddered—"with the baby."

He put his head in his hands.

Charlie sat down on the couch beside him and started to put his arm around him, but Joel jerked away. "God," he moaned. "It should have been me instead of Samuel. Why didn't you pull him out? You should have left me for that second blast."

"Don't," Charlie said.

Joel grabbed his cane, pushed himself up, and started toward the door.

"Where are you going?"

"I have no idea," Joel said, grabbing the doorknob.

"Stop."

Joel turned. "Are you going to make me?"

Charlie wanted to say, *I'll take your sorry Hinaendt down.* But he didn't. He took a deep breath. "How about a nap? Here on the couch." If Joel didn't agree, he'd have to take his keys.

Joel, his back to the door, slumped against it.

"If I stay, will you go back and see what Shani needs?"

"No," Charlie said. "But I'll take you down so you can see what your wife needs. And your sons."

Joel slid to the floor, wincing as he tried to straighten his leg out. "I can't face them," he said. "Not yet. Come back for me tomorrow. I'll go then. I promise."

Charlie'd had enough psych training and experience to know Joel wasn't doing well. There was no way he could leave him, but Charlie nodded, just to get him to stay. "You can crash in the spare bedroom. And shower, if you want. I'll grab some sweats for you to wear."

Joel exhaled. "I'll sleep first." He had to be in a lot of pain.

Charlie extended his hand. Joel took it and pushed up on his cane with his other hand, placing his weight on his good leg. Charlie pulled his buddy up and then directed him down the hall to the spare bedroom, grabbing some ibuprofen and following behind.

"Go back to Lancaster," Joel said. "Tell Shani I'm sorry. Don't hang around here because of me."

"Sure thing," Charlie said. "I'll get the sweats for you."

He noted the safe was intact when he went into his room for the sweat pants. Once Joel was settled, Charlie went back into the living room, collapsed on the couch, and called Ron.

After he explained what had happened, he asked for Ron's advice.

"You should go back," Ron said. "I'll come over and stay with Joel until he wakes up. Then I'll take him to my place." Ron was in his late forties, married, kids out of the house. "We can figure out the rest tomorrow."

"Thank you," Charlie said. "I owe you."

Ron chuckled. "I'm doing this for Joel, not you. We'll get him through this."

Charlie called Shani next and explained what was going on. She thought having Ron involved was a good idea. Charlie could hear her take a deep breath on the other end of the line. "Would you leave him a note and tell him to call me when he wakes up?"

"Will do," Charlie said.

He showered and packed his bag while he waited for Ron. As soon as the chaplain arrived, Charlie headed out the door, but as he reached his truck his phone rang. *Eve.*

"I couldn't sleep," she said. "Did you find him?"

After a quick update he said he was on his way.

"Drive carefully," she said. "You have to be exhausted. I'll be praying for you."

"Denki." It had been so long since he knew he was in someone's prayers.

By the time he reached Lancaster County the roads were drying somewhat. When he reached the Lehman house, Eve hurried out carrying a basket. "We've been watching for you," she said as he jumped down from the truck. "Don't come in. The sooner you go see Shani and the baby the sooner you can get to Monika's and to bed."

She handed him the basket as Zane, dressed in an Amish shirt, pants, and suspenders, opened the passenger door and climbed into the truck.

"I made you sandwiches," Eve said. "And Monika's address is on the piece of paper."

"Denki," he said, wanting desperately to give her a hug.

She stepped away.

He climbed back into the truck. As he backed it around, Zane asked, "So what's with you and Eve?"

"What do you mean?"

"It's like you're in love or something."

Charlie cringed.

"Lila thinks so too," Zane said. "Her Dat hasn't been happy with you for a long time. He's just being nice right now because of the baby and the fire and everything."

"Is that so?" Hopefully it was more than that.

Zane nodded.

"Well," Charlie said, "I'll take any kindness I can get from Tim Lehman." As he turned onto the highway, he said, "Nice getup you have on."

Zane looped his fingers through the suspenders. "Lucky for me, Daniel's been growing too. It's his newest pair of pants. Eve made them."

"You gonna wear those to school on Monday?"

"Yep." Zane grinned. "For the fashion statement of the year." He brushed his long bangs back. "I should get a haircut first though."

"Definitely," Charlie said. "I can do it tonight. I'll borrow a bowl from Monika."

Zane laughed. Charlie would need to take him clothes shopping soon. Shani would need a few things too. He sighed. And so would Joel, although he needed a whole lot more than new clothes.

Fear gripped his chest, but then he remembered Eve was praying and he exhaled, relaxing his grip on the steering wheel as best he could.

ෲ 30

Shani scooted up in her hospital bed as Zane, followed by Charlie, hurried into her room. It was obvious how exhausted they both were, but Zane grinned from ear to ear as he touched the top of the baby's head. Shani eased the baby into Zane's arms, and he sat on the edge of the bed, gazing down at his little brother.

Charlie stifled a yawn but then grinned at Shani and her two boys. Of course Joel was the one who got to sleep. Her patience was running thin. Charlie wouldn't understand how badly Joel had let her down.

Maybe Joel was easing into being gone for good. First he'd stay at Charlie's. Then maybe he'd go farther. He had Army buddies scattered all over the States. Someone would take him in and help him get on his feet.

After a half-hour visit, Zane started yawning too, and Shani sent them both off to Monika's, thankful for her friend's generosity. "Come back in the morning," she said.

They all needed a good rest, but she slept fitfully. During the baby's four a.m. feeding, she felt lonelier than she ever had in her entire life. She'd been twenty when Zane was born; Joel had been twenty-three. They were young, true, but so happy.

Tears slipped down her face as she burped the baby. Who would have thought her marriage would come to this? When her mother had left all those years ago, her father had seemed to take everything in stride. He'd been so matter of fact, telling Shani it had nothing to do with her, that both he and her mother loved her very much, that sometimes adults stopped getting along and it was better for everyone—including their children —for them not to live together. Then he'd had the foresight to send her to her grandparents to be loved and cared for, for a time of healing.

At first her mother had moved into an apartment in downtown Seattle with her new boyfriend, the neighbor man she'd left with. But a year later, they broke up and she moved to California. A few months later she remarried. By the time Shani was in high school she'd stopped going down to visit. Her mother did come for her wedding—and cried —but it was pretty obvious they weren't tears of joy. Maybe they were tears of guilt. Or fear for Shani.

As Shani edged to the side of the hospital bed and lowered the baby back into his crib, she couldn't stop the tears. Once Baby Boy Beck was settled, she scooted back down in the bed, positioning her head on the pillow and then wiping her face with the sheet.

She wouldn't beg Joel to come back home. She'd already begged him to get help, over and over. If he didn't care enough to make their marriage work, she wasn't going to force him. She'd been doing everything herself anyway. The only difference was she wouldn't have to put up with his moping around.

A couple hours later, just after she finished eating breakfast, her dad called. She'd left a message for him soon after getting to the hospital and had been surprised when he hadn't gotten back to her right away. They agreed that since he already had a plane ticket to come out to Lancaster County in three weeks, long after the baby had been due, he'd just stick to that plan. He didn't seem too worried about the house, just thankful that they were all okay and that it was insured.

She didn't tell him Joel had fled to Philly, but before he hung up he said, "I regret not saying more last time I was out. I was worried about you, but I should have also told you I wished I would have handled things differently when your mother left."

"How's that, Dad?" He'd been so calm. She remembered him handling it perfectly.

"I was trying to be brave—for you. But I should have been honest. It was the most difficult thing I've ever gone through."

Shani swallowed hard, peering into the crib at the baby.

"I wasn't honest with your mother, either, and

I think if I had been, she might have come home. Looking back, I think we could have worked things out."

"But she left," Shani said. *With another man.*

"She was depressed," her father said. "At the time I didn't understand. I thought she was purposeful about it. I didn't consider that she was ill and that starting a relationship with someone else made her feel better, at least for a short time. Not that what she did wasn't horrible—it was. It's just that it took me a long time to acknowledge her pain." He paused a moment and then said, "Give Joel more time. He's been through a lot."

She suppressed a sob.

Full of concern, her father asked, "Are you okay, honey?"

She told him then about Joel smoking and starting the fire. About him going to Philly without even holding the baby. "He's a mess," she said.

"He'll get better," her dad replied. "Give him time."

Shani wanted to answer that she wasn't so sure. Instead she said, "I hope you're right."

Later that morning Charlie showed up at the hospital with a new infant car seat, along with a couple of changes of clothes for Zane. He'd also purchased a pair of sweats and some long-sleeved T-shirts for Shani and two granny nightgowns. "Everything's pretty smoky back at the house," he said. "I think it can all be cleaned, but it will take a while."

Shani thanked him profusely. She didn't know what she would've done without Charlie.

Zane dubbed his new brother Bub Belly—which he insisted was Pennsylvania Dutch for *baby*—and held him while the nurse discharged Shani. Then Charlie drove everyone to Monika's house.

Shani didn't want to ask Charlie if he'd heard from Joel since returning to Lancaster, not in front of Zane. Her son had gone through enough in the last two days without worrying that his parents' marriage was in jeopardy. Then again, not having Joel around would eventually make him wonder anyway.

When Charlie stopped the truck as close to Monika's back door as he could, the woman ran out, calling out a greeting, followed by Jenny. Monika opened the back door of the cab, unfastened the car seat, pulled it from the truck, and led the way up her back stairs and then into her kitchen, cooing at the baby as she walked. Windows along the east side filled the room with light and the pale yellow walls brightened it even more. Eve had said that Deacon King had been a construction contractor. He'd done a great job on his own home.

Monika placed the car seat on the counter. "What name have you chosen?"

"Bub Belly," Zane said.

"What?" Jenny asked.

Zane reddened. "Isn't that what you call a baby?"

"Oh," Monika said. "You mean *Boppli*."

Jenny laughed.

Monika smiled and said, "I like Bub Belly better than our word. As a nickname." She turned toward Shani.

"Joel and I haven't decided yet."

"Then Bub Belly it is," Monika said.

Shani smiled. She wasn't big on nicknames, but they had to call him something other than Baby Boy Beck.

"I should get going," Charlie said. He told them all good-bye, hugging each one, including Monika and the baby together. "I'll tell Joel to call when I see him," he said to Shani.

She bit her lip and then nodded. Charlie had retrieved her cell from the house that morning—and she guessed he'd gotten Joel's too. He hadn't called the day before, but she knew they needed to talk. She just wasn't sure what she needed to say.

After Charlie left, Monika led her down the hall while Zane stayed in the kitchen with Jenny. The house was fairly new with hardwood floors, high ceilings, and wide molding. The bedroom had a double bed and a crib. Shani sank down on the bed. "I'm overwhelmed by your goodness," she said to Monika.

"It's not my goodness," she replied. "It's God's. I just had the foresight to save the crib I had with the girls in hopes of having grandchildren sooner rather than later." She smiled. "I'll hold the baby while you get situated."

"Thank you," Shani said.

After settling Bub Belly in the crib, Shani lay down on the bed and fell into a deep sleep.

Joel finally called the next afternoon. "Hey," he said, his voice raw. "Are you okay?"

Frustration flooded over her. "I'm fine," she said, aware of the tension in her voice. "How are you?"

"I don't blame you for being ticked."

She didn't respond.

"To answer your question," he said, "I'm not doing that great—but you knew that. Charlie agrees. He sent me off to the chaplain's house."

Shani wanted to say something encouraging, but she couldn't force the words.

"The chaplain—Ron—made an appointment for me to see a therapist, on Tuesday."

"He got you into the VA that soon?" She couldn't help the surprise in her voice.

"No. It's a civilian counselor." He sighed.

"And you're going?"

"He's making me."

When she didn't respond, he added, "You have every right to be mad, Shani. I could have lost all of you—and it would have been all my fault."

"We need you, Joel," she said, but her voice sounded hollow.

"Thanks," he answered, but his word sounded insincere too. "I called the insurance company," he said, changing the subject. "And then the cleaners. Next we need to get bids on the repairs."

"Monika said Tim and Gideon cleaned out what they could and put up tarps. Eve said they're putting a demolition group together to go over on Friday and then a building crew to go over on Saturday."

Joel didn't answer for a long moment. Finally he asked, "Why would Tim do that?"

"Apparently it's the way they're raised. To help."

Joel whistled.

Frankly, she was surprised by Tim's generosity too. "I guess he's a good man deep down, even though he's so intimidating," Shani said. "So are you and Charlie doing all right?"

"Yeah," Joel said. "I know he was just trying to help. He said he'd give the gun back when the therapist says it's okay." Then he said, "I should go."

He hadn't asked about the baby. Or Zane. They needed to talk—about naming the baby, about the future. But it didn't seem to be the right time.

"Would you call me after the appointment with the counselor?"

"Sure," he answered.

Shani hung up feeling wrung out. She was so used to taking care of everything, but here she was—staying in someone else's home because hers was damaged by fire and smoke, dependent on people she barely knew, while her husband hid from his family. She swallowed hard, willing herself not to cry.

Monika hired a driver to take Zane to school while she took Jenny in the buggy. On Tuesday evening Joel called and said the appointment with the counselor had gone all right and he had another one in two days, adding that he'd stay in Philly for that, at least.

On Wednesday, Eve followed Monika home with Trudy after she dropped her nieces and nephews off at school. Eve spent most of her time holding Bub while Monika played with Trudy.

Eve asked about Joel and then Zane. The one person she didn't ask about was Charlie. Finally Monika did, keeping her eyes on Eve as she asked. As Eve's face reddened, Monika shook her head.

"What?" Eve asked.

"You can't fool me, Eve Lehman," Monika said. "I saw the way you were with him that day after the ice storm. No wonder you keep putting Gideon off."

"I don't know what—"

Monika interrupted her. "Don't lie to me."

The woman had Trudy sitting on the edge of the table in front of her. Shani shifted, wondering whether or not she should step in to help Eve.

Eve shook her head and finally said, "I didn't mean to be deceptive."

Monika just smiled, but Eve began to cry. "What am I going to do?"

"Now, now." Monika stood, put Trudy on her hip, and put her arm around Eve's shoulder. "You'll get over Charlie. Gideon's the right one for you. Like Deacon King was for me."

Shani decided not to say anything, not in front of Monika, and Eve soon composed herself and Monika sat back down. Eve asked the older woman about the new quilt she was making. Not another word was said about Charlie or Gideon.

Mostly that week, Shani rested, fed the baby, and ate Monika's good food. On Friday she asked if Gideon was okay with her staying at Monika's.

"Of course he is," she answered. "Why wouldn't he be?"

"Tim wouldn't be all right if I stayed at his house."

Monika smiled. "Gideon wouldn't either. They're all worried about Eve—and your influence on her."

"I haven't encouraged her to leave the Amish faith," Shani said. In fact, she'd warned Charlie away from Eve.

Monika nodded. "I believe you. And I also

440

believe that Eve will come through this—God's testing her, that's all. She'll do the right thing this time."

Shani didn't want to discuss Eve's love life with Monika, so she changed the subject. "Has Tim always been so on edge? Or is it just since Abra passed away?"

"Always," Monika answered. "He's dealing with his own—what do you call it? PTSD?"

Shani nodded. "Anything in particular?"

"Tim and Eve's mother was a sweet woman, but their father was a tyrant. I think that's why Eve rebelled like she did when she was a teenager—to show she couldn't be controlled. Tim, on the other hand, became like his father—harsh and legalistic. Abra, God rest her soul, put up with a lot."

Shani thought on that as she nursed the baby. Most people had some sort of sad story in their past. Joel certainly did. So did she.

Joel called on Thursday evening and said his counseling session had been hard. Then he said he wanted to go to drill on Saturday, just to see everyone. Shani said that would be fine. The truth was she felt more relaxed—even with a new baby —than she had since getting the call eight months ago that Joel had been injured. It was a relief not to be concerned about his day-to-day needs, and she was doing her best not to think too far into the future and worry about what it might hold.

• • •

Saturday morning, Monika loaded all of them into the buggy to go to the Lehmans' place. Three months ago Shani would never have considered riding in a buggy, let alone with a newborn on a January morning. But the baby was swaddled, and wool blankets covered both of them. If anything, she was afraid he was going to get overheated. On the way there her cell phone rang. It was Joel.

"Hey," he said. "I'm at drill with Charlie. It's been good to see everyone. It hit me that it would be a good idea for me to see Karina and meet Samuel's parents. Charlie said maybe you could call her . . ."

"Are you sure?"

"Yeah . . ."

"Did you talk to the counselor about it?"

"I did. And about Johnny."

Shani took a sharp breath, wondering at the connection between Joel's brother and what had happened in Iraq. "Really?" She glanced at Zane, who sat in the back next to Jenny. He didn't seem to be listening.

"Yeah. He said there's a link—in my mind, anyway."

"Oh," Shani said.

"So could you call Karina?"

"Sure."

"The sooner the better."

She exhaled in relief. "I'll give her a call." Maybe Joel *would* get better.

Shani called, but no one answered. She left a message, hoping Karina would call back before Joel changed his mind. She did a few minutes later, and Shani explained Joel's request.

Karina said she would love to meet Joel, and then said, "It just so happens I'm on my way to Eve's. My in-laws volunteered to help fix your house, through their church. I asked if I could tag along."

Touched, Shani said she'd speak with her in person in a few minutes. She quickly left Joel a message before she lost cell service, telling him Samuel's parents were helping fix up the house, and Karina would be there too. Then she left Karina's number and asked him to make the arrangements. A few minutes later Monika turned down the Lehmans' driveway.

Karina and her in-laws had just arrived. Her mother-in-law held Samantha, who looked healthy and happy. They all made a fuss over Bub Belly, and then Karina reintroduced Shani and said, "We'd all like to meet with Joel. Is he at your house?"

Shani explained he was in Philly, knowing it sounded odd since she'd just had a baby. "I left him your number," she said.

Shani headed into the living room with Bub, thinking about Samuel. Shani had both of her sons. And her husband was still alive.

She had a lot to be thankful for.

ಬಾ 31

After the noon meal was served and cleaned up and the babies were down for their naps, Karina, Mrs. Johnson, and Eve started down the lane to see if they could help at the Becks' house. Monika and Shani stayed behind to watch over the little ones.

Once the fire marshal said it was safe to enter the house and the professionals had come in and vacuumed up all the water, Eve had gathered all the Becks' clothes and bedding and had been soaking it, washing it, and drying it all week. Thankfully it had been sunny.

As they reached the house, Eve watched the men working on the back porch and exterior kitchen wall, calling out to each other, sawing, nailing, and generally making a racket. Zane, Daniel, and Simon were helping—running for supplies, cleaning up as the men worked, and poking at each other as they usually did. Gideon and Tim were clearly in charge—Reuben was overseeing the lumberyard for the day.

Shani had asked Eve to check the messages on their landline, so once they entered the house Eve headed to the back bedroom. There were three. One from Zane's school about classes being canceled after the ice storm. One from Shani's boss who said she'd try her cell. And then one from Joel, left that morning, saying he hadn't been able to reach Karina and if anyone happened to check the messages would they ask her to call him on his cell.

Eve went and got Karina and led her to the phone. Then, slipping on a pair of rubber gloves, she began scrubbing the closest living room wall with a paint thinner solution to get rid of the soot. Karina returned, spoke quietly with her mother-in-law, and then they both joined Eve in washing the wall. Eve decided if they wanted her to know what was going on they'd tell her. She had no reason to ask.

Over and over Eve's thoughts turned to Charlie. She hadn't talked to him all week, but she'd been praying for him. She wasn't sure what God was doing, but she did know she'd never loved anyone the way she loved him. Then her thoughts turned to the children. Trudy's giggles that morning when she woke. Lila's help to get everything ready. Simon's bright smile, and Daniel's hard work. Rose's constant chatter.

When they reached the hallway, Eve and Karina continued down it, providing more privacy. Karina asked how Charlie was, and Eve said he had his first day back at drill, but that she hadn't talked with him all week.

"Oh," she said. "I was hoping you two had worked things out."

Eve shook her head. "It was never like that—not really." Her heart ached at the possibility of it.

"My bad," Karina said. "I had this idea that maybe you'd move to Philly. I wanted you to know, if you needed a place to live, I'd love to have you stay with me."

"That's so kind of you," Eve said. "But I can't leave." At least not yet. "And really, Charlie and I are only friends."

Karina smiled. "You could have fooled me."

Eve changed the subject to Samantha, asking about her health. The two chatted for quite a while until they were interrupted by someone calling out, "Hallo!"

It sounded like Charlie. Eve dropped her sponge into the bucket and headed toward the front door, wiping her hands on her apron. Charlie's truck was parked in front of the house, and Shani's van was next to it. Charlie stood by as Joel climbed down from the driver's side. Charlie wore his Army uniform, a camouflage one, and tan-colored boots. He must have left drill early. Joel wore jeans and a coat and walked with his cane.

Gideon was striding toward them, followed by Tim. Eve stopped on the porch. She didn't see Zane or her nephews. They'd probably gone down to their fort along the creek, which was a good thing. It would be better if Simon didn't see Charlie in his uniform, especially not in front of Tim.

"Sorry about the uniform," Charlie said to Gideon. "We decided to come straight here at the last moment. I didn't have a chance to change."

Gideon didn't answer Charlie but extended his hand, first to Charlie and then to Joel. Tim followed the gesture, but afterward he looked Charlie up and down—from his cap to his boots— and frowned.

"Thank you so much," Joel said. "For everything you've done." He motioned toward the other men. "All of you." He looked much better than he had the night of the fire.

Charlie spotted Eve on the porch and started toward her. "Is Karina around?"

She nodded. "In the house with Samuel's mom."

"What about his dad?"

Eve nodded toward the back porch. "He's working with the men."

Charlie found him, while Gideon walked with Joel up the ramp and Tim headed back to work. A few minutes later Samuel's parents and Karina sat with Joel and Charlie in the living room on the smoky sheet-covered furniture.

"Thank you for meeting with me," Joel said.

Eve stepped into the hall, retrieved the sponge from the bucket, and got back to work. She could imagine Joel was telling them about the night Samuel had died, what Charlie had told her, but it wasn't her business to overhear what was being said. Eve prayed as she scrubbed. For Joel. For

447

Karina and Samuel's parents. For Shani and the boys. For Charlie. The movement of her arm helped her fight back her tears.

After Abra had died, several people told Eve it was God's will and that good would come from it. She knew God had allowed it, and had no doubt that some kind of good would come from Abra's death, that all of them who loved her—even Tim—would hopefully be more compassionate to others and loving toward each other. Actually, it had happened already—she'd seen it this week.

But it hadn't been God's original plan for Abra to suffer and die. And it hadn't been his plan for Samuel to be killed on a road in Iraq either. It was his plan to walk with the survivors through it, though, to comfort them, to know their pain. How God did it, Eve couldn't fathom, knowing all the hurts in the world and still bearing all of them.

After a while, Karina stepped into the hall. "We're going back to your home so Joel can see Shani and the baby. And meet Samantha."

"I'll go too," Eve said. "Trudy's probably awake."

She followed Karina into the living room. Samuel's mom was hugging Joel and both were crying. So was Samuel's dad, who stood with his hand on Joel's shoulder. Eve had never seen a man cry before, not even Tim when Abra died. Karina stopped, but Eve continued on to the front porch, nearly bumping into Charlie.

"Sorry," she said.

He turned toward her, his eyes red, and reached for her. She trailed her hand through his for a quick moment.

"I'll see you at the house?" he whispered.

"Jah," she answered. "Tell Karina I went on ahead. I'll go through the field and check on the boys."

She needed a moment to collect herself. Having Charlie near had lowered her guard—a dangerous thing with Gideon and Tim close by. She darted through the hedge and into the field. The warmth of the day was slipping away with the lowering sun. She crossed the field and then as she neared the creek, she called out, "Daniel? Simon?"

Someone darted through the brush along the creek.

"Zane!"

"Down here," he called out.

She slipped down the pathway to the fort but stopped halfway. It was twice the size it had been last time she'd seen it. They'd used plywood and boards for the walls and roof and hay as thatch. A wide doorway allowed a glimpse inside, all the way to the creek. Either they hadn't yet put a wall up on the other side or had chosen not to.

Rose stuck her head out of the doorway.

"What are you doing?" Eve asked.

"Playing."

"Did you come by yourself?" Eve stopped at the doorway.

"No, with Lila and Jenny. Monika said it was okay."

"Oh." Eve stepped inside the fort. The floor seemed sturdy enough and the wall seemed secure. "Where are the other kids?"

Rose giggled.

Standing beside Zane, Lila waved from the other side of the creek. Jenny stood behind Lila, her eyes on Zane, as Simon soared over the creek on a rope.

Eve's stomach lurched. "Come on," she said, catching Simon by the waist as he neared her. "Let's all go back to the house for a snack."

On the way she lectured them about using common sense. "Do you know what would happen if Simon fell and hit his head again?"

"Aenti, I'm not going to do that."

"You don't know that. Another concussion could cause lasting damage."

Simon made a face, but Zane said, "Sorry, Aenti. We stopped playing Roman soldiers and started playing Tarzan. There's not as much *fechta*."

Eve suppressed a laugh as Zane started to run and the others followed. He'd called her Aenti. And he thought playing Tarzan was better than playing Roman soldiers—not as much fighting. She thought of when she and Abra had watched an old movie about the ape-man, when they were on their Rumschpringe, and she guessed it was a better choice—as long as they didn't dress for the parts.

By the time they reached the house Lila had nearly caught up with Zane. Eve loved that her niece still ran and played like a child. Soon enough, she'd be forced to act like a young lady. But at this moment, Lila appeared fearless.

Eve longed for that. She'd been afraid for too long. If she truly loved the Lord with all her heart, soul, and mind, if she truly loved her neighbor and loved herself, then it was time to stop living in fear.

Lord, help me, she silently prayed. *Help me to trust you.* Increasing her pace, she stepped out of the shadows of the poplar trees along the creek. The afternoon sun warmed her face as she followed the children through the field and back to the house.

The others trickled over from the Becks' place. Charlie drove his truck and Joel drove the van over, with Karina and her mother-in-law riding along. Joel struggled up the stairs by himself, with Charlie close behind. Once they were in the living room, Charlie stood in the corner, away from the others. But even so, Simon looked up at him in awe. At least Tim wasn't around.

Shani appeared calm as Joel picked up the baby from the couch where he'd been napping and sat down beside her. He held the Boppli for a while, and then held Samantha too, in his other arm. Karina snapped a photo of the three with a small camera but then seemed to realize what she was doing and gave Eve a sheepish look.

"It's fine," Eve said. Photos were one of the things she missed the most from the Englisch world.

Samantha began to fuss, and her mother took her back.

After Eve gathered Trudy from her crib, changed her diaper, and brought her into the living room, the baby squealed in delight when she saw Joel and lunged toward him. He took her, and she pulled on his ear and lip and then turned her attention to the baby, in Joel's other arm, grabbing for his eye.

Eve scooped her up. "Show Joel how close you are to walking, little one," she said, kneeling on the floor. The baby toddled toward Charlie instead, and he squatted, putting out his hands for her. She practically ran for a few steps, giggling, her fine hair blowing up and down, and then collapsed on the floor in a heap. Charlie scooped her up.

Smiling at the two, Eve rose to her feet—and looked up to see Monika in the doorway to the kitchen, an expression of concern on her face. She motioned for Eve to follow her. As the two stood next to the sink, she whispered, "This isn't a passing thing is it?"

Eve shook her head. "Don't worry though, I won't leave. Tim would never let me see the children."

Monika shook her head. "I have no idea what you should do, really. And I shouldn't even be talking with you about this, but . . . Eve, you can't let someone else—certainly not your brother—make the most important decision of your life."

Eve clasped the edge of the counter.

"If you stay, it should be because that's what God wants from you. But if God intends you to leave, I'll take care of these children. And I'll do everything I can to see that Tim doesn't keep you out of their lives. You have my word."

Eve swiped at her eyes with her free hand.

"You are worthy of love, Eve Lehman," Monika said. "I hate to admit it, but I've been wrong all along about you and Gideon. It's obvious there's something special between you and Charlie. Don't you ever tell a soul I encouraged you to leave, but . . . well, I guess that's exactly what I'm telling you to do, if that's how you feel led."

Eve's face grew warm. Tim and the children were the only family she had.

"You're in a hard spot, jah," Monika said. "You have my prayers—that's for sure, prayers that you'll find the kind of love I had with Deacon King."

Eve turned as Charlie stepped into the kitchen with Trudy. His face reddened. "I'm sorry. I'll take her back in the living room and let you two talk."

"Actually, I need to speak with you," Eve whispered. "Meet me outside in a minute." Monika put out her hands for the baby and Charlie went back into the living room.

Eve grabbed her cape, walked into the living room, and said she was going to check on the older children, who'd gone back outside.

She found them playing along the fence. None of them acknowledged her. Lila ran to the buggy and climbed in. Zane followed, stepped up, and sat beside her. Where were they going in their play? Off to church? Walmart? The bank? An African jungle? Eve's heart hurt. If only life could stay so simple.

Monika said she would take care of Abra's children, and Eve believed she would. She thought of the quilt that she'd given Shani. Abra had made it with love, saying she'd prayed over every stitch, asking God for the right husband for Eve. She'd wanted Eve to marry. To have a family of her own. She'd said so in the note.

But Eve had given away her right to be happy all those years ago. How could she now claim something she didn't deserve?

She remembered Leona's words as they'd visited in her kitchen: *"For by grace are ye saved through faith; and that not of yourselves: it is the gift of God."* She believed that. In fact, she'd truly embraced it through the pain of the last few years. And then there was what she'd recited to Tim. *"Love thy neighbor as thyself."* True, she'd said it trying to get him to recognize God wanted him to love the Becks. But Christ's command for her to love herself was just as valid.

She walked down to the bottom of the steps. Maybe she didn't deserve God's forgiveness, but who was she to refuse his gift? Maybe she didn't deserve Charlie's love, but how could she offer him her own if she refused his?

And the truth was, she did want to offer him her love.

He came out the back door, whistling. She turned toward him. He stopped but then quickly descended the steps. The longer she waited the harder it would be. She would have to trust God with the children.

Eve turned toward Charlie. "I want to move to Philly."

"What?"

"Karina said I could live with her."

A smile spread across his face. "That's great. Have you talked it through with Tim?"

She exhaled. "No, but I've decided," she said. "I mean, I've decided to go. We'll have to figure out the rest . . . together."

Charlie stepped closer. "This is what you believe God wants?"

"Jah," she said. "It might take a while, to make

sure everyone is settled before I go." She choked on the words. "Monika said she'll take care of them. She has the time, and I believe Tim will let her." Tears stung her eyes.

"I want to be with you when you talk to Tim," Charlie said.

"No."

"You can't catch me!" Simon yelled.

Zane jumped from the buggy and zipped by Daniel, who tagged him. Jenny followed Zane. Lila darted behind the buggy to the chicken coop, and Zane took off after her, leaving Simon free to reach base. But instead he ran toward the house, most likely to be closer to Charlie.

Charlie brushed Eve's hand with his. "Please," he said. "I don't want you to face Tim alone."

"Dat!" Rose ran toward the driveway as Eve registered the sound of wheels rolling over the gravel. Glancing toward the wagon, she called for all the children. Zane and Lila started toward the house, followed by Daniel.

Eve turned toward the wagon. Tim and Gideon rode up front, and the back was filled with tools and ladders.

"We're nearly done," Tim said, stopping the wagon. He jumped down and patted Rose on the head. "A few more hours on Monday will finish it up."

"I can come back down and help," Charlie said. "I have the day off."

Tim nodded but didn't look happy. Neither did Gideon. Eve slipped up the steps and back into the house, followed by the children.

Eve had planned to tell Tim that evening when everyone left, but when he came into the house, followed by Gideon, he cornered her in the kitchen as she made the coffee. "What's going on?" he asked.

"About?" She stepped around him and reached for the kettle.

"You know."

Eve shifted her focus back to the coffee. As she poured the hot water, she said, "It's best if we talk later. This isn't anyone else's business."

"You think this isn't Gideon's business? Not after what he's done for us."

"Tim," Gideon said, "Eve's right."

The three older children, who'd been in the living room, drifted into the kitchen, followed by Charlie, Simon at his side.

Charlie stepped farther into the room. "Tim. Gideon."

Eve shook her head at him, hoping he wouldn't say anything more.

Tim glared at Charlie and then said, "No. Let's talk now."

Eve put the kettle back on the stove and faced her brother. "I'm going to move to Philadelphia. Not right away, but sometime in the future."

"You're leaving the church, then?"

"I'm not sure," she said. "But I need to figure out what God has for me."

Tim crossed his arms. "You know what he has for you."

Eve felt the old anger well inside her. Tim reminded her of her father's harshness. How he never cared about her opinion. Never saw her as anything more than his daughter. She pulled the note from Abra from her pocket.

Tim's eye's widened. "Give that to me."

She shook her head. "She wrote it to me. Were you going to tell me?"

His face hardened.

"You married the woman you loved. Don't you think I should have a chance with the man I love?"

Tim crossed his arms. "I didn't go against my family. And God and the church."

She took a deep breath. It had been foolish to try to talk with Tim at all. She said, "I'll wait to go until we can figure things out here. Until we can explain what's going on to the children and figure out what's best for Trudy."

"Where's Aenti going?" Rose wailed, as Monika stepped into the kitchen with Trudy in her arms.

"Hush," Lila said, putting her hands on her little sister's shoulders.

Tim pointed toward the back door. "Go now. It's time for Lila to grow up and do her job."

"Tim . . ." Gideon said.

"We don't need Eve anymore."

Rose began to cry, and Trudy curled her lower lip.

Monika stepped toward Tim. "Surely you can wait a couple of hours to discuss this."

He crossed his arms, shook his head, and then turned toward Simon. "Get away from Charlie," Tim barked. "He shouldn't have worn his uniform here. You have no idea what it represents."

Simon took a step backward, a look of shock on his face. His Dat had never spoken to him so harshly.

Eve searched Charlie's eyes.

"Go pack," he said to her, gently. Then he turned and headed to the doorway of the mud porch. Simon spun around toward him. Charlie smiled and motioned him toward the living room.

Eve headed toward the hallway, the patter of little feet behind her.

"Don't follow her," Tim snarled.

Rose began to wail.

Eve wanted to comfort her niece, her heart breaking, but instead she hurried to her room and packed quickly. When she was done, she grabbed the blanket in Trudy's crib, put it to her nose and inhaled. It wasn't the child's favorite blanket— just one of several. She stuffed it on top of the clothes and zipped her bag.

A knock fell on her door.

Thinking it was Monika, she said, "Come in."

It was Karina. "Here's a key," she said. "Make yourself at home. I'll be back tomorrow."

Eve gave her a quick hug. Eve grabbed her bag and returned to the living room. Karina and her in-laws were slipping out the front door. Shani, Joel, Zane, and the baby had already left.

Tim held a crying Trudy in the kitchen, and the other children must have all been sent to their rooms. Monika stood awkwardly by the door. "I'm praying for you," she said. "And the children."

Eve whispered, "Is it horrible of me to leave?"

Monika shook her head. "I'm sorry though. I think I encouraged you too soon. It was rash of me."

"No," Eve said. "It's been coming for months."

She stepped away. Charlie still stood in the doorway to the mud porch, standing next to Gideon. The older man shrugged and smiled slightly, with kindness in his eyes.

Eve turned toward Tim. "We need to put the children first. They need to see me."

"Go," he said, balancing the crying baby in one arm as he pointed toward the door.

Charlie stepped to her side. Gideon nodded at Eve but didn't say anything. He wasn't shaming her. He wasn't condemning her. Gideon Byler was a good man—he just wasn't the right man for her.

Grief and sadness mixed with a measure of

relief as Eve walked toward Charlie's truck. She held her head high. There would be no more pretending about whom she loved. No more hiding. No more secrets.

But the loss of the children was almost too much to bear. The death of Abra pierced her again. If only she had the photo of the two of them from so long ago. She feared the farther she traveled from Lancaster, the more distant the memories of her friend would become. She swallowed hard. If Tim didn't let her see the children, she'd become a distant memory to them too.

Shani called Charlie's cell phone as Joel drove the van to Monika's. Eve answered. Her voice sounded surprisingly strong considering the humiliation she'd just endured.

Shani glanced back at Zane.

Quietly she asked, "Are you okay?"

Eve took a moment to answer but then said, "Yes and no."

"So you're going to Karina's tonight?"

"Yes."

"Are you *going* to be okay?"

"Yes," Eve said, her voice strong. "But I'm worried about the kids."

"I know," Shani said. She couldn't imagine the kids without Eve, but she didn't want to make her friend feel worse. "I'll help if Tim will let me."

"Denki," Eve said. "Monika will too—she offered it before I decided to leave." Eve choked.

Shani said, "I'll call you tonight, once you're at Karina's. I have her landline number."

By the time they arrived at Monika's, the baby was crying. Shani hurried inside with him and into the bedroom, while Zane helped Joel up the back steps. As she fed the baby, Shani could hear Zane and Joel talking in the kitchen.

"Why'd you take off like that?" Zane asked.

"I needed to clear my head."

"But you left Mom when she needed you. And the baby."

"I shouldn't have," Joel answered. "I'm sorry."

There was a muffled noise, and Shani wondered if Zane was crying.

After a while he said, "You didn't even stick around to name him."

"Your mom and I are working on it. Do you have any suggestions?"

The baby began to cry, and Shani couldn't hear any more. A few minutes later, Joel came into the bedroom.

Shani asked, "What's Zane doing?"

"Chores."

Shani was grateful to Monika for keeping Zane busy. "So what shall we name the baby?"

"I still like Adam."

"What did Zane say?"

"That we should name him John—after Johnny."

"How does he know about your brother?"

"I told him. One night when you were working."

"Oh," Shani replied.

And then Joel said, "How about that as a middle name?"

"Adam John." She stroked the baby's head. "I like that." Looking up at Joel, she said. "Tell me about Johnny."

"I already did."

Thirteen years ago, before they'd married, he told Shani his little brother had died in a snowmobiling accident and that was why his parents weren't coming from Wisconsin to Seattle to celebrate their wedding. He wouldn't say any more at the time.

"Tell me again," Shani said.

It was late March, at the family cabin. Johnny was twelve, and Joel was seventeen. Joel explained that Johnny had raced ahead on his snowmobile, taking the lead for the first time. When Johnny accelerated and headed toward a jump, Joel yelled for him to skip it. He was concerned about the snow level being down. But Johnny kept going. Maybe he couldn't hear Joel. Or maybe he ignored him. But he took the jump and flipped the snowmobile. The machine landed on top of him. In a frenzy, Joel managed to get Johnny out from under the snowmobile and back to the cabin.

"He was still alive at that point," Joel said. "My dad was furious—with me. I hadn't protected him. I should have gone first. What was I thinking?"

Johnny died on the way to the hospital. Joel graduated two months later and joined the Army.

"Did your dad ever apologize for blaming you?" Shani asked.

Joel shook his head. "I doubt he even remembered what he said in the heat of the moment. We never talked about it. But that was the way it was in our family and in our church too. Someone was always to blame when something went wrong. If there was a tragedy, it was either because of unconfessed sin in someone's life or because they'd used poor judgment. It was probably easier for my dad to blame it on my judgment than to have others speculate about my sin, which would have been a worse reflection on him."

Joel sighed. "That's why the Amish bothered me. I thought they'd be like that. Always finding blame."

Shani nodded. And it seemed some were like that, with Gideon's concern that Simon had been injured because Tim favored him. And Tim blaming Zane for scaring the horse. And the way Tim treated Eve. But then they'd all been so generous with their time and resources.

Joel continued. "I can't figure them out—Tim's so harsh and judgmental toward Eve, but he's been nothing but kind to me—all things considered. And the fire was my fault. Eve, Lila, and Trudy could have been badly burned or killed, along with you and the boys, but Tim never once shamed me about it."

Shani shifted the baby to her shoulder. "I guess the Amish are as complicated as we are," she said.

Joel nodded. "The counselor thinks Samuel's death triggered a lot of stuff for me. I felt responsible—Samuel should have been in the driver's seat—and Johnny should have been behind me instead of leading the way. But Samuel was exhausted and I insisted on driving. If I hadn't, he'd still be alive."

And Joel would be dead. Shani squeezed his hand.

"Also," Joel said, "the counselor thinks that Zane being twelve has probably triggered stuff for me too. Johnny and I were close, really close. Zane and I were close—and now we're not. I don't blame him. I'm the one—"

"No one's to blame," Shani said. "It's life. We just have to figure out what to do now."

He dropped his eyes. "It might take a while to get this all figured out—and I'll probably never be the way I was. . . . I might always be jumpy. On edge." He brushed away a tear.

Shani squeezed his hand again. She knew that. No one weathered life without changing in some way.

"But I'll keep going to counseling," Joel said, meeting her gaze.

"Thank you," Shani said. She'd go too, if that would help.

"Do you want me to go back to Philly?" Joel asked.

"No," she said. "All I've ever wanted was for us to be together, to have our family intact." Then she asked, "Do you want all of us to go back together, to leave Lancaster County?"

"No. I mean, we might have to eventually, or go somewhere else if I can't find a job in the area. But for now let's stay here."

"We should be able to go back home soon." That's what Shani wanted more than anything—to go home with Joel and their boys. Maybe it wouldn't be home forever, but right now it was the only place she wanted to be.

She tugged on Joel's hand, pulling him closer until his head was tucked against her shoulder. She kissed the side of his face and lifted his chin and kissed her husband again, this time on the mouth. He kissed her back.

When they pulled away, she said, "I need you, as much as you can give."

He nodded. "I'll try—I promise."

She wouldn't think about the future. It was enough to think about right *now,* but she would keep fighting for her marriage. She would fight for Joel's healing. She'd stay by his side. *Please God,* she thought, realizing she was praying. *For better or worse. Show me how.*

She didn't understand prayer, and maybe she never would, but she knew she needed to talk to God. Not to shut him out. She knew she needed to strive to love him with all her heart, soul, and mind, no matter what heartaches life brought. And perhaps one of the greatest values of prayer was that it prepared her to do the right thing. To love God. To love Joel. To love her boys.

And to love her neighbor—meaning Tim, even though Eve was gone.

Shani wasn't sure, after Eve left like that, whether Tim would finish rebuilding the kitchen—but he did. And Gideon helped. Charlie showed up Monday, just like he said he would, and primed and painted, although Eve didn't come with him. Tim totally ignored Charlie, but according to Joel—who drove the van over to hang out and help where he could—Gideon talked with him. "And Charlie's whistling again," he said. "I didn't realize he hadn't been until I heard him today."

On Wednesday morning, after Joel returned from taking Zane and Jenny to each of their schools and Monika by the Lehmans' to watch Trudy, his cell phone rang.

It was obvious as Shani listened to his side of the conversation that it was the insurance adjustor. Joel stood, pushing down on his cane with his free hand, and then stepped away from the table as he listened.

Finally he said, "That's what I thought."

The fire marshal's report must have come through. When the call was over, Joel said, "I was right."

"So it was a cigarette."

Joel wrinkled his nose. "That's what you thought? That I was smoking while you were in labor?"

She nodded.

He shook his head. "It was the pail of ashes, from the stove." He sat back down at the table. "Not that it matters—it was still my fault."

Shani almost laughed. It probably shouldn't have mattered to her, but it did.

"I haven't smoked since that last time you got mad at me—and then had to help me get ready for bed." He gave her a wry smile. "After that I threw all of my cigarettes away," he said. "But the fire was still my fault."

Shani shook her head. "It was ridiculous of me to ask you to take the ashes out." One of them should have asked Zane. Joel couldn't maneuver the steps carrying the pail. He probably would have fallen again. "God's using what happened, right? We've gotten help. We're talking. Tim is repairing our house. Eve finally did what she needed to do. Let's move forward."

On Thursday Shani went into Philly with Joel to the counselor. She sat in the lobby with the baby and then went in at the end. The counselor recommended a therapist in Lancaster and Joel said he'd go until he figured out how to handle the stress of adjusting back to civilian life and what to do as far as a job.

They stayed at Monika's for another week and then returned home. Shani wondered if she'd get the quilt Abra had made back or not, but she didn't expect to. She wouldn't have blamed Tim at all if he kept it. But the evening of their first day back, Tim and his boys came down the lane carrying hampers filled with their clean clothes, towels, sheets, and bedding, including the quilt.

Shani's dad came out to visit for a week, relieved that Shani and Joel were working on their marriage. He finished painting the living room, along with finishing up the detail work outside.

As winter progressed, the Lehman kids played down by the creek with Zane when they could. They came into the house a few times, to use the bathroom and get a snack. Shani asked Lila if it was okay with their dad. Her face reddened and she said, "For a few minutes. He doesn't want us to hang around though."

Monika did take care of Trudy, sometimes at her house but mostly at the Lehmans' place. A few times, she ventured down the lane for a cup of coffee. The little girl was toddling everywhere now, but still wanted to sit on Joel's lap when she visited. Monika said she still appeared out of sorts and seemed to be mourning Eve. "It's a travesty," she said. "I've tried to talk with Tim, but he's as stubborn as ever."

"How's Gideon doing?" Shani asked.

Monika smiled a little. "He seems fine."

Life went on. Zane turned thirteen. The sheep had their lambs. Adam smiled. Raised his head. Reached for Zane.

Joel continued counseling and started thinking about what kind of work he wanted to do. They visited a nondenominational church a few miles away from the house—and kept going back. As Joel and Shani both recovered, they found new ways to relate. They were more careful with each other. Not as sure. But step-by-step, their marriage improved.

Trudy turned one in late February. Of course, the Becks weren't invited to the party—if there was one. It nearly broke Shani's heart to think of Eve not being with the little girl on her special day. She'd been with Abra the day Trudy was born; she should have been with the baby to celebrate her first year. But that, like so many things, wasn't meant to be.

Daffodils bloomed and then the tulips. Tim put in a huge garden, and Shani put in a tiny one. Joel stopped complaining about the smell of the dairy.

The first of April, Charlie called and asked if they could meet Eve and him for lunch the next Saturday. Shani recommended a pizza place near Valley Forge. They set a time, and then Shani asked, "Is something up?"

Charlie hesitated before answering. "We miss you guys. See you then."

As Shani hung up, she tried not to guess what else might be going on.

∾ 33

The next Saturday was sunny and bright as Eve and Charlie waited inside the foyer of the pizza place. Eve had talked to Shani a couple of times each week on the phone, but she hadn't seen her since leaving Juneberry Lane in January.

Eve stood at the window, her hands in the back pockets of her jeans. Charlie stepped beside her and put his arm around her, tugging on her hair a little as he did. She was getting used to wearing it long. She leaned into him, resting her head against his neck. He pulled her closer.

A blue van turned into the parking lot. "There they are," she said, grabbing his hand and rushing through the door. The van stopped, Zane climbed down, and ran toward Charlie. Eve waved at Joel in the driver's seat and hurried around to the other side, where Shani unbuckled Adam. She hugged her friend and then scooped up the baby into her arms. "He's so big." Her eyes didn't leave his face as she spoke. He smiled up at her and blew a bubble.

"Look at you," Shani said, "in your jeans and boots. And your hair—it's beautiful."

Eve smiled.

"You look so happy," Shani said.

Eve knew she was blushing. "I am."

The women waited as Joel pulled the van into a parking space, and then Charlie and Eve greeted him after he climbed down. Even though he leaned heavily on his cane, he appeared much stronger.

Once they were seated, Eve continued to hold the baby.

"How's Karina doing?" Joel asked.

"Good. She's gone back to work part time. Samantha is doing well in daycare."

"How's your job going?" Shani asked. Eve had gotten a position at the same daycare that Samantha attended.

"Fine. I've started working on my GED, and Charlie . . ." She paused as she reached over and patted his leg. "He's teaching me how to drive."

Joel groaned.

Eve laughed. "Jah, it's quite the ordeal. There are times I wish he didn't have that big old truck."

Charlie laughed. "Me too." She grinned at him.

After they'd ordered their food, Charlie said, "Although we really do miss you and wanted to see you, we also have an announcement to make."

Shani leaned forward. "We're all ears."

Charlie glanced at Eve. She took a deep breath and then, as she cradled the baby, said, "We're getting married."

"When?" Zane groaned.

"The end of May," Charlie answered.

"Wow." Shani leaned back against the booth,

looking at Eve's left hand. "That's a short engage-
ment. You don't even have a ring yet."

Eve smiled at Charlie.

"Believe me, I tried to give her a ring . . ."

"I'm not used to jewelry," Eve said. She could
only adjust to so much at a time.

"Why so soon?" Shani asked.

Joel cleared his throat and said, "Shani . . ."

Zane looked from his mom to his dad and
asked, "What's going on?"

Eve tried not to laugh. Shani's face reddened. "I
didn't mean to imply there might be a reason for
them to marry so soon." She smiled. "I'm just
used to being nosy."

"It's fine," Eve said. "We know it's right for us,
is all. There's no reason to wait." She'd never
been surer of anything. She wanted nothing more
than to spend the rest of her life with Charlie.

Shani leaned forward again and took Eve's
hand across the table. "We're so happy for you."

Eve patted her friend's hand. "Thank you. But
there's more." This was the hard part.

Charlie nodded and said, "We don't want you to
come to the wedding."

"What?" Joel pressed back against the bench.
"Of course we're coming to the wedding."

"Hear me out," Charlie said. "Tim's not going
to be happy. We think he'll be more likely to keep
a relationship with you—to allow Zane to play
with the kids and Monika to have a friendship

with you—all of that, if you don't come to the wedding."

"I can see that," Shani said.

"Me too." Zane's voice was so serious it nearly broke Eve's heart.

Joel crossed his arms. "I've never been noninvited to a wedding before, especially not to my best friend's."

Charlie said, "It's not that we don't want you there—out of anyone we want you the most."

"And Tim and the kids," Eve said, choking on the word *kids*. She could barely stand to think of them.

Everyone was silent for a long moment, and then Zane said, "Rose lost another tooth. And Trudy thinks she can run. Simon's almost as tall as Daniel, and both of them helped with calving, delivering a set of twins by themselves when Tim was at work."

Eve met the boy's eyes and smiled. Even though it hurt, she was so happy for his news. "Wow," Eve said. "What about Lila? How is she doing?"

Zane's face grew red, which made Eve smile even more. "She's fine," Zane managed to say. "She and Jenny are friends again."

Eve chuckled. "That must mean Jenny has given up on liking you."

Zane turned beet red.

"Is she after Daniel again?" Eve asked.

Zane shrugged.

Shani grinned and then, perhaps in an effort to save Zane from further embarrassment, asked Eve, "What are your plans after you get your GED?"

She inhaled and then said, "I hope to go on to college, to study education."

"Wonderful!" Shani beamed. "If anyone can do it, you can. What colleges are you looking at?"

"Eventually, Eastern Mennonite."

Shani leaned forward again. "In Lancaster?"

Eve nodded. "We're moving back, after the wedding."

"I have a lead on a job," Charlie added. "And we're looking at acreage not too far from Monika's."

"If I'm ever going to have a relationship with the kids, I need to be closer," Eve said. "I hope, in time, Tim will allow me to see them." She dropped her gaze to Adam. He was fast asleep in her arms.

Everyone was silent for a long moment, until Shani said, "I have something for you in the car." She glanced from Eve to Charlie. "For both of you."

Eve adjusted Adam, bringing him to her shoulder. "Why would you have something for us?"

"It's the shadow quilt Abra made for you."

"No, Shani," Eve said. "I gave it to you."

"We'll make another one together," she said.

"Once you move back to Lancaster. I'd prefer that, actually."

Abra's quilt had covered Shani and Joel through their darkest days. How could Eve not accept Shani's gift of hope and love? Her eyes began to swim.

"We'll learn to quilt together," she said to her friend. *In memory of Abra.*

ᘔ 34

The middle of April, Joel bought a used pickup to drive himself to physical therapy and counseling appointments. Shani headed back to work two days a week, worrying about how Joel would do caring for Adam and wondering how she'd do away from the baby. But all of them adjusted. Joel carried the baby around the house in the front pack, using his cane. Zane helped and became a pro at changing diapers.

Shani and Joel decided he'd wait until the end of August to find a job. Having the summer with the boys was more important than making more money—their savings would see them through until then. Plus, his disability benefits had finally kicked in.

He had his eye on a couple of nonprofit organizations for veterans—he was tracking their job listings and working on his résumé. Most surprising was that Joel's parents planned to come out for a visit in June, after Zane was out of school.

When Shani saw Monika, she didn't dare tell her about Eve and Charlie's plan to move back to Lancaster. She'd let them disclose that when they were ready. It was enough that Monika knew they were getting married. "What does Tim have to say about that?" Shani asked.

"Oh, you can imagine," Monika replied.

"How about Gideon?"

Monika paused a moment. "You know, he seems oddly fine with all of it. He's not one to gossip anyway, but I haven't heard a single negative comment from Gideon about Eve or Charlie or . . . any of you."

A couple of times, Tim ventured down to Joel and Shani's. Once when he was mending fence at their end of the field, and another time to ask to borrow their posthole digger. "One of the boys must have broken mine," he said. "Probably Daniel."

Shani guessed it was Simon. Daniel was the most conscientious child she'd ever met.

Both times Shani invited Tim in for coffee and he accepted. He commented on how big Adam was getting, and asked about Shani's dad. Then he said, "He seems like a good guy. Easier to get along with than your grandfather." Tim sighed. "Although, looking back I could have handled all of that better. I'm thankful to your father for renewing my lease."

Shani appreciated his honest words.

It was the beginning of May. The month Abra died. The month Samuel was killed. The month Joel was injured. The month of Mother's Day and Memorial Day. The month of losses.

On the anniversary of Samuel's death on the eleventh, Joel, Shani, and Adam drove into Philly and had dinner with Karina, Samantha, Charlie, and Eve. Zane somehow convinced Tim to let him stay with his kids for the evening. Shani doubted Zane told him she and Joel were going to Charlie's house.

Samantha was saying "Mama-mama," reaching for food, and acting like she wanted to take steps. No one talked about the night Samuel died, but they did talk about Samuel. Karina shared about meeting him in college. She said she was shocked when he joined the Army Reserve his third year, after 9/11. "I never expected that from him," Karina said. They'd moved to Philadelphia for him to go to grad school, which was how Samuel ended up in Charlie's unit.

Her little girl dropped a piece of a roll on the floor and then giggled. "He didn't want to name her Samantha," Karina said, bending down. "He said it sounded prideful. I hope he doesn't mind."

"Serves him right," Joel said.

Shani gasped. But then Karina laughed. Charlie raised his glass. "To Samuel."

They all raised their glasses in a toast.

Samantha giggled again.

On the way home Shani was thankful Zane hadn't come along, because Joel finally talked about that night.

Shani reached over and took his hand. He

squeezed it. "It should have been me," he said. "It's not that I cheated death—I cheated Samuel. He was just a big kid. Scared to death to be a dad. Afraid something was going to happen to Karina and the baby. He never should have died."

Shani held his hand and stayed quiet.

"That's where I get all messed up with people saying all things work together for good."

Shani waited for her husband to say more, but when he didn't she said, "The good that comes from it are the little things. All of us getting together tonight. You finally talking. The two of us trying to trust God. Getting help. Praying. Karina's generosity toward Eve. The empathy all of us have because of what we've gone through." She sighed. Her words sounded hollow. "The thing is, you did live. So the most honoring thing you can do, in regards to Samuel, is to live your life as best you can. That's the most honoring thing we can do as far as God goes too."

She felt sick to her stomach thinking about it—realizing how close she'd really come to losing Joel.

Her heart ached for Karina. And little Samantha. Just as others had come alongside her family, she determined to do what she could for the mother and daughter too.

The last Saturday of May, Zane was out doing his chores when Joel came out to the living room wearing his dress blues. Shani sat in the rocking chair, nursing the baby. "So you're going?"

"Yep," he said. "I'm not going to cower to Tim Lehman."

Shani shifted the baby to her shoulder. Tim had been fine with Zane staying when they went into Philly. He let Lila and Rose come over to make cookies two days ago. Yesterday he'd sent Simon over after he'd fallen a few feet from the silo. He'd only bumped his head, but Tim wanted Shani to make sure he didn't have another concussion. He'd been fine.

Shani didn't want to risk all of that. "Are you okay if Zane and I don't go with you?"

Joel nodded. "I don't think Tim cares as much about what I do. I'm going to be there for Charlie."

Shani kept patting the baby's back.

"Why are you going so early?" Shani asked. "The ceremony isn't until noon." It seemed a funny time to have a wedding, but after Eve told Shani Amish weddings started at nine, it made more sense.

Joel gripped his dress hat. "Charlie said if I insisted on attending, I might as well stand up with him. They're taking photos beforehand."

Shani wrinkled her nose. She'd give anything to see Charlie and Joel in their uniforms and Eve in her dress. Shani kept patting the baby's back. At least there would be pictures.

"Come here," she said. Joel complied. She patted the cushion beside her, and he sat. She turned toward him and touched the row of medals on the right side of his jacket. He'd added his purple heart. "I'm proud of you," she whispered.

He glanced down at his medals. "Not for these, I hope."

She took a deep breath. "Yes, for these. But also for the hard work you're doing. Mostly for wanting to come back to us. For finally coming home."

He put his arm around her and pulled her close, until their faces touched. She felt his tears first and then her own. Without speaking they both cried until Joel kissed her lips. And then, without saying a word, he stood, retrieved his cane from beside his recliner, and headed out the door. She listened to the thump of his steps down the ramp and the slam of his pickup door. Then he was gone.

A half hour later, when she finally got around to doing the dishes, Zane, Lila, and Simon burst through the back door. "Who's with Trudy?" Shani asked.

"Monika's over," Lila answered. "A driver brought her and Jenny early this morning."

"Is your dad at work?"

Lila shook her head. "He was vaccinating the calves. We were all helping, but he's done now. Reuben came to help too."

"Is Monika going home?"

"I don't think so," Lila said. "Jenny's helping her make a snack. Daniel stayed back with them." Rose giggled.

"I'll go down and say hello." Shani had spent the morning in sweats and a T-shirt, but the day was so nice she decided to put on a skirt and blouse. She packed the diaper bag and then decided to drive instead of walking with the children. That would give her more time, just in case Monika wasn't going to be around much longer.

When she knocked on the Lehmans' back door, Monika opened it quickly, a smile spreading across her face. "I was hoping you'd stop by." She took Adam from her immediately. "How's the little man?" she cooed at him.

He smiled and waved his arms around.

"Where's Trudy?" Shani asked.

"Daniel and Jenny took her out to the swing."

Tim had put a tire swing in the oak tree along the side of the house just last week. It seemed a good sign that he was thinking about the children, about them having some fun.

Monika looked up at Shani. "Today's the day, right?"

Shani nodded.

"Did Joel go?"

Shani nodded again.

"I'm just sick," Monika said, sitting down on a

484

kitchen chair and cradling the baby. "I thought I could have more influence on Tim, but he's the most stubborn person I know. You should be there with Eve. So should Tim."

"How could he be?"

"What do you mean?"

"Wouldn't he be . . . excommunicated? Is that it?"

Monika wrinkled her nose. "Shunned?"

That was the word she'd been looking for. Eve said she'd been shunned. Gideon had sent her a formal letter the month before, stating she'd "mocked the church" and "acted in a prideful way" by leaving her home, dressing in an immodest manner, learning to drive, and furthering her education. Eve said it was a formality she expected, and she didn't hold it against Gideon. Not at all.

"Yes, *shunned,*" Shani said. "That's the word."

"Who told you he'd be shunned?"

Shani tilted her head. Eve hadn't. And Tim hadn't either. "I guess I just assumed that was the reason Tim wouldn't go—besides, you know . . ." She wrinkled her nose. "Besides the fact that he's really mad at Eve."

A disgusted expression passed over Monika's face. "All of us have loved ones who have left. I have two brothers who did. One before he joined the church and one after. I still have a relationship with both of them. And attended both of their

485

weddings. No one ever said anything to me about it."

"Really?"

Monika nodded.

Shani knew the rules varied from district to district. "So, theoretically, Tim could go? As far as your group is concerned?"

Monika nodded again.

"I see," Shani said. "Where is he?"

"Out in the barn," Monika answered.

Shani started toward the door. She had a skirt on and sandals. Her blouse was still clean. She looked presentable for a wedding. And Adam would be fine in his baby shorts and T-shirt.

Monika stood. "He won't go."

Shani stopped, her hand on the knob. "I'm still going to ask."

"If he doesn't, you should."

"Eve doesn't want me to. She thinks it'll make Tim more likely to reject us . . ."

Monika swayed with the baby. "The sooner Tim Lehman gets over himself the better."

"I guess I'll decide after I talk to him," Shani said. She didn't want to jeopardize her relationship with his kids—but she didn't want to miss out on the most important day of Eve and Charlie's life together either.

As she stepped out the door, Monika called out, "If he balks, tell him to call Gideon. He'd tell him to go."

"Okay," Shani responded. As time went by, she liked Gideon more and more.

Tim and Reuben were in the office, going over some paperwork. "Hallo," Shani called out, as she entered. "How are you, Reuben?"

"*Gut*," he answered. "And you?"

"Great," she said. "Is your Dat manning the lumberyard all by himself today?"

Reuben nodded. "Tim's teaching me about farming."

"Oh," Shani said. She'd imagined him taking over the lumberyard but maybe that wasn't what he wanted. Then again, Gideon was still fairly young. He probably had a good twenty years or more of work left in him.

"Tim," Shani said. "May I talk with you a minute?"

He glanced toward the field. "Are the kids all right?"

She nodded, and then jerked her head toward the door. "In private."

As they stepped outside, the older kids ran by.

"Don't go anywhere," Shani said to Zane. "I need to talk with you next."

She followed Tim to the side of the barn and then squinted at him as she spoke. "Would you go to Eve's wedding with us?"

"Don't ask me that."

"She loves you. She loves your children." Shani paused for a moment, but when Tim didn't say anything, she kept on talking. "So she's shunned, but I know you can still have a relationship with her. I get that you can't ride in a car she's driving or sit at the same table with her, although I've heard sitting at one a few inches away is all right."

He crossed his arms.

"She's your only sister. Do you know what I would give for a sibling? Don't do this to her. To yourself. Or to your children."

"You don't know what you're talking about."

"Oh yeah? Call your bishop, then. Ask him if you can go."

"I don't need to involve Gideon, of all people, in this. I don't need to involve myself in this."

"Think about Abra," Shani said, tears welling in her eyes. Sometimes she had to remind herself that she never knew the woman. She seemed so real to her. "What would she want you to do?"

He didn't budge.

"Well, I'm going," Shani said. "And when I come back, I promise we'll pick up where we left off. You'll stop by and comment on how big Adam is getting. Your kids will traipse through my house. Trudy will practice her running across my kitchen floor. I'll stop by to have coffee with Monika—and harass you.

"We're neighbors, Tim Lehman. Don't you dare ruin it." Her eyes began to water. "Because you're a good man. You saved us more than once since we've been here. The ramp. The house. Supporting Joel." A tear trickled down her face. Then another. She brushed them away. "My family loves your family, and even though you might try to deny it, I think you like us a little too."

His hands dropped to his sides. He cleared his throat but didn't speak.

Shani opened her mouth to say more, but the words stuck in her throat. Embarrassed by her outburst, she marched off. Clearly she hadn't changed Tim's mind.

"Come on, Zane," she called out.

"What's going on?"

"I'll tell you in the car."

"I don't want to go."

"We're going," she said. But first she had to go get the baby from Monika.

Thankfully the woman met her halfway, and by the look on her face, Shani thought she'd probably overheard her conversation with Tim. She took the baby, gave Monika a hug, and then started toward the van.

Tim was marching toward the house, so Shani increased her speed. Zane stood a few feet away from it, with all of the children gathered around him. "I want to stay here," he said as Tim clomped up the back steps.

"Get in the van." Shani opened the sliding door and slid Adam into his car seat, fumbling to fasten the buckle.

"Are you all right?" It was Lila, her voice full of compassion.

Shani managed to get the car seat buckled and swiped at her eyes again. She turned toward the girl. "I'm fine. Just feeling . . . sad."

Lila hugged her.

"Thanks, sweetie," she said, hugging her back. She looked over the girl's head at Zane and mouthed, "Cooperate."

"Where are we going?"

"I'll tell you in the van," she said, letting go of Lila. "We'll see all of you soon." She felt horrible about leaving for Eve's wedding, leaving all of them behind.

She stepped around to the driver's side, climbed in, and started the engine. Finally Zane obeyed her.

"We're going to Eve and Charlie's wedding," she said after he shut the door.

He groaned. "I told you I didn't want to go. I hate weddings."

"You've never been to one."

He crossed his arms. She took a good look at him. He wore a torn T-shirt and mud-splattered jeans. He smelled like a boy who had been working and playing outside all morning—that mix of soil and sweat. It wasn't that she found it a bad smell, but he certainly wasn't cleaned up for a wedding.

"We'll have to go back to the house," she said.

"Why?"

"So you can change."

"Mom!" he wailed.

Ignoring him, she backed up the van.

As she did, Zane said, "Look."

"What?" she asked, still looking backward.

"Tim."

She braked and turned. Tim lumbered toward them—barefoot, shoes and socks in one hand, and his black hat and an envelope in the other. He wore a clean white shirt and clean trousers, with the suspenders hanging to his knees.

"Let him sit up front," Shani said. She wasn't going to get her hopes up. Maybe he wanted a ride to the lumberyard.

"Do I have to go?"

"Ask Tim if he cares if you stay."

Zane hopped out of the car and asked quickly.

"Monika won't mind," Tim said, as he looped his suspenders over his arms, positioning them on his shoulders.

"You be good," Shani said. "Call my cell if you need to."

He nodded, grinning from ear to ear and running backward. He waved and then took off after the other kids who'd gathered around the barn with Reuben.

Tim climbed in and slammed the door, pulling on one sock and then the other. When he had his shoes on, Shani said, "Fasten your seat belt."

He obliged.

"Where to?" Shani asked.

"The wedding," he answered.

Relief flooded over her. Tim didn't say another word the rest of the way to Philly. It wasn't until he saw Eve at a distance, under a tree in the side yard that Tim said, "I don't want her to see me before the service."

Shani led him around to the other side of the church, Adam in her arms, wondering what Tim's plan was. Her stomach fell. She wouldn't put it past Tim to make a scene.

Charlie stood ramrod straight as Joel adjusted his bow tie in the pastor's office. It wasn't often he wore his dress blues, and he never could get the tie right. Thankfully Joel was at his side to help. Just having his friend nearby made him feel calmer and more at ease.

This was the happiest day of his life—and yet it was also bittersweet. Eve was putting on a brave front, but just the thought of her walking down the aisle by herself made Charlie choke up. Tim should be walking her down. And Lila and Rose should be leading the way, and then Shani. None of it was the way it should be—but that seemed to be the way life was.

He swallowed hard.

He could barely believe he was marrying Eve. He would have a relationship like his grandparents, honest and loving. With a simple lifestyle. He'd already traded in his truck for an ordinary sedan. They'd have a computer for Eve's course work—but nothing else. They'd have a few animals and a garden. God willing, they'd have children to raise and love.

Above all, he'd cherish Eve.

"Having second thoughts?" Joel teased.

Charlie grinned. "Only about you talking me into inviting you."

Joel stepped away from him toward the window and then froze. "Uh-oh," he said.

Charlie stepped toward the window. "What?"

Joel put his arm out. "Stay back."

Charlie learned forward just in time to see Tim walk by, his black hat squarely on his head. "What's he doing here?"

Shani trailed behind him, carrying the baby. Joel groaned. "She said she wasn't coming."

Sweat beaded on Charlie's forehead. Would the pastor include that old line, *If anyone knows any reason why these two should not be wed, let him speak up now . . .* He doubted that was in Amish weddings. Maybe it was only included in TV weddings anymore.

Joel pressed up against the window with Charlie right behind him. Tim led the way around the corner of the church, toward the front. Charlie wondered if Eve was done with the photographs. He hoped so. She was supposed to wait in the nursery until it was time to start.

"What time is it?" Charlie asked.

Joel held out his arm. "Eleven fifty-five."

Tim was probably on his way to find Eve. Maybe he'd force her to go back with him. "Go guard the nursery door," Charlie said. "Don't let him in there."

Joel held up a hand. "What am I supposed to do? Take him out?"

Charlie shook his head. "Just look tough."

Joel stepped back and retrieved his cane, which had been propped up against the pastor's desk. He held it up. "My days of looking tough are over." Still, he squared his shoulders.

"Then I'll do it," Charlie said.

Joel shook his head. "I'll go recon."

Charlie stood back from the window, watching the other guests arrive. Finally he dug his phone from his pocket. Eleven fifty-nine. Weddings never started on time—but this one needed to.

The door started to open, and Charlie turned sharply, expecting Joel. It was the pastor. "Ready?" he asked.

He shook his head. "Joel will be right back."

The music in the sanctuary seemed to grow louder with each passing second. Where was Joel? Finally Charlie said, "I'll go look for him."

"No, you stay here," the pastor said. "I will. Any idea where he might be?"

"Somewhere near the nursery. . . ." Charlie hesitated and then added, "Eve's brother showed up. We're worried he's going to try to talk her into going back to Lancaster. Or force her too."

"I'd certainly be against him forcing her—but if he talks her into it, I don't see that there's much we could do."

Charlie exhaled and then said, "You're right."

"I'll go see if I can find Joel," the pastor said.

Charlie stepped back to the window and tried to pray—for God's will. Then for what was best for Eve. Finally he sat down in the pastor's chair and said out loud, "It's your deal, God. You know what I hope for, long for. But . . ." He couldn't say any more.

He heard Joel's cane in the hall before the door swung open. The pastor was behind him. "It took me a while to find him," Joel said. "He didn't go to the nursery. He's sitting in the back with Shani."

"Did you talk to her?" Charlie stood.

Joel shook his head. "I didn't want Tim to see me."

"Let's go," the pastor said. He led the way down the back hallway and then through the door to the front of the church. The pastor continued on to the pulpit, while Charlie and Joel stopped at their assigned places. The sun shone through the stained-glass windows of the sanctuary, bathing the room in jewel tones. Charlie couldn't see very well, but he could make out Tim's imposing form in the back pew. He sat on the inside edge, right next to the aisle. Maybe he planned to grab Eve's arm when she walked in and whisk her away. Charlie's heart beat faster as the organist began the processional, not sure what he'd do if his fears came true.

Karina, wearing a simple royal blue dress,

started down the aisle. Charlie shifted to the right so he could see the open doors to the foyer. Eve wasn't there. Karina smiled and then turned to go to her designated place. The music grew louder. Charlie's mom, his dad at her side, stood and smiled at him. He searched the back for Eve.

There she was, all alone, in her white dress and veil. She held her head high and took her first step toward him.

೩೮ 36

It all felt so foreign to Eve, so different than the weekday morning weddings she was used to. Charlie had lamented that no one was walking her down the aisle, but she didn't feel alone. Not at all. God walked beside her.

The guests were all standing. All but one.

She gasped. Tim sat in the last pew, looking straight ahead, his hat in his hands. Shani stood beside him, holding Adam, smiling at Eve as if everything were fine. Eve kept on walking, searching for Charlie at the front of the church. She couldn't see him above the heads of their guests.

She forced herself to breathe and slowed her steps. Charlie was her partner. But God was her strength. Her refuge in times of trouble.

And that's what her brother was—trouble.

She took another deep breath. But Tim *was* her brother. Her only sibling.

She reminded herself he had no control over her anymore—especially not on her wedding day.

When she reached the halfway point down the aisle, she could finally see Charlie. He looked so handsome in his dress uniform, bathed in the colored Licht pouring through the stained-glass window above him. His eyes lit up when he saw her. *Joy.* She felt it too. She smiled back at him. The music surged. She couldn't help but increase her pace. He stepped out to meet her, taking her hand and pulling her close. The pastor said, "We are gathered here today to witness the joining of two lives . . ."

She put Tim out of her mind and squeezed Charlie's hand, hoping he knew how much she loved him. How grateful she was for his love for her.

The ceremony proceeded. Karina took Eve's bouquet of roses. The pastor joined Eve and Charlie's hands together. First they said the Lord's Prayer together, in German. *"Vater unser im Himmel, geheiligt werde dein Name . . ."* The recitation honored Eve's heritage along with Charlie's grandparents.

Then they repeated their vows—Charlie first and then Eve. She only thought of Tim in the back of the church once, when she thought of his and Abra's wedding day, of Lila and Daniel sitting between Eve and Leona, eyes wide, staring at their Mamm and her new husband. Of course they couldn't comprehend any of it. They were just over a year old. They had no idea how much their lives were about to change.

Tears began to sting her eyes, and Eve blinked. Then she locked eyes with Charlie, and the sense of harmony, as beautiful as the colored Licht, returned.

Joel handed Charlie her ring—a simple wedding band. It had been their compromise. He slid it onto her finger as the light caught the gold, causing it to shimmer like starlight.

Next Karina handed Eve Charlie's ring, and she held it in her hand as she repeated after the pastor. "I give you this ring, committing my heart and soul to you." She slid the ring onto his finger and repeated, "I ask you to wear it as a reminder of the vows"—she met Charlie's eyes— "and promises we have spoken today." They were promises to Charlie that she would keep. They weren't made out of fear or under duress. They were made of her own volition—based on her trust in God.

Charlie clasped her hand and held it tight. He grinned as the pastor declared them husband and wife and then said, "You may kiss the bride."

Amish ceremonies didn't include a wedding kiss. Charlie raised her veil and gently brushed her lips. She squeezed his hand as they turned toward the congregation together. They'd have their time together, soon.

A moment later Eve and Charlie were sailing back up the aisle. She was aware of everyone she'd missed as she'd entered the sanctuary. Charlie's parents. Karina's in-laws. Charlie's chaplain friend, Ron, and his wife. Abra's parents. Shani beamed at her as Adam slept on her shoulder. Tim still had his head down, staring at the floor.

Eve and Charlie continued on to the foyer, and a moment later, Karina and Joel joined them. As the pastor invited the guests to move into the reception hall, Shani and Tim slipped out the door first. Tim had something in his hand—an envelope. Shani stepped aside, letting him go first.

Eve didn't budge, but by the time Tim reached her, she realized he hadn't come to shame her or drag her back. He'd brought her something. A card, perhaps.

He extended the envelope. "I found these the night I found the note from Abra. She wanted you to have these too."

She took it from him and pulled out a small stack of photographs. Her heart stopped for a moment. The first photo was of her and Abra, the one Patrick took all those years ago. Abra wore her blond hair long, and her blue eyes sparkled with life. Eve had her arm around her friend.

She flipped to the next. It was Lila and Daniel as toddlers. Then one of Simon as a baby. And one of Rose. The next one was of Abra and Trudy, in the hospital right after the baby had been born. They were still hopeful then that the chemo would work. That Abra would live.

The last one was of Eve and Abra together at a distance, taken at Leona and Eli's just a few weeks before Abra died. Leona must have taken all the photos, except the first, and given them to Abra. And now Tim was giving them to Eve.

She looked up at her brother. "Denki," she said as guests made their way around the small group. She swiped at her eyes.

Tim inhaled sharply. "I'm sorry I didn't give you the note and the photos that night. And I'm sorry for being so harsh with you, even after I'd read what Abra wrote."

"Denki," Eve said again, slipping the photos back into the envelope.

Tim raised his eyebrows and said softly, "Even though it was written to you, it meant so much for me to read that she loved me."

"She did love you," Eve said. "I knew she did—even without the note."

Tim tugged on his beard. "Knowing it inspired me to help the Becks—along with Christ's commandment to love our neighbors. But neither was enough for me to be honest with you. Or loving enough to release you of the promise you'd made."

"Did Abra tell you about it?" Eve asked.

He shook his head. "I didn't know until I read the note. Once I did, I thought you'd stay. You caught me off guard when you said you planned to move away. I didn't know you had the note until then. I thought I'd lost it that night of the storm."

Eve nodded.

Tim's voice was a near whisper. "The children miss you."

"I miss them." She wondered if Tim missed her too, but then she realized he did. He wouldn't have come if he didn't. The knowing of it made her heart ache.

"I heard you're moving back," he said.

Eve nodded.

"*Gut.*" He clutched his hat again with both hands. "I hope, maybe, that you'll pay us all a visit."

Relief flooded through Eve. It might be the most her brother would ever say to her, but it was enough. "Are you staying for the meal?" she asked. She'd organized the women in the church to make a traditional Amish wedding dinner.

Tim turned toward Shani. Both she and Joel, along with Charlie, stood only a few feet away.

Shani nodded. "Let's stay."

Joel started toward the fellowship hall. Shani motioned for Tim to go ahead, and then she followed with the baby. Charlie stepped forward and took Eve's hand. She sank against his shoulder, tears stinging her eyes. He kissed the top of her head and pulled her close.

It would never be perfect with Tim—but he would let her see the children. That was all that mattered.

Joel held the baby while Shani ate a piece of peach pie. She was stuffed after the roasted chicken, mashed potatoes, creamed celery, and yeast rolls, but she wasn't going to waste the most amazing pie she'd ever tasted. After she took the last bite, Joel said, "Let's go home."

She smiled and then searched the hall for Tim. He stood along the far wall, arms folded, talking with Samuel's father. Karina and her mother-in-law, who held onto Samantha's finger as she practiced her standing, sat at a table nearby.

Charlie and Eve stood near the head table, talking with Leona.

Shani put her fork down.

"I'll tell Tim we're ready," Joel said. "He can ride with me."

"Thank you," Shani said, reaching for the baby. "Maybe he'll actually talk with another man."

It took a while for Joel to pull Tim away. He seemed to be enjoying himself. He didn't hug Eve, but he did pat her on the shoulder, and then he shook Charlie's hand.

Gratitude swept over Shani. And there was more to be thankful for. Eve had passed her GED and her driver's tests. Charlie would start the new job in Lancaster in early July.

No doubt there would be more bumps in the road. In the meantime, she was thankful that the Lehman children were keeping Zane grounded and away from the drama of the Englisch world. He much preferred playing with them to video games and school dances.

Joel motioned toward the door, and Shani followed, stopping to hug Charlie and Eve on the way. "See you soon," Eve said, holding her and Adam tight.

Tim walked with Joel to his pickup, and a couple of minutes later they pulled around by her van while she buckled Adam into his car seat.

Then she followed her husband toward home. By the time they reached Lancaster County, the baby began to cry. By the time she turned onto Juneberry Lane, he was screaming.

"We'll be home soon," she cooed. "But first we need to stop at the neighbors." As she followed Joel down the Lehmans' driveway, the children started to run toward the pickup, followed by Monika, who had Trudy on her hip. Shani took Adam out of his car seat and positioned him on her shoulder. He immediately stopped crying.

"How was it?" Monika asked Tim.

"Different," he answered.

Monika searched Shani's face, and Shani smiled back at her, mouthing, "Everything's fine." Then she said out loud, "I can give you a ride home."

"Denki, but Jenny's spending the night with

Lila—we arranged that with Tim beforehand—and I already have a ride." The woman's eyes sparkled.

"Really?" Shani shifted Adam to her hip so he could see the others.

Monika grinned. "Gideon. He's taking me out to dinner."

Shani couldn't help but smile back. She hugged Monika, and the older woman began to laugh. "Stop," she said. "I don't want to make a big deal out of this. Not yet, anyway." She pulled away and said, "You and Joel go on home. You've had a long day."

Shani motioned to Zane and then asked, "Do you want a ride?"

"No, I'll run home." But he didn't. He continued his conversation with Simon.

Tim turned to Joel and shook his hand. "Denki," he said. "For everything. You and Shani have been good neighbors to my family—to all of us."

Rose slipped to Shani's side and hugged her. Shani hugged her back. And then Lila. Daniel stepped closer and she hugged him too. Then Simon. Finally she kissed Trudy, still in Monika's arms, on top of her head, silently vowing to care for each of the Lehman children as much as Tim would let her. Joel and Tim didn't say anything but their eyes were both shining.

Tim's voice had a roughness to it—but not a

sharpness—as he said, "I'm not saying every-thing's going to be smooth from now on."

"Of course not," Joel replied. "How could it?" They both laughed.

Zane took off running toward the field, and Simon and Daniel followed. Lila, Jenny, and Rose stayed behind.

Tim yelled, "Be back in fifteen minutes to do the chores!"

"Come down for supper when you're done," Shani said, a little surprised by her spontaneous invitation. She had hamburger patties in the freezer. They'd barbecue. "The girls can come down now with Trudy—they can help me."

Tim didn't answer for a long moment, and Shani's face began to grow warm. Maybe she was out of line to invite them. But then Tim said to Lila, "Go get Trudy's car seat. You girls go with Shani. The boys and I'll be down as soon as we're done."

"Denki," Joel said.

As she fastened Adam back into his car seat and Lila secured Trudy, Shani thought of Eve, after they'd first met, quoting the verse: *"Love thy neighbor as thyself."* Shani would strive to love Tim and the Lehman children, Monika and Gideon, and Eve and Charlie as herself. To want the best for them. To support them. To pray for them.

And Joel too. Especially Joel. And her own boys.

As she drove the van down Juneberry Lane, the green canopy of the maple trees swaying overhead, gratitude flooded through Shani. Her grandfather's farm had proven to be a place of healing for her family.

It wasn't a perfect place—but it was the right place. They'd found a home where they could learn to love. A place where hope and joy and peace could grow, thanks to their Amish neighbors.

Acknowledgments

My thanks to Laurie Snyder for reading an early draft of this story and to Melanie Dobson for leading me through a later draft. Both of you helped me immensely. My ongoing thanks to my Bethany House editors, Karen Schurrer and Dave Long, for all of your invaluable editorial advice and support.

My gratitude to Marietta Couch, who answers my questions about the Amish, reads for me, and is a kindred spirit and sweet friend.

I'm thankful to Jim and Marilyn Weisenburg for sharing their broken hearts and God's work in their lives through this last decade as they mourn their son, Staff Sgt. David J. Weisenburg, who was killed in Iraq. Your honesty has touched me deeply.

I'm also grateful to Deserae Schultz for sharing her experiences as a military spouse.

I am thankful, as always, for my four children and what I've seen through their eyes. All have bravely experienced what it's like to have a father mobilized and deployed.

Last but certainly not least, I'm grateful to my husband, Colonel Peter C. Gould, for answering my endless questions about Army life and medical issues. I'm also thankful for your many years of service, loyalty, leadership, and endless support.

About the Author

Leslie Gould is the coauthor, with Mindy Starns Clark, of the #1 CBA bestseller *The Amish Midwife*, a 2012 Christy Award winner; CBA bestseller *Courting Cate*, first in the COURTSHIPS OF LANCASTER COUNTY series; and *Beyond the Blue*, winner of the Romantic Times Reviewers' Choice for Best Inspirational Novel, 2006. She holds an MFA in creative writing and lives in Portland, Oregon, with her husband and four children.

Learn more about Leslie at
www.lesliegould.com.

Center Point Large Print
600 Brooks Road / PO Box 1
Thorndike, ME 04986-0001 USA

(207) 568-3717

US & Canada:
1 800 929-9108
www.centerpointlargeprint.com